THE ETHICS

OF MAGIC

A HAUNTED LAW FIRM NOVEL

THE ETHICS OF MAGIC

A HAUNTED LAW FIRM NOVEL

ROBERT L. ARRINGTON

Formatting: Enchanted Ink Publishing

ISBN: 978-0578-80743-0

Printed in the United States of America

TO THE LATE JAMES B. HARVEY.
WHO ALWAYS SAID I WOULD.

1

BRUSH UP
YOUR SHAKESPEARE

MITCH

Mitch McCaffrey pulled his Jeep Wrangler Sport up to his garage door, and without removing his hands from the steering wheel, told it to open. It did, and he pulled in next to the Lexus RX330 on the other side of the garage. He turned off the engine manually while telling the car door to open, and shoved mail he'd picked up at the cluster mailboxes at the entry to Highlands Estates into his jacket pocket.

Exiting the vehicle, he retrieved his gym bag and brief case from the trunk and told the garage door to shut. While the garage door was closing, he closed the car door with another short command, turned to the door to his home, and ordered it to open. That had been a trickier spell, because there were no electronics to command; but he'd finally mastered it.

He entered into a short hallway, where, his hands still full, he turned on the hall lights with additional incanted commands. He stopped off at the laundry room to put his soiled gym clothes in the hamper, and turned to his right down the adjoining hallway to his study. There he placed his brief case on his writing desk, and retrieved the mail from his pocket. Muttering a short sorting spell, he watched the mail sort itself into boxes marked "Bills", "Junk", and "Personal".

In the master bedroom beyond the study, he changed from his work clothes into a golf shirt, cargo shorts (since the day was warm for October), and sandals. It took only a few words to summon these from the closet and the chest of drawers. He stopped in the bathroom to brush his hair where pulling on the shirt, because Diana was coming for dinner. Studying himself briefly in the bathroom mirror, he reflected that he looked like what he was: A middle-aged Scots-Irish North Carolinian, no more than average in height, who tried to eat carefully and exercise regularly.

In fact, Mitch was 47, 5-9, blocky in build, a bit barrel-chested from years of pumping iron, dark haired with a touch of gray at the temples, his head rather square when viewed face-on, his features regular. His hazel eyes were starting to get a bit far-sighted, and he used reading glasses more and more. Nothing remarkable, he thought.

He walked back down the hall past the photos of his son Carson into the kitchen. He summoned the steaks in marinade from the refrigerator to the counter where they could come to room temperature, and made sure the mixed onions, peppers and zucchini from the Fresh Market had not gone bad. With a wave of his hand and glance, he floated a wine glass from one cabinet and an open bottle of merlot from another. Pouring the wine by hand (it was too much effort to do everything by magic), he opened the door that led off the kitchen to the deck.

He had picked his house in part for the view from the deck. Looking down, traffic was moving on the state highway that passed the near-by water park, and then rose up the mountain past the turn to the Gorge, and split at the High Country Resort into roads toward Boone and to Tennessee. The ridge that rose on the other side of the highway so close that you'd think you could touch it was splashed by autumn reds and yellows and oranges among the evergreens. A plume of smoke rose from a chimney still hidden in the foliage about half way up, and Mitch could smell the burning hardwood even from where he stood.

On his left was the gas grill, and he told it to ignite, so that the lava rocks would heat. He pulled a cushion from a hamper, and sat on one of the two aluminum chairs that flanked a small table to his right. Now he had a few minutes to think about the week, and the day, before Diana arrived. These would not be good thoughts.

He hadn't thought anything about the procuring event at the time it happened. He was teaching his last class before lunch on Wednesday. The class was in one of the lecture rooms in the new English and Languages Building on the main campus, laid out as a hemispherical amphitheater, with the lectern front and center, a screen for video and computer presentations behind the lecturer, and a whiteboard to one side. But it was not full, and students sat scattered around the classroom, at all levels.

The class was an English Literature course required for students who planned on transferring credits from Carolina Highlands Community College to a four-year school. It had been carefully designed to ensure full transfer of hours to all of the North Carolina state university campuses, and to most other universities as well. Mitch was giving an introductory lecture on Shakespeare, preparatory to the class reading three plays.

Mitch was most of the way through the lecture when a hand went up in the back of the room. He looked up to see the long brown right arm of Lottie Watkins. Lottie had not really ever been a problem in class, except for being told to put down her cell phone; but she was not doing particularly well. She was plenty smart, but did not put forth much effort. Mitch knew, or knew of her family. Her father was a successful ophthalmologist in Martintown, an African American whose father had owned a garage. He'd returned from residency in Boston with an Italian-descended wife, which had caused a bit of a stir, but not nearly as much of one as would have been the case in the past. Lottie had an older brother who had followed in his dad's footsteps to medical school at Johns Hopkins, and an older sister who was a senior at Vanderbilt.

Their baby sister, Charlotte, always called Lottie, was at Carolina Highlands for the simple reason her grades had not justified her admission to the colleges she really wanted. Judging by her performance in Mitch's class, she might not be able to get admitted as a JC transfer, either. She was a pretty young woman, with long black hair in ringlets and a flawless café au lait complexion, and evidently knew it. she and her coterie of self-perceived socialites flounced around campus, passing time until the next party. Or so Mitch understood from college scuttlebutt.

"Yes, Ms. Watkins." Mitch acknowledge the raised hand.

"Why are we reading some dead white guy like Shakespeare anyway? Why not someone more relevant?" She had made much the same point about Chaucer.

"Well, as I told you, Shakespeare is relevant to transferring your credits. But tell me, who would be more relevant?"

"Somebody like…" she hesitated. "Maya Angelou."

Now this was interesting. It gave Mitch the opportunity for a teaching moment.

"Well," he said, "Maya Angelou is a talented writer, but not English. Have you read her works?"

"Some." Mitch noticed Lottie didn't say what she'd read. While he suspected the truthful answer would be "none", he left the omission alone.

"Do you know what she wrote about William Shakespeare?"

"I doubt she wrote anything about him."

"But she did. She was so taken by Sonnet 72 that she wrote that reading it she almost thought William Shakespeare grew up a black girl in Arkansas. She certainly thought Shakespeare was relevant."

Lottie looked unimpressed, but Mitch plunged ahead. "In fact, that leads nicely to your assignment for next week. The essay was going to be a thousand words on why we still read and perform Williams Shakespeare. It still is for most of you.

"But for Lottie and anyone else who wants to do it, the assignment is to read Sonnet 72, which you can find on line, a write a thousand words about how Shakespeare could speak to a black girl growing up the 20th Century South." He looked around the classroom. "Who else wants to write on the same thing?"

Only two did. One was Fred Jones, a bright kid who always sat in front and always wanted to do something different from the others. The other was Brenda Jenkins, a quiet black girl who sat in the back away from Lottie.

The bell rung. "Remember," he called as the students rose. "One thousand words. Due a week from today."

Lottie rose to leave, followed by two of her buddies. Mitch noticed that she wore tight short shorts. That was a bit much, even for Indian Summer. If she were in the office technology segment (which she'd never enter in a million years), which had a strict professional dress code, an instructor would have sent her home. She gave him a nasty, narrow-eyed look over her shoulder as she exited the room.

And Mitch promptly forgot about it. Until today, Friday, when…

"Well, hello there," Diana said from the door to the kitchen, and he came back to the present.

DIANA

Diana Corcoran Winstead checked her reflection in the mirror, and applied a last touch up of lipstick. She was pleased with what she saw. Just the right amount of make-up, her blue eyes accented but definitely not slutty, her honey-blonde hair back in a pony-tail, the pull over shirt with only a modest scoop to the neck-line, showing only a hint of cleavage, but with a necklace and opal pendant pointing exactly where Mitch could look. The pastel-banded shirt went well with the tan Capri pants, which fit tight enough to be interesting, but not uncomfortable.

She stood to leave, wearing flats, for Heaven's sake, not heels; she wasn't going to the Ball, and didn't really like wearing heels anyway. She grabbed a clutch purse and an overnight bag off the bed. Tonight was not really an occasion, but Win had the kids at his new place down near Valdese; and her mother had gone with Frank, her boyfriend, to the West Brainerd football game in Asheville. No one likely to call or to ask questions. Not that her mother would ask many. But she made sure her cell phone was in her purse, just in case.

Diana made sure the front door was locked and left the home through the door from the kitchen into the garage. On the way, she added a bag of dinner rolls she had snagged at the bakery next to the "store". She backed out into the street, closed the garage door with the remote, and guided her Camry out of the subdivision onto the state highway. She drove past convenience stores, a laundry, and several restaurants, mostly fast food but including the Bean n' Bacon Coffee House & Diner she and her mother owned and ran together. They opened only for breakfast and lunch, and closed promptly at 3:00 every day, but of course there were usually late lunch customers who lingered. Her Mom had been a dear to close for her today, so she could get in an aerobics workout before getting ready for her evening with Mitch.

She passed Carolina Highlands Community College where Mitch taught and rounded the bend to start the incline up to the true High Country. High Country Estates, the gated community where Mitch lived, was on the right just as the grade began to be steep. Diana had the gate code. She drove through the gate, and up the hill, past the pool and clubhouse, then past gray brick homes, mostly duplexes but some free standing, all the way to the last unit on the left, which belonged to Mitch McCaffrey alone.

Mitch had bought the place about two years ago, right after he got the inheritance he wouldn't say much about, and not long before the two had begun dating. The Jeep and the Lexus had come along at about the same time. Yet Mitch still taught English at the Community College. Diana frowned. Well, he hadn't told her how much he had inherited from Dr. McCormick.

By the time she headed up the hill, long shadows were falling across the road. There were people walking along the side of the private drive, enjoying the Indian Summer evening. Some knew her and waved, and she smiled and waved back. She pulled into the short drive and parked in front of the garage. She took her purse and the small bag of rolls, but left the overnight bag, for now. She walked the few steps around to the left and opened the door with the key he had given her.

She continued through the abbreviated foyer with the coat closet and through the great room with the heavy leather-covered furniture and the Arts & Crafts dining table into the kitchen, and saw through the door that he was sitting on the deck, staring off into the distance. She spoke.

Mitch looked up and to his left with a somber expression clouding his square features. But he immediately broke into a wide, welcoming grin. "Wow," he said, looking her up and down, evoking a dimpling response. He rose, and opened the screen door to greet her.

"Well, thank you," she said, lifting her face for a chaste, welcoming kiss. But she noticed his face immediately flatten again.

"What's wrong?"

He didn't try to deny that something was. "Tell you later. Dinner first."

They had done similar dinners before. Diana knew where everything was, and would sauté the vegetables and mix the salad. Mitch would grill the steaks.

"Fine," she said. "Brought a couple of dinner rolls." She looked through the door to the deck and saw his barely-touched wine glass on the table. "Where's mine?"

"Coming right up." He reopened the wine and poured for her.

The lava rocks were hot. Preparing dinner did not take long. Diana heated the rolls in the toaster-oven, found the salad greens and vegetables already chopped in the refrigerator, added the vinaigrette they both liked, and quick-fried the onions and squash. Since it was just the two of them, she set the small breakfast table in the kitchen. All that remained was to fill water glasses and for Mitch to bring in the steaks.

They'd been able to chat about nothing much through the screen door while sipping wine and cooking. Diana had to work in the morning. No, Mitch was not going to Boone; the Apps were playing at Arkansas State this weekend. But the Tar Heels were on TV at 3:30, and he wanted to be back for that. She should come watch with him.

He was going hiking in the morning. No, not hunting; it wasn't deer season yet, and he didn't feel like cleaning squirrel.

Dinner was good, although Diana, as usual couldn't finish her steak. Surprisingly, Mitch didn't finish his, either. Something really must be troubling him.

"We can re-heat these tomorrow," he observed.

"Yes, we can." She took another sip of wine, then looked him squarely in the eyes. "Spill it."

"Spill what?"

"You know what I mean. Whatever is on your mind."

Mitch sighed and started with the Lottie Watkins story.

"That doesn't sound like anything much," Diana observed when he paused.

"It's not. Or shouldn't be. But this afternoon, not too long before I

7

came home, Monica Gilbert walked into my office, shut the door, and said we needed to talk."

"Who is Monica Gilbert?"

"The College Compliance Officer. She can be Bad News, and she was today."

Diana frowned in thought. "Monica Gilbert? She used to be Monica Murray, didn't she?"

Mitch spread his hands. "I don't know. Do you know her?"

"I didn't know she worked at the College. Let me check."

What with google, Facebook, and Twitter, you could find almost anyone quickly. Diana was already up, reaching for her phone.

A few seconds later, after a few keystrokes and clicks, she announced, "I was right. That's Monica Murray."

"Is that important, and do you know her?"

Diana snorted. "It could be, and yes."

It was Mitch's turn to be curious. "Tell you what, let's clean up, and finish this conversation in the den."

Diana let Mitch load the dishwasher. He was fastidious for a man and knew exactly how he wanted it. Diana put the leftover steaks on the platter, covered them with tinfoil, and placed them in the fridge.

"Do you want another glass of wine?" he asked.

Diana shook her head, causing the ponytail to wag from shoulder to shoulder. "No, tonight I'll be a bad girl and have a large Grand." She meant Grand Marnier.

Mitch's den was directly beneath the kitchen, and opened to the outside to a concrete pad that held more outdoor furniture and a real charcoal grill. Inside, the downstairs held a full bath, a guest bedroom, and the den, furnished with more Mission furniture, a wet bar, a large screen TV and a fireplace with gas logs. It was fully dark by now, and the October evening was chill, no matter the warm daylight hours. Mitch ignited the logs.

Diana settled onto a love seat; and, with a brief shudder, covered herself with an afghan while Mitch poured. He had removed two large snifters from a cupboard, and brought her drink, returning to the bar to pour his own, a snifter of the Bowmore single malt. She noticed he took a larger serving than usual. Another sign that something was wrong.

"All right," she said when he had settled in beside her. "Tell me the rest. Then I'll talk Monica to you."

"Okay. As I was saying, Monica came into my office, closed the door, and said we needed to talk. Considering her job, my antenna went up immediately. I said sure…."

MITCH

Mitch's office wasn't that big. Nobody's was. But it held a trio of molded plastic chairs in front of his desk. Monica pulled one of them back toward the wall, seated herself, and crossed her legs.

Monica Gilbert was tall, about five feet seven inches in her stocking feet, and she always wore stiletto heels. She was fond of tailored business suits with short skirts and wore one today. She was attractive. They had a history.

He leaned back in his desk chair and tried to concentrate on eye contact.

His eyes widened as Gina Tompkins and Lorna Krazynski opened the door and took the other two chairs. Lorna, who was actually a neighbor at High Country Estates, and taught in the English Department, was wearing her usual smock. Gina Tompkins, dressed in a floor length skirt, cream-colored blouse and tan sweater, was an instructor in the arts department. He knew she was one of Monica's buddies. Mitch did not know her well. She was about Mitch's age, with a pinched face showing premature wrinkles, mousy brown hair and reading glasses hung from a chain about her neck.

Monica pulled a sheet of paper from a slim folder and begin to read aloud: "This is an interview with Mitchell McCaffrey, a regular, full time member of the faculty of Carolina Highlands Community College, against whom a student complaint has been filed alleging misconduct by a faculty member. The interview will be conducted by a committee consisting of the college compliance officer and two members of the faculty selected by the compliance department" -- Mitch suppressed a smile at the word "department", which he knew consisted of Monica and her administrative assistant – "in accordance with college procedures and policies. This interview is not a hearing. It is not permitted to question the interviewers except to ask for clarification. It is not permitted to record this interview. The only record will be the interviewers' notes. The committee will interview other witnesses and will issue a report to the president of the college when these have been completed."

She looked up at Mitch. "Do you understand?" she asked.

Mitch nodded and said, "Yes, I do."

"Do you have a recording device?"

"I have my cell phone, but it's off," he lied. Knowing that Monica was coming, but not knowing she would bring anyone, he had, just before they arrived, turned on an old voice recorder and placed it in one of his desk drawers. He hoped it would work.

"Let me see it."

Mitch pulled the phone from a pocket and handed it to her.

"Mind if I keep this?"

"Yes, I do."

"So, you decline to surrender your phone?"

"I do. It's my property."

"The record will reflect that." She slid the phone across the table to him. "Leave it on the table. It will stay where we can see it."

Mitch twitched his shoulders in a semi-shrug.

After a tense moment, she said, "Let's get started."

"Now what's this about?" Mitch asked.

Monica leaned forward and snapped in a waspish tone, "There's been a complaint about you. It's serious."

"By whom?"

"Lottie Watkins. And two others."

Lottie had two friends that stuck to her like glue, Corrine and Darlene. Both were white. The three always sat together in the back of the classroom. They walked in together, dressed alike, talked alike, left together. None of them was doing well in class. Lottie was their clear leader. They had to be the other two.

"About what?" he asked, not bothering to get more names.

"Lottie thinks you may be a racist. She doesn't feel safe in your class."

"What?" He really was flabbergasted.

Monica stayed on the offensive. "Did you make fun of her and punish her when she asserted herself as an African-American?"

"I did not."

"She says you did. She said other students will back her up."

"Just a moment," Mitch said. "Is this about Maya Angelou and William Shakespeare?"

Monica nodded. "That's part of it."

Mitch chuckled and relaxed a little, drawing a sharp glance from Monica. "Let me tell you what happened."

He did, hoping that would put an end to the matter. It didn't.

"So, you did disrespect her when she brought up her racial background, and gave her an assignment as punishment?"

Mitch shook his head. He really wasn't believing this conversation. "You know that's not what I did. I told her about how the African American author she mentioned was inspired by Shakespeare. She got the same writing assignment as everyone else, with the only exception it had to tie into how Shakespeare influenced Angelou. Other students were given the option to do the same variation. Two did. One was white, the other black. That's what happened. That's all that happened."

"But you admit she had to do extra work." Monica pressed on.

"Well, she would need to read a sonnet. Five minutes. Ten tops."

Lorna leaned forward. "She feels threatened, Mitch."

"She's wrong."

"There's more," Monica said. "She also says you've sexually harassing her."

"Now just how am I managing to do that?"

"She says you ogle her. She's caught you looking at her body, at her legs. You looked at her legs Wednesday when she left the classroom. Didn't you?"

"I saw her leave the classroom. I watched all the students leave."

"But you did look at her legs?"

"I looked at her. She has legs. Most people do."

"Don't be a smart-ass. You need to watch yourself. You're staring at my legs now."

"No, I'm not." But he automatically raised his eyes to a point right about her forehead, as opposed to looking at her whole body seated across the desk from him.

He hadn't been staring at her. He'd just been zoning out.

Monica unleashed an indignant huff. "How dare you deny it?"

"Because it's not true." He needed to change the subject. "Look, this shouldn't be a big deal. I'll talk with these three. Clear up any misunderstanding."

Monica shook her head vigorously. "It's way too late for that, Mitch. They won't talk with you. They're afraid of you. This is too serious to be smoothed over."

Abruptly Gina asked, "Don't you understand that you've been singling out all three of those young women for harassment?"

He hadn't expected that. "I beg your pardon. I am not."

"All of them say you pick on them and embarrass them in class," Monica supplied.

Mitch opened his hands in explanation. "Look, none of them are doing well in the class. When they don't read the assigned materials, and can't answer questions, I suppose they don't like it. But if they're embarrassed, they're embarrassing themselves."

"Well," Monica continued, "they all tell us that they get called on more than anyone else in the class. That it's constant and demeaning."

Mitch hesitated. He didn't think he'd called on Lottie and her friends more than anyone else. No, he was sure he hadn't.

"That's not true," he said.

"The other women in the class agree with them," Monica said.

Yeah, I'll just bet they do, Mitch thought. There was no way the other female students could have all been interviewed. He said nothing.

"What really concerns us, though," Gina said, "is the way you comment about their bodies."

Now that was outrageous. "I do no such thing!"

"The witnesses all say you do," Gina told him. "Do you deny commenting about the way they dress?"

"What are you talking about?" he demanded, and added, "Yes, I do deny it."

"Oh, you didn't tell Corrine that she paid too much attention to her clothes?" Gina's smile implied gotcha.

Mitch thought, and felt a sinking in the pit of his stomach. "I – I may have told one of them that if she paid as much attention to the reading assignment as she did to her wardrobe, she'd do better…But I was talking about her work, not her body."

"She didn't take it that way," Gina said, adding, "and neither did anyone else. After all, you didn't say that to any of the men, did you?"

"None of them ever dressed as though they were paying attention," Mitch said, and immediately regretted it. He sounded too defensive, he thought. He didn't think he'd teased these girls, but they were making it sound as though he did.

"We also know you make sexist comments in class," Monica said. "What do you have to say about that?"

"That I don't know what you're talking about," he snapped back.

"Really. Do you deny speaking with approval about the way women were treated in Shakespeare's time, and suggesting your female students ought to be treated the same way?"

"Of course I deny it. You're really twisting things around. We discussed in class that women during Elizabethan times didn't have the same rights as women today. I told them that Elizabethan women still found ways to be important and influential, and they might imagine the strategies those women used when they read the plays."

"You meant selling their bodies to men, didn't you?" Gina demanded.

"No," he replied. "Not at all. There were many other ways than sex. They were mothers. Some of them were aristocrats. Elizabeth I was Queen of England, for heaven's sake."

"But you knew that sex was the first thing that would occur to them, didn't you?" Gina pressed.

Mitch hadn't expected this. "N-no," he stammered, but he wasn't sure he sounded convincing.

Lorna broke in for the first time, "Mitch, did you tell them the way women were treated then was reprehensible?"

Mitch stared at her. "I didn't have to tell them that," he said finally. "They knew it. What I said was that those were different times, and things that we would consider absurd or even ugly were accepted by everyone."

Lorna shook her head sadly, "So you didn't even try to tell them it was wrong."

"I told them that it was wrong by our standards but not by the standards of the day," he said in defense.

"And implied that one was as good as the other," said Gina. It was a statement, not a question.

"I don't believe I did that." He realized that sounded lame.

"But they thought that's what you were doing, Mitch," Lorna said softly. "Don't you know that if you're not teaching what's right, you're teaching what's wrong?"

He didn't answer. There wasn't any point.

Monica smirked and quickly moved on to another topic. "Why did you miss the required diversity training last spring?"

"I didn't miss it. I was a few minutes late because a conference with a student ran late. Some others came in late, as I recall."

"Don't deflect to others. You were required to be on time."

"I'm sorry."

Monica smirked. "Are you also sorry you made bigoted comments about transgendered people?"

"I didn't make bigoted comments."

Monica pulled another sheet of paper from her folder, positioned reading glasses at the end of her nose, asked, "Do you deny that you said you didn't accept gender fluidity?"

Mitch remembered what she was talking about. The instructor Monica had brought in from somewhere had picked on him for a question. It had been, "Do you accept that gender is fluid...Mr. Mc-Caffrey?"

Mitch gave the same answer now, "Well, I have my doubts that someone can change his or her gender back and forth based on mood."

"That's a bigoted statement. You realize that, don't you?"

"No, I don't. And anyway, it wouldn't affect how I treated a student in class."

"How could it not, if you don't respect transgendered rights?"

"My job is to teach English Literature. I would teach it the same way to a transgendered student as to anybody else. I respect every student in class and at the college."

Gina weighed in, "You didn't respect Lottie Watkins as an African American?"

"How did I not?"

"She says that she identifies as black, even though she is mixed race, and you don't recognize that."

This was exasperating, but Mitch answered, "I don't know how she can say that. Her ancestry has never come up."

"Well, if you question whether a biological man can identify as a woman, you'd have trouble with a girl who is partly white who identifies as black, wouldn't you?"

"Well, no. Lottie can identify as she pleases. Personally, I hope she loves her mother's side of the family, but that's her business."

"You hope she loves her mother's side of the family, but not her father's?"

"Oh, for heaven's sake. I didn't say that."

Gina was on a roll. "You voted for —"

Monica interrupted her. "We don't need to know how he votes, Gina. I'm sure he votes for the candidates that match his values."

Clever, he thought. Monica is sending a message while pretending she isn't. He decided to engage, anyway.

"Look, whom I voted for is none of your business, and it has nothing to do with what you are supposed to be investigating."

"So you would refuse to answer that question?"

"I would."

Monica placed a hand on one of Gina's and pressed firmly. This was going nowhere. They needed to move on.

There were more questions in the same vein. Had he ever told an ethnic joke? Yeah, he probably had, but never to students, in class or out. What did he tell, when, and to whom? He said he didn't remember, which was almost true, because he had no specific date, joke, or person.

He decided not to take this anymore. He picked up his phone and rose to his feet.

"Where are you going?" Monica demanded.

Mitch picked up his phone. "I will answer any relevant question about what happened last week or at any time on campus. I am not going to answer any more irrelevant questions. Good-bye."

"I'll report this to the president and recommend suspension."

"Do what you need to do."

He walked past them, out the door, and left the building.

"And that's what happened." Mitch finished.

Diana leaned toward him and, throwing off the afghan, hugged him. "You poor guy. No wonder you're upset."

Mitch sipped his scotch, which he hadn't touched while telling his story. "I am that. But tell me, how do you know Monica?"

Diana sank back under the afghan. "That's a bit of a story, too." She closed her eyes, remembering. Her eyes opened. "I was in high school with her."

DIANA

Diana closed her eyes for a moment, remembering.

"You know I started high school at Brainerd Central?" Seeing Mitch shake his head, she continued, "Well, I did. We actually lived in the West Brainerd district, but I was a pretty good point guard in Middle School, so people were willing to pull strings for me to go to Central. My parents and I were willing to go along because that was supposed to be the 'prestige' school."

Mitch nodded. That kind of thing was still going on. Brainerd County had three high schools. Central was located in Martintown, and most of its student body would have gone to the old Martintown High School before school consolidation. Many of the well to do, especially the "old families" still lived in Martintown, or right outside. Then there was West Brainerd, in the northwest part of the county, and South Brainerd, located in the southeast. There was no East Brainerd High. Mitch's son had gone to Central. Mitch had grown up in Buncombe County, which was to the west; but he had lived in Brainerd County a good while now.

"I showed up at Central 22 years ago, a sophomore from the Glen Arden community. That was where we lived then. We didn't live where Mom's house is now until Dad passed away, and Mom sold the big house; and we opened the Bean 'n Bacon.

"Monica Murray was two years older than me. She was a senior. She practically ran the school. At least that's the way it seemed to me. Her Dad was a bank president at the Western Piedmont Bank. Her family lived in Fairfield Estates. She and her Mom thought they were high society. She didn't like people from Glen Arden or Maple Hill." Maple Hill was another community in western Brainerd County. Mitch's home was in Maple Hill.

Mitch was looking at her intently. They had been together for two years, almost; but he hadn't heard any of this before.

"Monica was the Homecoming Queen. She was the Prom Chair. She was the Prom Queen. She was on the Student Council. She had a little clique of friends who thought they ruled the roost. She was the Anchor Club President, and ran it like a snooty sorority. Most of the girls were afraid of her, and a lot looked up to her.

"After all, she was tall and pretty and wore expensive clothes. She and her clique were brutal. Cruel people."

Mitch nodded. He understood. Monica evidently hadn't changed much, if at all.

Diana paused, suddenly back in a hallway with books in her arms, staring at a tall, elegant girl, flanked with two clones who fairly bristled at her.

"She couldn't do anything about the basketball team. And that didn't matter to her anyway. But the homecoming court, the Anchor Club – things like that, she sure could.

"I joined the French Club, and someone nominated me to be its representative on the homecoming court. Monica objected, because I was 'only a sophomore' and didn't really live in the district. She got her way. But a sophomore who was one of her friend's cousin represented another club.

"I didn't really care about the homecoming court, but come December, the Anchor Club was going to select new members. That would have been really nice. My grades were good, I was going to start on the girls' basketball team. The word was the club was going to invite me. Monica kept it from happening. Her justification was that the club needed to add an African American, and we didn't need the space that could be given to a black girl to 'that redneck from Glen Arden'."

Diana had been staring at the fire while speaking. She turned toward Mitch, blinking.

"My Dad was a pharmacist. He had a number of black customers. The 'racist' tag was completely false."

Diana turned her head back toward the fireplace. "The girl they picked was nice. I was glad for her. But I'd had enough of Monica. I transferred to West for spring semester.

"So yeah, I know Monica."

Mitch spoke softly, "Didn't you give her just what she wanted? I mean, when you transferred."

Diana didn't answer immediately. Her face still toward the fire, she finally said,

"I've thought about that. It was my only regret. But what about you?" She turned her whole torso to look Mitch in the eyes.

"I'll have to think about it. But I think she has it in for me."

"Why you?"

"She's got rid of people before. Last year I kept her from getting rid of one. I was on a hearing panel. It was a shop teacher who had tweeted about the need to defend the Second Amendment. I guess she thought an English teacher wouldn't care what happened to a shop teacher. But I thought, and Joe Michaels from the math department thought, that we shouldn't fire someone because he said something some other faculty members didn't like on his own time. Monica wasn't happy. I doubt she's forgotten it. And --" He hesitated.

"And what?" she asked.

"And nothing," he said. But she thought he was leaving out something.

Diana bit her lip thoughtfully. "You need a lawyer. You need Kathryn Turner."

"You mean the woman who represented the professor at UNC-Asheville?"

"That's the one."

Mitch shook his head. "I can't believe this will come to anything. It's such nonsense."

Diana threw off the afghan and leaned toward him.

"Promise me you'll thank about it."

Mitch looked at the ceiling, then back toward her. Time passed. "Okay," he said, "if anything else happens I'll think about it."

"Good." Diana slid over into the circle of his right arm. They sat silently for a while, her head on his shoulder.

Then she turned and invited a kiss. He responded.

"If we're going to fool around tonight," she whispered, "we don't need to waste time. This old girl has to go to work early in the morning."

Mitch chuckled, but without humor. "I don't know if I'd be any good tonight."

But he was. Oh, he definitely was.

SILVER THREADS AND GOLDEN NEEDLES

MITCH

Mitch awoke the next morning to the sound of running water. Diana was showering already. But then, she was due at the Bean n' Bacon by six, because she wanted to be there when the restaurant opened, even though there were others who had arrived still earlier. Mitch understood. No one who ran a successful business stayed away long.

He had no such early Saturday morning obligations; but he was usually an early riser, so he got up and dressed. He would shave and shower after Diana was on her way.

Mitch was surprised he'd slept as well as he did. Maybe it was the comfort of Diana lying beside him. Maybe it was the love-making. Maybe he'd just been tired. But he was glad of the sleep. He went to the kitchen to make coffee. Diana would take a cup with her, and eat at "the store". He'd eat a light breakfast.

The hike would give him plenty of time to think, and he needed to think. About what had happened. About Diana's advice. About what to do.

He hadn't told Diana everything...

By full daylight, Mitch was shaved, showered, and dressed for his hike. The forecast called for another warm day, but the higher temperatures would come in the afternoon. The morning air was much chillier, so he wore cargo pants, a long-sleeved chino shirt, and a lightweight jacket. He crammed a buck knife into one pocket and attached a holster with a water bottle to his belt. He stuck sunglasses into a pocket, and pulled on an Appalachian State ball cap. His house keys in another pocket, his cell phone clipped opposite the water bottle, and a long hiking stick he'd carved himself completed his preparation. Diana had long since departed for the Bean 'n Bacon. He texted her an "I love you", and walked out his front door, telling it to lock behind him and setting the security wards behind him.

One of the things that had attracted him about High Country Estates was that the developer had bought land to the top of the ridge and put in a graveled hiking trail leading to a metal observation tower at the summit. The maintenance costs added to the homeowners' association dues, but Mitch thought these amenities were worth the price. The trail wound a bit, was steep enough to be strenuous, but not too strenuous. The hike to the tower and back was about three quarters of a mile.

The morning was cool and crisp. The autumn foliage was lovely. There was no one else on the trail. He had time to sort things through. To do that properly, he had to go back four years. To right after the divorce.

He didn't blame Sarah Ellen for the divorce. He couldn't, not really. From her point of view, he was far too complacent. Even at the time, looking back, he realized he had not caught on to her hints. Because he had been happy, he'd thought she was.

What had troubled him, he thought as he stepped up the trail, stopping now and then to look up at the foliage, was not what she had said, but what she hadn't. And there was a lot of self-recrimination at his naivety. She had lied, and he hadn't even asked any questions. At least, not many. And he had blithely accepted all of the answers.

The marriage had begun, as marriages do, with so much hope. They had connected at Boone, at the beginning of their senior year at Appalachian. Mitch was the supposedly unlikely combination of an

English Lit major on an Army ROTC scholarship. Sarah Ellen was a nursing student. They'd met a few times earlier, but had being seeing other people. This time they really clicked.

For Mitch, it wasn't just physical attraction, although that had been there. Sarah Ellen was fairly tall for a woman, just an inch short of his 5-9, slender with almost curly brown hair and luminous brown eyes. But she was lively and fun and he loved talking with her. They were engaged by Christmas, and were married shortly after graduation and Mitch's commissioning.

Coming out of college in 1992, Mitch missed Desert Storm and was discharged too early for Kosovo. It turned out that he barely left North Carolina. After training, he spent most of his hitch at Fort Bragg. Sarah Ellen easily found nursing jobs in Fayetteville, interrupted only by Carson's coming along well before they really planned on children.

Mitch managed to get accepted into graduate school at Carolina, and took a few correspondence courses while in the Army. They moved to Chapel Hill after he was discharged. They arranged daycare for toddler Carson, and Sarah Ellen worked at North Carolina Memorial Hospital. A year and a half later, Mitch had his M.A.., a provisional teaching certificate, and a job at West Brainerd High. Sarah Ellen found work at the new hospital in Martintown.

In another three years, the position at Carolina Highlands opened up, offering, at the time, a nice increase in pay. He'd been there ever since, with the only interruption being in 2005 when his reserve commission was activated. He spent an unpleasant tour in Iraq, and then was back at Carolina Highlands.

He had looked into getting his PhD. twice, and was accepted at Tennessee and Wake Forest. But there was no certainty the advanced degree would lead to a job at a university, and the cost and the disruption would be significant.

And Mitch was happy. He liked teaching without having to publish. Brainerd County, especially the western and northwestern sections that extended into the mountains, was a lovely area. Recreation was good. As he remarked to Sarah Ellen more than once, they weren't wealthy, but they were comfortable.

They didn't fight. Sarah Ellen insisted they couldn't afford another child. Mitch would have liked a daughter, especially; but he respected Sarah Ellen's wishes. Carson was a good kid. And his wife didn't appear to have changed. She complained about not driving nicer cars, or not getting a bigger house. But she didn't nag.

Her job was time consuming. By the time they were approaching forty, she had a supervisory position at a cardiology practice. That made her income equal to his, and sometimes greater when she was bonused. She frequently worked late hours and weekends.

And he had had Carson's ball games, hiking, hunting, going to football games when she worked weekends, odd jobs around the house, not to mention lesson plans and grading papers. They didn't have as much time together, but he found Sarah Ellen affectionate when they were.

He was stunned when she told him she was leaving him for one of the cardiologists. The doctor, Jerry Williams, was leaving his wife, too; and they were going to move to Charlotte, where Jerry had a good offer from a practice there." Don't try to change my mind," she'd told him. "We're done." He was 42 years old.

By the time he was 43, the divorce was final. Carson was a freshman at Carolina. And Mitch was alone.

It wasn't the divorce so much as the lying, the being able to sleep with him and whisper "I love you" while sneaking trysts with Jerry Williams, the occasional dinners with Williams and his wife where they were all congenial company, but with Jerry and Sarah Ellen sharing their secrets and making their plans.

He admitted to having had "bad vibes" sometimes. He'd ignored them. He shouldn't have.

The divorce itself was not difficult, his lawyer had assured him, although it had been expensive enough. Sarah Ellen didn't need support. She didn't want alimony. She didn't want anything from his state retirement. Carson was 17, and would soon be 18 and in college. Mitch had to refinance the mortgage to buy her out of the house. She wanted some of the contents, mostly her own family heirlooms that she really ought to have had. That was about it.

But he was still having trouble sleeping. His friends said he ought to get counseling. He resisted. Surely he didn't need that. Then someone told him about Dr. McKenzie. McKenzie was a clinical psychologist who, he was told, could help when no one else could. He'd made an appointment, kept it.

And that had changed his life.

MITCH

By now, Mitch had reached the observation tower. He paused for a moment before taking the steps up. The trail had been pretty steep. The stainless steel and aluminum tower was blinding in the direct sunlight, and he put on his sunglasses. He took the stairs, still sorting his thoughts. When he reached the covered tower, he paused to let his gaze wander across to the opposite ridge, and up to his right.

The road below was invisible through the foliage, except where it turned off to the now closed water park and where the grade steepened just past that exit; but he could hear traffic moving below him, muted by distance but still audible. His eyes went back to the ridge, mostly evergreen but splashed with color. On the opposite side was Jonah's Cove, where James McKenzie had lived and worked.

McKenzie's home-office was a good little drive from the modest subdivision in the Glen Arden community where Mitch had lived at the time. He had to drive almost all the way to the lake, and then wind around to Jonah's Cove. A "cove" was a land-locked dip between ridges, with a narrow belt of asphalt road down the middle, and some paved but mostly macadam roads leading off the main road at nearly right angles. There was a country store in about the middle of the cove, a little brick Baptist Church at the far end. The rest was mostly farm and pasture. McKenzie's place was in stone cottage set into the slope at the end of a rare stretch of asphalt. Mitch thought the first time he saw it that Hobbits might live there. There was no parking except in the drive, and no sign until a visitor mounted the steps to the front porch. There, a modest plaque said simply,

James McKenzie, PhD.
Clinical Psychology

When Mitch arrived the first time, the door was open, and he entered into a short dark hallway. To his right was a parlor, the furnishings of which included a desk with a telephone, and an old-fashioned rolodex and IBM selectric typewriter. Behind it sat a pleasant looking woman with white hair and bifocals, wearing a white blouse and a cardigan draped over her shoulders fastened with a cameo broach. A placard on the desk said she was Mrs. Jones. Mitch later learned that she doubled (tripled?) as the widowed McKenzie's secretary, bookkeeper, and housekeeper.

After Mitch filled out a short questionnaire, and Mrs. Jones photocopied his insurance card on an old photocopier behind the desk, she wasted no time in ushering him into Dr. McKenzie's office, which was almost directly across the hall from the parlor. The office was large, severely furnished in dark stained wood, the walls lined with bookshelves. McKenzie rose from behind a cluttered mahogany desk. There were more bookshelves behind the desk, some with certificates and photographs and not books. He was a tall man, elderly but not frail (Mitch later learned he was over 80), a bit heavy set, craggy features under longish silver hair, and dressed in white shirt, tartan necktie, and tan button up sweater with leather elbow pads. McKenzie shook hands, inexplicably raising an eyebrow as he did so, offered coffee, and gestured at one of the overstuffed chairs in front of the desk.

And so his treatment began. McKenzie assured him that he usually didn't require many sessions, so not to worry about cost. He then asked Mitch to tell his story. He listened attentively, taking few notes, occasionally interrupting with polite questions. When Mitch had finished, McKenzie asked what he wanted from therapy.

Mitch didn't hesitate. "To sleep, to get on with life, to feel good about myself. To feel good about my life."

McKenzie nodded. He smiled from behind his reading glasses and said mildly, "Knowing what you want is half of the battle." They scheduled another session for the following week.

There wound up being only three sessions of therapy. The second session did not start well. McKenzie's questions were reasonable. His advice was mild. But Mitch was irritated. Nothing was happening he couldn't think through for himself. He wasn't feeling better, and his answers betrayed his irritation.

McKenzie sat back in his chair, removed his glasses, and said abruptly, in a clear, commanding voice, "Mitch, you must open your mind. Open it!" He made a motion with his hand, more a sign than a wave.

Immediately, Mitch felt as though something had broken through a barrier in his mind, and he felt a rush of well-being he couldn't explain. They continued their conversation, and he began to feel he really would sort things out. He couldn't explain to himself the breakthrough, but he told McKenzie about it. The psychologist did not seem surprised.

"Tell you what, Mitch," he said, "let's schedule one more session. If you still feel the same way, we may be able to wrap up."

Mitch agreed, and showed up again the following week.

As he seated himself, he noticed a decanter of what appeared to be whiskey on McKenzie's desk, along with two snifters. He also found an envelope on his chair. McKenzie asked him to hold it unopened for now.

They chatted for a few minutes. Mitch told McKenzie he felt he was well, and thanked him. The psychologist nodded and suggested they share a drink.

"This is Laphroaig single malt," he said. "I think you'll like it, if you haven't had it."

Mitch nodded, and McKenzie poured generous dollops into both snifters. "Would you open the letter?"

Mitch did. He found a letter with a single neatly printed word, "Venez".

"Do you speak French?"

Mitch laughed. "Badly."

"Point at the snifter on the right, and read it out loud."

Mitch read aloud as instructed. The snifter rose from the desk and floated to him. The glass hung there within his grasp until he plucked it from the air, sloshing a bit onto his hand.

His treatment had ended. His training was about to begin.

By now he was down the tower, down the trail, and nearly home. After being sure no one was around, he had allowed himself the guilty pleasure of creating an air cushion that allowed him to step off the tower and descend gently to the ground, as though on an elevator, ruefully acknowledging to himself that one had to take his pleasure where he found it. His walk back downhill had been entirely conventional. There was still no one else on the trail.

He hadn't reached a decision. He had a problem at work. He could walk away from his job, but he enjoyed teaching and didn't want to do that. Diana wanted him to hire a lawyer. Should he? Or should he use magic? The latter prospect made him nervous. It was risky. But it just might be necessary.

Because he thought Monica Gilbert might be a witch.

3

TAKING A CHANCE
ON LOVE

DIANA

The Bean 'n Bacon Coffee Shop & Diner was a rustic, cheery place, its exterior covered in siding to present a log cabin appearance, and the interior featuring a large fireplace and walls covered with old farm implements to present a country kitchen ambiance. In the morning, it offered pastries and breakfast, switching to other fare at lunch. It closed at 3:00 every afternoon. Newcomers to the Martintown area thought the restaurant was standard Southern cooking — which was partly right — until they learned about the upscale coffee bar that was Diana's pride and joy. ("Bean" stood for "coffee bean" and not pinto or navy beans.)

The Bean 'n Bacon's business was usually brisk on Saturdays, and Diana found the asphalt parking in front and to the right (left from within the store) of the building already held a number of cars when she pulled around to the graveled employee lot at the rear. Some customers were sitting in their cars, waiting for the restaurant to open; others were lined up at the door.

Entering from the rear entrance into the kitchen, Diana called a greeting to her Mother and to the employees at the grill, grabbed an apron, and walked to the coffee bar. Ginger, a young woman who had worked for them about a year, was filling the last of the dispensers with this morning's brews. Ginger was the chief barista, but Diana helped, especially at busy hours.

Satisfied that everything was ready, Diana walked over to the main entrance, flipped the sign on the door's glass window from "Closed" to "Open", and unlatched the doors. Customers began pouring in.

They were, as usual, an eclectic bunch. Early morning joggers with their phones, iPods, and earphones, dressed in everything from shorts to sweats. These headed straight for the coffee bar. Farmers, hunters, and fishermen, most sporting slouch hats or baseball caps, wearing a lot of denim, headed for tables for eggs, biscuits, omelets, pancakes or waffles.

These customers would continue until about ten or ten-thirty, when the breakfast crowd would thin out. The lunch crowd would start coming in about eleven, and on Saturdays would include parents escorting baseball, midget football, soccer, or basketball teams. By about two, the lunch crowd would thin out, too. The coffee bar usually stayed busy until closing.

As Diana filled coffee cups, made cappuccino or café mocha, and grabbed apple fritters or muffins for customers, she kept scanning the line at the bar for Kathryn Turner. She wanted to bend her ear about Mitch's situation at the college. Kathryn sometimes came in on Saturday's, early or late, and if the latter with her son after soccer. Diana's nine and seven-year olds were in soccer, too; but Win usually took them to Saturday games or practice, because Diana was busy at the Bean 'n Bacon. For all his faults, Win was good about the boys.

Then Diana remembered. Kathryn likely wouldn't come in today, at least with Jimmy, because the soccer game was down at Morganton. Win was getting Steve and Paul to the game this morning. Well, she might call Kathryn, weekend or not. She had a strong feeling Mitch was going to need a lawyer, and a good one at that.

By 10:15, Diana thought the coffee business has slowed enough to give Ginger a break. Fifteen minutes later, she was able to take one herself. She decided to go out back and see if she could raise Kathryn by phone. Her Mother stopped her on the way.

Margaret Corcoran at 62 was 25 years older than her daughter. Allowing for the difference in age, there was a strong family resemblance. Margaret's hair was shorter than Diana's, and frosted, and she was a bit plump because she was not as rigorous as her daughter at refraining from sampling the merchandise. But people could tell she was Diana's mother.

Mitch said that Diana looked like Mira Sorvino, "except shorter, younger, and better". When he said it around Margaret, she always asked, "What about me?" And Mitch would say, "You're not younger." And they all would laugh. Lately Diana had taken to saying, "Yeah, and I was married to Harvey Weinstein. Or his clone." And they would laugh again, but the laughter was a little forced.

Margaret caught Diana on the arm. "Did anything happen last night? Is it all right with you and Mitch?" Margaret liked Mitch a lot, and hoped he and Diana would marry. When she'd said as much to her daughter, Diana had told her to mind her own business, and then had spoiled the reprimand by saying, "We will. But not right now."

This morning Diana said, "Mom, don't tell anyone, but Mitch may have a situation at work. He didn't do anything wrong, but I'm worried for him. I'm going to check on him now and see how he's doing."

Diana exited the restaurant through the kitchen. In the employee parking lot, a couple of employees were smoking in the designated area. Diana said "hi" and walked around the dumpster so she could talk in private. She found Mitch's text in her message in-box, and texted back a smiley and a heart icon. Then she found Kathryn in her contacts list and placed the call. It went immediately to voice mail. Drat, Kathryn was probably in Morganton at the soccer game. She left a voicemail asking for a return call after 2:00 p.m. and went back to work. She felt a rare temptation to ask one of the smokers to "loan" her a smoke, but resisted it.

Kathryn called at 2:30.

KATHRYN

Kathryn Turner found Diana's voicemail on her phone, which had been on vibrate during the game, while stopped at the McDonald's off Exit 105 in Morganton. She had Jimmy and two of his teammates. They'd won the game, and were hungry. Kathryn ate a regular cheeseburger while the boys wolfed down quarter pounders. Boys! She didn't know where they put it. They'd won their game, and Jimmy had scored a goal, so they were in a good mood. But they'd still be hungry if they'd lost.

Kathryn liked Diana. They'd done the soccer mom thing together, when they had time; and one of Kathryn's law partners had handled Diana's divorce. She liked Mitch, too, from what she knew of him, which wasn't much. He'd been hanging out at the Bean 'n Bacon a few times when Kathryn had dropped in for breakfast or coffee. The voicemail didn't tell her much except that Diana thought Mitch needed to talk to a lawyer. Because Kathryn's practice was employment and civil rights, she assumed in must be something about his job.

She decided to get the kids to their next stop, which would be at the multiplex theater in Martintown, before returning the call, since Diana had asked her to call after 2:00 o'clock. Another parent would pick the boys up after the film, so Kathryn could go home after the stop. Like Mitch, she wanted to catch the Tar Heels on television. Unless he'd been called to the hospital, her husband George would be at home, already glued to the TV if he'd finished the yard work. He was a general surgeon.

Kathryn called from her car after dropping the kids at the theater. Diana answered on the fifth ring, explaining she had to go outside to take the call. After exchanging "how-are-you's", Diana told Kathryn what Mitch had told her the night before. It was a good, efficient account. Kathryn didn't have to interrupt with questions.

While Diana was talking, Kathryn wondered if she had a conflict of interest, and decided she didn't. She had been a consultant for the community college while it was setting up its paralegal studies curriculum a few years earlier, but that was over; and she hadn't learned anything confidential that would matter in representing Mitch.

From Diana's story, she wouldn't have thought there was anything much for Mitch to worry about, if she hadn't had the prior experience with the client in Asheville. Now she knew, from experience and not just from horror stories on the internet, how oppressive colleges could be in their enforcement of political correctness. And she still wasn't completely sure this thing with Mitch McCaffrey would present a legal issue.

"Well, I'll be glad to talk with Mitch," she said when Diana had finished, "but this seems so trivial, it's hard to believe they'll make it an issue."

"They will," said Diana.

"Why do you think so?" Kathryn was a bit surprised at the degree of Diana's conviction.

There was a pause on the line, followed by a sigh.

"Because I know Monica Gilbert."

MITCH

It was still early when Mitch completed his morning hike to the tower and back. As he approached his home, he saw someone standing at the door, a short stocky female with long dark hair, dressed in a loose smock, baggy pants, and tennis shoes. He knew her. It was Lorna Kaczynski, the only other member of the community college faculty who lived in High Country Estates. She was trying to peer through the single clear portion of the patterned glass in the door.

"Hello, Lorna," he called to her. She jerked upright, and he heard he sharp intake of breath.

"Mitch," she said in a reproachful tone, "you startled me."

"Sorry," Mitch said. Lorna was usually a likeable sort, an artsy person who was all about flowers and New Age music. But she hadn't been likeable yesterday.

"I just wanted to tell you," she said. "Did you know Lottie Watkins asked to transfer over to my section of English Lit?"

Mitch shook his head. "Are they going to let her?"

"Yes. I met with Dr. Phillips and Monica Gilbert yesterday. Monica strongly feels it's for the best. Lottie doesn't feel safe in your class."

"You know that's nonsense, don't you?" he asked.

"No...No, I don't." There was a tremor in her voice. "I...I shouldn't have come here. I'm sorry. I should go." She seemed in a near panic. She wheeled and started downhill.

She turned back to him, her face recapturing the slit-eyed glare.

"Someone is going to want to know why you harassed those girls. But I don't want to listen to do it today." She fled down the walk.

Well, he thought, lawyer or magic. It appeared he was going to need both. He knew what he'd just seen, the evident war going on inside his guest.

Lorna had been witched. She was being compelled.

And there was one more thing. It was time to tell Diana, tell her everything.

4

I'M TELLING YOU NOW

DIANA

Diana was able to leave the Bean 'n Bacon about 3:15. She took a call from one of her sons while on the way to her car. Steve wanted to know if he and Paul could stay up late that night to watch TV. She asked to speak with Win, and made their father promise to supervise what they watched, and then gave permission.

Privately, she was skeptical about Win's supervision; but she knew that any parent's television oversight was dubious. Win had promised to limit them to Netflix, and change the streaming selection to "kids", and he was good about keeping his promises concerning the boys.

That was about the only promise to her he was good at keeping. One of the many things that bonded her with Mitch, she reflected as she pulled out onto the highway, was the similarity of their marital experiences. Of course, Nathan ("Win") Winstead hadn't had a grand affair. He was a serial philanderer. He was a salesman at a medical supply company, and traveled a lot. And he evidently had had a girl at every stop.

God alone knew how many times he hadn't been caught. But she had caught him twice and taken him back both times. Three years ago, when she learned the 22-year-old secretary at his company's local office was going to have his baby, she'd had enough. Win had begged her for a while, but not too hard this time; and he had finally had given up and let her have the divorce.

Diana got custody of the kids. They sold the house and split the money, and she got part of his 401K. She didn't ask for alimony, but he kept the boys insured and paid his child support on time. Diana was lenient about visitation. She wouldn't keep the boys from their Dad. But she was hurt. It still hurt, at little. But Mitch had done a lot to fix that.

By the time she got to Mitch's place, the football game was well under way. She found Mitch on the deck, where he liked to watch the games in good weather. He'd put a flat screen on the wall above the gas grill, and had run a cable connection to it. He'd also had a pull screen installed that blocked the sunlight from reflecting on the screen.

He had a frosted glass and a bowl of chips beside him. She came out to kiss him hello, and he mouthed "game" to her. She made a face, but was glad he had something he could lose himself in for a while. At the commercial break, he told her there was a pitcher of margaritas in the refrigerator, and she went to get one.

She went back to the deck and sat at the chair on the other side of the table. "How's the game?" she asked.

"Too early to tell."

Carolina was playing Georgia Tech in Atlanta. She remembered hearing the game was a toss-up. She watched with him for a while. She wasn't a real big fan, and being a Lenoir-Rhyne grad, had no particular loyalty to the Tar Heels. But she wanted them to win if he did. Besides, Win was an N.C. State alumnus, and her instinct was to not like what Win liked, and like what he didn't. Within reason, of course.

At halftime, they traded information about the day. She told Mitch Kathryn Turner was willing to see him. He told her about Lorna, but she got the feeling he was leaving something important out.

As the second half wore on, the announcers droning and a breeze making a gentle rattle in the leaves of the trees below the deck, Diana found herself nodding off in the comfort of the seat cushions and a stool for her feet. She let it happen.

She woke with a bit of a start. She wasn't in the chair on the deck. It wasn't full dark, but the light through the windows suggested an advancing dusk. She was on a bed. Raising her head on an elbow and looking around, she realized she was in Mitch's bedroom, on his bed. The covers hadn't been turned down except to expose the pillow that had supported her head. She remembered nothing except falling asleep with the ball game and the breeze in the background, and then a lovely dream about floating than then alighting on a cool pillow.

Diana pushed herself up, and saw her shoes were positioned neatly by the side of the bed where she had been sleeping and that the door was shut. From down the hall, she could hear, barely, smooth jazz instrumental and a female vocalist who might be Diana Krall. She also thought she hear Mitch's voice. She rose and stepped into her shoes.

When she reached and opened the door, she smelled something good from the kitchen, and heard a faint sizzling sound that mingled with now more distinct music and Mitch's voice. She walked slowly down the hall toward the lit kitchen.

Just before she entered the kitchen, she heard "Good-bye, son." When she reached the door, the kitchen lights were abruptly blinding. As she blinked away the spots, she thought she saw a shallow frying pan lift itself from the stove, and empty itself onto a platter, which then floated over to a trivet on the breakfast table. She gasped.

Hearing her sharp intake of breath, Mitch came between her and what she'd just seen. He bent and kissed her on the cheek. "Welcome back, sleepyhead."

Diana was still blinking, and now sure she couldn't believe her eyes. "W-Who were you talking to?" she asked.

"Carson. I just wanted to check on him." Carson was now a graduate student at Virginia Tech, and had watched the game, too.

Diana decided to ignore the evident optical illusion. She must still be half asleep. "Is he okay? Who won the game? What's that I smell?"

Mitch gently steered her to a chair at the table with his hands on her shoulders. The table was set with plates. There was a platter of sputtering shredded meat, peppers and onions in the center. The bowl of chips had been refilled and moved to the breakfast table, and there was a covered dish that might be tortillas. There were two glasses of iced tea.

"I took the leftovers and made steak tacos. Let's eat."

"I thought we were going out tonight."

Seating himself opposite her and picking up a paper napkin, Mitch shook his head.

"We need to talk." Not, "let's stay in and just talk". But the ominous "we need to talk."

"Sounds serious."

"It is." His solemn face broke into a smile that might or might not have been forced. "But steak tacos first. I think you'll like them."

The tacos (they were really fajitas) were indeed good, and Diana found that she was hungry after the long nap. During the meal, they talked about trivia, like the scores of the Carolina game and the App State game, and how was Carson. But there was an undercurrent, a slight tension, about the coming talk.

When they were done, Mitch asked her lightly, "Well, shall be retire downstairs?"

"Well, let's clear the dishes first."

"Surely." He looked down at the dirty plates and platter, and muttered a word she couldn't catch under his breath. The dishware lifted smoothly off the table and deposited themselves neatly on the counter above the dishwasher. The empty tea glasses followed.

Mitch rose, eyes twinkling just a bit at Diana's gaping, bug-eyed stare. "You wouldn't believe how long it took for me to master that. I broke some glasses and plates, I promise you."

He walked to the kitchen counter and began running water over the plates. "I could do this the other way, too; but it's easier to do it by hand," he said apologetically.

Diana couldn't speak. She could only make noises while searching for words that wouldn't quite come out.

"Ready to go downstairs and hear the story?" he asked.

"Y-yes. But I'm going to need a drink to start," she managed.

"There is still part of the margarita pitcher in the fridge."

Diana shook her head emphatically. "No, sir. You're going to have to share your Scotch for this."

Mitch

Now that the decision had been reached to share his secret, which no living person in the world, other than Mitch himself knew, the primary emotion Mitch felt was relief. But there was apprehension, too. He had been postponing telling Diana because he was afraid of how she might react to the news.

But now the time had come to tell everything. Or almost everything.

This evening, back in the assuring atmosphere of his den, with its stained bookshelves, overstuffed furniture, the eclectic combination of rustic prints and sports photos on the walls, the wet bar, and smooth jazz still playing softly from satellite radio in the background, he took a deep breath, sent her a shifter of single malt the way McCormick had sent the glass to him, and, pouring for himself the old-fashioned way, readied himself to launch into the speech he had mentally rehearsed earlier.

But Diana spoke first. "Are you psychic? Is this, uh, ESP?"

She sat on the couch with her knees tucked up under and to the side. He still stood at the wet bar. There was a bit of a chill in the house after dark, and he sub-vocalized a command to ignite the gas logs before answering.

Finally, he said, nodding slightly, "You could call it that if you want. But I prefer the simpler, older term. It's magic."

"How long have you been like this? I mean, known how to do this? Your whole life?"

He sat beside her and set his snifter on a coaster. "No. Only a few years. Dr. McCormick taught me before he died."

Mitch started at the beginning. He told her about how Dr. McCormick discovered his ability while in therapy. And he told her about his training.

"When did you complete your training?"

He shook his head. "I never did, really. I was still getting trained when Jamie died in his sleep. That was three years ago. But I was pretty far along. Far enough, I guess."

Diana said nothing, just sat looking at him and nodding encouragement. He laughed suddenly.

"I had some …interesting… training accidents. But no one got hurt, thankfully." He laughed again. "Early on, I was going to use a spell to light charcoal out in back of my old house. I put the charcoal in one of those towers, but no kindling under it."

"Did it work?"

"Oh, it worked all right. The charcoal ignited at once, almost like black powder, and sent a flame about 20 feet straight up in the air. It left nothing but powdered charcoal dust. Nobody saw it, but the whole neighborhood heard it. I had a hard time explaining."

Diana was giggling. "Oh, I would have loved to have seen that."

She filled the pause while Mitch was retrieving his train of thought. "What did you do after Dr. McCormick died? Are you in touch with other magicians? And is that what you call them? Or is it wizards? Witches?"

Mitch shook his head again. "No. McCormick knew some people, but I never got any names. But he told me there are a lot of terms, and to pick the one I liked. His favorite as 'magic user' or just 'user'. I told him that calling myself a 'user' would be misunderstood."

They laughed together again.

"I've studied on my own since he died. Have you seen the old books he left me? I have them in the bookcase with the glass doors in the study. They're grimoires. Spell books. They're old, and some are in French or German or Latin. It's slow going."

"So, he left you the books in addition to the money?"

Mitch nodded. "He did. I was shocked. After taxes, I received just a little over two million dollars. I bought the house and the cars. The rest, most of it, is invested."

"Can't you just magic up some more."

Mitch walked back to the bar and splashed just a little more Scotch into his snifter. "Well, Dr. McCormick had talked with me a lot about being careful with spells. They can have unintended consequences. And he talked with me even more about the ethical use of magic. He said that magic is a tool that shouldn't be misused.

"It's like a carving knife. If you use it to carve a roast, you're just carving meat. If you use it to stab someone to death, you're a murderer.

"He told me that the only difference between so-called 'white magic' and 'black magic' was the intent of the spell. If the intent is to hurt someone it's black magic, and it ultimately changes the User into to a bad person. Like the guy in 'Breaking Bad'. A good person can't do evil things and remain good.

"He taught me that one had to use spells designed for personal benefit cautiously, and sparingly. And he said it helped if the benefit sought didn't hurt someone else in the process."

Mitch returned to the couch and sat silently for a long moment. Diana waited patiently.

"So, no, I'm not going to try to turn lead into gold or something. That might not work. It could even backfire and cause harm to me or someone else."

"That leads us to another topic."

DIANA

Diana had watched and listened to Mitch in a daze. One of his many attractions was his apparent contradictions. He was veteran who liked to hunt, and was not uncomfortable with firearms. One of his passions was following football. Yet he had a strong artsy side. He taught junior college English Literature. He was a jazz aficionado. Like her, he had been hurt emotionally, and was private about it, and about much else. He obviously had money that didn't come from his teaching position, but no one knew how much.

And now this. It was a lot to swallow, all at once. Too much.

She held up a hand when he said he had another topic. "Hold on. I have a few questions first."

He sighed in understanding. "Go ahead."

She held up a finger. "First question: Who else besides me knows about this?" Obviously, "this" was his magic.

"Now that Jamie McCormick is gone, no one in the world except me and now you."

"Okay. And that leads to questions two and three: Why me, and why now?"

"Three reasons. One. Because I'm in love with you. Two. Because I've been planning on letting you in on the secret for some time now.

Three. Because I've got a problem, and I'm going to need advice from someone I trust. All good reasons."

Diana smiled. "So, you're in love with me?"

"Well, I think I've told you that before." They both knew he had.

"You have. And thank you. The sentiment is mutual. But I'm not done with the questions." There was more she just had to know. Her brow wrinkled in thought. Where to begin?

He nodded encouragement.

"Okay," he said, and waited for her to continue.

"Can anybody be taught to use magic? For example, could you teach me?"

"I wish I could, but no. You have to have the Talent. It must be hereditary."

"Oh. Do you have a family history?"

"Well, Dad used to joke his grandmother was a witch. So maybe. I don't know. Nobody took the stories seriously, but I wonder…." They both knew a lot of strange stories come out of the mountains. Then he said, "Jamie told me I was the only person he'd met around here that he was sure had the Talent. I can feel it in other people. I felt it in him. Sometimes, say at a shopping mall or in a ball game crowd, I get a flash of someone, somewhere. But I've never known who it was. Now you…Diana, you're interesting. I don't get a sense of the Talent, but there's an undercurrent of something. But maybe that's mixed up in my feelings."

"An undercurrent. Wow. I'm flattered. Okay, next question: Have you ever used a spell on me?" There was a bit of a tremor in her voice, and she supposed he could guess what it was about.

Mitch laughed, "You mean have I used a seduction spell or something? Absolutely not. Remember I told you about using magic ethically? Well, seduction spells are out. Off limits." She exhaled in relief, realizing she'd been holding her breath.

"And truthfully," he went on, "manipulating people is not my strongest talent. I'm glad it's not."

"What is?"

Another laugh. "Manipulating machinery and electronics. But I will confess. I've used magic on you three times."

"Really? When?"

"Remember when we were at Bouchon for dinner when we started dating? When you got so emotional talking about your ex? You were embarrassed and upset, so I used a calming spell. I can handle those. Benign spell, benign motive.

"And then I put a safety spell on your car. It won't let you have an accident, or will try not to."

"Ha! But I can buy a car that can do that. Hey, wait, why is that funny?"

"Because that's what Dr. McCormick told me, that we — we magic users — have gradually been getting obsolete since the Industrial Revolution, and the pace has been picking up with computers."

"You mean you don't need magic powers if you can ask Siri? Or don't need a broomstick if you can grab a flight?"

"Something like that. But I'm not so sure. It's what gave me the idea to use magic on electronic devices. It works. For me at least."

"And what was the third time?"

"How do you think you got from the chair on the deck to the bedroom today?"

Diana started, remembering the dream. She recovered: "All right. Final question for now: Why didn't you tell me before?"

"I was afraid I would run you off."

She slid across the couch and circled his neck with her arms. Their eyes met.

"Don't you know, Mitch McCaffrey, that it takes more than a little magic to run me off?"

Mitch

When they came up for air, Diana changed the subject again.

"What was that other topic you wanted to bring up?"

Mitch hesitated. This was going to be a little difficult.

"Diana, you know I've always wanted to live my life, enjoy my work, and just be left alone, don't you? That's why I don't do controversial campus causes, have a blog, nothing that's visibly political. I have my opinions and keep them to myself."

Yes, she understood that.

"Well, now I'm facing one of these college p.c. witch hunts; and I don't like any of my alternatives.

"I can hire a lawyer. But litigation means people asking all kinds of questions. About the money. About my private life, my personal opinions. All designed to trip me up. A lawyer can't completely protect me."

"So what?" she interrupted. "So, they find out you inherited money. Big deal. They won't find out you're a magician. They won't even ask."

"That's true. But what I mean to say is that lawyers are expensive. What I have is a nice nest egg. How much of it do I want to spend on lawyers? I have my Mother. I have my son. I have you and your kids. I will have other uses for the money. I sure don't have enough to retire now. If they get rid of me, how can I get a job with a smeared reputation? And the best lawyer I can get may not be enough.

"I didn't tell you, but when Lorna came by today, I could tell she'd been spelled, was being manipulated. She's a pretty sensible person. I don't think she'd jump to conclusions on her own. It's like someone is taking no chances.

"You see, there are a certain number of faculty who will knee-jerk that any accusation of impure thought or speech ought to result in dismissal. But at Carolina Highlands, Monica can't count on that. There are trades and math instructors that don't always toe the party line. And there are others who are just fair minded. Usually. Lorna is one, but not now.

"I told you there are Users who are good at controlling other people. I think Monica is one.

"I think Monica is a witch."

5

IT ONLY HURTS WHEN I CRY

MITCH

Mitch and Diana slept late the next morning – at least late for them. Mitch was worn out after a long Saturday, which had ended, predictably enough, with them both entwined unclad between the sheets of his bed. He was awakened by feeling Diana leave his side, and sat to watch her sway toward the bathroom.

"You know," he called to her, "you have a perfect hourglass. Most women don't."

"I work at it," she called back, truthfully. "But how do you know how most women look without their clothes on?" He heard her turn on the shower.

"I am just making a reasonable deduction based upon other evidence," He said, getting up himself, and moving to the bathroom to brush his teeth and shave while she showered. He almost entered the shower with her, but decided there was no reason to tempt fate. They had planned on attended holy services, and really had no time to spare.

"Explain something to me," she said while they were dressing, she in one of the dresses she kept in Mitch's closet.

"Sure, if I can."

"I thought you said you could sense another magic user, but you said only that Monica 'might be' a witch. Why the hesitation?"

"Because it's almost imperceptible. Which means her Talent is weak or untrained – if that's the case, she might not even know – or that she knows how to mask it. I think masking's more likely."

"Can a User mask their talent?"

"Some can. At least Jamie said he could when he wanted. I can't, at least not well. I probably broadcast like the Voice of America."

"So, you think she's trying to hide it from you?"

"Maybe. She'd want to take me off guard if she tries something."

"What are you going to do?"

"About that? There's nothing I can do, other than to check the wards around the house, my car, and probably my office. About the rest, I probably ought to make an appointment with Kat Turner, just to be safe."

"I can call her for you, if you want, in the morning."

"That would be better. If you call for me, then I won't be over-heard, on purpose or by accident. I can e-mail you what my calendar looks like."

They passed a pleasant day together, going to the 11:00 o'clock communion service at St. Bartholomew's Episcopal Church and then to a pleasant extended lunch at Mario's in Martintown. They changed clothes at Mitch's house and took the same hike to the tower together that Mitch had walked alone the prior day.

Mitch drove to work the next morning hoping everything would blow over but knowing that it would not. He found out as soon as he reached his office at the college.

Faculty were allowed to lock their office doors at night or over weekends, but the cleaning service had passkeys and entered to clean nightly, relocking the door after finishing the office. Setting a Ward on his office was trickier than on his home, where he could set one that would bar admittance, period, and send him a warning if anyone tried. (He felt the warning as a tingling in his scalp.) It had taken him a while to master the spell for his office, settling for a spell that would leave a residue telling him that someone who shouldn't have entered had done so.

He felt the alert as soon as he inserted the key in the door. Someone other than the janitor had been inside. When he opened the door, nothing appeared to be missing or amiss. His bookshelves and desk drawers had not, apparently, been disturbed. But his office computer was sending a warning. He muttered a word that would unlock the Ward and the tingling stopped.

Mitch had always had an easier time spelling electronic devices than with inanimate objects. McCormick, who had sources he'd never revealed to Mitch, had speculated this was because magic worked at a quantum level, and that the active computer systems were easier for some Users. This didn't explain, he'd said, why that for some, it was just the reverse, or why Mitch had a harder time with live animals and people than with computers and cell phones. Maybe it was because the digital systems were simpler. Mitch didn't know.

Anyway, he'd placed the Ward on his office computer so that if someone tried to tamper with it, it would shut off and refuse to restart. Because the Ward was at the quantum level (he supposed), later examination by an IT professional wouldn't reveal an explanation in the hardware or the software. Mitch opened the computer and did a quick check to be sure. There was nothing he could see. He checked the browsing history on the browser and the sent items in his e-mail folder. Nothing. The Ward had held.

There was a knock at his door, and Mitch called out for whoever it was to come in. It was Don Kelly from the IT staff.

"I have a note that there's something wrong with your computer."

"Really? It's not from me."

Kelly shrugged. "It's just a note from Administration. It's not signed."

"May I see it?"

The note was typed on generic letterhead. When Mitch took it, he subvocalized an inspection spell, and was rewarded with a tingling. Whoever had typed this didn't mean him any good. He handed back the note, and gestured toward his desk

"Go ahead."

Kelly's hands sped over the key board and the mouse, flicking from program to program. He connected a diagnostic box he carried in a satchel and checked some more, while Mitch watched. After a few minutes, he got up and said, "Well, I don't know why I got this, but there's nothing wrong."

After Kelly left, Mitch picked up his lecture notes from the table to the right of his desk, re-set the Wards, and left for his first class.

MONICA AND BART

Monica Gilbert was meeting in her office with Bart Stevens. Stevens, a lanky, rather awkward looking man in denim trousers and a plaid shirt, taught graphic arts at the college. He was tech savvy – had to be, to teach graphic arts these days – but not on the IT staff. He and Monica saw eye to eye on what was wrong with the college and how it should be run. They did each other favors from time to time that only the two of them knew about.

"I don't understand it," Stevens was saying, brushing his longish graying hair back from his forehead. "It shut off as soon as I touched it. I couldn't restart it."

Monica frowned and tapped her pen on her desk. "I think maybe I do. I'll have to think about this. Did you use gloves?"

"Oh, yes." It was imperative that he not leave prints.

"Good. Do you still have the stick drive?"

He nodded. He removed the drive from his jacket pocket and handed to her. The drive had a number of documents, mostly alt-right rants they'd downloaded, that Stevens was going to upload into McCaffrey's "Documents" folder, as well as the URL's for the fake browsing history – more alt-right sites and some pornography, he was going to create. But the IT staff would find nothing this morning. Pity, Monica thought.

"Well, hang onto it." She handed back to him across the desk. "We still may be able to use it."

"Will do." He hesitated at the door, "Are we still on for Thursday night?"

Monica smiled and ran her tongue over her lips. "Maybe." Her voice had a coy lilt. "We'll see."

Stevens left and went straight to the canteen for coffee. The early morning rush was over, but there were still a number of students and faculty. He spoke or nodded to several. He had enough time to sip his brew and read the morning Charlotte newspaper before he had class. He leaned back in the formed plastic chair and didn't notice the stick drive slide from his pocket onto the floor, the sound of its strike and bounce masked by the rattle of his newspaper and the conversation and bustle of the canteen.

In a few minutes, he left and went to his class. He didn't miss the drive until afterwards. When he returned to the canteen, it wasn't there. He asked around, but no one had seen it. He decided not to tell Monica right away.

MITCH

The rest of the morning was uneventful. When his English Lit class met, Lottie Watkins wasn't there. Her usual companions sat in their usual seats, and greeted him with smug little smiles. He nodded to them. Then he continued with the study of "Romeo and Juliet".

After class, he was on his way back to his office when a student trotted up beside him.

"Mr. McCaffrey?" It was one of his composition students. What was his name?

"Darrell Russell, from Comp I," the young man supplied.

"Oh, sure, Darrell. What can I do for you?"

Russell pulled a stick drive from his pocket. "I found this in the canteen. It doesn't have a label, so I put it in my laptop. It's kind of strange, but it seems like it's yours. It has your name in it."

"Let me see it," said Mitch, puzzled, but already formulating a theory.

Russell handed the drive to him. Mitch almost dropped it. The drive fairly exuded malice. He frowned in thought.

"Tell you what. I don't recall putting anything on a stick drive recently, and I haven't been in the canteen today. But I'll take a look at it, and if there's anything to be concerned about, I'll let you know. Fair enough?"

Russell said it was.

Mitch decided to return to his office and see what was on the drive. But no, without knowing what it was, he couldn't risk connecting it to his office device. He would walk out to his car and put it in the glove box and examine it at home, this evening.

He did exactly that and warded the glove box and the car. No chances taken. On the way across the parking lot, he remembered he had downloaded a PowerPoint program on Milton to a stick drive. The drive should still be in his desk drawer. When he returned to his office, there was no warning when he unlocked the door, so one had been in recently.

But he couldn't find the stick drive in his desk drawer. He hadn't remembered to look for it this morning. He searched his desk drawer again, but nothing else was missing. If the drive in his car was the same one, someone must have removed it from his office and dropped it in the canteen. Now who had passkeys other than the cleaning service? Ah, of course. Compliance.

Darrell had said the drive was "kind of strange." What else was on it now?

Finding out had to wait. He had another class this afternoon. He called Diana on her cell. She answered immediately. She said she had an appointment with Kat Turner and one of her law partners for him Wednesday at 5:00, if that would work. It would.

As he was leaving the building that afternoon, he saw Brenda Jenkins, one of his students, waiting outside. She was the African-American girl who had asked for the Maya Angelou version of the essay assignment. Brenda was not a "looker" like Lottie Watkins, but was all the same a pleasant, open-faced young woman who was always neat and modest in her dress. Her answers in class were intelligent when he called on her, but she didn't raise her hand to volunteer often.

"Mr. McCaffrey," she called to him.

He stopped and turned, "Yes, Brenda."

She walked closer, looking around to be sure no one was near. No one was.

"I – I don't think I'm supposed to tell you this, but I thought I'd better."

It was Mitch's turn to glance around to be sure the conversation would be private.

"Go on."

"I was interviewed by Dr. Kaczynski this morning. She…she kept wanting me to say you gave the writing assignment to punish the black students. She kept asking me if I was afraid of you. She sounded pretty nervous about it.

"But, Mr. McCaffrey, I'm not afraid of you. I asked for that assignment because I wanted to learn why a black poet liked Shakespeare so much. I enjoyed writing it. I told Dr. Kaczynski that, but she wasn't happy. She wants me to meet with Ms. Gilbert. I don't want to, but I guess I better.

"I don't understand what's going on. Can you tell me?"

"No, Brenda, I can't." Mitch thought rapidly, knowing anyone could walk out the door and see them, hear them, at any time. He couldn't tell Brenda not to talk with Monica. That would be used against him. But if Monica got near Brenda, she would use a compulsion spell on her.

He knew what to do. He wasn't good at compulsion spells. But he did well at warding spells to protect someone from being compelled. He subvocalized a Ward on Brenda while appearing to think about what to tell her.

The spell concluded, he said, "Just tell Ms. Gilbert the truth, Brenda. Don't be afraid." The Ward he'd placed had an anti-panic component, thankfully.

Brenda nodded, and then smiled. "Yes, sir. I'm glad I told you."

"So am I, Brenda. And – thank you!"

They parted company and Mitch walked on to his car.

6

HELP!
I NEED SOMEBODY!

DIANA

Before she left work, Diana had texted Mitch reminding him to call her to let her know what happened. He called her from his car while she was on her way to exercise class.

"Why don't you come to dinner tonight?" she asked. " We're having your favorite beef stew."

Mondays were beef stew day and the Bean 'n Bacon, and the restaurant's beef stew had a wide following. She knew Mitch was fond of it, but didn't get a chance at lunch at the store often and that If Diana and her mother were serving it at home tonight, it meant there was enough left over for a family meal but not enough to carry over at the Bean 'n Bacon for another day. The stew was definitely an inducement.

But he said, "I don't think we should discuss this in front of Steve and Paul."

"We won't. We'll go out on the porch after dinner while they're doing homework. Hey, why don't you go on to the house now? Mom could use company."

Mitch agreed.

When Diana reached the soccer field, practice was just concluding. The field was an easy walk from the boys' school so no one had had to take them. Diana parked and exited the car, and immediately met Kathryn Turner and her son Jimmy coming up the walk. Steve and Paul were still on the field talking to the coach.

Kathryn, in tan tailored slacks and a blue blazer over a white shirt, had clearly not had time to go home and change clothes before picking up her son. She was two years younger than Diana, a slender, attractive woman with shoulder length light brown hair. In court, she frequently wore over-sized glasses she did not need, but wasn't wearing them now. When she saw Diana, she smiled and spoke immediately.

"How's the boyfriend?"

"Well, they tried to hack his computer today. I don't know any details."

Kathryn stopped and absently tousled Jimmy's head, making him wince and pull away. "Mom!"

Kathryn ignored his protest and continued, "Are you going to see Mitch tonight?" Diana nodded. "Well tell him to write up everything he remembers about everything that's happened and bring it to the meeting. I mean everything."

By now Paul and Steve were walking up. Diana promised she'd pass the directive on to Mitch. Kathryn's Lexus SUV was close by Diana's Camry, and Diana watched them get in their car.

"You can help Mitch, can't you?" She called as Kathryn was opening her door.

Kathryn paused and smiled. "Well, we'll certainly try. I promise."

Paul and Steve had heard more than Diana intended. "Help with what?" he demanded. He knew Mrs. Turner was a lawyer. "Is Uncle Mitch in trouble? Is he going to go jail?" At his age, everything lawyers did was criminal law. Television!

Diana winced. Me and my big mouth, she thought.

"Never you mind," she said, and added, "no, Uncle Mitch is not going to jail. He just needs advice."

"What kind of advice?" asked Steve, the seven year-old.

"Grown up advice. Now let's go home."

"Are you and Uncle Mitch going to get married?" Steve asked, when they were in the Camry and Diana was backing out.

"Would you mind if we did?" Why did this have to come up now?

Steve didn't hesitate. "No, Mom. I wouldn't. He's nice. But how would that work with Dad? Would I have two dads?"

"No, moron," Paul broke in with his nine- year-old maturity. "Then Uncle Mitch would be a ...step-father. Don't you know anything?"

Diana intervened. "You guys need to can it. Uncle Mitch is coming to dinner, and I don't want you bothering him."

But she was worried for Mitch. She couldn't help it.

When they arrived at her home, they found Mitch in the kitchen leaning up against the counter, drinking coffee and talking with Margaret, who was likewise drinking coffee while seated at the kitchen table. They broke off their conversation when the kids rushed in and ran straight to Mitch.

In his excitement, Steve had forgotten his Mom's admonition. "Uncle Mitch! Are you going to be our step-father?"

"Yeah," Margaret added. "Are you?"

"Mother!" Diana's hands flew to her face.

Mitch was laughing. "All right, y'all. Enough with the pressure." His eyes swept the two boys. "Suppose we men go watch Sports Center while dinner is cooking."

"Yeah!" Paul enthused, but Steve said, "I want cartoons!"

Mitch herded them toward the den, and mouthed "later" to Diana as they left the kitchen.

After dinner, Margaret hustled the boys off to their shared room to finish their homework before bed, while announcing she would retire also and read in bed for a while before turning off the light. Late nights were not a good idea for someone who owned a restaurant that opened early.

Mitch helped Diana clear the dishes and load the dishwasher while Diana brewed decaf coffee. They took their cups onto the porch. It was chill, and Diana wore a jacket. Before she seated herself on one of the matching rockers, she turned on the outdoor space heater.

Diana knew she shouldn't stay up late, either; but after Mitch took a seat in the other rocker, spoke the first thing on her mind, which wasn't, after all, the situation at the college.

"I am so sorry about Mom and the boys, pushing you to marry me like that. It's embarrassing."

Their eyes met in the dim light. Mitch said, calmly and softly, "Who says I have to be pushed? I think it's time we decided to go ahead."

This was heart-fluttering, if not exactly news; but Diana said, "Now I'm embarrassing myself, bringing this up when you've got that terrible thing at work."

Mitch was silent for moment, then said, matter-of-factly, "Nothing is more important than this. I want to marry you. You know that. We've talked about it before." And they had, agreeing they would, eventually. He continued, "But...I suppose this can keep a few days. I don't have a ring with me, after all."

Diana hoped the darkness hid the furious blush that heated her face. But she accepted the invitation to change the subject. "Okay, Mitch. Tell me about your day."

He did.

When he reached the part about the stick drive, she interrupted. "Where is it?"

"In my inside jacket pocket. I'm going to insert it in my home computer when I get home."

Diana fairly jumped to her feet. "You are not! Just a minute."

She went inside and found tissue paper and a small, clear freezer bag in the kitchen. Returning, she handed the tissue to Mitch, and said, "Here. Wrap the drive in this and give it to me."

"What are you doing?" he asked, but obeyed all the same.

She placed the tissue-wrapped drive in the bag and sealed it. "I'm securing this and I'll take it to Kathryn tomorrow. Even the finger-prints on it may be important. Or...do you have a way to see who had it?" She meant by magic.

"I tried. I can see the student who gave it to me. And I can see myself. And somebody else. But I can't see him clearly. I guess too many people have handled it. It has to be someone at the college, though."

"Anyway, I think your lawyers need to look at it first. They may be able to get prints."

"You watch too many cop shows," he jibed.

"Hush. Now what about that recording from Friday? We need to get that to Kathryn, too, before your meeting."

"I haven't hired her yet."

"I said 'hush'. She's your lawyer even if it's just a consultation." She giggled. "I do watch enough TV to know that. Now can you put the recording on a stick drive, too?"

"Just a minute." He took out his phone and stared hard at it. A sub-vocalized command brought up instructions on how to upload the recording to another device. "We have to upload it to a PC and then copy it to the stick."

"Let's go inside. We'll use mine."

She made Mitch wait in the kitchen while she brought her laptop and a thumb drive from her home office. When the recording had been copied to the drive, she placed it, too in the zip-lock bag.

"Okay, I'll get these to Kathryn's office tomorrow...What are you doing?" She was watching him stare, in turn, at her computer and at the freezer bag.

"I just put wards on your computer and the stick drives. They shouldn't be a problem except for someone who wants to hurt one of us, but if anyone has a problem, call me." He paused and grinned. "We can't be too careful. I watch television, too."

There was a long, deep good-night kiss, and Mitch left for home.

KATHRYN

On Wednesday afternoon, Kathryn Turner hung up from her husband, George, and turned to the papers on her desk before her. They finally had the evening straightened out. Diana Winfield, bless her, would pick up Jimmy after soccer practice when she retrieved her own boys and hand Jimmy off to George at Mario's. George was hopeless in the kitchen, and would be at the hospital until after 5:00.

That was the best they could manage tonight, with the 5:00 meeting with Mitch McCaffrey certain to take a while. But George and Kathryn were used to juggling family and work. It was difficult at times. George always seemed to have several surgeries scheduled whenever Kathryn had a multi-day trial. But they managed. They really did.

The papers stacked up in front of her included the firm's standard engagement agreement, a print-out of the conflicts-of-interest check that was routine before taking on a client, another print-out of the contents of the stick drive the student had given "the client" (as she already thought of Mitch), and a transcript of the recording Mitch had made of his interview.

As she knew it would, the conflicts check had Mitch's name in several places. Her senior partner, Becky Johnson, had represented Mitch in his divorce. A senior associate, Dennis Wilson, and prepared Mitch's Will. She had met Mitch when he went to soccer games with Diana, and one or two times at the Bean 'n Bacon. He seemed nice, but she didn't really know him. It helped that he was already a client of the firm. She was going to need his permission for her to review Dennis' file. The more one knew about a client, the lower the chances of nasty surprises.

But Mitch obviously had money he hadn't saved from his salary at Carolina Highlands Community College, although she'd no idea how much. When someone was facing litigation, that helped. Any type of litigation was ferociously expensive these days. But she needed to know how much Mitch was willing to spend on what was ahead of him. She wouldn't blame him if he just walked away.

Anyway, they would offer Mitch the full resources of the firm, if he wanted them. She had selected Marc Washington, a young associate, to help her with the case she thought was coming. And Bill Norville, the managing partner who was still Kathryn's mentor, would be available for back-up. That would make for more people in the initial consultation than she preferred, but it couldn't be helped. Jenny Jackson, Norville's paralegal whom Kathryn sometimes "borrowed", would be there, too.

Of the other papers, the contents of the stick drive were most interesting. Someone had gone to a great deal of trouble to create a fake internet identity for Mitch, and to plan embarrassing items on his work computer. He or she had gone so far as to create a Facebook identity with all kinds of kooky posts, "likes" and "shares". She had wondered why that couldn't have been done without using Mitch's computer, but their IT guy at the firm had told her that if the plant hadn't come from Mitch's device's URL, it could easily be proven fake.

Someone was prepared to play serious hardball in order to get rid of Mitch McCaffrey. In some ways, she was not surprised. She knew that college compliance officers, suffused with political correctness and sometimes reveling in exercising their power to enforce it, were frequently not above falsifying or manufacturing evidence. They had run into that in the prior case she had handled with Norville's assistance, although it had been a bitch to prove. But this...

What she was seeing seemed a bit extreme even for an administrator on a mission to purge the faculty of undesirables. This was, well, personal. Kathryn wanted to find out why.

Her computer said it was 4:50 when her phone beeped to tell her McCaffrey had arrived.

This was going to be an interesting con.

MITCH

Mitch arrived at the Melton, Norville offices in downtown Martintown across from the courthouse with not much time to spare. He'd been able to leave the college early enough; his last class of the day had concluded at 2:00, and he had only about an hour of absolutely necessary paperwork he needed to complete in his office.

But he'd wanted to squeeze in a quick workout. The gym, after all was on the way into town. Still, he really couldn't go in for his appointment without a shower and changing back into his business clothes. Thus it was about a quarter of five when he arrived, his hair still a bit damp. He hadn't been told to bring anything except his curriculum vitae, so all he had with him was a portfolio holding the c.v. and a pad of paper, and a pen.

There were only two other persons in the reception area at the law offices, a young couple who were evidently there to sign papers that had been left with the receptionist, and who quickly signed and left. He sat in one of the chairs provided and absently studied the photographs of the Carolina mountains that decorated the walls. The receptionist, a well-dressed pleasant looking woman of middle years, asked if he wanted coffee, water, or a soft drink, and he declined.

His surroundings were not unfamiliar. He'd been a client before. He had met Kathryn Turner a couple of times. He'd attended the Lisa Willingham lecture at the college a few weeks earlier, and Turner had introduced her. Come to think of it, he wondered why Monica and her stooges (as he thought of them) hadn't asked him about his attendance at the lecture, which had not made the campus leftists happy. Well, they may not have known he'd been there. He hadn't asked any questions, and had sat in the back of the theater where the event had been held.

He'd also met Bill Norville and the other senior partner, Jack Melton. They worked out at the same gym he used. Melton's wife Libby was his accountant; that was how he'd got to a Melton, Norville lawyer for his Will. Martintown wasn't all that big. The law firm, with somewhere between 20 and 25 lawyers, was good-sized for this part of the state, though – probably one of the biggest between Charlotte and Asheville. They must have clients from outside of Brainerd County as well as within, he thought.

His cell phone said it was precisely 5:00 when Kathryn entered the reception area personally to take him to the conference. The room to which she led him was through a door into a hallway into the first door to the left. They entered a large room dominated by a long conference table of some dark-grained wood, which he thought might be mahogany but could be something else, flanked by adjustable conference chairs on both sides and at either end. There were no exterior windows, but the wall facing the door was largely filled with a large screen flat television. The overall ambiance was elegant, but functional. There was an elaborate electronic communications work station at the center of the table, in front of whom sat a pretty woman with long, blonde hair and pert features, whom Mitch judged to be about 30. A note pad and pen were placed to her right.

Mitch was surprised at the number of people present. In addition to Kathryn, there was Bill Norville who sat at the far end of the table, turned out immaculately in a dark blue pin-striped suit and yellow silk tie. To Norville's left sat Dennis Wilson, an open-faced young man with already thinning sandy hair, whom he knew, and a still-younger African-American, the color of his skin a shade lighter than the table, with strong, blunt features, whom he did not know. Both of the younger men wore khaki trousers, blue Oxford shirts, rep ties, and blue blazers. Mitch wondered if he was seeing the firm uniform for male associate attorneys.

Kathryn made the introductions. The blonde woman was a paralegal named Jenny Jackson; the black man an associate named Marc Washington, who, she said, "works with me and Bill." All rose to shake hands.

Mitch shook his head and chuckled. "Am I worth all of this attention?" he asked.

"I'm only going to stay a minute," Dennis explained. "I just need you to confirm that it's okay if I share your Will file with Kathryn and her team."

"Concerned about my ability to pay a fee?"

"Not at all," Norville said immediately. "Your litigation team needs to know everything if they are to represent you properly. Now, as for me, I'm going to fade away after the conference, and you won't see me much anymore. Kathryn and Marc will handle your case. Let's all have a seat."

Kathryn sat to the left of the paralegal, leaving Mitch to sit alone on the side of the table with his back to the door and more mountain photography lining the wall on that side of the room.

Kathryn opened a portfolio containing a legal pad and electronic calculator and uncapped a felt-tipped pen. "Mitch," she opened in a brisk tone, "we're going to propose an engagement but we need to get some feel for the case first. To start, what about Dennis' question? May he share that information with the rest of us?"

"Will it still be confidential?"

"Absolutely, to the extent the law allows. We are all your attorneys, even if you decide not to engage us for the present matter after this meeting."

Mitch agreed.

Wilson rose. "That's all I need," he said. He wished Mitch luck on the way out.

When the door had closed, Kathryn continued, "Okay, next point: Contact information". She read off Mitch's telephone numbers, home address and office and home e-mail addresses. Was it still accurate? He said it was.

"Great. Important point: No communications via office telephone or e-mail. I assume you'll know why."

Mitch nodded.

"Another thing: Do you do social media. Facebook? Twitter?"

"No." He thought for a minute and said, "I'm a member of two sports message boards, one App, and one Carolina."

Norville interrupted, "Public or Private?" Kathryn, who wasn't much into sports, was puzzled. What was the difference?

"Private," Mitch said, "and only on my home computer."

"Good," Bill responded, "but be careful anyway. Stay away from anything political or controversial. But check them now and then to be sure no one is trying to hijack your user name."

Kathryn approved, but she still wasn't sure what a message board was. Well, Norville and Washington could tell her.

"All right," she said. "Let's get down to business."

KATHRYN

Kathryn had mapped out the agenda for the meeting in consultation with Bill Norville. First, they lead Mitch through the class that had started it all. They wanted to know about the reactions of other students.

She watched as Mitch knitted his brows in thought before answering. "When it happened, not many students were really engaged. They just sat. I didn't get any bad body language.

"When the alternate assignment was offered, I had a couple of volunteers. One was a go-getter who volunteers for everything. The other is a good student, but kind of shy. The papers were turned in today. Hers was one of her best."

"What is this girl's racial background?" Norville asked.

"She's black. African American."

Norville nodded and made a note. They all made notes, even though Jenny Jackson's keyboard was clicking away in taking notes for the whole team.

"Why didn't you make Lottie's assignment optional like the rest of them?" Kathryn asked.

Mitch answered immediately. "Because it was a good teaching moment. Lottie has been a mediocre student. She's plenty intelligent, but doesn't work hard. I was hoping this would really engage her."

Kathryn nodded in approval. Good answer, she thought.

They moved on to the interview. Kathryn asked Jenny to play the recording. They all listened. Kathryn had heard it before, as had Norville. Washington and Jackson were hearing it for the first time. Kathryn watched Mitch as the recording played. He was mostly impassive, but he looked as though he were eating lemons when the political questions were asked.

"We have some questions," Kathryn said when the recording concluded.

"Shoot."

Kathryn glanced at Norville and Washington. This was a part of the interview they had planned in advance.

"How did you vote in the presidential election?" she asked suddenly.

As expected, Mitch bridled. "I don't see how that's any of your business."

"Answer the question. We need to know."

"Why?"

"Never mind that now. Just answer."

He did.

"Are you a registered Republican?" Norville asked.

Mitch looked mystified, but didn't protest before answering this time. "Well, yes. Not always an enthusiastic one."

Washington cleared his throat, then asked, "Do you give money to Republicans?"

"Not much."

"How much? To whom?" Kathryn chimed in.

"Well, I gave a little to Richard Burr."

"Mark Meadows?" Norville asked. Meadows was their congressman.

"Some."

"How much?"

"I-I don't remember exactly. Less than $500.00."

"What about Will Sweetson?" Kathryn asked. Sweetson was their state senator.

"Oh, sure. Will is in the same firm as my accountant."

"Did you go to a Sweetson rally?" Washington asked.

"One. Diana and I went."

"Speaking of your girlfriend," Norville said, "you do know that she and her mother give to pro-life organizations, don't you?"

He said he did.

"Do you belong to the NRA?" This was from Washington.

He acknowledged it.

"Then why don't you have a sticker on your car?"

"I just don't put stickers on my car."

"Bullshit. You have App State and Carolina stickers."

"Okay. It's because I don't want to call attention to myself at the college." He swallowed, and then continued, "But before I answer anything else, you all are going to tell me why I'm being asked all of these political questions."

Kathryn nodded to Norville, who answered, "Because this is political."

Mitch's face moved, but Kathryn couldn't tell if he was registering surprise or something else. His features slumped as though he had failed at something.

She said softly, "Mitch, when this gets to a hearing – and it will – you won't be asked these questions. Monica and her little committee wouldn't have asked some of the questions they did if they knew they were being recorded. But a lot of what we've just covered is known around town already. Some of it, like your party registration, is public information. Gilbert will have a way of letting the hearing panel know.

"They're going to pretend that the hearing is about misconduct. It's not. If we are going to help you, we have to expose what Gilbert is really trying to do. So we have to know."

"I'm not sure I like that," Mitch told her.

"Oh, you won't like any of it," she answered. "But you're already there.

"We still have a few questions – not political. Then I'm going to let Marc explain a little bit of the law to you, and then we'll talk about where we're headed and what can be done."

Mitch nodded.

"Where did you get your money?" Norville wanted to know, when they were again seated.

"Don't you know? Dennis knows."

"Remember, you only now approved sharing the information with us," Kathryn reminded him.

He told them about the McCormick bequest.

"McCormick's probate file is public record. It may come out now, if anyone looks. Will that bother you?"

"It will bother me some. I'd rather it not come out."

"Tell us why," she pressed him.

"I have never wanted publicity. I want my life to be as private as possible. I've always wanted to be 'under the radar'."

She guessed that made sense. "Marc, go ahead and tell Mitch what the law is."

Washington cleared his throat again. He was obviously the young associate attorney in a conference with senior counsel, and just a little bit uncomfortable in the spotlight.

"You may already know some of this, Professor McCaffrey," he began.

"Mister McCaffrey, or just Mitch," Mitch interrupted. "Community college instructors don't get to call themselves "professor'."

"Yes, sir." He looked down at a neatly typed sheet containing his notes, and continued, "Well, as you know, community college faculty members are retained on annual renewable contracts. They don't have tenure rights. And they can always be dismissed for cause.

"Therefore, the tenure statutes have no application. But because community college teachers are public employees, they do have due process rights. You're entitled to notice of any charges against you and to a hearing before a panel appointed by the college president. You've probably ready it in the college Policies and Procedures Manual."

Mitch said he had, and added, "But don't kid yourself. President Daniels appoints whomever Monica Gilbert tells her to appoint. Monica always picks the ones she wants."

"We're aware of that," Norville said. "Go on, Marc."

"The president doesn't have to accept the panel's recommendation, whatever it is; but we can expect that she will. There is no direct appeal from the president's ruling, but there is another way to challenge it."

"Marc, let me interrupt for a minute," Norville cut in. "Mitch, college hearing panels, everywhere really, are notorious kangaroo courts. This next part is important."

"There is a federal statute that protects citizens from violations of their constitutional rights by state and local officials. It's Section 1983 of Title 42 of the United States Code." He stopped and grinned. "Congress passed this law right after the Civil War to protect black folks from being run over by state officials. But it protects everyone.

"So, if the college violates your due process rights, by not giving you a fair procedure or by violating a liberty interest like freedom of speech, you can sue in court under that federal law. You have two years after a final determination by the college to do that."

"I don't want a federal lawsuit. That will get in the newspapers and on television." Mitch's tone sounded final.

"This matter may get publicity anyway," Kathryn warned him. "TV Channel 13 is always nosing around college campuses for news.

"But you don't have to decide now. Our point is this: If we can build a record that your due process rights were violated by not giving you a proper hearing, or that the real reason behind the accusation is to violate your free speech rights, then there is the possibility that we can scare the panel or the president into backing off, because they'll think a federal lawsuit will follow. We can also build a record that let us evaluate your chances in federal court.

"That's why we asked the 'political' questions. And there will be more to cover with you, such as whether your teaching methods or reading assignments have ever been challenged for improper reasons."

She paused and took a sip of water, then said, looking McCaffrey directly in the eyes, "None of what's ahead of you is easy. None of it is cheap. You need to understand that. The people in this conference don't know how much money you have. We don't need exact numbers.

"But it appears you don't have to have this job. So our question is this: Do you have the cojones to see this through?"

Mitch finished his coffee before answering. "I don't know. I honestly don't know. I'll need to think about it. And I want to talk with Diana. And my son. I don't have fabulous wealth. I don't know how much of my nest egg I can spend."

"We understand," Kathryn said. She pushed a folder across the table to him. "Our standard firm engagement letter and our rate schedule are in this folder. You will have the right to approve or disapprove of measures that will involve additional costs. It has a place for your signature. Read it. Think about it. Call me if you have any questions.

"And call us immediately if anything else happens."

Mitch opened and closed the folder.

"I won't you all to understand a few things about me," he said. "May I tell you now?"

"Of course," Kathryn told him.

Mitch looked at the ceiling in thought.

"You have to understand that I love teaching, and I love living and teaching here. I always have. It was part of what ended my marriage, because it wasn't enough for Sarah Ellen. I still live mostly on my salary, you know. The money is invested and isn't touched except for a few things.

"And I've always wanted to be left alone. I'm a traditional person. And…I guess you'd call me a libertarian. Well…that doesn't go over too well on college campuses these days.

"It wasn't too bad at App when I was an undergraduate. When I got into grad school at Carolina, it was a lot worse. I figured that out fast, because I was coming out of the military and that alone made me suspect with some – a lot of – people.

"My solution was to keep my mouth shut. I didn't join anything. I didn't talk politics or policy with anyone, except a few people outside the department that I trusted. There is so much pressure to conform. And it's worse now."

He heard Washington snort and looked up sharply.

"Try being black," Marc said.

Mitch studied the young man for a moment, and slowly nodded.

"I'll bet," He said. "Anyway, I've tried to keep it up. I'm still not a talker or a joiner. It's always worked. At least until now." He shook his head sadly. "I guess I feel like a failure. I honestly didn't think I did anything wrong, even by their standards. This is like a bad dream."

Kathryn started to respond, but Norville beat her to it. "Mitch, the harassment claim is weak. We know that. Hell, Monica knows that. But one thing you need to understand: For someone like her to want to hurt you, you don't have to do anything wrong. You just have to not be one of them."

Kathryn spoke to Bill as well as to Mitch, noting to herself that the two seemed to share a pretty good idea of who "they" and "them" were. "Bill, that's right. But this is personal, too. I want to explore that with you more, Mitch, next time we meet. We haven't even talked about the thumb drive they tried to plant. That had to come from Gilbert. Didn't it, Mitch?"

"Yes, she has a buddy who teaches computers."

"What kind of buddy?" She waved off the question. "We'll drill down into that next time. And yes, I think there will be a next time. But it's past dinner time, and let's wrap up for now. You have enough to think about."

They all rose and shook hands again. She showed Mitch to the door and returned to the conference room to retrieve her notes.

Jenny had taken her laptop and gone, doubtless out the back door into employee parking. Norville had disappeared, too. But Marc Washington was still there.

"Do you think he will hire us?" Marc asked.

Kathryn hesitated. "I…think so. But I'm not sure."

"Can we help him if he does?"

Kathryn closed her portfolio. "I don't know that either."

7

BLOWING IN THE WIND

MITCH

When Mitch left the law offices, he found two text messages on his cell phone. One was from Diana, asking, "How did it go? Call me." The other was from his son, Carson, who wanted to schedule a Skype for tomorrow night. He didn't say why.

Mitch immediately texted Carson a "Sure. When?" He quickly realized several things. First, he was hungry. He could solve that by picking up a pizza. Second, he dreaded telling Carson about what was going on with his job. Third, he really needed to talk with Diana.

He called Diana before he left the parking lot . He told her the meeting was good, but he had a lot to think about.

After a pause, she said, "Well, let me give you two more."

"Okay. What?"

"One. Could you really stand to do without teaching? Two. If not you, who?"

But he was already thinking about both.

MONICA

Monica Gilbert was not having a good Thursday afternoon. Things were not going well with the Mitch McCaffrey prosecution, as she already thought of it.

It had started with the college president right after lunch. Claire Daniels had met with her privately in her office down the hall from Monica's, and turned down her recommendation to suspend McCaffrey. She had sat there behind her desk with her substantial backside doubtless overflowing her chair, toying with a letter opener, and said, "No."

"Monica, you know that with the lottery scholarships, more kids are going to community college before transferring. We're just not as trade heavy as we used to be. We don't have enough English teachers for someone to take over his courses."

"But he wouldn't answer questions. And, Claire, he's dangerous."

Claire had never turned her down before.

"From what you told me, he answered on everything important. And the only people who think he's dangerous are Lottie Watkins and her best buddies. Those three have been in and out of academic trouble ever since they've been here. No. I'll look at it again after you've issued a report. You haven't finished the interviews, have you?"

Monica admitted she hadn't. "But there's already enough to tell he's a racist."

Claire set down the letter opener. "Really? Based on one assignment that included an essay on a black poet?"

Monica was growing angry, which she knew was a mistake. But she pressed on. "Come on, Claire. You know there's more to it than that. The assignment was designed to glorify a dead, white male. And look how archaic and patriarchal his lesson plans are. Nothing about Milton's bigotry. Nothing about the sexism and racism in Shakespeare. He might as well have been teaching in 1917."

"His colleagues can take it up in peer review," Claire responded mildly. "Maybe his contract won't be renewed next spring. But I'm not going to suspend him. Not yet."

Monica considered working a compulsion. No, she thought. Not now. Claire might be right. She needed support from Mitch's peers. And more evidence. Well, she would get both.

She decided to start with Lorna Kaczynski, and that had not gone as well as she would have liked, either. She'd e-mailed Lorna, asking her to drop by the compliance office; and Lorna had dutifully showed up about mid-afternoon, as always dressed in her frumpy New Age hippie best of flowing printed skirt and a blousy sweater that was too heavy for the warm weather, out of breath, a film of sweat glistening below the frizzy hair above her forehead.

Once she had settled in the chair opposite Monica, Lorna had breathlessly begun at once. "Monica, do we really need to dismiss Mitch McCaffrey? Maybe we should just arrange to have him apologize and get training or something. I mean, he's a popular teacher. He's always been so helpful me. He's a nice guy. Really. I'm sure this is just a misunderstanding."

Monica had had to force down her anger and present herself calmly, resenting the impulse to renew the compulsion she'd had to use earlier. This would work better if Lorna was persuaded. She had to have someone from the English Department on the hearing panel, and no more than one from the investigating committee. Lorna had to be it.

"Lorna, I'm surprised at you. Haven't you complained to me before about how old-fashioned and politically incorrect McCaffrey is in the classroom?"

Lorna frowned. "Well, yes, he's very traditional. But that's not really misconduct, is it?"

"It is if it makes African Americans and women uncomfortable. And that's what he did. You know it. You're not having any trouble with Lottie, are you?"

"Well, no. But I'm not getting much out of her, either, so far. She just sits in class on her phone, texting away, with this little smug smile on her face."

"That's no reason to tolerate a racist. And one who demeans women at that."

"I don't think Mitch is a racist. He's never said anything —"

Monica cut her off. "Lorna, Lorna. Don't you understand that the stealth racists, the ones who hide in the closet, are in some ways the most dangerous of all?

"Just look at whom you're defending. You can tell what he is by how he teaches. Nothing about Milton's religious bigotry. Not one word about Hamlet's abuse of Ophelia. Lorna, these young people deserve more than just reading assignments. We need to teach them the right values. You know that."

"I know," Lorna acknowledged, but went on stubbornly, "but I've never heard of Mitch teaching wrong values."

Monica leaned back in her swivel chair with a loud, long sigh. "Lorna, think about what you just said. Not teaching the correct values is teaching the wrong values. Our children, even our young adults, must have a safe space, and they must have proper guidance. They don't get either from Mitch McCaffrey."

"Well, I don't know —"

"Yes, you do."

Lorna wrung her hands. Really. "This is so hard."

Monica decided to ease up for now. She'd planted the seeds. She had to have Lorna, and would compel her if she had to. But persons under compulsion weren't reliable. It would be better to convince her.

"Well, think about it, while we finish the interviews."

"I will," Lorna promised, and left.

Monica shut the door behind Lorna, and returned to her desk to think. She glanced at the digital clock on her desk. She would see Bart tonight, and maybe he had figured out something.

She was going to get Mitch McCaffrey. Mostly because she knew that at heart, he really was a racist and a sexist. But partly because he had turned up his nose at her. Men just didn't do that. And partly because his little girlfriend had never bent the knee to her. And no one did that to her. Not if she could help it.

Her brow wrinkled in thought. Mitch might be a challenge. He fairly radiated magic. But she didn't know how skilled he was.

But he must have spelled his computer. Otherwise, Bart would have been able to plant what they'd worked out. Monica didn't feel guilty about that. She was only exposing what he was so cleverly hiding.

She wished she were a better trained witch. The only person with the Talent she had ever really known was her Mother, who was now in a nursing home and suffering from advanced dementia. Mama was really only a hedge witch.

Still, she was glad of what her mother had taught her. Compulsion spells were useful at managing people. Especially men. (This would be easier if Claire were a man.) And the preservation spell was better at anti-aging than cosmetics or even exercise, although she used both. She knew she looked good, and looked younger than her 39 years. That was satisfying. And valuable.

She had never had many serious rivals. That little minx Diana Winstead had been one. Oh, Monica had been, still was, prettier – taller, longer legs, every bit as curvy, her features more sculpted, her natural dark chestnut hair more striking. She knew that. But Diana still had turned heads, had her followers. Monica could not tolerate that.

And so she'd run Diana off. But that wasn't enough. She had needed Diana to knuckle under, and had never forgotten that she hadn't. She had never been able to spell Diana, and couldn't figure out why not. She didn't project an iota of magic.

Maybe Diana would knuckle under this time. She'd love to hear her beg for Mitch's job.

Wait a minute. Diana might be a chink in Mitch's armor. Hadn't she heard Diana and her mother had allowed political rallies at the Ben 'n Bacon after hours? The wrong rallies at that. She should check that out. Her friend Sylvia ought to know. If Mitch was involved with a fascist, wasn't he one himself?

She'd have to talk with Bart about that.

MONICA AND BART

Bart Stevens had been one of Monica's easier conquests. And one of the most useful. She didn't really find him attractive, but he would do. Before he'd gone into teaching, he had been a hacker. Still was, really, and good at it. He'd planted fake evidence for her before and covered their tracks. He'd also read private e-mails for her.

He also was committed to the right causes. He was not a member of Anitfa, but he was sympathetic. The sex had helped him push through the riskier parts, but he had never done anything for her of which he disapproved. She'd never had to compel him.

Bart was married to a little mouse of a woman who reminded Monica of a younger, thinner Lorna Kaczynski. Laura Stevens was devoted to her mostly awful water colors and to their two children, and wasn't hard to fool. Jimmy really did work nights at the college sometimes, so he could park in his reserved slot, and walk through the building to where Monica could pick him up. They'd dive to her house and close the garage door before entering. She would drive him back to his car later.

Their meetings were sometimes about sex, sometimes about business, but usually both. Tonight it would be both if she liked what he had to say.

Monica had tried marriage and parenthood, and neither had suited her. Her engineer husband Mark was boring and easily compelled. Her son Bobby was too much like his father, and showed not a jot of Talent. She hadn't objected when the boy wanted to stay with his father. She saw him sometimes because it would have looked odd to be totally disinterested, but neither she nor Bobby enjoyed the visits. He wanted to play computer games and she let him. That made it easier.

Bart was more interesting. They had something in common other than sex.

Tonight she got right down to business when he had slumped way down in the passenger's seat of her Prius, a baseball hat pulled over his brows.

"What do you have for me?"

She heard a loud sigh. "Not much yet. I don't know what he's done to his work computer, but I can't do a thing with it. Funny thing is, IT reported it A-OK when I faked a maintenance call for him.

"I tired hacking into his home computer through the internet, but it's protected, too. I'm not sure how. Nothing I know about, that's for sure. I tried sending him a file that would let me in with a fake e-mail address, but I guess he's too savvy to open it."

He turned his head to her in apology. "I can keep trying." He didn't mention the missing thumb drive, and hoped he wouldn't have to do so.

"Do you still have the stuff we put together?"

"Yeah," he answered truthfully. It was in a secure folder on his personal laptop.

After a moment, Monica said slowly, "Let's try something different. See what you can find on line about his girlfriend."

"The woman at the Bean 'n Bacon?"

"That's the one. Diana Winstead. Maybe we can get in the back-door."

Monica pulled into her garage and closed the door.

"Now," she said before leaving the vehicle, "let's do something more…fun."

Stevens was okay with that. More than okay.

MITCH

In contrast to Monica, Mitch had a good day. Nothing bad happened. He met with his composition classes, graded papers, read a professional journal. At lunch, he spoke briefly with one of his buddies about the Saturday ball game trip to Boone.

He called Diana from the gym parking lot after his workout. She was with the boys tonight while her mom was at a bridge club meeting. He told her about the call he planned with Carson, wondered what his son wanted to talk about.

"You're going to tell him, aren't you?" she asked.

"I'm planning on it. Actually, I'd like to know what he thinks about my options."

"Well, he's a smart kid. I'll bet he has something worthwhile to say."

At home, Mitch prepared himself a quick dinner of salad and pasta with take-out meatballs from Mario's. He glanced and the clock on the kitchen wall as he put up the dishes. It was time for the Skype session with Carson.

Carson was at his apartment in Blacksburg, where he lived alone. He had taken his degree in Computer Science at Carolina the previous spring, and was beginning a Master's at Virginia Tech. The apartment around him was neat as a pin, except for a gym bag that had been tossed on a chair. In that, he was like his father.

But in appearance, Mitch saw more of tall, slender, dark Sarah Ellen in his son than he saw of himself. He wondered fleetingly about how Sarah Ellen was doing; he hadn't spoken with her in a while.

They talked about Carson's classes and about football for a few minutes.

Then, there was a brief but awkward pause, then Carson said, "You remember I told you about my girlfriend Lisa, don't you?"

Mitched said he did, and Carson hesitated again, and continued, "Well, I thought you ought to know that we're getting pretty serious. Like, you know, wedding bells serious."

Mitch had never met Lisa Paginelli. He had only heard Carson talk about her. But he was going to be positive about the news.

"Well, son," he said, "I think you have good judgment. I feel sure you've made a good choice."

Carson's face lit up, and he ran on for a few minutes about just how fine Lisa was. Then he asked, "How about you and Diana?"

He and Diana had always got on well.

"You know we've been serious for a while," his father said. "And I think there is a wedding on our future, too. But there's something I have to work through first."

The ice broken, he told Carson the story of the past few days. All of it except for any mention of magic or witchcraft. Carson, as far as he knew, didn't know about that.

"And so," he concluded, "I don't know what to do. I can fight whatever Monica has up her sleeve with a lawyer. But it will be honking expensive. I might not be successful, and that might make it worse."

Carson had been sipping on a tall something in a Starbuck's cup. He took a final drink, set down the cup, and looked direct at his father through the screen.

"Dad, you ought to fight this."

"You seem awfully sure."

"Dad, I am. All the time you were talking, I've been thinking. I always took to heart what you told me about surviving as a conservative at college by keeping my mouth shut. I always did that.

"But I'm getting tired of it. It's not right. I'm not a fascist or a racist or a sexist or any 'ist'. I'm tired of being told I am one if I don't toe someone else's line. Tech isn't as bad as Carolina that way, but it's pretty bad here, too. And it's getting worse."

Mitch opened his mouth to respond, but Carson held up a hand.

"I'm not through, Dad. Next year, I'm going to get a degree and I'll have to get a job. Things are getting bad in business, too. Look what went on at Google. It all started at the colleges.

"And that's where it has to end. In the colleges. Somebody has to stand up to them. You can. I don't know how much money you have. I don't need to know. I am real grateful for the help you're giving me. I'll tell you that. But I know you can afford a lawyer.

"If you don't fight something like this, what about the poor guy who doesn't have any money? Who's going give him any hope?

"If you don't fight, who will?"

Mitch was chuckling in spite of himself. "Diana told me the same thing."

"Well, she called me."

"You got this speech from her?"

"Not a bit of it. I had a long talk with her about what I've seen at school this summer. She knew I would agree with her. She just wanted to give me a head's up.

"I've had my say. It's up to you."

"Thanks for the advice, son."

"That's a switch, huh?

They laughed and signed off. Mitch went the den, poured a single malt and sat long in thought. Then he went to his study, opened a manila folder and wrote quickly. He closed the folder and headed for bed.

He slept well that night. Surprisingly well.

KATHRYN

Kathryn Turner walked from her car to the door to the law offices in bright autumn sunshine. It had rained sometime during the night, and the rain had washed the Indian Summer away, leaving a distinct chill in the air. She liked it.

She dropped by the front desk to check in, and was handed a plain tan folder. She knew what she would find before opening it, and was both please and apprehensive.

It was Mitch McCaffrey's signed engagement.

"Darlene," she told the receptionist, "buzz Marc and tell him to see me as soon as he can. We have work to do."

8

WHEN ALL IS SAID AND DONE

MITCH

Friday was another day in which nothing happened. Mitch was thankful for it, because he knew it wouldn't last. He'd just have to live with the anxiety of wondering when the other shoe would drop.

His English lit class met in the late morning as usual, minus Lottie and her two shadows; and he had a good time teaching. The class was reading Romeo and Juliet, and there was some spirited discussion of the two main characters' ages, and the differences between 16th Century Europe and the present day. Mitch was glad to see the usually shy Brenda Jenkins chime in. That kind of class was up-lifting, so Mitch was in a good mood when he headed to the canteen for a snack and some coffee afterwards. There, he ran into Don Kelly.

"Hi, Mitch. Any issues with your computer?"

"Nope," Mitch told him, then asked, "Are you going to Boone tomorrow?" Kelly was another Mountaineer fan.

Don shook his head sadly. "Can't make it. The game is too early, what with all I have to do around the house and in the yard. "I'll catch it on the radio, or maybe TV, if I finish soon enough. What about you?"

"I'm going to meet Ben and Lonnie at the Bean 'n Bacon early, and motor on up."

"Wish I could go. Do you think we can take Wake Forest?"

"Good chance. Go Apps!"

Mitch didn't notice Bart Stevens standing close by.

Monica

While Mitch was exchanging texts with his attorney, Monica was lunching with Sylvia Sonenberg at the Martintown Country Club. Sylvia was a crisp, thin, severely dressed woman with short bobbed hair streaked with gray. She looks like money, Monica thought, knowing her lunch companion, a lumber company heiress, was just what she looked like.

More importantly, Sylvia was a college benefactor and the chair of the Brainerd County Democratic party executive committee. She had been a reliable ally in the past. And she did not disappoint today.

Sylvia was a gold-mine of information about Margaret Corcoran and Diana Winstead. It turned out they permitted a gun-club affiliated with the NRA to meet at their restaurant, and had allowed political rallies at the Bean n' Bacon for the wrong candidates.

"But can you use this information?" Sylvia asked when her information had been exhausted. "It doesn't tie to the college."

Monica lips curled in a smirk. "Not on the record. But I'll make sure the hearing panel knows." The smirk became a laugh in which Sylvia joined. "Oh, I will certainly do that." Then she added with less humor. "I don't want to leave anything to chance. He'll get a lawyer. He has money, I understand."

"I wouldn't know," sniffed Sylvia. "But if he gets a lawyer, it'll probably be that nasty Bill Norville."

"Probably," Monica agreed. Neither could stand Norville's incandescent conservatism. "Or that young partner of his, Turner."

All in all, it was an entirely satisfactory lunch.

Just before Monica left the table, she received a text from Bart. He had an idea he thought she would like. She did.

After all, she thought on the way to her car, one didn't need the Craft for everything.

MITCH

Saturday dawned clear and chilly. Perfect football weather, Mitch thought as he looked out the window, happy to submerge his free-floating anxiety with giddy anticipation of the game. Showering and shaving quickly, he threw on cargo pants, a tee shirt and an App State hoody, and pulled on running shoes.

He partially filled a hamper with paper napkins and plates, plastic forks, and Appalachian stadium cups, adding a small bottle of vodka and a bottle of bloody Mary Mix. The rest of the tailgate would come at the Bean 'n Bacon, or be brought by Lonnie and Ben. This was one of the infamous noon kick-offs dictated by television, so the tailgate would have a breakfast slant.

The hamper went in the back of the Lexus along with a folding table and chairs; and Mitch, after making sure he had the tickets and the parking pass, was off.

Lonnie and Ben were already at the Bean 'n Bacon. Mitch collected a kiss from Diana to go with the large bag of ham, sausage and chicken biscuits for the hamper she handed them. All three men ordered large coffees to go.

Lonnie had a cooler holding bottled water and six packs of Coke and Catawba Brewing White Zombie beer that went into the Lexus beside the hamper. The drive to Boone would take about an hour, so they would have time to tailgate before kick-off, unless they got caught in traffic.

Sure enough, they beat most of the game traffic.

Mitch's membership in the Yosef's Club gave him a spot in the big parking lot close to the stadium. It was a glorious day for a tailgate. The sky was a crystalline blue, and there was still lots of color on the surrounding mountains. They set up the folding table and chairs and took out the hamper and cooler. Mitch made everyone a Bloody Mary. The biscuits were still warm.

Ben had brought a radio, and turned on the Saturday pre-game show. It competed with classic rock and roll blaring from where a nearby group had set up. The lot filled rapidly. Fans wandered around, stopping to talk with those they knew. Some had tickets to sell. Others were buying.

Some of the fans were wearing Wake Forest gear. They were in a good mood, exchanging good-natured gibes with the App fans. Mitch noticed one who walked around snapping photos, a lot of photos. Well, good for him.

There was still an empty space next to the Land Rover, and Mitch's group stood there, talking football and sipping their drinks. The grinning photographer, a plump middle-aged man wearing a Wake sweatshirt and baseball cap, brushed by on his way through the empty space to the next row with a smiling "excuse me". Mitch ignored a brief tingle. It was just a fan.

Mitch had noticed a young man in front of them walking from car to car with a sheaf of flyers in his hand. Now and then he stopped and offered one to a cluster of fans, who sometimes accepted and sometimes waved him off. As he came nearer, Mitch noticed he was unkempt, in ragged blue jeans and jacket over a Grateful Dead tee shirt, sporting a scruffy mustache and goatee.

When he reached Mitch's group he walked directly to Mitch, although Ben and Lonnie were closer.

"Have one of these, buddy," he said, shoving a flyer into Mitch's hand.

Mitch's witch sense tingled. And when he looked at the paper, he saw it depicted crossed Confederate and Nazi flags over all-caps bold print that read: "WHITE PEOPLE —AN ENDANGERED SPECIES". He wadded the paper up, dropped it and ground it beneath his heel.

"Get out of here!" he said. But the young man had moved on, quickly disappearing into a press of students who were walking by.

Mitch hadn't noticed the snapping of the camera behind him before he got rid of the flyer.

On the way to the stadium, he asked one of the fans who had taken a flyer from the young Nazi why he had done so.

"Why not?" The fan appeared genuinely puzzled. "It was just a flyer for a country music festival in Blowing Rock."

Now why had he been picked for the Nazi propaganda?

The question almost answered itself. Someone was trying to set him up. But he didn't know how. He hadn't been about to keep the flyer.

He remembered to put a ward on his car as well as locking it.

It had been a good game. Everyone agreed with that. But the App fans were disappointed. Their team had lost to a good Wake Forest team by a point, and they had badly wanted a win.

Mitch, Ben, and Lonnie were animatedly discussing the "what if's" when they returned to Mitch's car. Mitch unlocked the car (and released the ward, although Ben and Lonnie didn't know it). They opened the rear storage and retrieved beverages from the cooler, water for Mitch because he was driving, beer poured into cups for the other two. They continued to discuss the game while waiting for traffic to clear out. Mitch looked for the crumpled flyer but didn't find it, but he noticed something else.

At the rear of the car, there was a crumpled Confederate flag decal on the pavement. It was still sticky. He found adhesive on the rear window where someone had tried to attach it. The way the ward worked, protecting the vehicle from malicious intent, told him someone had tried to attach the decal who wished him, or someone associated with the vehicle, ill.

He closed his eyes and concentrated, receiving an image of the stout photographer in Wake Forest gear and the skinny guy with the flyers. He recognized neither.

Ben and Lonnie were giving him puzzled looks. "Anything wrong?" Lonnie asked.

"No." He quietly washed the decal's adhesive away with water from his bottle, and placed it in the pocket of his hoodie. Maybe he could learn more later.

But he was sure someone was trying to manufacture evidence. He'd have to tell his lawyers.

DIANA

Diana did not see Mitch Saturday evening. She knew that by the time she finished at the Bean 'n Bacon, went to her exercise class, and picked up the boys from soccer, she would be exhausted and he would be in front of the television in Full Football Mode, in which she might as well have been part of the furniture. When she retrieved Paul and Steve, who were as usual hanging with Jimmy Turner after the game, she offered to take the three of them to a movie, so Kathryn and Dr. George could have an impromptu date night dinner.

She texted him, "tough luck". He immediately responded, and added he had something to tell her. She started to ask what, but decided to simply text back, "See you tomorrow. Kisses."

She took the boys home, where Kathryn and her husband called for Jimmy only a short time later. They declined her offer to come in for coffee. Kathryn said nothing about Mitch's case, and Diana decided not to ask, even though she wanted to.

As she readied for bed, she realized she was irked, upset. She was peeved at Mitch. With everything that was going on in his life, how could he just immerse himself in college football as though everything were all right?

She knew she wasn't being fair. Then she realized what the problem really was.

She was scared.

Scared this thing at the college wouldn't end well for Mitch. Scared that it would leave him at loose ends with no purpose in life.

And scared about what that would do to them. To her.

Now mad at herself for her fear and her unhappiness, she cried on her pillow and went to sleep.

The next morning brought another clear, cool late October day. Diana rousted Paul and Steve for breakfast and made them get ready for church afterwards. She and Myra took them to Sunday School at the First Methodist Church of Glen Arden, where the Corcoran family had attended church ever since Diana's Savannah Irish great-grandfather's conversion from Roman Catholicism in the 1920's. Supposedly he had converted for her great-grandmother's sake.

Diana found herself enjoying the service. It was odd, she thought, how troubles that seemed over-powering late at night were better in the morning. When they returned from church, she had time to feed the boys lunch before changing clothes to await Mitch. They were going to drive to Black Mountain to visit Mitch's mom, and then he had promised her dinner at Bouchon in Asheville, which was a French Provencal bistro they both liked.

"I'll have to invite Mom to join us," he had told her. "But she won't go."

Well, it would be all right if Joanna McCaffrey took them up on it. She liked Mitch's mother. One of the many things that had drawn her to Mitch was they had so much in common. Not just the circumstances of their divorce. They'd both lost their fathers relatively early in life.

Neither father had left their families destitute. But it had affected their options. In Mitch's case, it had meant Army ROTC at Appalachian State, to be able to attend college. For his younger brother, Johnny, it had meant two years at the then smaller Carolina Highlands Community College before following in his brother's footsteps to Boone.

Diana's older brother Rob had been through school, married, and living in Nashville when her father had passed. But he had his own family on the way, and hadn't been able to offer much help. Diana's dad had left enough for her mother to open the Bean 'n Bacon, if she downsized houses. Diana had postponed college to help with the restaurant. Only later had she been able, by commuting and on-line classes, get her business degree from Lenoir Rhyne.

It had all worked out. Neither mother had ever re-married, although Diana's mother had her boyfriends. Mitch's mother, to her knowledge, had been content with her memories and her position as an elementary school teacher.

Mitch arrived about two in the afternoon driving the Lexus. The trip to Black Mountain and Asheville was downhill on a state road to I-40, then west on the interstate. The line of demarcation between the mountains and the Piedmont was supposedly Martintown, with the eastern and southern parts of Brainerd County in the rolling but steepening Piedmont hills, and the western and northern sections in the mountains. All of the roads they would travel were good.

Joanna McCaffrey now lived in an upscale assisted living complex in Black Mountain, courtesy of selling her house some help from

Mitch's inheritance. She had been reluctant to leave the house where she'd raised her family, but had finally agreed to take the unit. She'd admitted her quality of life had improved, having found a number of friends.

They called it assisted living, Diana reflected as she and Mitch were seated on a sofa that was actually more the size of a love seat; but Joanna did not appear she required much assistance. The unit, really an efficiency apartment, was well furnished and neat as a pin.

So was its occupant. At 82, Joanna McCaffrey was a still attractive, white-haired lady to whom Mitch bore a strong resemblance. Today she wore pumps, khaki pants, and a green sweater fastened with a brooch over a white blouse. She offered them iced tea.

The conversation quickly turned to family. Mitch's brother Johnny was going to visit next month and spend a day with Joanna before joining Mitch for a ball game in Boone. He had called earlier that week, and he and his family were fine.

"And how are you doing, Mitch?" his mother asked.

Mitch and Diana exchanged glances. Diana was again a bit put out with Mitch, because he had stubbornly refused to tell her what had happened in Boone until later, claiming, "we have the whole rest of the day". But they had agreed to say nothing of the complaint against Mitch to his mother for now.

Joanna accepted the assurance of "fine", but had noticed the look that had passed between Diana and her son.

The time passed quickly while they caught up. As expected, Joanna turned down the invitation to dinner in Asheville.

Diana and Mitch left a few minutes later. She waited until when they were in the car, and said immediately, "Okay, Mitch, spill it. I want to know what happened yesterday. Right now."

He told her as they were pulling out of the assisted living complex onto the road that would take them back to the interstate.

"Mitch, this is getting frightening. Someone – it has to be Monica – really has it in for you. Do you know why?"

"Well, I'll tell you what my lawyers say." Mitch repeated to her what Bill Norville had suggested.

"I'm sure that's part of it," Diana replied, "but I think there's something personal to it. Do you know what it is?"

After a pause, he said, "No."

She thought there was something he wasn't telling, but before she could press him, she noticed a strip shopping center to the right with a store that looked interesting.

"Mitch, pull into that strip center, please. There's a store I want to go in."

He did as she requested. "Which one?"

Diana pointed. "There."

The sign said in gaudy gold leaf, "MOUNTAIN MAGIC", adding below in smaller print, "Lore and Games for All Ages."

"I might find something for the boys," she explained. "It's open."

Mitch looked at the store dubiously. But he said, "Okay. There's a used book store next door. I'll go in there."

MITCH

Mitch parked directly in from of Mountain Magic, intending to walk Diana to the door and turn right to the adjoining bookstore. But as they approached the clear window with the store's name emblazoned on it, he felt a tingling. Not of magic.He sensed no real magic emanating from the store. No, what he felt was the same tingle he'd received Saturday. There was someone inside who wished him ill.

He stopped at the door and peered inside. There were tables with board games like "Dungeons and Dragons" and other tables with video games. There were racks of what appeared to be comic books, and other book shelves he couldn't make out through the glare of the late afternoon sunlight. There appeared to be a counter in the back, staffed by a young man in a tee shirt with a scruffy beard.

Where had he seen him? Wait a minute. The tailgate yesterday. The Nazi flyer.

He moved aside for Diana. "Go on in, honey," he said. "I'll be in, in a minute."

He stepped back and took out his phone, and opened the camera. He muttered a quick spell to lessen the glare and snapped two pictures of the front window, and another two of the door, making sure he got the street address printed on the latter.

Before he went inside, he sub-vocalized another spell, concentrating because he hadn't used it much. It was a glamour. Whoever saw him wouldn't notice anything unusual. They wouldn't notice anything at all. His features would be indistinct and unmemorable. Another magic user would see through it with no difficulty. But he'd detected no magic in the store.

Entering, he moved to Diana's side at a table where she was looking at video games. She glanced up and gave a start, peering at him sharply.

"I decided this store was more interesting than the bookstore," he said, knowing the glamour was likely confusing her but she would be assured by his voice. "It's a charming shop," he continued more loudly, but not shouting.

"It is. But I think these games are a little old for the boys." His eyes followed her pointing fingers. The games on this table all said, "Ages 12 and above."

"I agree. But let's look around. You can always ask the clerk."

She walked to another table while he inspected the bookshelves. Most of the offerings were regional lore ranging from local ghost stories to mountain recipes. One shelf was labeled, "Beware! Grimoires." But he sensed they were fake. There were several shelves of graphic novels. And a whole case of action figures from Harry Potter, The Lord of the Rings, and The Hobbit, not to mention DC and Marvel Comics.

He turned to see Diana clutching the new Harry Potter book. "I've been meaning to get this for the boys. But I don't see any games for kids their age."

"Well, as I said, let's ask the Clerk."

They walked to the counter at the back of the store, where they found Mr. Scruffy looking at the clock on the while behind him. Mitch saw it was just a few minutes until Sunday closing, according to the hours he'd seen on the front door. He and Diana were the only customers in the store. The sales clerk turned to Diana and Mitch, revealing he wore a Led Zeppelin shirt today, and showing no recognition when he glanced at Mitch.

Diana explained what she was looking for.

Scruffy nodded. "I can't think of anything. But let me get the owner."

Scruffy left the salesroom through a door in the back, and they could hear low voices for a minute. Then he returned with a smiling, slightly overweight, middle-aged man with thinning reddish hair, wearing wire-rimmed glasses and an Argyll sweater. He was evidently a little warm in the latter, as there were sweat beads at his receding hairline.

There was another quick tingle. This was Mr. Wake Forest Photographer from the tailgate. He smiled at Diana, his eyes touching Mitch but not lingering.

"No, we don't carry much in games for younger kids," Photo-bug told her. "Our regular customers just don't buy them."

"Well, I'll just get the book, then," Diana said. "I know you need to close up."

While Scruffy was ringing up the sale, Mitch spoke for the first time, taking a chance, but only a small one, that his voice would be familiar.

"You have a nice store," he said. "Do you have a card, or something that would show your webpage – if you have one?"

"Sure do", said Photo-bug. He pointed to a holder beside the cash register. Mitch retrieved one, noting it gave the store's name, followed by "Arthur Jenkins, Prop." That must be Photo-bug.

"Do you mind if a take a few photos?" Mitch said. "We can show them to our friends in Hickory."

Diana opened her mouth, closed it. She had tumbled to there being something up.

"Not at all! Not at all," Jenkins (as Mitch supposed him to be) said. Mitch pulled out his phone, snapping shots of the tables and shelves, and one each of Jenkins and his scruffy sales clerk.

He'd watched Diana pay in cash, so no one had seen any identification. He offered his hand to Jenkins, pulling a name out of the air as he did.

"Mike Martin," he said. "This is Ruth, my fiancé." Diana, bless her, didn't bat an eye.

Jenkins took Mitch's hand and then offered his to Ruth, introducing Mr. Scruffy as Peter Felton. Mitch and Diana shook hands with Felton, too.

"Thanks so much," Diana chirped, offering her best, sweetest smile. "We'll get out and let you nice people close up."

"What was that all about?" Diana asked when they were in the car. "You better be glad I figured out you wanted to keep our names secret." She blinked as she looked over at Mitch, who removed the glamour just as he looked over.

"I'll explain on the road," Mitch said. "I don't want to take any chances here."

By the time they reached Bouchon, he'd explained fully.

"Mitch, you need to get this information to Kathryn immediately," Diana told him as they walked from the Ransom Street garage to the restaurant. "I wouldn't even wait for your meeting Tuesday."

"You're right. I'll call Monday."

Then they were able to enjoy dinner and the ride back.

9

KNOWING ME, KNOWING YOU

MONICA

Monica Gilbert was having a most satisfactory Monday morning. She had met with Bart Stevens and now had both an electronic copy and several prints of Mitch McCaffrey exchanging Nazi literature with a young man in a parking lot. It was not clear from the photograph who was handing whom the flyer.

"This probably won't hold up," Stevens had warned. "We can't tie it to anything, because we haven't been able to penetrate his devices."

"It doesn't matter," Monica had said. "It's bad enough that he took it. We'll make sure the faculty and especially the hearing panel know about this. At the least, it will distract him and make him spend time trying to refute it.

"Why don't you float this around some of the faculty we can trust. Tell them to keep it quiet for now."

And she had just hung up from the last of McCaffrey's former students she'd decided to contact. Once Stevens had helped her hack into records, it wasn't hard to figure whom. She was looking for women or minorities who had done poorly in his classes. Not the "D" students. Those would be too obvious. No, what she had needed were former students on the college transfer track who had "hooked" his English Lit course. The ones for whom a "C" on hours needed for transfer might make the difference between being accepted at Carolina or Western Carolina.

It hadn't been hard to suggest to them that McCaffrey's conduct had been inappropriate. One was willing to say she had the distinct impression that her grade would have been better if she'd offered to sleep with him. It hadn't even required compulsion. Only a gentle push, a suggestion, which about all she could manage over the telephone anyway.

She had notes of her interviews. All of them had promised a statement by e-mail. They wouldn't be under oath; but compliance with the rules of evidence wasn't necessary, at least at this point. This was excellent.

She'd met with the committee this morning. Gina had been an aggressive interviewer, Lorna less so. She could wish for more witnesses, but they had enough to file a report. Lottie and her shadows were, she thought, pretty solid. She hadn't got anywhere with most of the others, but you always had some that were too timid, and even some who were too reactionary. There were others whose interview notes could be... massaged..., yes that was the word, without too much risk.

And that, she reflected, was exactly the problem with Mitchell McCaffrey. Really more than his rejection of her, although she still didn't like it. He'd been discrete about it, so no one knew. He hadn't publicly humiliated her. If that had been all, she could overlook if not forgive it.

But McCaffrey, when it came down to it, was an irresponsible teacher. They had such a wonderful opportunity here to mold students. Most of the kids here were from local families. Many had grown up redneck. They were here to get their start in higher education at low cost.

But they had to be taught properly. They had to be taught correctly. They had to be kept safe from dangerous ideas and turned into good progressive thinkers. This wasn't happening in McCaffrey's classes.

She didn't have any evidence he was overtly feeding them right wing propaganda. In fact, she was pretty sure he wasn't. The kids interviewed, the ones she couldn't use, all had said Mitch refused to discuss current political issues in his classes. He always turned the discussions to what was going on at the time of Milton, Shakespeare, or Chaucer.

In other words, he was being covert. Teaching the course without providing proper judgment was just perpetuating the racism, the sexism, the homophobia of those dead white men who wrote the plays and the poems. It was covert right-wing propaganda. The college should not, could not, continue to tolerate it.

She had no sympathy for Mitch McCaffrey. He didn't need this position. He was supposed to have money. The college could fill that job with someone who would teach the right values, preferably with a woman or a minority who would improve the gender and ethnic faculty balance.

She would write the report this afternoon. It would recommend termination. Gina and Lorna would sign, the first enthusiastically, the second reluctantly; but Lorna would sign all the same.

She permitted herself a smile. They had left him alone for days. He probably was feeling safe, that it would blow over. Well, it wouldn't. He was going to find out, probably by the end of the week.

But now for lunch. Sylvia was going to join her again. She hoped they had that young server again at the Club. He was hot. Maybe…

MARC AND KATHRYN

On Tuesday evening, Kathryn and Marc paid a visit to Mitch in his home. Marc thought it had gone well.

"What do you think?" Kathryn asked him at the office the following morning. He knew what she meant

"I like him. I want to help him. And I love his house! I forgot to ask him about his hunting rifles. I saw them in a case in the basement, down the hall. I want to come back and see them."

Leave to a man to go straight for the macho stuff. She asked, "Do you think he's telling us everything?"

"I thought you and Mr. Norville said nobody tells you everything."

"They don't. But I'm asking about Mitch specifically."

Marc considered, then said, "Well he didn't want to talk about those old books. And I don't understand why he doesn't want his computer inspected. And…and…Kathryn…do you really think he does his own housecleaning?"

"Good work. That's exactly what I picked up on. But what I can't figure out is why it bothers me."

"Do you think there's anything bad on his computer?"

"Could be, but I doubt it. It's something else I haven't figured out." She sighed. "Okay, Marc, finish up checking out Felton and Jenkins. Let me know what you find. Let's get the contacts with the former students going right away.

"We'll save the current students for later. You get to do the interviews." She shot him a wicked smile. "Including Lottie and her group."

Marc started. "Ms. T- I mean Kathryn — shouldn't a woman do that?"

Kathryn snorted. "You don't understand young women as well as you may think. But we'll send Tiffany with you, or Jenny if Bill can spare her." Tiffany was a paralegal that primarily reported to Kathryn.

10

WHERE HAVE ALL THE FLOWERS GONE?

MITCH

Mitch had just backed out of his garage the next morning when his phone rang. He punched the icon on his dash that would enable him to talk over his car microphone and speakers, expecting to hear Diana's voice.

"Good morning," he said, not adding a "darling" or a "sweetheart" this once. It was good that he didn't.

It was Kathryn Turner.

"Mitch, can you do lunch today or tomorrow? I want to follow up with something I thought about last night. I can get a private room at Tremaine's." Tremaine's was Martintown's effort at upscale dining.

Mitch thought. "Today would be better. But shouldn't it wait until something definite happens?"

There was a pause on the line. "Well, it could. And I thought about it. But I'd rather go ahead. We may be pressed for time after the college president schedules a hearing. What about noon sharp? Just ask for the room reserved for Melton, Norville's use."

Mitch was puzzled, but agreed. No point in hiring a lawyer if you weren't going to take any recommendations.

Mitch's lit class ended at 11:00. The class had finished with Romeo and Juliet, and were now reading King Lear, which they did not like as much. He'd suggested the play had relevance to them because surely they had issues with parents much as Lear's daughters had issues with their father. Then they'd perked up. When he reached his office, he found nothing to delay his making his lunch appointment.

Tremaine's was not that busy. He didn't see anyone waiting on a table that he knew; and when he asked for the law firm's reserved room, the hostess led him there immediately. Kathryn was already there, tapping on her phone. When he entered, she rose before he could wave her to keep her chair and shook hands.

"Why do I feel this meeting is about bad news?" he asked when the hostess had left with their drink orders.

Kathryn responded with the wry smile for which she was noted.

"Why do clients always assume that?" she asked, rhetorically. "I don't have any news. I do have some questions, but let's wait until we've ordered."

They ordered light lunches, a bowl of the onion soup for Mitch and a Caesar salad with grilled chicken for Kathryn. The server left a basket of bread and departed.

"So why are we here?" Mitch asked when the door had closed behind the server.

Kathryn leaned forward slightly, far enough to make a point, but not far enough to be intimidating.

. "I didn't want to press you on this in front of Marc," she said. "But I have the feeling this thing with Monica Gilbert is not just about enforcing a politically correct agenda. It's personal, too. I think there is something, maybe more than one something, you're not telling us. I want to know what it is."

He started to protest. But no, she was right. He respected her instincts. He'd hired the right lawyer. He wasn't about to tell her everything. She'd think he was nuts. But some of it. Yes, he ought to tell her some of it.

"Okay, I...do have something to tell you that you ought to know.."

"And oh, before you do, In need to tell you I'm going to send a forensic IT analyst and a paralegal over to your office in the morning, if there's a good time, just to be sure nothing's been tampered with."

"Nothing has," Mitch assured her. "I check it every day."

"I believe you. But we'll do this all the same. I'm worried about what they might plant when you're not there to check. We're going to do an inventory. With pictures. We can't image your computer because it's college property, but the guy I'm sending can check everything and print-screen your directories."

"When I'm not there?"

"Mitch, I know we're getting side-tracked, but please understand. Monica Gilbert and maybe some others are really after your job. Her committee will report against you, and recommend suspension pending a hearing. You'll be escorted out of the building and your access to anything but public space will be revoked. I'm surprised it hasn't happened already. We shouldn't delay this."

Mitch had known this was coming, and here it was, just about. He knew Kathryn was on his side, and he ought to take her recommendation. "Well...okay. Early is good. My first class isn't until 10:00. Have them call my cell and I'll go out and get them."

Kathryn nodded and sipped her water. "Now," she said briskly, "tell me what you haven't been telling."

"Well, she has a history with Diana," he began.

Kathryn's brows lifted. Diana was a friend, but she'd heard nothing about any connection with Monica.

He told her the same story Diana had told him.

Their orders arrived. When Denise had left again, she looked thoughtfully at Mitch, and said, "That's an interesting story. And it explains part of what I am looking for." She took a forkful of salad, chewed, swallowed. "But I think there's more than that."

She took another swallow of San Pellegrino, then made direct eye contact.

"Does Monica Gilbert have a history with you?"

For a moment, Mitch thought Kathryn Turner must have some Talent. But no, he was picking up nothing. It was just really good intuition. He'd hoped to avoid telling what he was about to say, but she was right. It could be important, and she needed to know.

"Well," he began...

The divorce was not final, but it was close. He had just started his sessions with Dr. Fitzpatrick. He was coping by doing his job, and by exercise. His visits to the gym relieved a lot of stress.

It was a Friday afternoon. He didn't have a spotter for the free weights, so he was concentrating on the Nautilus machines. He noticed a woman who hadn't been there before.

Actually, everyone noticed her. The men looked at one another with sly smiles. The women, when they thought no one was looking, rolled their eyes. She was rather tall, pretty with an aquiline nose and a mop of dark red hair.

And her figure was spectacular. She wore tight leggings and a halter top over a sports bra that exposed a lot of cleavage. He had seen other women who came tricked out in a similar fashion, there to be seen and envied or lusted after as much as to work out.

But he recognized this one. She had been introduced at a faculty cocktail party as the new compliance officer only a few weeks earlier. He remembered that she had come in wearing an expensive business suit with a remarkably short skirt. It had reminded him of the outfit he'd seen one of Michael Jackson's lawyers wear on television. But Brainerd County wasn't California.

In a way, she was amusing. She was working out, all right. But she was making sure she used the machines that would work her pectoral muscles, causing her breasts to lift suggestively, if one were male, provoking the rolled eyes and sly grins, of which she was fully aware, if he read her occasional upward twitching of the lips correctly.

Of course, he was sneaking looks. Everyone was.

He went on with his routine. He was nearly finished, with only one more set on the crunch, machine, when he saw her walking toward him.

"You're the English teacher, aren't you?" she asked. Her voice was a husky contralto. "At the college, I mean."

"Yes," he responded, looking up and offering a hand that he supposed wasn't too sweaty. She took it firmly. "Mitch McCaffrey. And you're the new compliance officer, Ms...." He looked resolutely at her green eyes, refusing to let them drop.

"Gilbert," she smiled at him, and he thought her mouth a bit cruel. "Monica Gilbert."

"I've been watching you," she said after a moment. "You're pretty impressive. On the machines, I mean." But he didn't think that was her intent.

"Thank you. So are you," he said honestly.

She nodded, accepting the compliment without modesty, real or false.

"I've been thinking. Suppose we get a drink after we're done. You could fill me in on the school."

Of course, he was tempted. Of course, he was. But there was something about her. It may have been the Talent then untapped within him. But he thought he was being invited into dangerous waters.

"I'm sorry," he said. "I have an appointment with my therapist right after I get through here. I'd better hurry my shower our I'll be late." It was an excuse. A lie, actually. He didn't have an appointment that evening. He was going to the West Brainerd football game. Or had planned to. Maybe he would just go home.

"That's too bad," she responded. "Another time, perhaps?" She really said "perhaps".

He decided to be honest.

"Monica, to tell the truth, I'm just winding up a divorce; and I'm not in a good place right now. I don't know when I'll feel more social. But I'm not really, not now."

"I see," she said, coloring slightly, and not from exercise. He supposed men just didn't turn her down, and probably few did. But he thought he saw more anger than embarrassment in her demeanor. "Well, I hope you have a good session with your therapist."

Then, before she turned, she looked at him intently for a moment, brows knotted. He felt a brief pressure in his forehead, but her face relaxed into puzzlement, and the pressure subsided. "And have a nice weekend," she said, and turned and walked away, rolling her hips. He supposed she wanted him to know what he was missing.

"She never approached me again, and she was always correct in dealing with me. At least until now. But she was always cool," Mitch finished. "I don't know if what I told you is important. But it happened.

"She moved on to other men. More than one, I've heard. But she just gave me a bad feeling. I really wasn't interested. Tempted, yes, but not interested – if that makes any sense.

"I took Diana to a few cocktail parties for faculty after we started seeing each other. Monica didn't attend any of them. So I never knew they knew each other."

What he'd thought was a bad feeling was that she'd tried to put a compulsion on him, he realized now, and either his natural Talent had fended it off, or she'd just thought better of it. But he wasn't about to tell Kathryn that.

"Well, it does explain why there seems to be a special interest in this 'prosecution'", Kathryn said softly. "But I hope the story hasn't been too upsetting. I'm afraid you've let your soup cool."

Mitch looked at the table. His soup was mostly untouched, and the ice cubes in his tea had melted.

Well, he hadn't been hungry anyway.

"Thank you for telling me, "said Kathryn. "All information helps. I think this will help more than you think."

He wondered if she realized that she still didn't have all of the information.

And wouldn't.

DIANA

Diana had been apprehensive all morning – actually, since the day before. Maybe that was why she wasn't surprised when Mitch called to ask her to join him for take-out that evening, because "there's something I told Kathryn that I need to tell you."

"Why haven't you told me before?"

"I didn't want to worry you with it."

"Pretty lame, McCaffrey."

"I know. But…Diana, something has just occurred to me that could be important."

"Something about Monica?" she asked.

"No. Something about you."

Of course she'd agreed. Mom could handle the kids one evening. And damn it! Men were so infuriating. Getting protective for no reason. She was eaten up with curiosity, and she shouldn't have had to be.

By the time she reached Mitch's home a few hours later, much of her irritation, although not her curiosity, had subsided. She had done some serious thinking during her exercise class, and she finally had a better handle on what was really bugging her. She'd bring it up tonight after Mitch had brought her up to speed on his case. Part of it was that she missed him when they were apart, even for a few days. How were they going to solve that?

While they were eating the Thai take-out Mitch had picked up, Mitch told her about what had happened at the gym during his divorce. What she heard pissed her off. Really pissed her off.

"That...minx," she said. "That bitch. She didn't even work out there regularly, did she?"

"No. I'd never seen her there before. And I didn't see her again after."

Diana was surprised at how angry the story made her. Not at Mitch. At Monica. Then something occurred to her. "Tell me, what about this story is important about me?"

Mitch had the wine bottle pour for himself this time. He took a sip, obviously stalling so he could get what he wanted to say exactly right.

"Okay, you remember what I told you about Monica trying a compulsion spell on me?" He'd left that out in the version of the story he'd told Kathryn.

She nodded.

"I wasn't trained. I didn't even know I had the Talent. But somehow I resisted compulsion....Now, you also remember I told you that I couldn't detect any of the Talent in you?"

"Yes." She was starting to see where he was going.

"Well, I'm starting to re-think that, a little. There are those who can't use magic, but who can resist it. I think you may be one of them.

"One other thing I told you before. I don't believe in using a compulsion spell, except maybe in self-defense. I was taught it's unethical. I've never tried to compel you. Honest."

She waved a hand dismissively, showing him she understood. What was he driving at now?

"I want to do an experiment. I'm going to try a compulsion spell on you now. It's going to be something innocuous. Are you game?"

"You better not make me take my clothes off, or hop around on one foot."

He laughed. "I've never had to compel you to take your clothes off. You've always volunteered."

She laughed, too. "All right. Go ahead."

She watched as he sat back, holding his wine glass up to his face, not drinking, but hiding his lips. His brows knitted in concentration.

The plate in front of her on the table still held a half-eaten portion of steamed rice. Mitch had placed a bottle of Kikkoman's low-sodium soy sauce on the table, to her left by the salt and pepper. She found herself staring at the bottle of soy sauce, wanting to pick it up and pour from it on the rice.

She reached for the bottle, touched it.

No. She didn't want any more rice. She didn't like soy sauce anyway. Why would she even think – oh.

She folded her hand on the table and looked up at Mitch's eyes. "Was that it? Did I pass?"

"You sure did. Tell me, what did you feel?"

"It was a little strange. More than a little. I was expecting something stronger, and at first I didn't feel anything. I was looking at the table, and all of a sudden I saw the soy sauce and decided I would pour it on the rice. I started to pick it up, and then – well, it was like waking up. I just realized I didn't want any soy sauce. So I didn't get any."

"Now back in high school, did you ever have a moment like that with Monica?"

She had leaned forward to speak, and sat back with a gasp. "Good Lord, Mitch, that's been, what, 17 or 18 years ago. I can't remember. How could I – wait a minute." She'd just thought of something. "Yes-s. It was in cheerleading try outs, and all of a sudden I wanted to trip one of the other girls. I saw Monica smirking at me, and – just like that" – she snapped her fingers – "I didn't want to do that. Do you think…?"

"I do. Monica tried to compel you, and couldn't."

"But how is that important now?"

"It's both good and bad. I'd thought Monica might try to get at me by working a compulsion on you. She can't. That's good. But she might try to get at me by hurting you somehow. That's bad.

"I've already warded your car. I'm going to ward you, though it doesn't appear you need it. I'm going to drop by tomorrow and ward your Mom and the boys. But you all still need to be careful. Not all mischief is magical."

Diana felt tears prickle. She blinked, and asked, "Mitch, what are we doing?"

"Huh? What do you mean?"

"Well, here we are with me afraid for you. And now you tell me to be afraid for the boys. And you have all this money. And this...this magic.

"We could take the boys and move to the coast. We could kiss all of this good-bye. Or you could magic your way out of this thing. Instead, you're dealing with lawyers, and we all feel threatened and I'm still working six days a week and I want to know why. Why?" She was sobbing now and knew she must look awful.

Mitch reached for her hand across the table. She let him take and squeeze it.

"Do you think I don't stay up worrying about the same thing, honey?" he asked. "I promise you I do.

"But I decided to fight this thing because I realized you and Carson are right. Somebody has to stand up to these bullies. If somebody doesn't, it'll get worse.

"And you? I've seen how proud you are of the business you've worked to build, and taking care of your sons. That's why I didn't tell you the details about the money. I didn't want you to lose that."

She nodded, blinking tears. "But —"

"Darling, I want to see you with more time to spend with me and to enjoy life. But I want it to be on your terms, our terms, not because Monica Gilbert has driven us away. Magic? I want to be careful about magic. It can backfire on you. And if you use it hatefully, it will make you hateful.

"So I'm going to have to think about it. There may be something else I can do. But I'd rather handle this through the lawyers if I can."

He squeezed her hand again, harder, but not painfully.

"But I promise you this. We will get through this."

And she believed him. And she loved him. She placed her other hand over his and squeezed back.

And then she felt a burst of anger, righteous, white-hot. Staring through the tears that still flowed directly into Mitch's intent eyes, she said, "We just can't let that witch win. We can't. We won't."

They sat in silence, united, sharing emotion, a feeling of unity that was not sexual, but all the more intense.

Then they cleared the dishes, kissed, and she left with promises for tomorrow.

They knew the other shoe was going to drop soon.

11

BLOWING IN THE WIND

MITCH

Mitch hadn't been in his office long the next morning, had just started reviewing his notes for his comp class in fact, when his cell phone rang. It was Jenny Jackson from Melton, Norville. She said they had just parked in the public lot.

"I'll come out and get you," he offered.

"No, don't. We know where your office is. We're coming in through different entrances. There'll be two knocks on your door."

The first knock was Jenny and another paralegal named Tiffany DeRatt. He didn't have to be introduced to her because she'd been a student a few years earlier. She was pretty, slender, African American, with tight blue-black curls, and dressed like Jenny in what appeared to be the firm paralegal uniform of dark pantsuit over a white blouse, wearing minimal jewelry, although a diamond stud graced one nostril.

"Hi, Mr. McCaffrey," she said, shaking hands. "I wanted to be one of your witnesses, but Kat and Marc said it wouldn't work because I work for them."

Jenny placed a brief case on a chair, and, opening it, revealed a digital camera, a portable electronic Dictaphone, and two legal pads and pens. She grabbed the camera while Tiffany took out a pad and pen.

"Guy" – whoever Guy was – "is running a little bit behind us. So, we're going to do the inventory first," Jenny said.

She stepped back and took a wide-angle shot of the office from the door, then began snapping pictures of each wall. She took close ups of the bookshelves so titles could be read.

"Do the books belong to you?" she asked.

"Most of them," Mitch told her.

While Jenny was taking photos, Tiffany was making a list. Looking over her shoulder, Mitch saw the date in the upper right-hand corner, and below that "Wall 1", then a space, "Wall 2", and so on. She added, "Bookshelf 1" and Bookshelf 2", with a number of blank lines underneath each, and then "Desk".

She went back and listed all of the diplomas and certificates on the wall behind his desk, including his teaching awards. He had photos of the stadiums in Boone in Chapel Hill on one wall, and she listed them.

Jenny took two shots of the desk top, then opened each drawer and starting snapping photos. She set the camera on the desk and asked Tiffany for the Dictaphone. She began rapid-fire dictation while Tiffany checked off location on the pad, covering each wall and each bookshelf, including the professional journals that were stacked on the lower shelves. Tiffany took each volume off the shelf and flipped through it for inserted papers. There were a couple. She showed them to Jenny, who added that information to the dictated summary.

The two then moved to the desk, going through each drawer. They even counted sheets of paper and pens and pencils. He wondered if they were going to count paper clips, but didn't. Sometimes they asked him to clarify what a document was, and he told them. Then they each initialed each page of pad that had writing, and asked Mitch to do the same. At last, everything went back in the briefcase.

Just as Jenny was closing the briefcase, there was another knock at the door. Tiffany opened it and admitted a man carrying a square black leather case. He was about Mitch's age, was dressed in jeans, a blue oxford shirt and a denim jacket. He was wiry, with graying pale brown hair, wire rimmed glasses and a brushy gray moustache. Tiffany introduced him as Guy Polizotto, with Computer Security Solutions.

Polizotto went straight to work. First, he checked behind all of the wall hangings, looking for bugs. He stood on a chair and lifted the cover to the overhead florescent light for the same thing. After confirming the two paralegals had seen the shelf behind every book or magazine, he pulled each bookcase out far enough to look behind.

He didn't find anything. Mitch had known he wouldn't. He had placed a ward on the office, and the Ward would have told him if something malicious had happened while he was out.

"Now let's look at that computer," Polizotto said, and Mitch moved aside while he sat down at the swivel chair behind the desk, placing the black case on the floor to his right. Mitch didn't have to remove the Ward on the computer, because Polizzotto wasn't hostile, but did have to give him his PIN to unlock the screen.

The other three watched while Polizzotto first printed, using "Print Screen" on the keyboard and the printer attached to the desktop device, the opening screen, and then did the same with every screen he opened. He studied the contents of Mitch's "documents" folder carefully, stopping to ask questions every so often. None of the folders contained much of anything personal. Mitch confirmed that anything like that would be on his laptop at home.

"What are these?" he asked when he opened the "Passwords" folder.

"Just my passwords to the state's and college's materials for faculty members," Mitch replied. "Most of the materials, like the faculty policy manual, are publicly available anyway."

"That's right," Jenny confirmed. "We already have copies of those."

The screen printing continued. He opened the dropdown menu for "favorites" on the browser. There weren't many. The college and state sites, a link to the Modern Languages Institute and another to the Southern Association of Colleges and Schools page. And –

"What are 'App Talk' and 'Heel Prints'?"

"Oh, those are private message boards for Appalachian State and Carolina," Mitch told him.

"Are they password protected?"

"Yes."

"Are the passwords written down? Or saved?"

"Saved."

"Change them today. And don't save them on this device."

Finally, Polizotto hooked two wires from his case to the tower, and then did mysterious things while the other three whispered small talk. At length he was satisfied. Mitch, who had been looking at his watch, was happy to hear it. He had to get to his class.

"Well," Polizotto said, removing the cables he'd attached, "I wish I could image the whole device, but we better not because you don't own it. But I didn't see anything suspicious....Now, when can I get by to check your home computer?"

Mitch decided that evening worked as well as anything.

When they left and he locked the office to go to his class, Mitch was relieved. He'd leave the Ward on the computer, but he couldn't be sure Monica couldn't take it off if she got hold of it. He believed what Kathryn had told him about what was probably coming. He wondered if he should start removing the books that were his. But no, he'd have been told if that was recommended, and doing so on his own initiative would, well, look as though he were guilty of something.

Polizzotto's inspection of his home security system and his home computer that evening went without a hitch. But he had a feeling, not necessarily from the Talent, that something was about to happen, probably the next day. When he made his good-night call to Diana, he said as much.

"Well, darling, you're ready for it," Diana said. "No. I should have said we're ready for."

Mitch really didn't think he was. But he had reached a decision while they were talking. He not only needed to work with his lawyers. He needed to brainstorm something else.

MONICA

Monica Gilbert began her Friday pleased overall, but still a little exasperated. McCaffrey was about to be suspended, and Claire was going to appoint a hearing panel that Monica would handpick for her (as she always did). She was on her way to getting her way.

But she'd had more pushback than she thought. Gina had been right with her all the way, but Lorna had needed pushing in how they worded the investigatory report and recommendation. And for a minute, she'd thought she was going to have to compel Claire on the suspension.

"You don't know how hard it's going to be to cover his classes," she'd protested.

"Don't you have an adjunct or two you can call?" Monica had asked, possibly more snappish than she should.

"We're working on it," the college president said. She'd just been on the phone with the department head discussing options.

"Claire, you — we — don't have any choice. Our report says there is cause to believe this man violated the sexual harassment policy with students, and reason to believe his students may not be safe in his classes. It says that his teaching methods are contrary to college values —"

"Are they?" Claire had asked.

"The hearing panel could find they are. You can't keep him in the classroom with these charges pending."

Sighing, Claire had relented. "I suppose not."

So now it was all lined up. They'd do this after McCaffrey's final class this afternoon. They'd called a private security firm to escort him out. He'd be given the notice of suspension pending hearing and a copy of the committee report. They wouldn't let him remove anything except his photos and diplomas; everything else would be sent to him after "Compliance" — meaning Monica and Sharon, her administrative assistant, who was completely reliable — had "inspected" the contents of the office.

They'd take Mitch's keys and change the locks anyway. The IT Department would inspect his computer, but she'd find a way for Stevens to get another shot at it.

Sitting at her desk, she smiled. This was going to be…fun. She summoned Sharon on the intercom, and quickly gave instructions.

She didn't know that while Sharon was completely reliable to be on her side, Claire's assistant Peggy was not. Because Claire had to sign the suspension letter and direct Human Resources to process the paperwork, Peggy knew what was going to happen.

Mitch McCaffrey had worked hard with Peggy's nephew to get him in Western Carolina three years earlier. Peggy hadn't forgotten.

MARC

When Marc Washington left the state courthouse at about 10:30 Friday morning, he thought he had the pressure work for today behind him. Fridays were the day of the week that the Superior Court judges heard motions, and he'd been sent by Bill Norville to defend a motion to compel discovery filed by a plaintiff in an age discrimination case.

The hearing went well. The judge tossed the other lawyer a few bones, requiring the production of a few more documents, and otherwise denied the motion. Norville had told Marc to be prepared for the judge to "divide the baby". But Marc was pretty pleased. The "other side", as lawyers called it, hadn't got much of the baby. A toe maybe, or a lock of hair.

He drove back to the office, at first thinking about writing up the order from the hearing, but letting his mind wander to Tiffany DeRatt. Marc thought Tiffany was…pretty appealing. But.

But Melton, Norville had a pretty clear relationships policy that precluded dating subordinate employees. Tiffany did not directly report to Marc, but rather to Kathryn Turner. That didn't fully answer the question, though, because Marc, as a lawyer had authority to give her directives in any case in which he was assisting Kathryn.

So maybe he should leave it alone. Probably he should leave it alone. After all, he didn't know how Tiffany felt about him. Well, he sort of did. Her signals had been positive. But she wouldn't get fired if they got involved and it went sideways. Marc would.

No, he should look elsewhere, he thought as he parked his vehicle.

He was a bit startled when he walked into the office, and Betty, the receptionist said, "You're to see Tiffany immediately. It's urgent."

"But I need to report to Mr. Norville," he protested.

Betty, a matronly type in her early 50's, smiled and said, "Honey, you better see Tiffany first. I was told to tell you anything else can wait."

"Who told you?"

"Tiffany herself. She's the one who took the call from Mr. McCaffrey. She texted Kathryn, and these instructions are coming from her."

Marc felt his eyes widen. Kathryn was in Charlotte for continuing professional education, and Jenny had decided this – whatever this was – was important enough to interrupt a partner. It must be the college had acted. It had to be.

He went directly to Tiffany's cubicle.

"What's up, Tiff?" he asked.

"We're going to Carolina Highlands. Mr. McCaffrey has found out through the grapevine that they're going to suspend him this afternoon, and Ms. Turner wants Melton, Norville boots on the ground when it happens."

"Do I have time to unload my briefcase and tell Mr. Norville about the hearing?"

Tiffany consulted the clock on her cell phone. She seldom wore a watch. It was now 11:15. "Yes. But don't waste time. I'll be in your office to bring you up to speed in 15 minutes."

Marc quickly unloaded his briefcase and e-mailed Norville and their client about the mostly favorable ruling. He made himself the task reminder to draft an Order.

He was ready when Tiffany entered a few minutes early. Today was "casual Friday", but she wore the paralegal uniform of conservative pantsuit, this time beige, all the same. Marc noticed for the nth time how pretty she was.

But her manner was all efficiency.

"Someone at the college got word to Mr. McCaffrey that they are going to suspend him after his last class this afternoon," she said. "He called Kathryn, and they put the call through to me. I put him on hold and texted Kathryn on my cell.

"She told me that you and I are to go directly to the school and stay in his office. His last class ends at 3:00 and they expect to be waiting on him at his office. We'll be waiting on them."

"What does she want us to do?"

"She said to protect the client." Tiffany flashed him a bright smile. "She said you'd know what to do."

Marc felt a surge of adrenalin greater than the one before court this morning. This time, there would be no judge to referee, no court rules. Just him. Well, he had Tiff, and she actually had two years of time in service on him, even though she wasn't a lawyer. And he had talked with Kathryn about how she expected this to come down.

"Uh," he asked, playing for time while he gathered his thoughts, "do we have time for lunch?"

"We can get something at Subway on the way," Tiffany answered. "We're supposed to meet Mr. McCaffrey at his office at one o'clock."

"Tiff, I need your help," he said.

She flashed the smile again. "Of course. Why do you think Kathryn asked me to go?"

"What do we need to take?"

"Ms. Turner told me to always take a voice recorder in case we get the chance to use it. I have an app on my phone, but I'd better put a portable Dictaphone in my purse. No camera. We'll use our phones if we need pictures. And of course we need something to write on."

"Did Kathryn say anything else?"

Tiffany frowned, then said, "Yes. I almost forgot. She said to be sure his office was as secure as possible, and to officially protest if they wouldn't allow him to remove all of his stuff today."

"I thought you and Jenny had scotched that yesterday."

This time the smile was a wide grin. "We're trying to set them up, silly."

Marc didn't take offense. She had been at this business longer than she had.

"Does she think we'll have any trouble getting in?"

"She thinks not. People come and go all the time. And they don't know that we know. But we need to use the side entrance. I know the way."

"What about the letter?"

They had pre-drafted a letter notifying the college of their representation, and formally requesting access to evidence supporting the charges against Mitch.

Tiffany shook her head. "No. Kathryn hasn't signed it yet, and it's not dated. She said it's better if it's hand-delivered come Monday."

Marc stood, picked up his own briefcase and shoved a couple of pads into it, along with a couple of pens.

"Okay," he said, "let's go. Oh… we better be sure we have our business cards."

Tiffany stood, too. "Always, Lawyer Washington. A good lawyer – or a good paralegal – is never without them." She actually winked at him. "An ambulance might drive by."

They decided they had time to actually eat at the Subway. Marc was glad, because eating while driving was a dicey proposition. It would spoil the effect of confronting the college's goons – that was how he thought of them – if he did it with oil or mayo dribbled on his tie.

"What kind of a teacher was our client?" he asked as they drove from their fast food stop to the campus.

"A good one," Tiffany said without hesitation. "I was in Paralegal Studies, so I had him for English Comp. He was interested in all of his students, made a point to know what certificate or degree we were there to get."

"No trouble with him?"

She arched an eyebrow. "You mean harassment?"

He nodded.

"Definitely not. Nothing racist, either, as far as I could see." She smiled at a memory. "I wrote an essay for Black History Month. I got a B+, and a note that said I should read Frederick Douglass."

"Did you?"

"I did, some. Did you know he was a big fan of the Second Amendment? He thought black people should be able to protect themselves."

"I did know that." Marc had read Douglass himself. He wondered if he had just scored style points with Tiffany. Not that it matters, he quickly thought.

As Tiffany suggested, they parked in the public lot at entered the building that held Mitch's office through a side door, which was open during school hours, and walked quietly and quickly down a corridor, through double doors, and up a staircase. Tiffany had made the trip before and led the way,

There were students and faculty in the hallway. Most were about their business and paid them no mind.

When they knocked on the door to Mitch's office, his voice told them to enter. Mitch was seated behind his desk, wearing a bemused smile.

"I was wondering," he said when they were seated, "if I'll see this office again after today."

They nodded, but didn't answer right away. They didn't know.

But finally, Marc said, "You will if we have anything to say about it."

MARC AND TIFFANY

"What are you going to do today?" Mitch asked.

Marc looked at Tiffany, and she nodded for him to go ahead, widening her eyes as though to say, "Hey, you're the lawyer. I just work here."

Clearing his throat, Marc said, "Well, sir, we're here for two reasons. First, we want to be sure no one takes an improper advantage of you. Second, we're witnesses to whatever happens. We'll record or video it if we can."

"I thought lawyers can't testify," Mitch said.

"That's not quite true. It is true that I won't be able to testify and still appear for you as legal counsel. But that's part of why Ms. DeRatt is here with me."

"Do you think it's going to be that bad?" Mitch asked. "I mean, they can just give me a notice to clean out my office and leave."

Nodding, Marc explained, "They can. But we think they'll make more of a production out of it. Escort you out. And they can do that. We want to be sure that they don't overreach — try to confiscate your personal property or something."

"Well, I'll feel better with y'all here," Mitch said. "What if they meet me in the hall after class and just send me out of the building then?"

Marc bit his lip. That hadn't occurred to him. He lifted his head to the ceiling in thought. "Well," he said after a moment, "they'll still come here. And we'll be waiting."

They talked quietly before Mitch had to leave for class. He wanted to know about Marc's background, and they spoke for while about how Marc's alma mater was until recently Appalachian's big rival. He asked Tiffany how she was doing, and wanted to know if she had a boyfriend.

"Just curious," he added quickly. "I'm taken and not fishing."

Tiffany laughed. "Not at present, Mr. McCaffrey. Not right now." She did not look at Marc when she said it.

Well, that's interesting, Marc thought, in spite of his earlier resolve.

It wasn't long before Mitch left for what was going to be the last class he would teach, at least for a while. He said he would come back directly after class, and asked them to lock the door behind him, since he always locked it himself when he was out.

After he was gone, Marc and Tiffany talked in low voices, so that no one in the hallway could overhear. They made sure they had the Dictaphone and their cell phones fully charged.

The conversation came to a lull. They were out of speculation about how this thing with Mitch's suspension might come down.

Tiffany gave Marc a long look, and then a dimpled smile. "Marc…"

"Uh-huh." He looked directly at her with raised eyebrows.

The smile broadened. "I just want you to know that I can read the firm policy manual as well as you can. So…no. We can't. We both need our jobs."

Then she winked. "But you are cute."

Marc gaped a moment, then rallied. "I thought people our age didn't use 'cute'. It's out of date."

"My mother taught me that 'hot' is low-class and I was not to use it. Besides, 'cute' is much better. I don't want to stoke your ego."

They were interrupted by the sound of a key turning in the door lock. The door opened to reveal a tall dark-haired woman in stiletto heels and a dark purple suit with a short skirt. They immediately recognized her as Monica Gilbert. She was flanked by two beefy looking men in private Security Firm uniforms. Behind them stood another man is business casual dress they didn't recognize.

Mark stood while they took in him and Tiffany with open mouths.

"Hello," he said.

MONICA

Monica had lingered at lunch. The McCaffrey suspension was all set up, and she had nothing else pressing on her calendar. She had taken Sharon with her, and they chatted amiably, and had even indulged in a second glass of wine, which was strictly against college policy, but they had a private room at Tremaine's and no one would know. Then they ordered coffee and continued to chat to lose their wine buzz, which took still more time.

By the time they were back at Carolina Highlands, it was time to meet the security detail she had ordered, and to pick up the signed letter of suspension from Claire's office. Sharon excused herself to visit the restroom (and lose some wine and coffee) while Monica walked on to the president's office down the hall.

She secured the paperwork and told the guards she'd brief them on the way to Mitch's office. She wanted to be there when McCaffrey returned from class. She turned off her cell phone so nothing would interrupt her.

In a few minutes, she and her entourage reached McCaffrey's office, and...

MARC

When Marc hear the key turn in the door, he immediately realized it was probably not the client, because the 2:00 p.m. class was still in progress. Thus, he wasn't completely surprised when he saw who was at the door.

But from the wide-eyed expression on her face, Monica Gilbert was surprised. She recovered quickly, though. Her carefully made-up and attractive face twisting in rage, she rapped out, loud and shrill, "Who the hell are you?"

Marc reminded himself that it was important to appear cool and confident, whether he actually felt cool and confident or not. Bill Norville and Kathryn Turner had drilled that into him.

Forcing a smile, he stepped forward and offered a business card he produced from a coat pocket. "Good afternoon. I'm Marc Washington and this is Ms. DeRatt." He pronounced Tiffany's name as she did, in common with most North Carolinians, whether white or black, DEE-rat. "We're Mr. McCaffrey's lawyers." He paused and corrected himself. "Well, I'm one of them, anyway. Ms. DeRatt is my paralegal." Well, technically, Tiffany was Kathryn Turner's paralegal; but this bunch wouldn't know that, or care.

"So you say," Gilbert sniffed.

"We do say, ma'am," he said, keeping his tone low and calm, and internally wondering how he did it. "Our client will confirm it."

Monica stepped into the office, and responded, "Well, whether he will or won't, you're not supposed to be here. You need to leave." She looked down at the proffered card but did not accept it.

Marc stood his ground, as the two security guards, still looking confused, stepped in to stand beside Monica. The other guy remained in the hallway, shuffling his feet.

"We need to speak with Mr. McCaffrey first," Marc said.

"Actually, you don't. If you don't leave immediately, I'll have these gentlemen remove you."

Marc risked a glance at Tiffany, who had also risen. She nodded. Hopefully that meant she had turned on and locked the Dictaphone and was getting this. He saw that she had her phone in her hand.

Monica noticed the glance, and wheeled on Tiffany. "What are you doing, young lady?" she demanded. Her high cheek-boned face was flushed beyond the rouge.

Tiffany said, in a sweet and demure voice, "Why, I'm videoing what's happening, Ms. Gilbert. That's what Ms. Turner has trained me to do." Marc wondered if she really had the video app going. He later found that she did.

"You can't do that!" Monica turned to the guard on the left. "Get that phone away from her."

The guard, looking uncomfortable, said, "Ma'am, we can offer protection and observation. We can't make arrests. And we aren't authorized to take any property except a weapon." He swallowed hard. Marc felt sorry for him. These guys were obviously retired cops, who didn't expect any real trouble, ever.

"We can call the police," the man continued. "Do you want us to do that?"

"Not yet," Monica snapped. "But I'll have you do it if these two don't leave right now." She turned back to Marc. "Do you want to be arrested for trespassing?"

At that moment, a new voice came from the hallway. "What's going on here?"

It was Mitch.

Monica wheeled on him. "We were just asking your...visitors...to leave. Then we have some things to take up with you.

"Confidentially," she added. She was squeezing a manila folder in one hand with a white-knuckled grip.

Mitch politely but firmly pushed his way past the guards into his office and walked to stand behind his desk, setting down the textbook and class materials he was carrying.

"Surely not too confidential for my lawyers to hear," he said.

Monica, ignoring Tiffany and Marc for now, snapped, "Absolutely too confidential for that. You have no right to legal counsel at this meeting."

Technically that was true. But Marc had another card to play. "Weingarten – "he began. He referred to a well-known Labor Board decision.

Monica was really agitated by now. "Don't give me that, counselor. That case doesn't require any such thing."

Oh, puke, Marc thought. She knows that. But she would. He turned to Mitch, "Mr. McCaffrey, you're entitled to have a co-worker witness if this is any sort of a disciplinary meeting. Is there anyone?"

But Monica was wise to that ploy, too. "Mr. Jefferson---"

"Washington," he supplied, suspecting the error was deliberate.

"Whatever your name is, you know Mr. McCaffrey is a public employee, and that law doesn't apply to him." Which was true. "Now you and Miss Video here need to leave right now, or I will call the police."

"I don't understand, ma'am," Marc said, keeping his voice even and as calm as possible. "What do you need to do with our client? And can't we sit in, just out of courtesy?"

"No, you can't!" Monica's face was crimson by now. "You have ten seconds to start moving."

She looked directly into Marc's eyes with intensity that made him, first uncomfortable, and then...as though he were being pushed by something inside his head. And then suddenly, the feeling passed. He wasn't being pushed any more.

He saw Gilbert turn back toward Mitch, who was looking at her with a slight smile. They locked eyes for a moment. Then she sighed and took a step back. Now what was that all about?

"Can't we at least inventory our client's office first?" Marc asked, forcing a plaintive tone.

"You may not! We'll do that – oh, go! Now!"

Marc picked up his briefcase and motioned to Tiffany to precede him. She was continuing to point the phone, so Marc assumed she really was making a video.

Monica stared at Tiffany and her phone, and looked back toward Mitch, who kept the amused smile. Why was he smiling? There was something in this by play he didn't understand.

"Mr. McCaffrey, call us when your meeting is over," Marc said on the way out.

Mitch said he would.

When they passed the man in the hall, Marc, figuring what the hell, asked, "Who are you?"

The unknown man, plump and middle-aged, whispered, "IT", and looked at his shoes.

Then Marc and Tiffany were walking briskly down the hallway and out of the building toward Marc's car. Marc looked at his watch. It was not quite 3:20. The whole exchange had been less than a quarter hour. Marc wanted a tissue, feeling sweat prickling the hairline at his brow.

"Got it all?" he whispered to Tiffany as they exited the same door they had entered.

"I think so," she whispered back.

"Good girl!"

She punched him on the arm. "Good boy!" And they exchanged smiles.

12

WHEN WILL THE GOOD APPLES FALL?

MITCH

When Marc and Tiffany left his office, Mitch was feeling both apprehension and relief. And a little satisfaction that he had caught and blocked Monica's compulsion spell on Marc Washington. He wasn't going to enjoy this meeting, but he was relieved to be getting over with it.

Monica left the guards in the room, and brought in Don Kelly from the hallway. There were only two chairs in the room beside the swivel chair behind Mitch's desk. She took one, and gestured for Don to take the other. He did, not meeting Mitch's eyes and squirming. The guards stood by the door.

A small crowd had gathered outside, mostly students and staff attracted by the uniforms and the exchange between Monica and Marc. She commanded the guards to shut the door.

"Let's get this over with," she said. "These gentlemen will be witnesses."

"Get what over with?" Mitch asked. "You haven't told me yet."

"I think you know," she said evenly, placing the folder on her side of the desk.

"Don't I get any witnesses?" Mitch asked, unable to resist a smile as he said it.

"Are you questioning the honesty of these gentlemen?" Monica pretended outrage.

"No. I would just like a witness I pick."

"Well, that's not your prerogative. Shall we get started?"

Marc leaned back in his chair, keeping the smile. Damned if he was going to appear shocked or upset. "Might as well."

"Uhh, look," Don broke in, "if Mr. McCaffrey wants someone else, I can leave and go get one."

Yeah, Don, Mitch thought, I'll just bet you would. But Monica of course nixed it. "Keep your seat," she told Don, louder than necessary.

The papers Monica gave Mitch were what he had been told to expect. There was another copy of the Notice of Complaint. There was the Investigating Committee's Report, several pages long. Mitch read over it quickly.

He had expected it, but it was still hurtful and, to his thinking outrageous. He not only had harassed Lottie, but also her two friends. Moreover, he had a history of harassing female students. His classroom was not safe. Students were not safe around him. He had made statements, both inside and outside of class, that were racist, sexist, and homophobic. He thought, really?

Here was one hadn't expected: He had run his class room as an instrument of extremist political propaganda, and had repressed dissent, especially from progressive students. How had they come up with that?

The Committee recommended cancellation of his contract and termination from college employment. A separate Notice stated that college policy, a copy of which was attached, requiring a hearing before an impartial panel of his faculty peers, to be appointed by the president, to review the evidence and to make a final recommendation to the president. He would be given notice of the hearing and an opportunity to be heard and present evidence. He was entitled to be represented by counsel. Pending the president's final decision, he would remain on paid leave.

There were receipts he was expected to sign for all of this. He signed them.

And there was a final document that directed him to discuss the charge with no persons other than his lawyers, and that he agreed to refrain from doing so. Kathryn had warned him that he might be presented with something like this. On that paper, he didn't sign the blank, but rather wrote at the bottom of the page, "I have read this", and initialed it.

"You must sign as instructed," Monica said.

"I'm not going to," Mitch said, keeping the smile plastered on his face while he sub-vocalized a Ward for Don and the guards. Monica's eyes widened. She knew what he was doing and couldn't stop him.

"Mr. McCaffrey, I'm warning you," she said.

"Ha! About what? You can't have me arrested for not signing this one. And you certainly can't have me shot." He looked pointedly at the guards. "You're not going to shoot anyone, are you, gentlemen?"

They shuffled from one foot to the other and said nothing.

"By the way, I do get copies of all of this, don't I?"

"Here. These are yours." Monica spoke tight-lipped, for once looking older than she was, and slid copies across the desk to him. She drew a deep breath and said, "I'm required to ask you before these witnesses if you understand what you have read and been told today."

"Oh, I understand. I don't agree with it."

"It's not necessary that you do. Now, if there's nothing else to say, these gentlemen" — she twisted in her seat and waved at the security guards — "will oversee your removing your personal effects and escort you from the building. Mr. Kelly will take charge of, and inspect your computer."

"May I have a representative present for that?"

"Are you impugning Mr. Kelly's integrity?"

"No. I'm impugning yours."

Monica jumped to her feet. "You heard that!" She looked down at Kelly and around to the guards. She was loud enough to be heard in the hallway.

Mitch paid no attention. "When can I get my books?"

Monica looked down at him. Her smile, he thought, was actually…

evil. "When we are through inspecting them and verifying ownership, we'll have them shipped to you."

"I don't suppose I get to be present for the inspection?"

"No. Anything else?"

Mitch leaned forward over the desk, clasping his hands in front. He knew his lawyers wouldn't like what he was about to say, but he said it anyway.

"Tell me, Monica," he said, keeping his tone as matter-of-fact as possible, "do you really need to do this just because I turned you down?"

"You heard that, too! You heard that, too!" She shouted, saying it twice this time and waving her arms in a circle.

Mitch saw her blink back tears. He had no sympathy.

"I try to have a professional meeting with you, and you lie and insult me this way," she sobbed.

Yeah, right, Mitch thought. He knew crocodile tears when he saw them.

It didn't take much to empty his things from the office, if no books were being removed. The diplomas and certificates were bulky, but nothing else was. There was a desk clock, now stopped because it needed a battery. A stand for a pen. A letter opener. These had been given to him by students. A few other nick-knacks. All told, it filled two boxes. The guards carried them when they left. Kelly had already disconnected the computer and was ready to carry it out.

Monica's screeching had attracted a crowd, and numerous eyes followed them as they exited the building. A few tried to ask Mitch what was going on, but he shook his head. "Can't discuss it now," he said.

He was glad he had driven the Lexus today. He could put his stuff in the back, and he'd suspected he might have to do so. The Wrangler would have been a problem. It was a bright day, a bit breezy and chilly, but fine. He opened the gate, and the guards placed the boxes in the storage space. He noted their name tags said "David Mooney" and "Bill Johnson".

"Thank you, gentlemen," Mitch said.

"No problem," Mooney said and turned away. Johnson half-turned, and then reversed it.

"Did she really offer to fuck you?" he asked.

"Bill!" the other cautioned.

Mitch didn't respond, only grinned.

"And you turned her down?" Johnson persisted, ignoring his colleague's hand on his shoulder.

Mitch shrugged.

This time Johnson did turn away. "I don't blame you," he called over his shoulder, "she's a real barracuda. She bites."

Mitch couldn't help but chuckle as he saw them walk away, Mooney whispering furiously to Johnson.

A small crowd of students had followed them out, but had hung back too far away (he believed) to have heard what had just been said. They started forward.

"Not now, y'all," he called, waving them back.

Several shouted "good luck", and he thanked them.

When he was in his vehicle, he called the law office. Marc was on the phone, but Tiffany asked that he drive in, so they could make copies of the suspension and hearing papers.

He was surprised to find he was in an amazingly good mood as he left the parking lot. He had held his own with Monica. And –

There was one more thing. He now knew he was a stronger magic user than she was.

This was going to be interesting. It might – just might – even be fun. At least a little.

MITCH

When Mitch reached the Melton, Norville offices, he was immediately ushered into a conference room where Marc and Tiffany were waiting. The first thing they wanted was to see the papers Monica had given Mitch, which they read quickly. Marc paused a couple of times to ask a question about what he thought they meant by this allegation or that. Some Mitch could answer. A couple, like the "stifling progressive opinions" charge, mystified him.

Marc punched the intercom to summon an administrative assistant. When she arrived, Marc told her to copy and scan the documents, and send the scan to Tiffany for indexing. When the assistant had left,

Marc asked him what had happened. Tiffany recorded and took notes on the conference.

"You said what?" Marc interrupted when he reached the parting salvo he'd aimed at Monica Gilbert. He gaped at Mitch incredulously.

Tiffany snorted, then tittered, and then giggled.

"Tiff! That's enough," Marc said.

"Yes, sir," she said, but snorted again before composing herself. Marc sent her another sharp look. "Well, it is funny," she protested.

Mitch found himself smiling, too. He had enjoyed that part, he had to admit.

"It won't be funny at the hearing," Marc warned. "It'll be used against you, Mitch. They'll use it to show you are capable of harassment and crude behavior."

Mitch felt his smile fade. But darn it, getting Monica's goat had been satisfying.

"I understand," he said. Then, after a moment, he added, "But I did turn her down."

"I thought so," Tiffany said, earning another stare from Marc, who asked, "No witnesses, I assume."

"Well, no."

"Then it doesn't help, that I can see. Now tell me how she responded again."

Mitch walked them back through his description of the event. He added the exchange with the two security guards outside. Tiffany tittered again, earning another scowl from Marc, who sat back in his chair and rubbed his chin.

"Well, this does tell us something that might useful," he said.

Mitch nodded. "I think I know what it is."

Marc raised his brows and motioned for Mitch to go ahead.

"Now we know she can be rattled. She can be goaded into acting out."

Mitch left the offices after making an appointment for early Monday afternoon. It might as well be early; he wasn't going to work that day, or any day for a while. Marc told him he didn't want to map out anything for Mitch until a senior attorney was present.

At home, he dressed casually in denim trousers and an App State hoody over a tee shirt, trading his dress shoes for sneakers. While he was changing clothes, he spelled on the gas grill and turned the oven to pre-heat the same way, and commanded the marinated chicken and root vegetables out of the refrigerator while walking down the hallway.

He'd been practicing his magic and decided to test his ability to fine tune spells for simple household tasks. While he was opening a wine bottle, he spelled the romaine lettuce, onions, and Caesar dressing out of the fridge, and made the salad mix itself in a bowl he spelled over to the table.

He set the table the same way. He decided to place the vegetables in the oven by hand, but he made the wine pour itself. He tuned jazz on Sirius XM by magic. He needed to wait a few minutes for the chicken to reach room temperature. He decided to take his wine outside and prepare the grill top himself. It wasn't that cool outside, yet.

As an afterthought, he told grill tongs and salad tongs to leave the kitchen drawers for their places on the salad and beside the warming chicken.

His mind roamed back to the day's events, and to speculation about what was next in his case.

He hadn't re-set the security system, and the Ward he'd placed on the house warned only of malicious attempted entry. Diana had let herself in, cat-footed to the deck, and placed his arms around his waist, before he knew she was there. He'd been that deep in thought.

"Hello, handsome," she said. "Penny for your thoughts."

He turned, immediately pleased she'd taken the time to look so good. Her hair was freshly washed, and brushed her shoulders. Her make-up was perfect. Matching his casual look, she wore sequined jeans and a fluffy sky-blue (he automatically thought "Carolina Blue") sweater.

"Hello yourself, gorgeous," he responded, gathering her for a kiss, but taking care that the tongs with marinade and chicken drippings didn't brush her back. "Ready for a glass of wine?"

When she nodded, he summoned the wine bottle and a glass from the kitchen.

"Pretty slick," she acknowledged, then: "I'm still not used to this stuff, you know."

"The wine or the magic?"

"The magic, silly."

While they ate, he told her about what had happened at the college. She was nodding gravely until he reached his closing confrontation with Monica. Then she surprised him.

She was sipping from her wine glass, and snorted it out her nostrils, causing her to grab her napkin while she doubled over in a fit of uncontrolled pealing laughter. It went on for a while, completely halting his story. She was visibly trying to control it, but it kept erupting until she got the hiccups and he had to spell them gone so she could finish her dinner.

Mitch was non-plused. "Honey, what in the world?"

"I-I'm sorry. I'm sorry. It's — just so funny." She nearly started again.

"I'm afraid to tell what Johnson the security guard said."

But she made him; and this time, she did start again. It didn't last quite as long.

"I got fussed at for saying that by my lawyers," he said. He explained what Marc had told him.

She sobered, and then tittered again. "Oh, sweetheart, I am so sorry. I know this is serious. But — well, if you didn't want to win this case so much, knowing that you really got Monica's goat would almost be worth it to me, no matter what happens."

While he stared at her, she continued. "I know this doesn't make sense, but …well, after all these years, it's like I finally got mine back from her."

"It does make sense, actually." He understood. Monica was rejected, and she was accepted.

"Darling, you know I'm in this to win. We already discussed that. I may have hurt myself today. If I did, I'll live with it. But I'm going to need your help."

He reached across the table to take her hand. "I need to know more about Monica."

DIANA

They had finished dinner and retired downstairs before they picked up the thread of the conversation again. During the rest of dinner, she'd tried to find out what Mitch was doing tomorrow morning if he wasn't going deer hunting. He'd only told her he had some errands to run.

She gathered the errands had something to do with her, but decided not to press him.

After they had settled into the den, as she thought of it (although Mitch pretentiously wanted to call it the "library"), she with a short glass of Campari over ice, he with his customary single malt, she decided she shouldn't wait for Mitch to prompt her.

"What do you want to know about Monica?" she asked.

He placed his snifter, as yet untouched, on the coffee table, and, elbows on knees, folded his hand beneath his chin.

"Well," he began, "I know she's from Martintown, went to high school here, has degrees from Agnes Scott and Virginia, and worked for one of the community colleges in the Triad before she came here. That's in her college bio. I've heard she is divorced, but I haven't heard about any kids.

"But what I hope you can help me with is early background. You went to school with her, after all."

"Not for long."

"I hope long enough. What about her parents? Brothers and sisters? What were they like? Where are they now?"

"Okay, I told you her dad was president of Western Piedmont Bank. Owned a good chunk of it, too. They lived in a big house in the Park Ridge Section of town – you know, that's where the really well to do live. Many still do."

Mitch nodded, and she went on, "I think she still lives in that house – moved back here when her father died several years ago. He got a big pile of money when Bank of America bought Western Piedmont. I'm sure she got a nice inheritance."

"Where was her father from?"

"Here. Old family. I think her grandfather was a doctor."

"What about her mother?"

"Let me think….Oh, I think I know where you're coming from. You want to know how she got to be a witch."

Mitch nodded, sipping his scotch.

"You know, you maybe should talk with Mom. She'll know more than I do. I only saw her mother a couple of time. She was pretty – Monica looks a lot like her. She showed up at cheerleader try-outs – some kind of volunteer judge -- and wasn't nice at all.

"I remember Mom said she didn't like her. Said she put on all kind of airs in Junior League now she'd married money, but was 'white trash' at heart. She wasn't from Brainerd County. Mom said she grew up way up off Jonah's Ridge, over the county line, and probably didn't have an inside toilet. I don't know if that's true, or if it was just Mom."

"Is she still living?"

"I think she's in a nursing home somewhere. Marion, maybe? You hear stuff at the store, but sometimes it's hard to remember if it didn't seem important. You can talk to Mom, or I can see what I can find out from her tomorrow."

"Please do. Anything else?"

"Let's see." She sipped her Campari thoughtfully, then sat up straight.

"Yes, there is. Mom told me it was a good idea to stay clear of Merinda Martin. That was her mother's name. I remember now."

"Did she say why?"

"Yes." Diana looked directly at Mitch. "She said people who got on Merinda's bad side tended to have accidents."

MONICA

Monica was not happy as she drove home from work. She was angry. She was furious at Mitch McCaffrey. Now she wanted rid of him more than ever. She was angry with the security guards and with Don Kelly for standing there and not jumping to her defense. She was mad at herself for letting Mitch get her goat when she was in control, and letting the students and staff in the hallway see her bat back tears as she power-walked back to her office.

She was mad at Mitch's lawyer, and his cute little paralegal with the cell phone taking videos. What really irked her was that she had never really mastered using the Power on electronic devices, but she didn't enjoy realizing that. It felt better to be angry at the paralegal, and promise herself revenge.

Still, she thought as she pulled her Prius into her garage, she now had Mitch McCaffrey out of the college; and she'd see to it that he never came back. She didn't care how much Claire griped about the difficulty in hiring a replacement. It couldn't be all that hard. The new hire might not be experienced. But it was a real opportunity to improve the diversity of the faculty. Hire a woman, maybe a black or Hispanic woman. Even if the English Department already had a majority of women, the overall college didn't, if you counted the trades.

The death march of Mitch McCaffrey's employment with Carolina Highlands Community College had begun. And she could move it a little forward tonight. She had a date with someone who could help. But she needed to be composed and chic when she was with him. Time to shrug off the frustration of the afternoon.

She went directly to her bedroom after letting herself into the house where she'd grown up, not even bothering to check the mail that her maid Maria had placed on the kitchen counter. She could get that later. Instead, she asked Maria set out a little black dress while Monica attended to her shower and her evening cosmetics.

She liked having a live-in maid, especially one as efficient, grateful, and stunning as Maria. The house was certainly big enough. She ordinarily wouldn't have liked the competition of another attractive woman in the house, but she'd found Maria useful at distracting men she didn't care to fool with herself. Maria was Puerto Rican, so she didn't have a problem with INS and didn't expose Monica to scrutiny that way. Maria was well paid, and should be happy. Regardless, she was obedient.

Her date was John Kingsley (King) Armistead, who was the Human Resources Director at Southeastern Electronics, the company that had provided a tremendous shot in the arm to the Brainerd County economy when it had opened five years ago. Southeastern was not, in some respects, a progressive company. One of its goals was to manufacture computer chips for military aircraft that now had to be imported from China.

But King made sure its HR policies were very progressive, selling his department's approach as being necessary for risk management and avoidance. They were sometimes at odds with their own management team, but had been able to exert remarkable influence and control. And the company was a significant contributor to the college's scholarship fund. It had influence.

King had shown interest in Monica for some time. He was a few years older than she, divorced as she was (not that it would really have mattered to her if he were married), and attractive enough despite a hairline that was beginning to recede and the beginnings (but only the bare beginnings) of a paunch. They belonged to the same Rotary Club, and it had been ridiculously easy to suggest to him at lunch Wednesday that he ought to ask her out. It hadn't really taken a compulsion, just a nudge. His own lust had done the rest.

She'd come home in time not to rush. She took her time in the shower, drying her hair, and removing and replacing her cosmetics. She took a moment to bolster her preservation spell. She couldn't actually reverse aging, but the preservation spell was working well enough. It had certainly worked okay with her mother, who was physically going strong despite having dementia so far advanced that, in light of her age, could only be classic Alzheimer's.

She wished she could ask her mother's advice about the Power, but there wouldn't be any point. She usually didn't recognize Monica. But the Power was still there. The staff at the home complained about all of the accidents that happened around her. But they really didn't blame her mother. How could they? If only they knew.

She finished dressing in the dress Maria had laid out for her, deciding to wear hose this time, although she hated hose. Completing her outfit with black stiletto heels, pearls and a clutch purse, she made her way to her home office to await King. She buzzed Maria on the intercom that her dad had installed years ago, which still worked, and instructed her to dress in her formal maid's dress, and to "kick it up a notch." Maria knew that meant to leave the blouse unbuttoned a little way, to get the man's attention and move his mind in the direction Monica wanted, but not enough to upstage her.

She didn't have to wait long. When the doorbell rang, Maria knew to show King to the parlor, where she would keep him waiting just long enough. After a discrete few minutes, she entered her mother's parlor, and found him admiring a Delacroix print of a chateau on the Loire.

"Like that?" she asked.

"A great deal," he replied. "But not as much as I like what I see now."

She gave him her most dazzling smile, but all she said was, "Shall we go? I'm famished." She called Maria, who had been waiting on a bench just outside, to bring her coat. This scenario had been scripted an enacted a number of times.

He drove her to the Resort restaurant at the top of the Ridge in his red Mercedes convertible, but thankfully kept the retractable folding hardtop up because of the evening chill. Indian summer was definitely over, likely for good. They passed the entrance to High Country Estates, causing her to cast a hate-filled glance to where she knew Mitch lived.

That little red-neck whore Diana was doubtless with him tonight. She hoped they were anxious and had no joy of each other.

King, who thought he was regaling her with stories of how his week had gone, did not notice her momentary distraction. It was good that men were so self-centered, and yet so pliable.

The restaurant was lovely, all stained cedar and dark burnished furniture with muted lighting, the outdoor tables, less formal, warmed by gas torchiers. They rejected these, however, to sit inside, where a talented and pretty vocalist sang torch songs, accompanied by a piano.

After they had ordered, King got around to asking about her week. She'd thought he would get to that eventually.

She sighed over her glass of New Zealand pinot noir. "All right, I guess." She proceeded to fill him in on the accusations against McCaffrey, omitting any detail from today's uncomfortable suspension. She included the evidence, as her committee saw it, and her own interpretation. Her story didn't leave any room for doubt, at least for someone who was wired to think correctly. And King was.

"Well," he said, when she had finished, "that is a concern, if you have someone like that on the faculty. But from what you say, it seems open and shut."

She sighed again. "I wish. I'm worried about Claire, though."

He looked surprised. "The college president? I would think she'd be firmly in your corner on something like this."

Another sigh would have been too much. Monica merely grimaced.

"Oh, her heart's in the right place," she said. "But she worries so much about the cost of keeping someone on suspension. And about the difficulty replacing an experienced instructor. The final decision is hers. I'm concerned she'll be content with a slap on the wrist. A warning and training or something.

"That won't cut it with this guy. It'll roll off him like water off a duck's back. And then we'll be stuck with him. We'll keep someone like him on the faculty. How will that look to the students we're trying to mold? How will that look to good progressive employers like your company that we depend on for help?"

King sat back, visibly a little alarmed, and obviously wanting to impress her, just as she intended. Image was everything. He firmly believed it. Better leave nothing to doubt. And this woman needed support so much.

She almost regretted he was so …easy, even before he spoke.

"I definitely see what you mean," he said. "Maybe I can help. I'll speak with her. Southeastern Electronics' continued financial support could be at stake.

"Could be. I'll have to say it that way. It's not my sole decision. And we have some board members who are — not enlightened, shall we say?"

She smiled over the rim of the wine glass. This was all she needed — for now. And she hadn't used even a touch of the Power. It was all her. She felt a rush of complete satisfaction that she could bend him so easily without it.

"Thank you, King. Thank you so much." She actually meant it, since his cooperation was not compelled, except by …her.

Their food came right after. Afterwards, there was dancing on the small dance floor, and she let his hand, when their backs were turned toward the empty outdoor seating and away from the dining room or even the band, drop comfortably to her rump.

Later, when they returned to her home, and Maria had served brandy in the parlor and then she led him to her bedroom, she allowed more liberties, everything, in fact. They were adults, after all. She'd been momentarily irked that his eyes lingered too long on Maria when she brought the snifters of Courvoisier. But she could overlook that from a healthy male from whom she wanted something, even if she wouldn't forgive it.

She found the rest of the night pleasurable and moderately amusing. But she made sure he thought it was more than that for her, and she was sure it was for him.

The next morning, after she had fed him fruit and a croissant and coffee and a small glass of champagne, and she'd kissed him good-bye with just the right combination of promise and tease, she returned to bed. She required more sleep.

She didn't see Maria spit on her little black dress before she placed it in the wash.

DIANA

As Diana rode to church with Mitch Sunday morning, she felt a little overwhelmed and, to be honest with herself, more than a little giddy. She couldn't keep her eyes from returning to the ring finger of her left hand, which had been bare for the past three years, but now…now it wore a real sparkler.

Her goofy smile faded for a moment when she remembered how much hope, and optimism —and love — she'd had when that finger had held such a ring the first time, only to see them disappear with hurt, and disappointment, and anger. She looked over and smiled at Mitch, who smiled back, possibly guessing her thoughts, and rallied. This time, it would be different.

She should have realized something was up when he had insisted on calling for her at home rather than her driving to his place, and telling her she ought to "dress up a little bit'. But he'd been through so much, she really didn't see how he could concentrate on anything but what had happened, and was going to happen. He had fooled her. Maybe, she thought, she'd really known and had wanted to be fooled.

And then there was such a wonderful dinner, and then the ring.

Maybe, Diana thought as they pulled into the church parking lot, the good apples are falling on my side of the fence.

13

WISHIN' AND HOPIN'

KATHRYN

Kathryn Turner surveyed the conference room to be sure that everything was ready for the Mitch McCaffrey conference. It seemed to be.

There was a short stack of papers for the client. The first was a copy of the letter over her signature that had been hand-delivered to both Claire Daniels and Monica Gilbert. It notified the college of the firm's representation and demanded access to the investigatory file on Mitch and to his office computer. The second was the firm's first monthly invoice.

The white board had been uncovered and markers and erasers set out. A laptop computer had been connected to a large television screen on another wall. There were pads, pens and pencils. Coffee, condiments, ice, water and soft drinks were on a sideboard, and there were bowls of mints on the conference table. The "paper file" was on another corner of the table. It was already pretty big, if you counted the witness notebook that went with it.

Her litigation team trouped in. Tiffany DeRatt was the first. She carried another evidence binder, and seated herself behind the laptop. They could put documents on the screen, or could pass around the notebook. She was followed by Jenny Jackson, on loan from Bill Norville, who took a pad and pen and seated herself beside Tiffany.

Marc Washington followed in less than a minute. He carried a pad with scribblings. He and Tiffany had been interviewing witnesses, and would interview more. He went to the far end of the table in front of the whiteboard. Bill Norville was the last to enter. He wasn't on the team, really, but had agreed to sit in, again. Instead of his usual charcoal gray or blue pin-stripe, today Norville wore a navy cardigan sweater over a blue oxford cloth shirt, with a rep tie. He had been Kathryn's mentor — still was, really. But he was edging closer to retirement, now. Well, she corrected the thought, semi-retirement. Lawyers rarely completely retired.

She nodded and spoke to all of them, asking Marc if he and Tiffany could report on witnesses interviewed to date. They could.

They were ready when the phone's intercom buzzed to let them know the client had arrived. Time to really get to work.

When Mitch entered and shook hands all around, then accepted a bottle of water, and took a seat to Kathryn's right at the end of the table opposite Marc, Kathryn thought he appeared amazingly calm and relaxed. Most clients, even the well to do, who were caught for the first time in the coils of the legal system were more apprehensive.

He reviewed his copy of the letter to the college, merely nodding as he read it and making no comment or asking any questions. He flipped through the invoice the same way, and told her he would send payment immediately. That was not necessary, but no law firm ever turned it down.

"All right," she said, "let's see if we can project a timetable, shall we?" Hearing no dissent, she continued, "We should get a letter in a couple of days, acknowledging receipt of our letter. I think they will probably give us witness statements, if they have them, but deny everything else. Agree?" Her eyes shifted from Norville to Washington.

"I think they'll probably give us interviewers' notes," Norville said. "The University did in the Jenkins case."

"But that was a tenure case. Without the tenure statute, the community college, especially with Gilbert calling the shots, will be bolder, I think."

"Uhh…" Marc began.

"Yes?" Kathryn arched an eyebrow. "Go on." Sometimes an associate had to be pushed, especially if he was going to be contradicting a partner.

"Well," Marc said, "I took a look at the State Board regs." He was referring to the North Carolina State Board for Community Colleges. "They acknowledge that faculty subject to dismissal are entitled to due process. If they don't let us see the evidence they have against Marc, they're subject to denial of procedural due process. Mr. McCaffrey has the right to confrontation of his accusers."

"But that's at the hearing," Kathryn observed.

"True," Norville said. "But I don't think going to bring in every person they interviewed. They're going to put the investigation committee in the witness chair and ask them to summarize their evidence. I think we'll get the notes. At least some of them. They may try to withhold the ones they don't like."

Mitch cleared his throat. "Far be it from me to question my own panel of experts," he said, "but can they do that – read their notes, I mean? I thought that was 'hearsay'." He smiled sheepishly. "Well, I do read Grisham."

"That's a great question, Mitch," she said. "But the answer is 'yes'. You're entitled to minimal due process, but the court rules of evidence don't apply in the hearing. To get those, you have to be in court. If this hearing goes south on us, and the odds are that it will, you have to go on to the next step, which is to file a federal civil rights suit. Remember that the operative word in 'minimal due process' is 'minimal'."

"But I don't want to file a suit. I want to win it here, at this hearing." He sipped his water and smiled again. "I have confidence in my lawyers."

"Kathryn," Norville said, ignoring the pressure Mitch's "confidence" was placing on the legal team, "that's the reason I think we'll get the notes, although I grant Gilbert might try to shred the ones she doesn't like. Might, but even that's risky for her. We're going to find out the names of the people they talked to.

"If Gilbert has any sense – and I don't think she's stupid – she'll contact the State Board's Office of Legal Affairs, and they're savvy enough not to hand you a due process issue. They might try it with a lawyer with no civil rights track record, but not with us. They're well aware of the Jenkins case.

"It might take you two tries, though. Marc better have a memo on the law and the regs ready to throw at them."

"Already done," Marc said. "Tiffany has a copy in the file." He and DeRatt exchanged a nod and smiles.

"Okay," Kathryn said, "we get the interview notes. Does everyone agree they don't let us access the computer?"

"I think it depends on whether they try to plant something on it," said Marc. "We know from the stick drive Mr. McCaffrey got hold of they've tried once. If they do that, they'll give us access for the same reason Mr. Norville said about the interview notes. If they don't, they might anyway because they know inspection is wasting our time."

"I'm really not worried about that," Mitch said, earning a sharp look from Kathryn.

"Why not?" she demanded.

Mitch opened his hands in a pantomime shrug. "I just don't think they will."

"Mitch, have you done something to that computer?" She couldn't imagine what, since the firm had had it inspected and the IT guy hadn't found anything.

"No," Mitch said quickly, but she thought he looked sheepish. He wasn't telling her something. But what?

"Even if they do," he continued, "can't we pull that stick drive out on them?"

"Yes," she said, "and we will. But they'll claim we manufactured it."

The room was silent for a moment, and then she went on, "All right, let's get back to the timetable. I think Bill is right that they won't hand us any procedural issue we might try to take to court. I think we're looking at a hearing after the first of the year."

"Claire Daniels won't want to do that," Mitch said.

"Why not?"

"Because college policy says they have to suspend me with pay while this stuff is going on. She's having to pay for an adjunct to take my classes now, plus paying me. She won't want to do that for another semester, or even another half semester. It messes with her budget."

Well, that made sense, Kathryn thought, then said, "But when could they do it? Any time before Thanksgiving would be too quick. Tiff, pull up a calendar."

Tiffany immediately opened Outlook and projected a calendar on the screen. She changed the setting from "daily" to "monthly" and arrowed the month to "November."

"Hmm," Kathryn said after a moment. "We have an early Thanksgiving this year. Move over to December." Tiffany obeyed. "What about the second full week in December? Even the Friday is several days before Christmas break. If Mitch is right, do you think they might try to set it then?"

"Well, that's final exam week," Mitch offered. "They might have trouble getting a hearing panel from the faculty. But I think they could probably do it. Especially since Monica will pick the hearing panel."

"I thought the college president did that," Marc said.

Mitch snorted. "She does. But she'll name the members Monica tells her to name. She always does."

Kathryn agreed with her client, but couldn't resist adding, "Now do you see why we're telling you the odds are against you at this hearing?"

Mitch didn't look perturbed. "I've known that all along. But we're going to beat the odds."

Kathryn sighed. Surely her client wasn't that confident. "Okay team," she pressed on, "there may be a hearing before Christmas. At this point, we have to plan on it. Now let's review the evidence..."

The meeting ended right before 5:00. Kathryn thought it had gone pretty well. Marc had done a good job getting favorable statements from a number of Mitch's former students, and now he and the two paralegals were going to move on to present students, including Lottie and her "besties". Now that should be interesting.

Mitch was going to place discrete calls to selected faculty colleagues to ask if they would help. Kathryn told him he really must come up with one or two, which would be a challenge because they would be scared.

The whole team was concerned about damaging evidence being

planted in Mitch's office. The inventory Jenny and Tiffany had taken would help. They weren't sure what to do about the attempt to fake evidence at the tailgate, because these guys were hostile witnesses and couldn't be subpoenaed to this hearing. They all decided to give it some thought.

She and Bill had explained that this process was a sort of dance in which the college would try to make the case against him a simple case of harassment, while at the same time sending a subtle message to the stacked hearing panel that Mitch was "one of them" who ought to be disposed of. The defense team, on the other hand, would be trying to unmask what was going on so that the panel and especially the college president would decide that dismissing Mitch would be too risky, too open to challenge in court.

She thought he understood. He still didn't look that nervous.. That might be good, or it might mean the nerves would hit later. She'd seen both in clients.

Remember," she told Mitch as the meeting broke up, "we're in this to win it for you. Sooner or later," she added.

"Sooner," Mitch had said. "It needs to be sooner."

Talk about pressure.

CLAIRE

Claire Daniels sat at her desk, staring at Monica Gilbert and her assistant Sharon seated across from her, waiting for Peggy to place and connect the long- distance call to the Office of Legal Affairs at the State Board offices in Raleigh. Lawrence Kincaid, whose title was Director of Legal Affairs, was expecting the call.

Before her on her desk was the entire McCaffrey file. It included the letter from Kathryn Gilbert that had been hand-delivered to her, with a copy to Monica, this morning. Their response to the letter was on the call agenda; she'd e-mailed a scan of it to Larry this morning.

She looked up from the file to see Monica glaring at her. She'd just told Gilbert about the four students, all enrolled in McCaffrey's English Lit class, who had showed up at her office right before lunch, all of them unhappy with Mitch McCaffrey's suspension and all of them wanting to know what was going on. Two of them were women; and one of these, Brenda Jenkins, was black. They had all said they wanted to help Mr. McCaffrey if they could.

"That's not what they said in their interviews," Monica had snapped – meaning, Claire thought, that it wasn't what Monica and her team had written down.

"I expect not," Claire had responded. "But I wanted to tell you, because you know they will find Kat Turner, or that Kat will find them."

Monica had nodded. There was no point in arguing with the undeniable. But she'd wanted to know what Claire had told them.

"I thanked them for their concern, and for coming to see me. I told them that complaints against the faculty were handled as confidentially as possible, and that I couldn't tell them any of the particulars right now, but there would be an announcement when a decision is made."

"Why didn't you caution them about talking with McCaffrey or his lawyers?"

Claire had raised an eyebrow. "Now how could I do that? We don't want to be accused of hiding anything, or of witness-tampering."

"That's not witness tampering!" Monica had snarled, and then just glared at Claire while they waited for the call.

The phone rang. Peggy said Mr. Kincaid was on the line. Claire punched the loudspeaker button with relief.

Claire thanked him for scheduling the call so quickly, and introduced the persons on the call from her end. Kincaid had invited Megan Stennis to sit in with him. Claire was pleased with the choice. She knew Megan, who she thought was a level-headed person, and who had almost as much experience in Legal Affairs as Larry. She had worked with both many times. In her mind's eye, she could see them both, huddled around a similar speaker-phone. Larry with his usual rumpled suit, his shock of almost white hair, and his old-fashioned wire framed glasses straight from the Reagan administration. Megan, barely five feet tall, a little plump (as she was herself), graying hair dyed dark, and tiny reading glasses perpetually on the bridge of her nose.

She noted from Monica's frown that Gilbert was not pleased. She and Meg had probably clashed before.

They reviewed the particulars of the McCaffrey complaint. That didn't take long; it had been e-mailed to Legal Affairs the previous week, so the two lawyers had read it. Claire then asked for advice on what to do about Turner's demands for copies of evidence and turn-over of the computer.

"Say 'no'!" Monica injected immediately, earning a stare from Claire at the vehemence.

"I don't think that's a good idea, Monica," Kincaid's voice came from over the speaker.

"Why not?" Monica demanded before Claire could say anything.

The voice this time was Megan Stennis'. "Because we don't want to hand a good lawyer like Kathryn Turner a due process issue. We don't want to be in federal court defending a claim that the instructor was denied confrontation, or adequate notice of the particulars of the evidence against him."

"That's right," Kincaid continued. "Our recommendation is to give them copies of the interview notes and witness statements. As for the computer, has the IT inspection been completed?"

"Not yet," Monica said. As far as Claire knew, that was true.

"Well," Kincaid said, "wait until that's been done. If there's nothing on the computer we're going to use, say no, and give Turner a copy of your IT report. If there is, say, 'yes' – at McCaffrey's expense, of course."

"It'll take a few days," Monica said.

"That's fine. Go ahead and send them the other stuff first. Put them off on the computer."

Based on body language, Monica didn't like what she'd been told. But she didn't argue.

"Let's see," Kincaid, "we're going to need to get you a hearing counsel to work with Monica."

"I want Barry Feldman," Monica said quickly.

Claire had met Feldman at system meetings. He had written the recommended speech codes that all of the colleges in the system had rushed into effect, and had been forced to revise after the state legis-lature had enacted the Higher Education Free Speech Act. Of course that's who Monica would want.

Kincaid's response was so quick that he must have known this was coming.

"I don't think that's the best choice, Monica."

"Why not?" Gilbert wasn't giving Claire a chance to say anything.

"Barry is competent," Kincaid admitted. "And he's dedicated. But Monica, he's like you. He's a zealot."

"Well, we need zealots," Monica fired back.

"Sometimes we do. But in this case, Ms. Gilbert" — he switched to formal address to make his point — "you're going to need a balance wheel. As I said, the college doesn't need to hand the instructor's lawyer any arguments she can take to court. We don't want any hereafters. As Megan and I understand it, this is a fairly popular instructor, and ———"

"He is," Claire confirmed, accepting Monica's dirty look with indifference.

"———we want to be sure whatever the hearing panel does sticks. So I think Megan or I should do this. Probably Meg. I get tied down here too much."

He plunged on, "Now we need to settle on the hearing panel. Any objections, Claire, to the ones Ms. Gilbert recommended?"

Claire bit her lip, which Kincaid couldn't see, and hesitated, which he and Megan doubtless noticed. All of the members Monica had picked out were zealously left-wing or feminist, or both, but...she really couldn't oppose them.

"No," she said at last. "Not really. I do worry a little about there not being a man." She was playing for time, and hoping one of the lawyers would rescue her. Neither did.

Monica had offered three names. Marcia Phillips, the Department Head, was appropriate. The other two were Donna Powell from the Music Department, and Teresa Moretz from Nursing.

"Well, we don't have an African American, either," Monica fleered.

"Well, we'll go with these names, then," said Kincaid. "But better get an alternate, in case one of them has to withdraw for some reason. Gets sick, whatever."

"I'll find somebody," Gilbert promised.

"All right, then," Kincaid continued, "we need a hearing date. I don't see how we can do this before the first of the year."

"We have to," Claire broke in. She'd known this was coming. "Larry, you know how budget-limited we are. The college can't afford to pay an adjunct and paid leave to McCaffrey for the rest of this term and the next. We need this decided before the spring term begins."

"Well," Kincaid said, "let's look at the calendar....Now, I see Thanksgiving is early this year. That gives us the second full week in December, which is a week usually too close to Christmas Break, I mean Winter Break. Will that work?"

"Yes," said Monica.

"No," Claire said at the same time, and then added, "That's exam week."

"I know," Kincaid acknowledged. "But that's the best we can do if you want this done this term. You'll just have to make it work."

Claire was sure her sigh was audible over the phone. "I suppose we must."

"There's just one thing," Kincaid said. "That lets me out as hearing counsel. I have to go with the Chairman to budget meetings with the state senate higher education committee that week. No getting around it."

"I'm out that week, too, unless something happens," Megan added. "I have another hearing in Wilmington."

Ahh-ohh, Claire thought. I think I know what's next.

"Well, Monica," Kincaid said, going back to her first name, "it looks like you get your way. You get Barry Feldman after all. I'll tell him and have him call you."

Monica flashed a triumphant smile, looking directly at Claire.

"But I want regular reports," Kincaid said. "Including the evening of the first day of the hearing."

That rubbed the smile off Monica's face, but she nodded and said, "I understand."

"The first day?" asked Claire. "Is this going to take more than a day?"

"Oh, yes," Larry told her. "At least two days, or I miss my best guess."

The call ended.

When Claire escorted Monica and Sharon out of the office, Peggy had a written phone message for her. A reporter for Channel 13 wanted the college to confirm that McCaffrey had been suspended for misconduct.

Lovely, Claire thought, just lovely.

"Call her back and tell her we'll get her a response tomorrow," Claire directed. "Monica, get on the phone to Public Affairs and have them draft a press release. Tell them to run it by Larry or Megan."

"Why not Barry?" Monica asked. There was not quite a tease in her voice.

"Larry or Meg," Claire repeated. "Larry or Megan."

14

THEY CAN'T TAKE THAT AWAY FROM ME

MITCH

Mitch was barely out of the parking lot at Melton, Norville when his cell phone rang. He didn't recognize the number and almost didn't accept the call. But he didn't remember Kathryn's cell number and maybe it was her. She might have forgotten something she wanted to tell him. So he answered.

Instead, it was Peggy Sturgill, Claire Daniels' administrative assistant. She said she was calling from her car, and proceeded to tell her about the four students who had visited Claire's office that morning. She remembered the names, and he would, too.

"I whispered to them on the way out to call Kathryn Turner," she said. "I hope that was all right."

He assured her that it was. "But be careful, Peg," he added. "I wouldn't want you to get fired over me."

"I will. But there's one more thing you need to know. We got a call from Channel 13 on your case. You know, that woman who does the investigative reporting for them, or thinks she does."

Mitch felt a rock drop to the bottom of his stomach. Kathryn had told him to expect it, but he didn't want to be on the news. He did know whom Peggy was talking about.

"Mary Marletti?" he prompted.

"That's the one. I don't know how she found out. I guess Monica must have leaked it to her. I thought you ought to know. The reporter will probably call you, too."

Mitch glumly had to agree with her. And he certainly needed to tell his lawyers.

After thanking Peggy and disconnecting, he told his telephone to call Kathryn Turner. The nice thing about using magic was that he didn't have to grab his phone and push an icon to give the command. He picked her cell phone number because he wasn't sure she'd still be at the office.

But she was. She answered after several rings.

"I'm sitting here with Marc talking about your case," she said. "What's up?"

He told her, the bad news and the good.

"I'm going to put the phone on 'speaker'," she said. "Now tell Marc the same things you just told me."

He did. "I assume I should just say, 'no comment' if the TV station calls me," he concluded.

Kathryn surprised him by saying, "No, some people will take that to mean you're guilty. You don't want to say much, but you've got to say more than just 'no comment'. We have to get out ahead of this, a little. Let me think for a minute."

By this time Mitch was almost to the turn off to High Country Estates. What if a reporter was waiting on him at home? He decided to pull off into a Minute Market lot while he was talking to Kathryn.

After a moment, she said, "First of all, don't accept any calls if you don't know the number. Do you have a land line?"

"Not anymore."

"Good. It's less likely they can get your cell number. Now...where are you now?"

He told her.

"Would anyone give the TV station the gate code at your place?"

"No, I don't think so." A wave of relief passed over him. He had forgotten the gate.

"Well, if a TV truck follows you in, or something, or they catch you outside the supermarket, or somewhere, here's what you say:

"'I did not do anything wrong. I did not violate college policy. I am confident a hearing will confirm that. I am unable to say anything else at this time because the college has advised me this is a confidential process. I am deeply disappointed that someone at the college has not respected the confidentiality.' Can you remember that?"

Mitch thought he could, if he remained calm, and he had already remembered a calming spell he could use on himself. But he asked anyway, "I think so, but can you e-mail it to me?"

"Of course. Now buck up, Mitch. We thought this was coming. We'll decide here whether we should send this to the media for you. In the meantime, if you talk with a reporter, stick to the script. Don't say anything else. Tell them you're acting on our advice if you need to. Trust us, and call us if you need us. You have my number, and Marc's."

Mitch felt better after getting Kathryn's advice. But he knew some reporter would find him sooner or later, and he dreaded it. He also dreaded the questions he'd get from his friends when this hit the news in a few minutes, or tonight.

He'd have to get used to it. Maybe…maybe there was a spell for dealing with the media, or something close enough to work. He'd look for one.

KATHRYN AND MARC

"Did you write down what I told him to say?" Kathryn asked when Mitch had hung up.

"No," Marc admitted. "I think I remember it, but can you give it to me again?"

After Marc had it on paper, Kathryn said, "E-mail this to Mitch. Copy me, Tiffany, Jenny and Bill. We'll get a press release out tomorrow."

"May I ask a question?" Marc asked as he rose to do her bidding.

"Ask."

"Why did you advise the client not to take calls from the media? Why not let him get it over with, since you went ahead and told him what to say?"

"That's two questions, but good ones," Kathryn said, smiling. "Two reasons, Marc: First, it's just hit Mitch that his friends, his fiancé, her kids, the people he goes to church with, are all going to hear this. He's upset. He should be. I want to give him some time to process this development. The reporter won't want to accept his statement. She'll keep pressing him. He's more likely to say something else, something he shouldn't, if he talks when he's upset.

"Second, if we can get our press release out before they can get hold of him, there's a chance – slight, but a chance – they'll accept the press release and leave him alone, especially since the press release will be on our letterhead. They'll know he's lawyered up and been told not to talk.'

Marc was nodding. "Makes sense," he told her. "Thank you. I'll take care of the e-mail before I leave for dinner."

"Oh my God!" Kathryn said suddenly, rising from behind her desk. Marc wheeled. "What's wrong?"

"I just realized I'm late to pick up Jimmy from soccer practice."

DIANA

Diana missed the six o'clock news because she was picking up Paul and Steve from soccer. She knew what was going to be on it, because Mitch had called her, and then she had run into Kathryn Turner at the soccer field.

The two had stood aside from their kids and talked briefly in low tones.

"Be careful yourself," Kathryn had cautioned her. "Martintown isn't all that big. A lot of people know you and Mitch are an item. A fair number know you're engaged." She could see Kathryn's wry smile in the gloom. "That diamond isn't exactly invisible. The TV station may try to call you. Or even show up at the Bean n' Bacon."

"Do you really think so?" That a reporter would seek her out hadn't occurred to her.

"Well, I wouldn't rule it out."

"What should I do? What should I say?"

"What would you want to say?"

"That this is just awful, there's not a word of truth to it; and that vicious…witch Monica Gilbert has just trumped this up."

"I'm glad I ran into you then. It's okay to say you don't believe the accusations against Mitch. Then you should just stop and say you've nothing else to say about it, and ask them not to trouble you any further. Don't get suckered into a conversation."

"What else could they ask me?"

"Whether it's true you and Mitch are engaged to be married, and whether this charge will affect that."

"Well, we are and it won't!" Diana had snapped back. "Can I say that?"

Kathryn bit her lip. "Yes, you can say that. But then repeat you won't answer any more questions."

While Diana was nodding her understanding, Kathryn continued, "You also have to figure out what to tell your sons. They're going to be asked about it at school. I'll leave that to you. You're the mommy."

Diana had decided to get it over with, with the boys in the car on the way home. They didn't understand what "harassment" was, and when she'd explained as best she could, they were indignant. Uncle Mitch wouldn't do anything like that. He just wouldn't.

"Everybody knows he's gone on you, Mom," Paul had said. "He wouldn't do anything to mess that up."

She had told him to tell anyone who asked that they were sure Uncle Mitch wasn't guilty and they had nothing else to say. She'd made them promise not to talk to a reporter.

When they arrived at home, Margaret had seen the six o'clock news and confirmed the Mitch report was on it. They decided not to discuss it with the kids at dinner, other than to tell them, no, they couldn't stay up for the ten o'clock news.

Now, with Paul and Steve in their rooms, supposedly doing homework, and the dishes cleared, Diana sat at the kitchen table with an open iPad to find the report on the featured stories link on the TV 13 web page. It was there.

"And now here's Mary Marletti to tell us what's going on at Carolina Highlands," the anchor said when she clicked on the link, a photo of the entrance to the college on the screen behind him.

The screen shifted to Mary Marletti's perky dark brown bob and olive features.

"TV 13 can confirm that English Instructor Mitchell McCaffrey has been suspended from his teaching duties and faces a hearing to determine whether his appointment should be revoked. No particulars have been released to the public. But TV 13 News has learned that a number of female students have accused the 47 year-old and long-time instructor of sexual harassment."

That was it. That was quite enough. Diana closed the iPad.

She had to admit that when she'd first learned of the news report she had been angry at Mitch. Angry at him for involving her in this mess, when he could have kept it quiet and walked away. But she'd quickly realized that was unfair, irrational. She herself had encouraged Mitch to fight.

But the anger was still there. Anger at the students who were willing to tell lies to mess with a teacher. Anger at a school administration that was too sanctimoniously politically correct and too cowardly to put a stop to this insanity. And most of all anger at the person she knew to be the orchestrator of this witch hunt. Monica Gilbert. Monica, who was the real witch.

Diana had a better word for Monica that rhymed with "witch" and began with another letter. Monica the bitch. Any ugly word for an ugly person, on the inside if not on the outside.

Well, Monica was not going to win. Somehow, they'd beat her at her own game. Diana didn't know how, but vowed to herself that they would. That she would by herself if need be.

I will not let that bitch take my life away from me, she thought. I won't. She can't because I won't let her.

Before she went to bed, she called Mitch, and told him exactly that. She hoped he felt better for hearing it.

Because she sure felt better for saying it.

15

OVER THE RIVER AND THROUGH THE WOODS

MITCH

Early on Friday morning, Mitch met Ben and Lonnie at the parking lot of the Bean n' Bacon. He had persuaded them to take a day off to go deer hunting, because there would be fewer hunters in the woods and because it would leave Saturday open for football. It hadn't taken much persuading.

Mitch bagged a finely racked buck, and Lonnie duplicated his effort. But they were far apart. By the time they had texted one another about their kills, and field dressed the carcasses and informed Ben, also by text, it was already early afternoon. By the time they had both carcasses to the truck, which was easier, but not easy, with Ben helping, the sun had already disappeared over South Ridge.

They had enough time to bring their kills to a butcher that would complete carving up the carcasses and freezer wrap the meat. From there it would go to the big freezer at the Bean n' Bacon, where a fair amount of the venison would supplement the turkey at the big annual Thanksgiving Day feast in a couple of weeks.

When the deer were covered in tarps in the bed of the pick-up, Lonnie opened a cooler and pulled out three Sweetwater IPA's. Mitch and Ben accepted gratefully.

They chatted idly about the hunt for a few minutes, with Lonnie chiding Ben that North Carolina wasn't Wyoming, and that he'd do better without the scope. Mitch decided it was time to ask them what he needed to find out.

"Hey, guys," he said. "You remember that tailgate at Boone a few weeks ago?"

They did.

"And do you remember the man who handed me that Nazi flyer?"

"Yeah" Lonnie said. "Damned punk."

"Sure," Ben agreed. "Scruffy little asshole."

"What about the guy who was wandering around taking pictures at about that same time?"

They had to think about that. Finally, Ben said, "You mean the guy in the Wake sweatshirt?"

"That's the one."

"Yeah, I think I remember him," Lonnie said.

"Do you think you'd recognize them if you saw them again?" Mitch had to admit he was enjoying playing investigator.

"The Nazi for sure," Ben said. "Not as sure about the other. But I might."

"Same," said Lonnie.

"Okay, then look at these." Mitch opened the gallery app on his phone and brought up the photos he'd taken at the fantasy store in Black Mountain. Ben and Lonnie passed the phone back and forth a couple of times.

"That's Mr. Nazi," Ben said, handing the phone back to Mitch. "And I'm pretty sure the other guy was the Wake fan we saw. Where did you take these?"

"I'll tell you, but let's hear from Lonnie first."

"I agree," Lonnie said. "Those are the guys. I'm sure."

"Gentlemen, I think what you saw at the tailgate was an attempted set up planned out by someone – I think I know whom – at the college. They're going to try to pretend I'm a Nazi, or a white supremacist, or something."

"Those assholes!" Lonnie said.

Ben: "Yeah."

"But I got lucky. Diana wanted to go into a store when we were in Black Mountain, and there they were. I pretended to play tourist and take pictures."

"But how did they not recognize you?" Ben wanted to know.

He couldn't tell them the real reason, so he was evasive. "I don't know, but if they did, I couldn't tell it."

Mitch couldn't resist a wide grin. They looked at him with raised brows.

"Boys," he said, "I'm not sure, but I think you may have just become witnesses."

They groaned simultaneously.

But he knew they would do it.

DIANA

As Diana drove to Mitch's house the next evening, she was affectionately fuming about her fiancé. She had wanted to take him out to dinner Friday evening, using her car to avoid anyone unpleasant who might recognize either of his; but no, he didn't get back from his hunting expedition (and from running the deer carcasses by the butcher) in time for it to make sense. And of course today, they had to wait until his football games were over, which made going to Asheville or Morganton impractical.

For the life of her, she still couldn't figure out how someone with so many important things on his mind could just submerge it all in his hobbies. She had to admit she was glad he could, but she still didn't quite understand it.

So help me, she thought, if he's not ready because a game ran late or comes out boozy from drinking all afternoon in front of the TV, I'll smack him a good one.

But Mitch answered the door immediately, clearly sober, scrubbed, and handsome in his sport shirt, sweater, khakis and tassel loafers, with an App State windbreaker over one arm and a wide grin. She decided to forgive him. For now, anyway. But they were not going to talk football all during dinner, she told him immediately. He readily agreed, but still managed to get in that the Apps were closing in on the Sun Belt title, and the Tar Heels were better than expected, right after he kissed her hello.

"Okay, buddy," she said, unable to keep from smiling back, "that's enough football. Got it?"

He said he did.

Diana had selected dinner at Mario's. The main dining room was mostly a pizzeria, but there was a smaller dining room in the rear that featured a more upscale menu. Seating in the back was limited, but it was more private, yet not private enough for Diana's purposes. But she'd found a better option. It was possible, with reservations to eat at a small table in the kitchen, where the customers could see the food prepared. Eating there could get a little noisy, but the noise assured privacy.

And Pete Mastroianni had assured her he would let her and Mitch in though the employee's entrance in the rear parking lot, usually reserved for employees.

Piero Mastroianni had opened Mario's thirty years ago. The family hailed from Naples via New York City. The local newspaper had once asked Pete why he called the restaurant "Mario's", when no one in the family was named "Mario". Why not "Piero's" or even "Pete's"? He'd said he had an uncle named Mario back in Italy.

Diana had known the Mastroianni family practically her whole life. She had gone to school with Pete's kids, Robert and Sophia. Robert now helped manage the restaurant. Sophia was married and living in Florida. Pete Mastroianni was also active in the local restaurant association, where he and Margaret Corcoran had become friends.

By the time Diana pulled her Camry into the rear parking lot, it was almost fully dark at this time of year, and no one seemed to pay attention as she and Mitch pulled into an empty space, and, after exiting the car, rapped on the back door with the sign "Restaurant Employees Only." After a second knock, a beaming Robert admitted them and led them to a table for two against a wall, away from the door into the dining area, so they would not be seen.

The restaurant smells of garlic, tomato sauce, and baking bread were wonderful. Robert quickly produced menus, a basket of garlic bread sticks and a bottle of Chianti. Despite the kitchen noises, they could hear the combination of soft classical music and Frank Sinatra the restaurant used. The meal was off to a good start.

They ordered one of the house specials, the seafood pasta for two, which consisted of oysters, shrimp, clams, mussels, and conch steamed over spicy marinara sauce, and served with the sauce over linguine, preceded by Caesar salad made from scratch at the table, and accompanied by the wine. It was, they agreed, as delicious as advertised. They decided to finish with coffee and tiramisu.

Desert and just arrived when it happened. Their server, a part-time Carolina Highlands student named Freddie Barnes had appeared with the tiramisu and placed on a folding stand next to the table while he removed the remains of their entrees, which he would place on a metal table behind him before carrying them to be washed. She had just whispered to Mitch how wonderful it was to have a lovely quiet meal with no reporters or cameras.

They first heard it as a commotion in the main dining room that was low at first, and louder as it drew closer. There were shouts of "where are they?" and "where is he?". Then the swinging door to the kitchen burst open and a group of six – no seven, she realized later – shoved their way in.

They saw Mitch and Diana immediately. Then the shouting began, a mixed chant of "Racist!" and "Abuser!" and "Sexist!" depending on the shouter. They were a mixed group, three women and four men, some well-dressed, others sloppy in sweats or tattered jeans. All were flushed and wild-eyed. None looked college-aged. More like late twenty or thirty-somethings. Diana knew none of them. She looked at Mitch and he shook his head slightly. Evidently, he didn't know any of them, either.

The apparent leader was a woman. She was one of the well-dressed ones, of medium height for a woman, her dark brown hair tied back, wearing a bulky green sweater and cord pants tucked into tall boots. She might have been pretty in repose, but it was impossible to tell with her face contorted in rage.

"Do you think you can harass and abuse those girls, and then hide from us?" she shouted at Mitch, who said nothing. She advanced on the table where he and Diana still sat, staring in disbelief.

Freddie moved to block her. "Now, ma'am, you're going to need to –"

The woman, whoever she was, shoved him to get him out of her way. Freddie hadn't expected that. He still had the dishware from dinner balanced precariously in both hands. He was a skinny young man, who looked still younger despite a wispy brown beard. He staggered back until he hit the metal table, dropping the dishes.

Marinara sauce, oyster, clam and mussel shells splattered on the floor, some of it splashing the woman's boots. Flatware clattered on the tile. One of the plates shattered. That brought Mitch to his feet.

One of the men, tall, bushy-bearded, and not so well dressed in faded jeans, tennis shoes, and a gray hoody, stepped past the woman to tower over Mitch. "You racist, abusive son-of-a-bitch!" he shouted. "You leave Melissa alone! Pick on me."

But Mitch slid to the side to steady a trembling Freddie. He looked calmly at the big man, and said, "I'm not picking on anyone. But leave this young man out of it."

"No," said a voice from behind Mitch. "Just leave. Period. All of you. Now."

It was Robert Mastroianni. The Mastroianni's, while not big men, were bulky. Robert had played football at West Brainerd, on the line. He stood beside Mitch. But the group of – what were they? Protesters? That didn't sound right, Diana thought, despite the pounding of her heart and the blood roaring in her ears. This bunch didn't act like they were going anywhere.

"No peace for child abusers!" a skinny woman shouted. Then the "racist-sexist" chant began again.

"I'm telling you for the last time," Robert warned. "Leave now, or I'll –"

"Do what?" the big guy in the hoody sneered. "Make us? Try it. Just try it. It's our right to protest racists and Nazis."

The chant continued while he and Robert continued their staring match.

Diana saw Mitch standing to one side. She had learned to tell when he was casting a spell. But what was he up to?

She looked back to the crowd who had shoved into the kitchen.

One was standing in the doorway so as to hold the door partly open. Behind him, she could see a crowd of servers and some customers watching anxiously. One seemed to be talking on a cell phone. Another appeared to be using hers to take photos. As she watched, the ones in the rear seemed to relax. Their shoulders slumped. They quit shouting. Only Melissa and the big guy in the hoody were still talking, she directing barbs at Mitch, he snarling at Robert Mastroianni.

Then, from around the grills and oven, pushing their way past the small crowd of cooks who had stopped work to watch, Pete himself appeared, followed by four Brainerd County Sheriff's deputies.

"All right," one wearing a sergeant's stripes bellowed, "what's going on here?" Diana knew him. He was a frequent customer at the Bean n' Bacon. His name tag said "Benson" and she remembered his first name was Les.

Melissa, the hoody guy, and Robert all started to talk at once. Only she, Mitch, and Freddie were silent.

"QUIET!" Les bellowed again. He looked around and his eyes settled on Diana.

"Ms. Winstead," he said when there was a bit of quiet, even though the big hoody man was still mumbling, "tell me what happened here."

Diana took a deep breath and then related what had happened as quickly as she could, but leaving out nothing. The woman called "Melissa" tried to interrupt several times with either "No!" or "So?", but Benson told her to be quiet. When Diana was finished, Benson turned to Robert.

"Is that what happened, Rob?" he asked.

"Yeah, best as I saw it."

"Anybody saying anything different?" He looked directly at Melissa, who was still seething.

"We were just protesting," she said. "This man harassed young women. And he's a closet Nazi. He can't sneak off without being challenged."

"Yeah!" chimed in the rest, but they continued to look, well, a little subdued. Diana notices Mitch was continuing to stare at Melissa.

Benson hooked his thumbs in his belt. "Y'all can protest all you want, but you can't barge into a restaurant and disrupt everyone else's evening. Now you need to get out…Unless Mr. Mastroianni here wants to prefer charges.

Robert rubbed his chin. Finally, he said. "Only one." He pointed at Melissa. I want her charged with vandalism and for assaulting my employee."

"What?" the woman shrieked.

"Are you sure, Robert?"

Robert exchanged a glance with his father, who nodded.

"I'm sure," he said, then added, "unless she'll apologize to our guests here and signs off to pay for the broken dishes. I'll drop it then."

"I will not," Melissa said.

"If you don't, and Mr. Mastroianni insists he'll press charges, ma'am, I'll have to cuff you."

"But…but," Melissa sputtered. She looked at Mitch, and then seemed to deflate, sort of like the others had, Diana noticed. Sighing, she said. "All right. I'll do it." Rallying, she said to Benson, but without her former fire, "Just wait until I tell Sylvia. You'll get a boycott. This doesn't happen anywhere else."

Benson smiled. "This is Brainerd County, ma'am."

The others waited for Melissa Deever, who produced a card saying she worked in the Southeastern Electronics Human Resources Department, and signed a promise to pay damages scrawled on its back. She also made an obviously insincere apology to Freddie, who only nodded. Then the deputies escorted them through the restaurant and out the door.

Mitch apologized to the Mastroianni's for the scene. "Do you want us to stay away?"

Pete said, "Not on your life. Come anytime." He snorted, "Boycott hell. I'm not afraid of Sylvia Sonnenberg."

Diana recognized the name. Sonnenberg had money, and was supposed to be some kind of mover and shaker in local Democratic politics. But she and Mitch were both ready to leave. They declined desert. Robert insisted on giving them a tiramisu take-out. After paying, they left, only to see a TV 13 Truck parked in back.

They declined an interview. Mitch suggested they talk to Robert and Freddie. But they had to push their way past the reporters.

Once they were on the road, Diana asked immediately, "What were you doing, Mitch? I know you were doing something. I say all those assholes calm down. Even Melissa Tompkins, at least a little."

"It was a calming spell," Mitch replied. "I didn't want a fight. Even if Robert and I could have held our own."

"You can do that?"

"Yeah. I've had that spell for a while. I am better at it now....I've been practicing. But it still took longer than I'd like with Deever."

She risked taking her eyes off the road long enough to give him a sharp look, and saw a grim smile.

"Have you got better at anything else?" she asked.

He didn't answer right away. After a long pause, he said only, "Maybe."

Channel 13
News Report

Anchor: And now here's Mary Marletti with the latest on the suspended Carolina Highlands Instructor, Mitchell McCaffrey.

Marletti (standing in the Mario's parking lot): Apparently, Gina, a group of seven protesters showed up here at Mario's restaurant outside Martintown tonight to confront McCaffrey and his fiancé, Diana Winstead while they were having dinner at a private table in the kitchen. We've learned the owner summoned the Brainerd County Sheriff 's department (screen shifts to two squad cars), but (screen returns to Marletti) we've learned that no charges were brought and the protesters have been released. McCaffrey and Winstead (screen shifts to McCaffrey and Winstead leaving restaurant) declined interviews, but one of the protestors, Melissa Deever, was willing to talk with us. (Screen shifts to Marletti standing with Deever.)

Deever: We know that Mitch McCaffrey is a closet racist and a white supremacist with ties to the alt right. He may be a Nazi. He harassed young women he was supposed to teach. Someone like that can't be allowed to teach young people. He can't expect to be left alone as long as he peddles hate in our community college. (Screen shifts back to Marletti.)

Marletti: We asked restaurant owner Pete Mastroianni about this, and why McCaffrey is welcome in his restaurant. Here's what he had to say. (Screen shifts to Marletti standing with Mastroianni.)

Mastroianni: Mary, I don't believe a word of it. Mitch McCaffrey has been a customer for years. He's taught a number of our employees, men and women, black and white. They all speak highly of him. Diana Winstead is a great gal. She wouldn't give the time of day to a Nazi, or someone who harassed his students. Somebody has made this stuff up. I wish I knew who. They wouldn't be welcome at Mario's. But Mitch and Diana are welcome any time. Now those people who disrupted my restaurant don't need to come back. (Screen splits to show Anchor and Marletti only.)

Anchor: Mary, when are we going to learn more about this, or what the truth of the allegations is?

Marletti: We don't know, Gina. The college has not made public when McCaffrey's hearing will be held. And it's not a public hearing. We may not know until the college president issues a ruling. But TV 13 will report all information as it becomes available.

16

STOP IN THE
NAME OF LOVE

KATHRYN

"If you'll confirm in writing that the office will be secured, we can agree to leave it all there for now." She was on the telephone with Barry Feldman, who had called to tell her he would be appearing for Carolina Highlands at the McCaffrey hearing, and she was referring to Mitch's books that had remained in his office.

"It'll save the time it will take to move them back after he's reinstated," she continued. She really didn't enjoy this kind of sparring with opposing counsel; but she really didn't know Feldman, and wanted to take his temperature a little bit.

"I really don't think that's likely at all," Feldman replied. "If you look at the evidence the college has on him…well, it's pretty bad." He sounded earnest, but most lawyers were good at that.

"I wouldn't know," Kathryn purred with feigned innocence. "We haven't seen the files we requested yet. We are going to get them, aren't we?"

"Hasn't Monica sent them over yet?" Feldman asked, probably

feigning innocence himself. "They were supposed to send that with the Notice of Hearing."

They had already discussed the hearing date, the second Tuesday in December, and agreed that it would be prudent to reserve Wednesday of that week, too. They'd also discussed the hearing room at the college, and how it ought to be configured. That part of the call had gone well.

"No," Kathryn answered. "We don't have them."

"Well, I'll have that done right away. E-mail okay?"

She said it was.

"Now going back to his books, I'll discuss leaving them there with the folks at the college. But there's no reason not to turn them over to your client. The inventory of his office has been completed."

"We're going to be getting a copy of that, too, aren't we? Immediately, I mean?"

"Oh, yes. I'll e-mail it to you today."

They moved on to discuss exchange of witness and exhibit lists, and agreed on ten days before the hearing. Kathryn wanted fourteen days, and Barry had at first said a week. So they split the difference.

They wound up the call pretty quickly after that. At least it had been cordial. Calls to opposing counsel weren't always. She made a note to check out Feldman with some lawyers she knew at his old firm in Raleigh, where he'd worked before joining the Legal Affairs group for the community college system.

Otherwise, the case was going pretty well. Marc and Tiffany had made good progress on their interviews. A number of students had come to them. A few wouldn't return calls. Most hadn't known anything, or said they didn't. At least these wouldn't hurt. In theory, at least. If they were telling the truth.

But they hadn't talked to Lottie and her friends yet. They needed to do that. Try, at least.

She sent out an e-mail reporting on the call, and to schedule another team meeting. It should be lawyers only at first. Mitch should be scheduled to come in right afterwards.

Right after she clicked "send", her phone rang. The call was from the front desk.

"There's someone on hold who wants to talk with you. She says you don't know her, but it's about the McCaffrey case."

"Who is it?"

"She says her name is 'Maria.'"

"That rings no bells, but put her through."

Melissa and King

Melissa Deever was not having a good time. She was sitting with her boss, J. Kingsley Armistead, behind closed doors in his office. But she was afraid he could be heard in the secretarial pool down the hall.

"What in the bloody hell did you think you were doing?" Armistead practically yelled at her. "What?"

Melissa decided she'd better be meek. Keeping her eyes downcast, she said, "We all thought we were doing the right thing by confronting him."

"Just who is 'we'?" he demanded.

"Just some people I know. We're progressives. We all believe racist, sexist pigs have to be outed."

"In public? Taking the lead yourself? Associating Southeastern Electronics name with it?"

"I didn't say I was there on behalf of Southeastern," she protested.

"You gave out your business card. You allowed yourself to be interviewed on television."

"I'm sorry," she almost whimpered.

"Sorry doesn't cut it. Even without the card, you'd have been recognized. Haven't you got any common sense at all? No. Don't answer that. Obviously you don't."

She tried to defend herself. "King...I mean Mr. Armistead," she corrected, seeing his glare darken still more. "We all know that people like that can't be allowed to teach young people."

Armistead allowed his features to relax, and when he spoke, the volume dropped. "Of course we do. But this has to be done the right way. We have to get along in this place. We get government contracts, and guess who runs the government right now?

"I've planned to drop a word to Claire Daniels about this, to tell her Southeastern would take a dim view of their allowing that kind of person to continue teaching. I'm still going to do that."

"But you! You've made it harder! Don't you dare pull a stunt like this again. Do you hear me? Do you?"

Melissa sighed with relief. This was going to be a reprimand, not a termination.

"I understand."

Marc and Tiffany

Late in the afternoon of the following Friday, Marc Washington and Tiffany DeRatt were in Marc's new Honda Fit, speeding down the four-lane state connector road to its intersection with Highway I-40, there to turn toward Asheville on a mission to interview witnesses.

The witnesses were Lottie Watkins and her satellites, Corrine Jacobs and Darlene Parker. They had decided not to approach anyone on campus, and the whole team had decided phone calls would go un-answered and voice-mails un-returned. One of the friendly witnesses told them that the three frequently hung out at the Lab, a restaurant and bar on Lexington Avenue, on Friday evenings, and had found out by cautious eavesdropping that this evening would be one of those.

Maybe they'd get lucky and one or more of them would talk. Maybe not. But at least they could see these girls in one of their elements and size them up. Kathryn had decided it was worth the trip. Tiffany had her cell phone camera and voice recorder ready. They'd get something, surely. Even hostility was worth something.

The week had gone pretty well so far, in terms of progress on this case, Marc decided. He and Tiffany still had a couple of names to call, students or former students the investigation committee mentioned in their report. Tiffany still had to finish the report on interviews to date for him to edit and pass on to Kathryn. But so far, so good.

No one had been really happy with the TV report of the incident at Mario's. But, as Bill Norville had observed, it was pretty much a wash. Pete Mastroianni's interview balanced Melissa Deever's. And Southeastern Electronics had already announced it did not endorse Deever's tactics, and her interview did not reflect company policy.

More troubling had been some of the evidence disclosed by the college as having been gathered in the inspection of the client's office, which they were now discussing as they drove. The college claimed to have found a small stack of neo-Nazi flyers in Mitch's desk. Monica Gilbert claimed to have received an anonymous e-mail with an attached photo of Mitch and a bearded young man, both of whom had their hands on the same flyer. It was impossible to tell who was handing the flyer to whom, but the inference, from finding the stack in the desk, was that Mitch was doing the distributing.

"But," Tiffany protested, "doesn't the inventory we took before the college suspended him refute that? And what about Mitch's photos from Black Mountain and his friends' testimony? Doesn't that make the evidence look like a plant?"

"It does to me," Marc replied. "And it would to a jury, black or white. But to Gilbert's hand-picked stooges on the hearing panel? Bill and Kathryn think it will be enough for them to think Mitch might be alt-right, so they can seize on something else to get rid of him. You know, 'we can't take a chance on having someone who even might be like that on the faculty.' Something like that."

After a moment, he added, "Heck, they think that just thinking Mitch is fairly conservative might be enough to poison the well. And that really is true."

"You mean they'll find him guilty of harassment, whether he is or not, just because they don't like his politics?"

"That's what we're afraid of."

"But that evidence is so…nothing," Tiffany objected again. "I mean, Lottie didn't feel safe because he asked her to read a sonnet? She thought he was looking at her legs, when he couldn't see them until she stood up and walked out?"

They had checked at Mitch's suggestion, and sure enough, someone standing at the lectern couldn't see the lower body and legs of someone seated at the back.

But Marc simply said, "Yes."

"What about Claire Daniels?" Tiffany said. "Could she overrule the panel if we offer a strong defense?"

"Tiff, our team is split on that. She has the legal authority to do that, for sure. The client and Kathryn think she might. But Mr. Norville doesn't think she'd dare go against the panel, because the other radicals on the faculty would pitch a fit."

Tiffany nodded thoughtfully. "Well, when I was there, she had the reputation of being pretty liberal, but not extreme."

"I feel sorry for her," Marc says. "She had to keep the public in a conservative area like we live in happy, and also has to keep the progressive faculty happy. She has to be perpetually purple."

Tiffany laughed, and Marc stole a glance at her. Damn, she was pretty. And a sharp dresser, too, in her tailored Navy-blue pant suit and gold chain. They hadn't had time to change after work. Marc's sole concession to looking casual had been to remove his rep tie. He still had the oxford shirt, blazer and cords. Tiffany hadn't tried to change anything.

Down, boy, he thought. She's off limits. But he stole another look and saw an imitation of Kathryn's wry smile, which she wiped from her face when she caught him looking.

By the time they arrived and had parked in the Civic Center garage, the dusk was almost full-blown night. As they walked down Walnut Street to the Lab, which was a favorite hang-out of the students at the branch of the University in Asheville (the ones of drinking age, anyway), the buzz and clatter from inside gave notice the place was already pretty busy.

"We'll sit at bar, ask for menus, and look around until they find them," Marc said. "Remember, we're supposed to look like we're on a date at first glance."

Tiffany stopped abruptly and grabbed his arm. "You mean we're not? How dare you trifle with my affections?"

They laughed again. Then, her smile fading, she asked, "How do these girls get to drink, anyway? Are any of them 21?"

"No, they're close, but not there. I bet they have fake ids."

"That will fool anybody?" She asked, dubious.

"Well, if offered in dark, busy and crowed bar. Especially by a pretty girl to a male bartender."

"I'll get a pic of them drinking, then, if we don't get anything else."

By this time, they were there. And it was dark inside, and noisy, and crowded. But they found two empty seats at the bar, ordered a beer for Marc and a glass of wine for Tiffany, and started looking around.

They found them almost by accident when Tiffany, who was seated to Marc's right, looked past him back to the front of the bar facing Lexington Avenue. The Lab kept that front open to the air deep into November, and opened it again in March, using portable heaters to warm the adjacent seating area.

There was a series of chairs up against the wall, which was not quite chest high, with the restaurant open to the air from there to the ceiling. Customers could sit there and watch the traffic on Lexington.

Tiffany grabbed Marc's arm and told him to look back to his left.

"All the way to the front," she hissed.

There they were, sitting in a row, almost in uniform with tight jeans molding their butts to the stools, and fluffy but tight sweaters.

"The one on the right is Lottie," she said.

"I thought you didn't know her."

"I've seen the photos. And she looks like her sister. Her sister's a little darker, though. This one looks even more like her mother."

Marc turned back toward her. "We can't be obvious. You keep on looking toward me, when we talk, but keep your eyes on them. I'll look back every now and then, pretending I want to see something outside. Tell me anything you see."

Tiffany giggled. "Yes, Mr. Secret Agent Man."

Marc nursed his beer. He had to drive back. Tiffany sipped her wine. The barkeep asked if they wanted to order food, and Marc asked for corn chips and queso. They didn't want to get bogged down with a meal. They'd grab a sandwich on the way back.

After a few minutes, Marc said, "Take your phone, stand up and step back to take my picture. Be sure to get them in the background."

She did, and their subjects obliged them when the camera flashed and turned, stood up and waved. They laughed and raised what had to be pints of beer when Tiffany, grinning, snapped a shot of the three, then turned and seated themselves again.

"Fake ids, I reckon," said Tiffany.

"Male server, no doubt," said Marc, and was confirmed when a young man in a Lab logo'd apron dropped by where they sat, evidently to check on them.

"Okay," Tiffany said when their chips came, "so we've caught them drinking with faked ids. Is that going to help?"

Marc made a wry face. "A little. It shows they don't mind breaking the law. It shows they don't mind lying."

"Does it show they'd lie about harassment?" she asked.

"Well, Kathryn will say it doesn't recommend them."

"Are we going to try to talk with them?"

"Yeah. On our way out."

She punched him lightly on the arm. "Oh-oh. One of them may be leaving."

Marc turned and pretended to look at the foot traffic on the street. One of the three girls – Corrine, he thought – and risen and walked out the door. But she walked around on the sidewalk to where she faced her buds and lit a cigarette. She stood there laughing and talking while she smoked.

Their server brought another round of beer – no, one of the glasses looked like a Coke – and removed their empties.

"They're here for a while," Marc said. "And at least they have enough sense for one to be a designated driver. We'll leave after I pay, and try to strike up a conversation on the way out. Don't forget to turn on the voice recorder."

"How are going to approach them?"

Marc considered. "Maybe if we walk around to where Corrine was standing...but we have to find an excuse to stop."

Tiffany frowned in thought. "I can stop to smoke."

"You smoke?"

"Not often. But asking Corrine if I can bum a cig would be a perfect ice-breaker."

"We'll do it."

Marc called for the check, paid with cash, including the tip, and they rose from their seats.

"Well," he said, "here goes nothing."

They left the bar and turned left on Lexington. The foot traffic was light. When they reached were their subjects were sitting, Tiffany touched Marc on the arm, stage whispered, "just a sec, hon", and approached Corrine.

"Excuse me" she said. "I'm sorry to bother you, but I happened to see you having a cigarette. I am dying for a smoke. You wouldn't let me bum one, would you."

Corrine smiled up at her. "Why sure, honey."

She handed over a cigarette and her lighter. Tiffany stepped back next to Marc where smoking on the walk was permitted, and lit up.

"Ahh," she said, "that's good." She handed the butane lighter to Marc, and commanded, "Give this back to the lady, honey. I have to stand here."

Marc stepped forward and handed her Corrine the lighter. "Thanks," he said. "Tiffany here falls off the wagon every now and then."

They all laughed. "Corrine is never on the wagon," Lottie told him. "She's a bad girl." They all laughed again.

Marc stepped back beside Tiffany. Before he could say anything else, the third girl – Darlene Parker, that was her name – asked, "Hey, could you guys take our picture?" She held up her cell phone.

"Why, sure," Marc said.

He took two shots and returned the phone. "Where are y'all from?" he asked.

"Martintown," Darlene told him. "What about you all?"

"Why that's a coincidence," Tiffany said. "So are we?"

Introductions followed. Marc noticed their names did not ring a bell.

"What are y'all doing here?" Lottie asked.

"Same as you," Tiffany said. "Friday night on the town. Say, could I get another cig?"

Darlene handed one to her, asking, "So what do you guys do? Work? School?" Tiffany and Marc were both young enough to still be students.

"Well," Marc said, "I'm a lawyer. Tiffany's a paralegal."

That got their antenna up. "Who with?" Lottie asked, her voice brittle.

"We're with Melton, Norville, Jennings & Johnson," Marc said as affably as he could make his voice, "and we'd like to talk with you all."

"About"– Corrine began, but Lottie interrupted.

"You want to talk about the McCaffrey case, don't you?" she asked, her voice pure ice. "Nothin' doin'. We don't have to talk with you. We don't have to talk with anyone. Ms. Gilbert said so."

"That's true," Marc said, his voice level. "You don't. But we think you ought to, if you don't have anything to hide."

Lottie's stunning face was a mask of rage. "Get away from us! If you don't, I'll call the manager."

Tiffany took a step forward. "We'll go," she said. "But you know, I had Mr. McCaffrey for comp when I was at Carolina Highlands. He helped me a lot. Y'all ought to be ashamed. You're messin' with a good man."

Corrine's face was a blank. Darlene, the one who was drinking Coke, looked uncomfortable, shifting on her stool. But Lottie stood firm.

"I said leave," she commanded.

Marc held up his hands in surrender. "Okay, okay. We're going." He gave them what he thought was his most evil smile. "See you at the hearing."

Marc started down the street, but Tiffany hung back after starting to follow him.

"Let me give you girls some advice," she said, her eyes moving from face to face. "Y'all need to quit running in a pack. You're gonna get each other in trouble sooner or later. If you're not already."

She turned to follow Marc, but Lottie called after her, "Is he your boss?"

Tiffany stopped and turned. "One of them."

Lottie's eyes were fixed beyond her, to where Marc stood waiting, looking back quizzically. "Lucky girl! He's hot."

Tiffany hoped she was dark enough not to show the blush, but she felt the heat on her cheeks. She didn't think Marc had heard that. Good.

But the voice recorder was still running, she realized.

Marc's car was only a few minutes away. They didn't say anything to each other while they found it and left the garage, still nothing while Marc got them back on the interstate, and turned them back towards home. Marc finally asked if a McDonald's drive through was okay, and she said it was. They found one three exits back down the road.

Tiffany tried to break the ice after they had their sandwiches, his Big Mac and her grilled chicken.

"You're not much of a date," she accused.

Marc protested that he wasn't a date at all, and the fast food was due to Bill Norville's miserly associate pay and expense account policy, but it sounded lame to both of them, particularly since neither was really true.

"So now we know," Marc said as they re-entered Highway I-40.

"Yes. Now we know. Was this trip worthwhile?"

"I think so. We had to find out if they would talk with us. We've confirmed they're party girls who aren't exactly tearful harassment victims. And that Lottie, as we thought, is the ring-leader."

They ate their sandwiches as they drove. Marc swore softly once when mustard dripped on his shirt, and she handed him a napkin to wipe it off. They didn't talk for a long time.

They were almost to the turn off to the connector road to Martintown when Tiffany broke the silence.

"I've been thinking…" she trailed off.

"About what?"

"Lottie. Her parents. What do you think about inter-racial relationships?"

"Fine with me," he said, shrugging. "There are plenty of them these days. It ain't like it was in the old days."

"I know. What would your parents think if you dated a white chick, even married one? I don't think mine would like it."

Marc considered. "They'd be okay with it." He hesitated. "But you know, I've never thought about trying to find a white girl. I just haven't considered it."

"What? You mean you'd turn down Jennifer Lawrence?"

He burst out laughing. "I didn't say that. But…for whatever reason, I just haven't seen myself with a white girl."

"What about Lottie Watkins? She'd only half white."

"Lottie Watkins? Are you crazy?"

Tiffany appeared to think about his answer.

"Good," she said at last, and added nothing.

They talked a little about the case while they finished the drive, but there were long pauses in the conversation.

But when Marc pulled into her apartment parking lot to let her out, she leaned over and kissed him gently on the lips.

"I won't tell anybody if you don't," she whispered. "Good night."

She was out of the car and had shut the door before he could say anything else. Marc sat still for a full minute, and then touched a finger to his lips, and put the car in gear to drive home.

17

COME YE THANKFUL PEOPLE, COME

MONICA

Monica Gilbert was almost to Raleigh. It had not been a fun drive. Traffic on the day before Thanksgiving had been awful. It still was, and she was now stuck in it. There was evidently and accident somewhere ahead, and I-40, for the time being, was a parking lot. She'd programed the GPS on her phone to give her the shortest route to her destination without using the interstate; but she had to get to an exit before it would be of any use, and east-bound traffic, at the moment, was not moving at all.

She still didn't regret accepting Barry Feldman's invitation. He'd suggested she visit for the holiday. They could discuss the McCaffrey case in person and make it a working break. He'd take her to the Carolina Club in Chapel Hill for Thanksgiving dinner. She wouldn't need to get a hotel because he had plenty of room at his condo. Staying there wouldn't exactly conform to college policy, but no one had to know.

She smiled to herself. How true that he had plenty of room, since he didn't expect them to require more than one bedroom. She sighed.

Men were so predictable. Feldman was a little younger than she was, and she had to admit he was rather attractive – tall and slender with a neat, dark beard and blue eyes. And she didn't mind making her body work for her, especially if she got some pleasure out of it herself. It saved compulsion spells, which were tricky, or at least made them easier. A nudge, and not a shove. But sometimes it got…tiresome.

But she hadn't hesitated to accept the invitation. She really had nothing else to do. Seeing her mother, who rarely knew her these days, at the nursing home was pointless and depressing. She could have wrangled an invitation from one of her colleagues at the college, but that would have been boring.

The two other men she'd been dangling, Bart Stevens and King Armistead, were not options this weekend. Bart would be with his hippie wife. King had his own family obligations. Besides, both had been disappointing lately.

That silly woman who worked with King had not been helpful. The episode at Mario's had made McCaffrey and his strumpet objects of sympathy in the eyes of the public, not objects of scorn. When she found that Bart had put Melissa Deever and her crowd up to it with his Antifa connections, Monica had been furious.

And then King had been a wimp, refusing to fire the woman, and telling Monica he'd better put off talking to Claire until things settled down. She almost had used a compulsion spell on him then. Useless. The corporate drone was useless. Well, maybe not totally. She had got him to promise to call Claire next week. All she had to do was promise another dinner date.

Still, she thought, things hadn't gone as smoothly as she'd have liked. Fortunately, Lottie Watkins had had enough judgment to call her first, before unleashing the tweet storm she'd planned about Turner's associate trying to interview her. Better save that outrage for the hearing.

Bart had managed to try again with McCaffrey's computer, but got nowhere. Whatever anti-hacking spell Mitch had placed on it was too strong. She probably shouldn't blame Bart for that, because she hadn't been able to touch the spell herself. But she still was unhappy about it.

There was still some time before the pre-hearing disclosures. They'd try again.

Traffic finally begin to move and she placed her car in gear. She wouldn't need the back roads after all. Good. She had to pee, and for that, magic was no help at all.

DIANA

Diana's alarm buzzed at 6:30 on Thanksgiving morning. This was an hour and a half later than her normal time to arise on days the restaurant would be open, but she needed to get up at least somewhat early to begin preparation for the crowd that would begin showing up at the Bean n' Bacon about noon.

She and her mother had been hosting Thanksgiving dinner for the staff and selected friends and customers and their families for years. They always smoked – slow roasted really; there was only a light smoky flavor to the meat – two or three large turkeys. Most of the guests brought covered dishes or desserts. Usually someone brought a baked ham. Once she had started seeing Mitch seriously, he would prepare, if he had the meat, a venison roast or two to supplement the fowl, using the same huge gas grill located behind the restaurant as would be used to roast the turkeys.

This year, because they had more guests than usual, there were three turkeys, and three venison roasts of varying sizes. She had confirmed that two guests would bring hams. There would be plenty of food, and also wine, beer, iced tea, coffee, and soft drinks. The kids (and some of the adults) would throw around a football and play cornhole in the parking lot out back. And someone would turn on the televisions in the restaurant to watch football. It would be a lot of fun.

The turkeys had to be roasted first. She and Margaret had stuffed them with oyster, sausage and cornbread stuffing the afternoon before, and they were waiting in the walk-in cooler. Mitch had promised her to meet her at the Bean n' Bacon to get started. He was actually going to be there before she arrived, to turn on the grill and position the pans to catch the drippings.

She showered and dressed quickly. She didn't bother with makeup, because she was going to take her kit and apply it later at the store. Mitch was going to wait with her for Margaret and the boys to arrive after breakfast, and then go home to pick up Carson and Lisa. After dressing, she quietly left the house. She'd get coffee and a sweet roll or something at the store.

The roads were almost empty, and daylight was just breaking as she drove, headlights on, to the Bean n' Bacon, reflecting on the evening before, when Mitch had brought Carson and Lisa to visit and share Thai take-out. The conversation had been brisk and at times boisterous, with lots of oohing and ahhing over the two engagement rings. She liked Lisa. She thought Lisa liked her.

Thankfully, there hadn't been much talk about the impending hearing at the college, and when the subject had come up, Mitch didn't seem upset or terribly concerned. In fact, for the past several days, he had seemed quietly confident, but hadn't given any reason. That worried her. But then, she'd have been even more worried if he were distraught.

That's the problem, she thought as she pulled into the Bean n' Bacon lot just as the sun cleared the ridge and bathed it in dazzling and nearly blinding sunlight. Everything, anything, would be worrying. She was going to have to come to terms with that if she were going to make it through the next few weeks without becoming a nervous wreck.

As promised, Mitch's Lexus was already in the rear lot, and Mitch himself was adjusting the flame on the grill. He greeted her with a quick kiss, and followed her into the restaurant, where he went straight into the kitchen to secure an apron, a grill cleaning pad, and a heavy-duty grilling fork. He left the last of these on the counter, and immediately turned back outside to clean the grill. They hadn't said more than "sleep well? Uh-huh".

While he was outside, Diana turned on the satellite radio connected to the restaurant speaker system, and turned it to a smooth jazz station instead of the Country-Western station that usually played for customers. Then she removed the turkeys, who were already in their aluminum pans, from the walk-in cooler and placed them on the counter. Mitch returned shortly and washed his hands.

"The grates are clean, honey," he said, "and the heat's turned way up."

"Okay," she replied. "Help me with the turkeys."

They carried two of the turkeys to the grill and placed them on the side where the burners remained unlit, so they could roast on indirect heat. Mitch went back for the third turkey, which he placed beside the first two. He closed the lid, using a mitten to grasp the metal handle. They would let the interior heat reach 400 degrees Fahrenheit and stay there for 30 minutes, then turn down the gas so that the turkey slow-roasted thereafter.

The venison wouldn't go on until hours later. The goal there was for center sections that were medium rare. Mitch would have to use tongs to raise the grates to position the drip pans for those. The roasts could stay in the cooler for a while, now, and removed later to come to room temperature before roasting.

They stood together without speaking for a couple of minutes, enjoying the crisp air and the view of the ridge. Most of the leaves had fallen, but there were still some flashes of red, orange and yellow up there. The forecast called for fine weather today, but a rapidly moving rain front tonight, followed by much cooler weather all across the state. They were going to need to bundle up for the ballgame Saturday.

Inside, Diana walked to the coffee bar and started a pot of coffee. Later, she'd make enough to fill a large urn. They were not doing designer coffee today, because of the number of people coming. Today the urn would hold standard coffee, but good quality. She and her mother didn't stint on the grade of coffee they served, which was a good Counter-Culture blend and, as Margaret joked, "about the only thing counter-culture around here."

When she finished, she walked to the cooler and produced a bottle of Freixenet and another of orange juice, holding them up for Mitch's inspection.

"Why the hell not?" Mitch responded, glancing at his watch. "We've got time."

Diana produced two champagne flutes from a cabinet and poured for them. They sat on stools at the coffee bar and sipped their Mimosas while they watched the pot fill with coffee and inhaled the fragrance of brewing.

"Darling," Diana said, "I want to ask you something."

"Ask away."

"You seem," she hesitated, "you seem almost un-naturally calm about this hearing. It worries me a little. You're not zoned out, are you? In denial or something?"

Mitch's eyes met hers directly. "No, sweetheart, I'm not. Honest I'm not. I know the deck is stacked against me still."

He reached for the champagne bottle and poured himself another Mimosa, adding plenty of orange juice, before continuing.

"Part of my attitude comes from deciding to be fine with this no matter how it turns out. I really will. There is too much good in my life to let this thing ruin it.

"Part of it is that I really do have confidence in my lawyers. They're really on top of this. And…part of it is that I just have a feeling we're going to catch a break. Just a feeling, but pretty strong."

"A magic feeling?"

"No," he said, a little too quickly. She was immediately suspicious but decided not to press him. "Just a feeling," he repeated. "Now, this is magic." Sub-vocally, he told the champagne to re-fill her glass and then return to the cooler, the door to which opened for the bottle, and closed when it was on a shelf.

She decided to ignore his showing off for her. "If it doesn't turn out well, are you going to sue?"

He took longer to answer this time. "I…I don't know. I don't really want to. But Kathryn will recommend it, I feel sure. Carson will want me to. But hopefully, it won't come to that."

Diana, not fully satisfied but now fairly confident her lover wasn't depressive, decided to drop it. But she knew two things. One, something was up. Two, Mitch was hopeful about it but not completely confident. She decided to change the subject.

"Speaking of Kathryn, she and her family will be here."

They had decided to ask his legal team.

"Oh, good," he said. "What about the others?"

"All of the rest have family commitments. That includes the paralegals."

"Marc, too?" he asked.

"Marc, too. He drove to Orangeburg yesterday."

The coffee was ready and Mitch, again using magic, brought them mugs and cream. "You better enjoy this now. I won't be able to do this after while."

After one mug of coffee, he went outside and returned to announce he'd turned the gas flame to a lower setting.

"Can you help me set up the dining room?" she asked. They needed to push tables together to create a long buffet table, with plastic utensils and cups, and heavy paper platters at one end, and place tablecloths there and everywhere else.

He could. Once she showed him where everything was, he did it with style, by spelling it done. It made her laugh to see the tablecloths unfold, tables push themselves together and utensils and plates transport themselves.

"You have been practicing," she said around giggles.

"I've had plenty of time to do it."

"You can have a job here, bussing tables and cleaning up, if the college releases you. Good hours. Solid minimum wage. Wonderful bosses. You'd like it."

"Benefits?" he asked, arching his brows.

"Pretty good," she said. "Regular sex with one the owners. Of course, you have to marry her."

"I'll take the job." And they both laughed.

Then they heard Margaret's car pull up outside, and Paul and Steve's voices calling out greetings a moment later.

"You're going to have to help unload the rest of Mom's food the hard way," Diana offered.

"You mean the old-fashioned way."

But it didn't take long, and then it was time for him to go get Carson and Lisa.

The Watkins

Henry and Dorothy Watkins were on their way home from attending Thanksgiving Day services at St. Timothy's Episcopal Church. St. Timothy's was the old, traditional parish with the church located in the tony section of Martintown. (St. Bartholomew's, where Mitch attended, was a newer, smaller parish located between the Glen Arden and Maple Oak communities.) They were discussing the service for now, but both knew the subject would soon shift to their children. It usually did.

"I thought it was a nice, traditional Thanksgiving service," Dr. Watkins was saying. "Today is not the time for anything controversial."

He was at odds with the Rector in a good-natured way much of the time. She was new to the parish, and some of her more radical notions did not always sit well with the communicants. Henry Watkins, who had grown up AME, and had become an Episcopalian as a compromise with his wife, who had been reared Roman Catholic, was all right with the occasional sermon on civil rights. How could he not be? But he thought it was a bit much when the topic strayed into the "right" to "gender fluidity", which, as a medical doctor, he just thought counter-factual. As for Dorothy, she still was taken a little aback by the notion of a female priest, but she kept quiet about it – except sometimes to Henry.

"I agree," Dorothy said in a low tone, as though distracted. Henry looked over at his wife. He had been stunned by her beauty when he'd met the young nurse all these years ago, and he still was. She was older, her raven's wing hair carrying just a touch of gray, and a few pounds heavier. But still…

Their daughter Charlotte – Lottie – looked so heartbreaking like her it was almost uncanny. He could sense that Lottie was about to become the subject of the conversation. And as it turned out, he was right.

"Henry," Dorothy began, in the tone that told him he was about to be scolded. "Honey, I want you to ease up on Lottie today. We have all of the kids here for Thanksgiving, and I want a nice friendly, family dinner. Please."

Their son Robert and their older daughter Becky had managed to come home. They had missed church services, pleading being tired from their trips. As for Lottie, well, she slept late almost all the time. Getting her to church was an ordeal under the best of circumstances. At least there were no boyfriends and girlfriends to manage. Robert and Becky didn't have anyone they were serious enough about to ask. Lottie was between guys – for the moment. So it would be just family.

He said, "Yes, dear." He said that a lot. Then, against his better judgment, he added, "But she'd better not expect wine this afternoon.

Not after that stunt she and those girls pulled in Asheville." He was taking the family to the Country Club this afternoon. That would spare Dorothy from cooking a big meal, and managing leftovers.

"Oh, honey," Dorothy protested. "Give her a break. She's all upset. She's been harassed at school."

"Hmmph," her husband said. "Maybe. I've had my doubts."

"Why Henry Watkins! I'm shocked. You of all people. Did you know the college has evidence the man is secretly a white supremacist? Imagine Lottie being taught by someone like that. And what he did was offensive. Giving her extra work because she mentioned a black writer."

Henry knew he was entering dangerous waters, but pressed on anyway. "Dorothy, it seems to me our Charlotte hasn't had anything but breaks. We've spoiled her rotten. You've spoiled her rotten. You know we've caught her lying plenty of times. And frankly, dear, Charlotte isn't black except when it suits her and she thinks she can get something out of it.

"This whole story bothers me. The teacher seems like a good guy. He's been there for years. He's taught black kids before. He had to have served with African Americans in the Army."

Dorothy, if she'd be honest, knew what he said was true. All of their children were clearly mixed race, but their youngest was colored much closer to Dorothy's pale olive Mediterranean than to his own shade of milk chocolate, close enough to have "passed" as white back when anyone cared about such things. Most of her friends were white. Most of her boyfriends were white. She only pulled out being African American when there was something to be gained by it.

But Dorothy wasn't going to be honest about it. And, as he feared, she was going to be emotional. She started crying.

"I just don't see how you can be so mean to your own daughter," she said between sniffles. "You can't even give her the benefit of the doubt." Just a hint of Jersey had crept into her speech. That was a bad sign. She sniffed again, and then rattled off a couple of sentences in Italian that he couldn't follow. That was a worse one.

"Okay, honey," he said. "You win. We'll back her up as much as we can. And I promise not to jump her this afternoon. I do."

But privately, he thought, I don't want her to embarrass herself if this claim of hers turns out to be false. Maybe I ought to speak with this Mitch McCaffrey. Or maybe not.

He'd think about it, he decided.

MITCH AND DIANA

Mitch was having a good day. The venison had come steaming off the grill just as he'd planned, well done toward the tip and medium rare at the center. And the turkeys had come out fine, too.

By the time he'd returned to the Bean n' Bacon with Carson and Lisa following him, Ben and Lonnie were there with their families, and had pitched in to set up bins filled with ice for soft drinks, beer and white wine outside in back, and folding tables for cups. Their kids were already working with Diana's to set up two corn-hole games. Everyone was excited to meet Lisa.

Other guests began arriving shortly thereafter. Some had brought snacks to tide everyone over pending dinner, and bowls for chips and salsa and onion dip joined the plastic cups on the tables outside. Chatter was constant, and more guests arrived steadily. Kathryn Turner and her husband and son were some of the last to arrive, Kathryn with a large bowl of three-bean salad.

The kids and some of the adults played corn hole. Jimmy Turner had brought a football, and he and Diana's boys had thrown it around the parking lot, bouncing it off a couple of cars before their mothers came out and made them move to the grassy strip beyond the lot. He'd noticed Kathryn and Diana quietly talking, but couldn't hear the conversation. Probably about him. He'd find out later.

He talked with George Turner for a long time, while Mitch sipped a beer and Dr. Turner almost apologetically settled for a Coke Life, explaining that he was on-call at the hospital today, of all days, so alcohol was completely off limits. George turned out to be an App State fan, and they had a good time speculating which bowl game the Mountaineers might land in. They watched as some of the restaurant employees who had a small blue grass band set up in a corner of the restaurant for later on.

By the time dinner was ready at 3:00 p.m., Mitch thought the day was darned near perfect. The only thing, the only person, missing was his mother. Not that she hadn't been invited, and not that he wouldn't have made the time to go get her, or send Carson for her. But when he had called, she told him that Diana's Thanksgiving parties were lovely, but there were too many people for her. She said that the facility where she lived had a perfectly nice Thanksgiving meal planned, with turkey and cranberry sauce and everything; and she and the other widows were going to meet in the main dining room and then play Scrabble and then watch "Momma Mia" in the theater.

She'd be perfectly fine, thank you, but it would be nice if Carson could bring his girl by tomorrow before they left for Chapel Hill and yes, she knew that was going in the wrong direction, but it was really a short drive and it needn't be a long visit. Thankfully, Carson and Lisa had laughed and said they'd be glad to go. So that was all right.

Sure enough, George Turner got a call from the hospital, fortunately after he'd almost finished his meal. Diana assured him she'd find a way to get Kathryn and Jimmy home. By that time, the musicians were about ready to start; and one of them called out for someone to turn down the volume on the Cowboys game so everyone could hear the music.

A big man with red hair and a red face, wearing bib overalls and a MAGA baseball cap, stepped up to the microphone, a banjo draped over a shoulder. Mitch recognized him as another cook, Billy Johnson.

"All right, folks," Johnson yelled into the mic, "let's make Brainerd County GREAT again."

Amid some applause, and some groans, the band launched to "Fox on the Run", and soon there was a lot of toe tapping, clapping and a fair amount of picture taking, with cell phones and digital cameras. He liked the tune, always had.

> *She walked through the corn leading down to the river.*
> *Her hair shone like gold in the hot mornin' sun.*
> *She took all the love a pore boy could give her.*
> *And left me to die, like a fox on the run.*
> *Like a fox, like a fox, like a fox*
> *ON THE RUN!*

Camera flashes continued. Mitch felt a mild tingling, a sign from the Ward he'd place on himself that someone close by meant him ill. No magic appeared to be involved. Looking around, he decided the apparent source was a teen-aged girl with braces and a frizzy hair-do, sitting with a woman who was obviously her mother, based on the same hair-style and color, and a stocky man of middle years in a checked shirt. She was holding up her cell phone and apparently making a video recording. The camera appeared to be focused on the lead singer in overalls, wearing the MAGA hat.

He leaned over and whispered to Diana, "Who is the girl making the video?" He gestured toward the girl as unobtrusively as possible.

Diana finally found the person he meant. "I don't remember her name. That's her mother with her. She's Missy Barton, one of our part-time baristas. Pretty artsy. The man with her is Missy's boyfriend. She's divorced. I don't remember his name, but I think he's a Martintown fire fighter."

The song ended and the band launched into another. The girl put down her phone. The feeling gradually subsided.

The party began to break up about 7:00. By that time, the ballgame was over, and the band looked tired. The guests were, as usual, really good about helping clean up. Those who had brought covered dishes took them with them. There was a little leftover turkey that Margaret parceled out to those who wanted to take any. Mitch had already turned off the grill, and went out and locked it closed.

Mitch drove home himself, carrying a Tupperware container with a bit of the venison and an unopened bottle of red wine in the floorboard of the back seat. Clouds were coming in, and the predicted rain would start soon. But it had been an almost perfect day, he decided.

Except for that girl making the video. He wondered what was up with that.

He'd mention it to Kathryn.

18

THERE'S GOT TO BE A MORNING AFTER

MONICA AND BARRY

Monica and Barry sat in his study in his condo outside Raleigh. She was packed, dressed, and ready for the trip back to Martintown, but they needed to go over the McCaffrey evidence first. Witness and exhibit disclosures were due the following Wednesday.

There hadn't been any business to speak of Wednesday evening and Thursday. Those days had been all about small talk, food and sex. She had found it all quite satisfactory, even if she had had to bring all of the imagination to the sex. Evidently, he hadn't any; but he'd seemed to enjoy hers. She certainly had.

Yesterday's dinner at the Carolina Club had been especially good. Barry hadn't been able to believe her consumption at the buffet.

"Where do you put it?" he'd asked, subconsciously patting his own beginnings of a paunch. "You stay so slim."

She'd only smiled. She wished her mother had been able to teach her more, but she'd taught her that much. Of course, she couldn't tell Barry how she did it. Maybe she could give him some magical help with his own weight before leaving. But maybe not. He hadn't quite earned it yet.

Now, after a leisurely breakfast, and a great deal of good coffee (his coffee was good; she'd give him that), it was time to be all business. She sat across from him at his desk, her lap-top open before her. His was open, too, but pushed to the side. He had pulled out a legal pad and a felt tipped pen. They reviewed the evidence quickly. He had already studied everything she'd sent him.

But they covered all of it. They'd have the investigators' testimony. Monica felt they could cover it all with her and Gina. They wouldn't use Lorna unless they had to; she was too soft-hearted. They had three statements from former female students who didn't like Mitch. One of them would testify in person. They had what had been found in doing the inventory of Mitch's office. She thought that was important.

"Kathryn Turner will insist that's a plant," Barry warned.

"Let her," Monica snorted. "We want to plant in the panel's mind just who McCaffrey is. They won't be able to prove it's a plant. And Turner's team will have to spend time defending it."

"Uhh, Monica, it's not a plant, is it?"

She sat back, feigning indignation. "Of course not! You don't think I'd do anything like that, do you?"

"Just checking." They exchanged smiles. He was fulfilling his ethical duty as a lawyer to verify evidence as best he could. She knew that. She also knew that they both knew the evidence had been planted. He just had to have cover if there was a slip. But there wouldn't be.

Then there was the testimony of the young women they'd been calling the three little pigs – Lottie, Darlene and Corrine. None of them were fat girls. But their academic records were hardly exemplary, and they were known as party rockets. Still, as Monica said, they had rights. And McCaffrey had violated those rights.

"How solid are they?" Barry asked.

"Solid enough," Monica said. "Especially Lottie. She's quite the little actress. If anything, you'll have to caution her not to be too dramatic. And she's really the complainant. Everyone else is just corroborating her. But I think we can nail McCaffrey with her testimony, especially if we can make the Panel understand that he's just not desirable in that position."

Barry nodded. "Yes, that's the plan."

"So," she asked, "what do you think?"

He leaned back in his swivel chair and tapped his teeth with the cap of his pen. "Well," he said, "I've seen stronger cases. The evidence of his white nationalist tendencies will be disputed, and what we claim is harassment is open to interpretation."

Monica made a sour face. She hadn't wanted to hear that. She was sitting with crossed legs, and leaned forward, clasping her hands over the top knee.

"It'll be enough for the Panel. They're solid. Look, Barry, you understand as well as anybody that even if McCaffrey were not an overt male-privileged white nationalist, he's one at heart.. He's not progressive in his teaching. He just throws all of these dead, white male writers at his students. We can't have someone like that teaching our young people. This Panel will get that."

"I do understand that. I believe what you say about the Panel. It's not the Panel that concerns me. It's what comes after. Kathryn Turner will do her best to paint this hearing as a witch hunt you drummed up with Lottie Watkins for her to punish him for her bad grades and for you to get rid of someone you didn't like because he wouldn't toe your line." He held up a hand. "I'm not saying I agree. I'm saying that's what she'll do.

"She's not thinking about the Panel. She's thinking about a jury. We won't do nearly as well with a Western North Carolina jury if we leave ourselves open to a civil rights suit.

"Hell, Turner's already taken money off the state doing just that up in Asheville. The AG's office is wary of her. They've already called me to caution me, and asked if I need help."

"Do you?"

"No, I don't think so. But Larry Kincaid and Megan Stennis have me on a pretty tight leash. They want regular reports. Claire Daniels has asked them to do that. I'm a little worried about her, too."

"Claire? She's a wuss. She won't dare go against a faculty panel finding."

"She might if Larry or Megan tell her the risk of a 1983 suit is too great. So we need to make our proof as strong as possible."

"We will," Monica said. "We will – if you have the balls for the fight."

He ignored the jibe. "I do. But I do have a concern about the Panel."

"What? I told you they will be solidly with us."

"I believe you. But you don't have anyone with any real experience chairing a hearing panel. I'm concerned Turner and Norville will cross them up."

Monica bit her lip. "It won't be Norville. I understand he's on his way to retirement. She's using that young associate who harassed our girls in Asheville."

"The black guy?"

"Yeah, Washington...But I see what you're talking about." She thought for a minute. "Say, don't the rules entitle the panel to a non-voting procedural adviser?"

"They do," he agreed. "But who could we get?"

"Don't you have anybody on staff?"

It was Barry's turn to stop in thought. Suddenly, he snapped his fingers. "I have just the person, if I can get Larry to approve it. A young woman just joined us who had been with a plaintiffs' civil rights firm. Her name is Rachel Jordan. She'd be perfect if Larry will approve bringing her."

"What if Claire makes the request herself?"

"Do you think she will?"

"If I suggest it in the right way. Won't Turner protest that, though?"

"She will, but so what? It's not illegal. Now...is there anything else?"

"I want another go at his computer."

"I thought your IT guy said it's clean."

"I just don't think he's sophisticated enough. I want someone else to look at it."

"Who?"

"Bart Stevens. He's with the college in graphic arts. A real computer whiz."

"Well, if he thinks he's found anything, tell him to stop and get a forensics specialist in. I'll e-mail you a reference this afternoon. But call me first."

"Of course," she purred.

"And Monica – don't plant anything. It's not worth it."

"I told you I don't do stuff like that." They exchanged smiles again.

Monica looked at her watch. "Okay, if we're done for now, I need to get on the road."

She stood and accepted a hug when he walked around, but didn't kiss him. He looked disappointed. Good. He needed to stay hungry.

She let him carry her bags to her car, and hugged him again, kissing him lightly this time. Then she left.

She didn't tell him that one reason she had to get back is that she needed to get Bart Stevens in line.

And he didn't tell her that what he'd told her the college must not appear to do was exactly what she'd said they were going to do. He realized that that's what they always did, and he didn't even disagree with it. Faculties needed to be purged of reactionaries.

But if you were too obvious about it, you got sued. Sometimes, you lost the suit. That worried him.

Of course, he reflected, if suit were filed, it would be the AG's problem, not his. In the meantime, he'd keep Monica happy.

He had to do it, though, without getting in trouble with Larry.

And that worried him, too.

MARC

On Saturday, after hugging his mother and his kid sister, and shaking hands with his Dad, Marc left his parents' home in Orangeburg to drive back to Martintown. Actually, he was going to stop in Asheville for the night, and would meet Tiffany; but he didn't tell them that. He sighed at the realization they couldn't keep their relationship a secret much longer. He dreaded approaching Norville about it. Maybe they could go to Kathryn first. Yes, he decided, Kathryn would be better.

He looked forward to seeing Tiff, but he had a few hours of windshield time before he would. At least, traveling Saturday instead of Sunday, the traffic shouldn't be so bad today. His visit with his family had been good. He'd had a good time with his father yesterday, watching football on TV.

Marc was through the Columbia interchanges and on his way to Spartanburg by the time he'd relived his afternoon with his Dad. When his phone rang, he gave a start. He wasn't expecting a call. Maybe it was Tiff.

He punched the Bluetooth connection on the steering column. "Hello."

"Hi," came a sultry female voice. "This is Charlotte."

"Beg your pardon." Charlotte who?

"You know. Charlotte Watkins."

Wait a minute. "Lottie?"

"Uh-huh."

How did she get his number? Oh, it was on the business card he'd left for the girls at the Lab, the one he didn't think they'd taken.

"I thought you didn't want to talk with us."

"I might talk with you, if you'll buy me a drink.... Just you," she added.

"You know I'm not allowed to do that."

"I guess you don't want to talk with me then."

"I do want to talk with you. Can you come by the office?"

"I was thinking of someplace more private."

"That's not a good idea."

"Well, I guess we just can't talk. I'm disappointed."

Damn it, nobody had taught him how to handle something like this. Not in law school. Not at the firm. Yet, he had to keep her engaged some way.

"Hey, listen. Are you on a cell phone?" he asked.

"Uh-huhhh," she drawled it out.

"Okay, I'll have your number on my phone. If I can think of some place suitable, I'll call you."

"Maybe I'll answer," she teased. "Maybe I won't. Will it be someplace fun?"

"I'll let you know."

He disconnected thinking he'd lost whatever contest the call represented. Hell and damn.

Maybe Tiffany could think of something.

MARC AND TIFFANY

Marc and Tiffany were at the rooftop bar of the Indigo Hotel when he brought up the call from Lottie. They had shared a delightful dinner at Vinny's on Merriman Avenue, and had walked around downtown for a while, bundled against the sudden cold front, before returning to the hotel. They sat as close as possible to one of the space heaters that enabled the Indigo to keep the bar open to the air on a night like this.

Tiffany was not exactly over-joyed by the news.

"You're not really planning to talk with her, are you?" she hissed across the table.

"I don't know. I might learn something important." He felt he ought to defend himself.

"What you're going to learn, Mister Washington," she shot back, "is that she's contacting you to get you in trouble. If you meet with her by yourself, you will get in trouble. She'll claim you harassed her, or threatened her, or both. She'll record it and edit the recording. She'll file a bar complaint, or the college will. You'll have to get out of the case. You'll get fired. Christ, you should have hung up on her! Don't you have any sense?"

Marc squirmed in his chair. There was a fair amount of truth in what she was saying. But still, if he could find a way...

Tiffany was just warming up, though. "But you, you want to meet with her. Alone. You're nuts." She scowled at him. "Or are you just thinking about her big off-white boobs? Is that it?"

Marc couldn't help but giggle at her choice of terminology. It wasn't even fair. Lottie certainly was well-endowed, but he hadn't been thinking about that. Well, not much. Maybe a little. But his reaction made things worse.

"It's not funny!" she almost screamed at him, causing other patrons to turn and look at them.

Marc forced the grin off his face.

"Hold on," he said, throwing up a hand. "I know it's not funny. And no, I wasn't thinking of her...looks. Hell's bells, I haven't met with her yet."

"And you won't, Marc Washington. Not without me with you."

"She'll leave if I bring someone with me. Especially you. She knows you, remember?"

"Well, I guarantee you Kathryn won't approve it unless you bring a witness. You better not do anything like this without Kathryn knowing. You hear me, buddyrow?"

"I hear you. I really do. But I can't help but think this might be important."

"She's just trolling."

"Probably. But it might be useful to catch her at it."

That made Tiffany pause. "I hadn't thought of that," she admitted. She sipped her wine, neglected during her outburst, while she thought. "Hey!" She actually smiled.

"Hey what?"

"You said she knows me. She doesn't know Jenny Jackson."

"She'd still leave."

"Only if she knew a witness was there."

Marc's grin now matched hers.

"Let me think," he said. "There's a Starbucks on the east side of town. I could suggest she meet me there. Jenny could go in, in advance, and set up a laptop, and pretend to work. Maybe get on the internet. I'd be sure to get there ahead of Lottie and make sure we sit near-by. Jenny would see the whole thing, and maybe hear part of it. It could work."

"And you're going to record it anyhow, aren't you? Belt and suspenders."

"Oh, yes. Thanks, Tiff. You're great."

"We still better run this by Kathryn," she warned.

"Oh, for sure. And...speaking of talking with Kathryn." He trailed off and took a slug of his Crown and 7 to fortify himself.

Then he began. Their server, who was relieved they were not going to argue loudly after all, had been about to approach them to see if they needed anything else. But she backed off.

They were whispering across the table and gazing into each other's eyes.

19

SECRET AGENT MAN

MITCH

Mitch met Peggy Sturgill and her husband Fred at the Minute Market just down the road from the entrance to High Country Estates right at dusk on Sunday. They would take her car to the college campus. She said that she frequently came in on weekends, and wouldn't create any suspicion. Fred sometimes went with her, and he would stay hunched down in her car while she and Mitch went inside. Fred, who was a mechanic for the local Toyota dealership, was of similar height and build, and they had arranged to dress similarly, in dark hoodies. Mitch would later also hide his face behind a glamour, but of course he didn't tell them that.

There were few cars in the college lot. There was a security guard on patrol, but he recognized Peggy and just waved. She parked in her usual reserved space outside the administration building. She had a key to a side door, and she and Mitch walked inside, quickly, but not too quickly. Fred sat outside and streamed an NFL game on his android, using ear buds so there would be no sound.

The administration building at Carolina Highlands, like the campus as a whole, was modern and utilitarian rather than charming and traditional. Some of the hallway bulletin boards had Thanksgiving decorations that would soon be replaced. They walked quickly to the president's office suite by the dim light of the emergency bulbs that lit automatically when the main lighting was off, a little apprehensive that they would find Claire Daniels there, but they didn't.

After turning on the lights in her own work area that fronted the president's office, Peggy admitted herself to Claire's office and returned after only a short delay with a master electronic key card that would let them into the IT Support offices, which were located one floor down at the lowest level. She didn't have to lead him there. He had been in the offices before, seeking assistance from the IT Department.

The key admitted him with no problems and he flipped on the overhead fluorescents out of necessity. He hoped he could find his desktop. The first desk he came to was the Department secretary's. Beyond it was the IT Director's. Would it be in there? No, he decided; if they hadn't locked it up, it would be in a work area. He tried another door and found another office. Still another door yielded the same result.

The fourth door had the prize. He saw what he was sure his own desktop, keyboard and screen connected, at a low table against the far wall in what was obviously a workshop, with a long central metal table and a bunch of shelves on the side walls filled with electronic odds and ends. There was a metal folding chair in front of the table with what he hoped was "his" office computer. Someone had evidently been working at it.

Turning on only one bank of the overhead lights, he sat in the chair and, first pulling on latex gloves purchased at the local Walgreen's, powered up the computer. Yes, he saw as soon as the desktop screen appeared, it was his. He sensed immediately his Ward was still in place, and a quick check of his folders and browsing history showed that nobody had messed with it yet.

Mitch took a deep breath before continuing. He was taking a risk. He was going to have to remove the Ward. That meant that Monica's minions could get in and work mischief. But there was just a chance she'd figure out a way to break the blocking spell herself. He had had a lot of time since his suspension to think and to practice spell-casting. And he had an idea. He had decided it was worth it to try. After all, Kathryn's sending her own consultant to inspect his device before he got suspended was sort of a safety net. And if what he was going to do worked, it could make a big difference.

He had found the spell thumbing through the binders Dr. McCormick had left. It had been developed in Russia in the late 19th Century by a magic user who was a member of the Social Revolutionary Party. He didn't recognize the name, or know whether the wizard (he might as well call him that, although McCormick had disdained the term) was an aristocrat or from the bourgeoisie.

But whoever he was, this man had come up with what he called a replacement spell. The Okhrana, the Tsar's secret police, had not been above planting seditious documents, even forged documents, in the papers of persons that were under suspicion. It made arrest and conviction easier. The spell was designed to transform any such planted document into something else. The original spell-caster's favorite choice was poetry.

The original grimoire from which this was taken was in a ratty-looking leather bound volume, written in Russian using the Cyrillic alphabet, which Mitch could not read at all. But the English translation had appeared complete, as best he could tell. The practice sessions had worked, too, first with printed documents, and then with his home computer. The latter had actually worked better, but then he had always had a gift for manipulating electronic devices and software with spell casting.

It would have been nice to have figured this out before they had planted the printed flyers, but he hadn't. Besides, it probably wouldn't have mattered because they made the plants in Monica's office and not really in his, he reflected.

The original magician's notes had said it helped to pray before using the spell, so he quietly uttered the Lord's Prayer and crossed himself before beginning. He removed the Ward.

Taking another breath, he opened the browser and found the site he was seeking. Document by document, he chanted the opening part of the spell, not bothering to sub-vocalize because he was alone. Then he opened his "Documents" folder and uttered the closing words.

Next, he went back to his browser and found the files he wanted on YouTube. He repeated the process so these files would appear on the browsing history at the right time.

The final step was to set the time for the spell to go into effect. The long dead Russian had realized that this was important. If the spell took effect too soon, the Okhrana would see the replacement documents in time to in turn replace them with something else. He chanted the timing spell so that the rest would go into effect in three days, late in the evening on Wednesday. After the pre-hearing disclosures. He hoped. There was no way to test it.

He powered off the computer, and retraced his steps, turning off the lights and re-locking the doors as he left. Fleetingly, he wondered if these spells had survived the Revolution, had been known to the NKVD and the KGB. He supposed not. When he reached Peggy's office, he found her sitting at her desk, her own computer powered up, busy at her keyboard. She was actually working, he realized.

"Well, that didn't take long, whatever you did," she whispered. Mitch had been gone only about thirty minutes.

"I just checked my computer," he said in the same tone. "Thanks. It's okay for now."

"I hope it stays that way," she responded.

"Me, too."

They encountered no one on the way out. When they reached Peggy's vehicle, they found Fred had turned off his phone and was fuming that the Carolina Panthers had lost. Mitch commiserated with him.

When they turned out of the college campus onto the main road, they saw a car turning in. Mitch's personal Ward tingled. He was sure it was Monica's Prius.

This could have been a close call, he realized.

MONICA AND BART

Less than an hour before, Monica and Bart had sat sipping coffee at the Panera Bread Company in downtown Martintown. There were few other customers. Monica was also eating a sweet roll.

"I want to take another shot at McCaffrey's computer," she said.

Stevens said, "Sure, but do you think it's worth it? We'll get accused of planting stuff."

"Let them. The Panel will ignore it." She realized she really was as confident as she sounded. "But it does worry me that our lawyer wants us to bring in a forensics firm to confirm it. That could blow everything."

Stevens sipped his coffee. "Did he require you to use any particular firm?"

"He e-mailed me the contact information for one in Charlotte."

"But you can hire another one, can't you?"

She considered. "Well, yes, if they're qualified. Why?"

"Because we need to use Ron McKay's firm in Asheville. McKay's reliable."

"How do you know?"

"I know him. He's one of us. He subscribes to Jacobin." He referred to the radical socialist magazine. "You won't have to make the computer available to the McCaffrey team before the hearing. All they'll have is Ron's Report, and it'll be what you want."

Monica considered. It was tempting.

But she said, "I don't know. Barry Feldman keeps warning me that we have to beware of a 'civil rights' lawsuit after the hearing." She hoped he heard the quotation marks. As though somebody like McCaffrey could claim a violation of civil rights. She continued, "If that happens, we will have to make the computer available to their own specialist. Won't the plant come out then?"

Bart's lip curled up in a smug smile. "Leave that to McKay. He's good."

Her eyes searched his. "You're sure."

"As I can be."

"Can you still make the insertions?"

"If I can get in."

Monica took a large bite of the sweet roll, chewed. After swallowing, she said, "If we're going to do it, it had better be tonight. Are you ready?"

He nodded. "Oh, yes. That is, if afterwards, you are?" He cocked his head and smiled.

She eyed him coldly for a moment, then burst out laughing. "You're insatiable," she accused. "But why not? If it works, you'll have earned some...benefit."

"Are you going to finish that?" He pointed to the remnants of the roll.

"Oh yes. It's good."

He eyed her appraisingly. "Honestly, Monica, I don't see how you avoid being chubby, or at least a little plump, the way you eat."

Her lips twitched in amusement. "I have a raging metabolism, I suppose...Let me powder my nose, and I'll call Maria to let her know we may have a guest later this evening. We can take my car to the college."

Four hours later, Monica was feeling pleased with herself – and with Bart Stevens. He'd had no trouble, once she'd admitted him to the IT Department, in getting into McCaffrey's computer and implanting some things that would make the hearing much more...difficult for him. She knew she'd be accused of planting the documents and links, but she didn't care. If Bart's connection was as good as advertised, nobody would ever prove it.

She was too tired to take Stevens to her bed. It had been an exhausting holiday weekend. He had to settle for a snifter of her brandy, a few kisses and caresses, all delivered in her parlor, and a promise for later. That would have to be enough for him. He pouted a little bit when she rang for Maria to show him out, but he went.

And then he had to piss her off by giving Maria the eye, when she appeared to show him out. She promised herself he'd pay for that, at a time of her own choosing. Yet...Maria was an enticing little piece, even to her, she had to admit. Sometime, she'd have to explore that possibility. But tonight...well, she was tired.

But she decided to plant the seed by giving the young woman a hug that was longer than necessary and a squeeze to the rump, when Maria returned to announce that Stevens was gone, and ask her if she needed anything else. She felt Maria's curvy body stiffen and decided to break it off and just say, "No, dear. Nothing. Thank you...Oh, please turn down the bed for me."

It was just as well for her that she didn't see the finger Maria shot at the closed door to parlor after leaving, or learn about the text message her maid sent after she was asleep. A text to Kathryn Turner.

20

SILHOUETTES

KATHRYN

It is axiomatic with lawyers, Kathryn thought, that any time you think you have a morning set aside to quietly work on something, you will be immediately besieged by e-mails and phone calls from other clients, or opposing counsel in other cases, demanding your immediate attention with apparently desperate urgency. The e-mails and calls turned up like bad pennies, and with respect to clients, you could usually predict who was going to call.

So why did it always take her by surprise?

This Monday had been one of those mornings. She had a team meeting, lawyers and paralegals only, scheduled for that afternoon at 3:00, and she had planned to use this morning to outline their evidence, and began writing up the outlines for direct and cross-examination of witnesses.

It was now 11:00 and she hadn't even scratched. Here it was only an hour before lunch and she hadn't worked on Mitch's case at all.

Kathryn sighed and opened her word processor – again. Maybe there wouldn't be any more interruptions.

There was a knock at her door, and she looked up to see Marc Washington, Tiffany DeRatt, and Jenny Jackson standing in the doorway.

"Could we talk for a minute?" Mark asked.

"Can't it wait until the team meeting this afternoon?" Kathryn snapped, then went on, her voice softened, "I'm sorry to snap at you, but you just wouldn't believe my morning. Really, can it wait?"

"It could," Marc responded, "but we all think that when you've heard it, you'll agree it shouldn't."

Kathryn reluctantly turned away from the computer desktop. "All right," she said in resignation, "Shut the door and go ahead."

They all pulled up chairs, Marc in the middle, and both Tiffany and Jenny turned to look at him expectantly. He realized he had to be the point man in this meeting, and hesitantly told Kathryn about his call from Lottie Watkins, and the idea he and Tiffany had to follow up on it. He told her Jenny was willing to be involved, and she nodded when he said it.

"This may not come to anything, but we think it can be done at relatively low risk. It's not like we're interviewing someone's client. Lottie is just a witness. Maybe she'll give us something. We all think it's worth a try."

"What do you think Lottie will want out of a meeting with you?" Kathryn asked him.

Marc was hopeful that being African American, the blush wouldn't show; but he felt the heat creep up his face. But he said, "I honestly don't know. Tiffany thinks she's trying to set me up. Maybe she just wants to flirt. But we all agree that if I can get her talking, she might slip and tell us something."

Kathryn considered. "You may be right...unless Monica Gilbert put her up to this, and is orchestrating the whole thing. That's possible. If it's anybody on her side, it's Monica. I don't trust Barry Feldman, but I don't think he'd do this."

"I don't think it's Gilbert," Marc said. "My read on Lottie is that she is a fairly frivolous young girl, and this is something she's doing to amuse herself. She may just want to see if I'll meet with her."

"I think Marc's right," Tiffany put in. "Lottie thinks she's irresistible, and can get any man wound around her finger. She's trying to prove she can do it with Marc. But it that's what it is, or if she really is trying to set Marc up, catching her in front of a witness would be worth something to us, wouldn't it?" Seeing Kathryn's nod, she continued. "I can't be the witness. She knows me and would walk out if she saw me there. But Jenny can do it."

Kathryn sat for a full minute, drumming her fingertips on her desk.

"All right," she said. "Go ahead. Marc, when you call her, use the speaker phone with Tiffany or Jenny sitting there. If she'll meet, the Starbuck's is fine. You and Jenny shouldn't go together, and she should be set up there when you arrive. But Marc, you have to maneuver Lottie to sit close to Jenny. She should always be close enough to at least see you.

"If anything 'funny' happens, terminate the meeting. Assume she is recording you. Call her today. If you reach her and she agrees to meet, you can report in the meeting today. Try to meet with her before the session with the client Friday afternoon."

They all nodded agreement.

"Good luck," she said. "Now all of you get out and let me work." Then, remembering a mental note she'd made to herself, she added, "No, wait just a second. Tiffany, I want you to check out a Bart Stevens, who teaches at Carolina Highlands. He may have something to do with computers. See what you can find online and call the client to see what he knows. Do this soonest.

"I also want you to see what you can find out about Monica Gilbert's maid. Try Mitch first. He may have heard something. But be discrete, okay?"

"Got it, boss," Tiffany acknowledged.

The team convened on schedule in the same conference room in which they'd held the previous McCaffrey case meetings. Kathryn positioned herself at the end near the whiteboard. Tiffany had the two banker's boxes that held the file (if one could still call it that). All had their laptops. Jenny had seen to it that water and coffee were available on the sideboard.

"All right," Kathryn began. "Let's start by hearing from Marc on whether there will be a meeting with Lottie Watkins. That is, Marc, if you know."

"Sure," he said. "You all should have an e-mail in your in-box I just sent a few minutes ago. Anyway, I left a voicemail for her to call me right before lunch, and gave both my office and cell numbers. She called my cell less than an hour ago.

"We're going to meet at the Starbuck's we talked about Wednesday at 3:30. It shouldn't be too crowded then. She told me she would meet with just me, and nobody else. I assured her I wouldn't bring anybody with me. That's true. Sort of."

Kathryn turned to Jenny. "Be sure you're there by 3:00. Try to set up your laptop so you can appear to be working, or at least playing on it. Working is okay, but don't let anyone see the screen. Pick a place where Marc has some alternatives to sit close to you.

"Marc, I suggest you get there at 3:20 or so. Go get a table where Jenny can see you and Lottie. She can sneak peaks while looking at her screen. It would be nice if she could hear you, too, but I doubt that's possible. Be sure to use your voice recorder yourself."

"I'll be able to hear them," Jenny said.

"How?"

I have a directional mic. I can put it in a case so it will look like an iPod. I'll use earbuds, and everyone around me will think I'm listening to music."

Kathryn was mildly surprised. "Oh? Where did you get that?"

"Amazon. I've used it before for Bill…Mr. Norville."

"Oh." Kathryn decided not to ask anything else about the microphone. Instead, she rose from her chair, picked up a marker, and wrote "Witness and Exhibit Disclosures" on the whiteboard. "Okay, people, let's move along. These are due Wednesday. Do we have drafts?"

"We do." Tiffany passed copies of two short documents to everyone. There was silence while everyone read them.

"I assume you've already seen these, Marc," Kathryn said when she had finished review; and when he had nodded assent, continued, "I see only one problem. Tiff, you have the stick drive someone passed on to the client on the exhibit list, the one with the alt-right and Nazi stuff. We don't need to disclose this now. We don't know for sure that they'll pull anything with his computer."

"Don't we lose the right to offer it if we don't disclose it now?" Marc asked. "That's why I told Tiff to leave it on."

"No, check my letter to Feldman. Both sides have until close of business Friday to disclose rebuttal exhibits and witnesses. We can list the drive then if we need to. For the same reason, we need to save our IT Expert for rebuttal. Take his name off the Witness list." She paused, thinking. "I might as well tell you…"

She quickly took them through her communications with Maria.

"Maria doesn't know exactly what they've done. She only knows they were excited about something in Mitch's computer. We need to proceed just as I said, but we're going to wind up with rebuttal exhibits and a rebuttal witness. I'd bet on it.

"By the way, Tiff. Anything on Maria? She wouldn't even give me her last name."

"No, ma'am. The client said he would check with some people. All he'd heard was that Monica has a Latina housemaid."

"What about Stevens?"

"I've got a lot more on him. Mitch has met him. He teaches computer graphics, knows a lot about computers and working with software. The client says he's seen with Gilbert a lot, lunch and so on.

"Stevens is pretty outspoken about his politics. Lots of liberal bumper stickers on his car. His social media activity is pretty left-wing, too."

"Thanks. Keep trying on Maria. Now, if there is nothing else on these disclosures…"

She went back to the Board and wrote "Hearing Notebooks."

"Tiffany, we can't finalize them until sometime next week, but I want Marc and me to have notebooks with dividers for witness and exhibit lists for both sides, witness outlines – by name – and opening and closing. You can start on these immediately."

"Got it," Tiffany acknowledged.

Still at the board, Kathryn wrote, "Hearing Staffing."

"Obviously, Marc and I. Ordinarily one of you would be hearing paralegal. But we've had to list you as witnesses because of the evidence plant. Jenny, please check with Jack Melton to see if I can borrow someone from his section."

Knowing it would be done, she didn't wait for an answer before writing, "CHCC Witnesses" and a colon. We don't have their list, but we have the Report Gilbert and her minions wrote. Marc, whom do you think they'll call?"

Marc said immediately, "They're going to depend a lot on written statements, I think. But they'll need at least one of the client's former students they dug up to testify live. I think the most likely one is Amanda Atkinson."

Kathryn wrote in that name. "Why?"

"Two reasons. One, she's relatively local. She teaches Middle School in McDowell County. Two, she's a true believer. She's all into Mitch's closet racism and sexism because he didn't teach to the Left and because of his 'white male privilege'. You can tell that from her witness statement. And she really goes wild on Facebook and Twitter."

"Do we have the screen shots printed out? And did we list them?"

"They're in a folder," Tiffany said. "And yes, they're on the exhibit list. Should we move them to rebuttal?"

"No, at the least they'll offer her written statement. But let me see the folder."

Tiffany went to one of the boxes, pulled out a slim file folder, and handed it to Kathryn. Sure enough, the posts were full of "believe women" and "white privilege'.

"We'd better be careful with these," she observed. "Our panel may agree with them. But...maybe they'll say so on the record."

Hesitating only a moment, she placed her initials by the witness' name. "I'll cross this one."

Then she wrote the names of Lottie, Corrine, and Darlene. "Do we agree all of them will testify?"

"At least two of them," Marc said. "The statements from the other current students are pretty tame, and I don't think they'll want to expose them to cross examination. But I'm not sure about Darlene. I think she's the weak link."

"I agree," Tiffany chimed in. "When we approached them in Asheville, her body language wasn't defiant. More like, 'Oh hell, what have I got myself into?'"

Kathryn considered. "Tiffany, if that's the case, why don't you take another shot at her? Give her a call. See if she'll meet by herself with you and Marc."

"Got it." Tiffany's keyboard rattled with another note.

Kathryn wrote Marc's initials by all three names. "Marc, why don't you do the cross on these girls?"

Marc started. "Me? Including Lottie?" When Kathryn only nodded, he asked, "Shouldn't a woman cross examine them?"

"That's a good point. But I think you might get more from them. Just a hunch. Let me see your outlines."

She wrote the names of Lorna Kaczynski, Gina Tompkins, and Monica Gilbert.

"What about these? All to testify?"

Marc said, "Again, I think just two. Kaczynski is the client's neighbor. I don't think they'll use her. I think they'll lead with Tompkins and finish with Gilbert, if they don't finish with Lottie."

"I tend to agree. Okay, I'll do the cross on these." She added her initials. "Anybody else?"

"No, I don't think so," Mark said. "Not unless they have an IT Expert. We'll know Wednesday."

"Let's move on." She wrote another heading, "McCaffrey Witnesses."

"So who are we going to use?"

They rattled off names. Mitch, obviously, and he would be their final witness. Kathryn would do his direct examination. They decided they would use Brenda Watkins as their lead witness. Kathryn would ask her, too. There were three more current students, and they picked out one, Fred Jones, for live testimony. Marc would ask Jones at the hearing. They'd offer the statements of the other two. They had several former students. They picked out one, a woman who was local. That was another Kathryn witness.

Ben and Lonnie would be Marc's witnesses. So would their IT expert. They decided to call only one current faculty member, a man who taught math. They'd been disappointed here. Most of the faculty witnesses they'd tried had expressed sympathy but were unwilling to get involved. Kathryn would take him.

Tiffany would be Marc's witness and Jenny, Kathryn's.

"All, right," Kathryn concluded. "Good meeting. We'll cover the game plan with the client when we meet Friday. Good luck with Lottie Wednesday. Next week is for witness prep. Anything else for now?"

"Uhh, court reporter?" Marc asked.

"Taken care of, boss." Tiffany grinned at him.

MONICA

Monica Gilbert and Barry Feldman were having a meeting like the one chaired by Kathryn, but not in person. They were using Skype.

Monica began the call with an update on McCaffrey's computer. She promised she'd have Sharon put what they'd "found" in a zip file and e-mail it to Barry right away, and apologized for not doing it sooner.

"We still need to have an IT Forensics consultant look at the computer," Feldman cautioned. "Did you contact the group I gave you?"

"No, we're using someone closer that one of our computer instructors knows, from Asheville. I just now sent you the link to their webpage. The guy's already been here and will have a report tomorrow. Don't worry. He's fully qualified."

She saw Barry turn to his second screen and open an e-mail. He clicked on the link, and read, his lips moving silently.

"Okay," he said. "This outfit is not on our approved contractor list, but they do appear qualified. I can justify it by claiming we needed speed. But Monica --" The look he gave her was stern – "we're not doing anything funny, are we? You know what I mean."

Monica let her jaw drop in exasperation. "We've already discussed this, and I already told you. Absolutely not."

"I know," he said, "but it looks odd that you and your graphics teacher could find things that your IT Department couldn't, and find it less than two weeks before the hearing. You understand that, don't you?"

"I do. And we can't really explain it ourselves. All I can think of is that McCaffrey had somebody do something to his computer, and it wore off." She couldn't tell him that what must have worn off was a spell she didn't understand.

"Well, let me have your guy's report. You know, don't you, that we'll get an immediate demand to let their forensics examiner look at it."

"We don't have to do that, do we?"

"Not now. But we will if this ever gets in court. That's why I want to be sure we're not pushing the envelope."

"Don't worry," she smiled at him, "everything will be fine." Well, it will be if Bart's contact came through like Bart said he would, she thought. "It's not going to court anyway. At heart, McCaffrey is a wimp. Turner may recommend it, but he won't do it."

"Well, Larry is telling me to play this as though he is."

Monica decided not to respond to that comment, but to ask about something else. "Speaking of Larry Kincaid, do we have approval on the hearing panel adviser from Legal?"

"Yeah, I think so. I'm supposed to meet with him right after you and I get through. Evidently, you got Claire Daniels to ask for it like you said. He's okay with it, but he's not sold on Rachel Jordan."

"Why not?"

"He knows she's capable, but he says she thinks too much like me – and you."

"Well, that's good, isn't it?"

"Larry says not if the record looks too much like an orchestrated screw job. I think I can get him to go for using Rachel. There really isn't anybody else. I'll text you tonight."

"Okay, he said when she didn't comment, "now let's talk about our witnesses."

They got on the same page concerning witnesses pretty quickly. They would lead off with Gina, who would summarize the investigation and introduce written witness statements. The next witness would be the teacher from Marion, the former student. Sharon would be called to cover what had been found in McCaffrey's office. They'd follow that up with the IT consultant, assuming his report was good.

Then would come the guts of the case, three complaining students. Corrine first, then Darlene, and finally Lottie.

"Any concerns about them?" Feldman asked.

"Only about Darlene. Corrine and Lottie, especially Lottie, both want McCaffrey's ass on a spear. Darlene may just be going along. If there's a weak link, it's her. But I think she'll come around if we work with her." Darlene was so weak willed, a compulsion spell, which was sometimes hard to maintain, ought to be easy, she thought, but of course didn't tell Barry.

They both agreed they would prepare Lorna but wouldn't use her unless they had to. Monica was relieved that Feldman agreed with her about Lorna. Lorna was flighty, erratic. Monica could tell that while she'd signed off on the report, Lorna had mixed feelings about terminating Mitch's contract. She'd had to use a compulsion a couple of times to get the signature, and didn't want to risk holding another while Lorna was being cross-examined.

Monica herself would be called last, to sum everything up and explain why the termination was justified. That is, unless, Lottie was so good it was better to end with her. They'd decide on the spot.

By this time, it was getting close to Barry's meeting with Kincaid. They hadn't yet discussed the McCaffrey witnesses, but they could do that once the disclosures came down.

"When are you coming here?" Monica asked.

"Next Tuesday night. That will leave plenty of time to help you prep witnesses. We can do the last-minute stuff the following Monday, and then the hearing Tuesday and Wednesday."

"What about Rachel?"

"She'll come in the Sunday before the hearing. She won't need more than one day to go over the hearing protocols with the Panel. If she comes, that is. But I think she will."

Monica was pleased. The call had gone well.

"Oh, we are so going to kick their asses," she gloated at the end.

"I hope we do." As a lawyer, Feldman was much more cautious.

"We will, darling. We will." The endearment was a promise, as he well knew.

Monica smiled when the call terminated. Yes, it was always good to hold out a carrot.

KATHRYN

Wednesday at noon, Kathryn met her husband for lunch at the cafeteria at Brainerd County Memorial Hospital. George had had two surgeries that morning, and part of the reason she was there was to just spend a little time with him, as they rarely were able to do during week-days. But she had another purpose.

Tiffany DeRatt had found out, after Mitch had quietly checked with Peggy Sturgill by text, and Peggy had asked some discrete questions, that the "Maria" who had called and texted her was likely Maria Rivera. Rivera was actually a part-time student at Carolina Highlands, taking nursing courses on Monday, Wednesday and Friday mornings, and on a partial scholarship funded by the hospital's foundation. Eventually, she would become a registered nurse. In the meantime, she was a maid.

Kathryn hoped that if she had lunch with her husband at the hospital cafeteria, she should run into Rivera there. Sure enough, the nursing student and house maid came in just as she and George were finishing.

Rivera agreed for Kathryn to sit with her, but she was clearly apprehensive, her dark eyes darting to surrounding tables, and her head on a swivel to see if they were being observed. Equally clearly, she detested Monica Gilbert, but was also terrified of her. She insisted she knew nothing she hadn't already told Kathryn.

"Why did you reach out to me?" Kathryn asked at last, making her tone as gentle as possible.

There was a long pause, and then Maria said, "She uses people. She uses me. And I think what she is doing to this man may be very bad."

"Will you help us by testifying about that at his hearing?"

Kathryn saw the young woman blink back tears.

"No, I can't. I need my job. And I really don't know." She was pleading now.

"Then why did you contact me?"

"Because I don't like to be used as …bait for her men, to distract them. I don't like having to play a game with her myself."

"Will you get word to me if you learn anything else?" Kathryn asked. "That's all I need, really." It was probably all she could get.

This time, Maria responded immediately. "Yes," she said, and then, abruptly and with feeling, "She is a puta!...And I think maybe a bruja. She eats like a pig and gains no weight."

Kathryn thanked her and left. She didn't leave a card. Maria already knew how to find her.

Kathryn's foreign language in school had been French. Her Spanish was limited. She understood what a puta was, but had to look up the other word on her phone when she reached her car.

Bruja. Witch.

Well, she thought as she turned on the ignition, her wry smile only for herself this time, this case was at least interesting.

She had to admit that.

MARC

At 3:10 that afternoon, Marc pulled into the parking lot at Starbuck's. There were a number of cars there, but the place was not nearly full. He was a little early, so he sat in his Camry for several minutes, thinking about how the conversation might go, before he got out. He thought it would be better to have a table before Lottie arrived – if she actually showed up – so she would be forced to join him.

When he entered, he saw that Jenny Jackson had taken a small table toward the rear of the shop, close to the restrooms, but sitting with her back to the counter and facing the window. There was a table close by the window – which was a glass wall, really – directly in her line of sight. She had an open laptop in front of her, buds in her ears, and what looked like it might have been an iPod to her right; but he knew it to be the directional mic.

Lottie was definitely not there yet.

As he walked to the counter and ordered a vente Café Mocha, Marc reflected that Jenny Jackson might be wasted as a paralegal. She could have been a private investigator. He knew she was forty, maybe a little older, but she looked younger. She had crimped her long blonde hair, and dressed herself in boots and stone-washed jeans with fake wear at the knees, over which she wore a fluffy Bohemian waste-length blue sweater with large perforations.

The effect of a studious retro-hippy was completed by enormous round spectacles that he knew were just clear glass. She appeared intent on her screen and keyboard, and he knew only from a quick glance up at him that she acknowledged his arrival.

He walked without looking at her to the table for two against the window, and sat with his face to the door, but immediately took out his phone and began checking his messages and e-mails. There were a number of each, and he plunged into them. This wasn't his only case.

"Well, hello there, Counselor."

He looked up with a start to see Lottie standing in front of him, her fine regular features split with a wide smile. As always, she was dressed as provocatively as weather and circumstances would permit. They were at the tail end of November, and the time for short shorts and halter tops had long passed; but she made do with tight jeans and soft zip-up leather buskins with moderate heels, and a burgundy sweater with a v-neck showing a remarkable amount of cleavage. Marc tried not to gape, then suppressed a smile at what Tiffany had said about Lottie's rack.

"Hello, yourself," he said. "What can I get you?" He nodded at the counter.

"Whatever you're having," Lottie said. "I sure you have good taste. In coffee, I mean." Her smile turned wicked.

Business was still light, but it nonetheless took a couple of minutes to get the café Mocha. He looked back at the table. Lottie had seated herself opposite his coffee drink, and was paying no attention to Jenny, who was tapping a toe to whatever was streaming through the ear buds, and clicking away on her laptop.

He brought Lottie's drink to the table, and resumed his seat.

"Thank you for meeting with me," he said.

"Thank you for coming alone," she replied. "I've been wanting to talk with you."

She didn't say about what, so Marc supplied, "Are you ready to talk about Mitch McCaffrey?"

"No. Absolutely not. I told you I have nothing to say about that, and I meant it."

"You'll have something to say week after next. You might as well tell me now."

The wicked smile seemed frozen on her face. "But I won't." Yet she made no effort to leave.

"I don't understand," he said, seriously. "Then what do you want to talk about?"

She interrupted the challenging smile only to sip delicately at her coffee. "I want to get to know you," she said. "Tell me about yourself."

Marc willed himself not to look at Jenny. She was probably enjoying this, he thought. He lacked the self-control to keep from shifting in his seat, squirming a little. But Kathryn and Bill Norville had taught him it was better sometimes to engage with a witness and let her guide the conversation. He decided to give her the truth.

Why not? It wouldn't compromise the McCaffrey case.

So he told her about growing up in Orangeburg, about his father being a college professor at S.C. State, and his mother much younger. He told her about his kid sister who was a junior at Clemson. About how he had been a good, but not highly recruited, high school football player who had managed a scholarship to Western Carolina.

He told her about how hard he'd studied to be able to get into law school at Tennessee, and about how hard the adjustment had been from college. And surprising himself, he told her about how the Black Law Student Association had been unhappy that he had joined the Federalist Society and wouldn't back all of their resolutions. His Dad and Mom had taught him to think for himself, he explained; and thinking for himself, knowing his bonding with his white teammates on the WCU football team, he just didn't buy that all white folks were racists, or that the solution for his people was to always bitch about racism. He explained that some of his classmates, white as well as black, had shunned him for thinking that way.

He wasn't sure why he opened up to her that way, didn't know how that would help what he was trying to do. But he did it. Her face and body language said she was interested, though, and she didn't interrupt.

"I just don't think anybody has the right to tell you what to think," he finished. "Or expect you to conform to what they say. I won't do it."

Lottie's lips were slightly parted, and for a moment he thought she was really going to respond to what he'd said. But she didn't.

Instead she asked, "Got a girl friend?"

Again, he shifted in his chair. This could get dangerous, with Jenny listening and probably transcribing all of this. But again he decided on the truth. Some of it, anyway.

"Maybe," he conceded. "But I don't need to be talking to you about it. I came here to talk about a hearing. The hearing," he amended.

"But we're not talking about that, are we?" She continued to smile, but the smile was softer, somehow, not wicked like before.

"No," he conceded, "but we should be,"

Again she wouldn't engage, but persisted in her prying. "It's not that girl who was with you in Asheville was it? She's pretty."

"No," he lied.

"But not as pretty as I am," she said. She looked directly into his eyes, and he struggled not to look away. "I might be interested, you know." Her voice was silky soft, deliberately seductive.

He had no trouble with that one, though. "No," he said. "That's out of the question."

"Why not?" she asked, maintaining the smile, teasing, sure she was playing with him, and getting away with it. And probably was.

But the answer was easy. "Because you're a witness in a case I'm helping handle. An important witness. I won't do anything unethical."

She regarded him with evident appraisal. "But that's not the only reason, is it?"

Marc took a deep breath. He still wasn't sure where this was going, or whether he was really learning anything. But he'd been using the truth so far, and he decided to stick with it.

"No, it's not." He took a moment to sip his by-now cool coffee, and plunged ahead. "Lottie, you are a pretty young woman. And I can tell you're smart. But you're spoiled and you're cruel. You're ready to take my client's job because you can. Just for kicks. It's all a joke to you. A party.

"Life isn't a party. It's serious. People get hurt. I won't ever get involved with someone who would do anything like that. Who would hurt somebody for fun."

He expected her to jump up and yell at him. Storm out. Throw coffee in his face.

But she didn't. She just stared at him with her lips trembling, and then started to cry softly, tears smearing her mascara. He was surprised to consciously notice for the first time that her eyes were large and wide and a soft, luminous brown.

"I'm sorry," he said, handing her a napkin. He didn't have anything else to offer. She took it and dabbed her eyes, continuing to sniffle. "I was too hard on you."

"No," she said, her voice breaking just a little bit. "It-it's all right... It's just that I've heard something like it before. A little bit like it, anyhow."

He decided to follow up. "Tell me about it."

She was the one to breathe deeply this time. "It was last year. I had a boyfriend. I really liked him. He was a senior at App, a white dude."

Marc waved off that datum. As though that could really matter these days, he thought. He didn't think this was going to be about race anyway. As it turned out, he was right.

"Go on," he said.

"I thought we were getting serious. I thought he was going to propose. But he broke up with me. Dumped me one night when we were out. He...said he liked me but I was a party girl. He was on his way to grad school at Carolina, and he couldn't be distracted by somebody like me."

She really did sob this time, and Marc noticed the baristas looking at them with some concern. He had willed himself not to look at Jenny Jackson, but he heard her keyboard continuing to click away. He allowed the pause to continue.

Finally, she continued, "He said he didn't trust me, that I would leave him for somebody more fun, and he wasn't going to risk getting hurt, not when his career and his student loans were on the line. He said it had been fun, but he was going to end it."

"What did you do about it?" Marc asked.

"I couldn't convince him I really wasn't what he thought. I tried. But I couldn't. And then I cried for a month. Like I'm crying now."

She blew her nose, and finished with a bleak smile, "So I decided that if that's what people thought of me, that I was just a party girl, I would be the best party girl around. If I was having fun, to hell with everybody."

"How's that working for you?" Marc asked, quietly.

She straightened, wiped her eyes with the napkin. "Good," she said. "Real good. You know, I thought you and I could have fun. But now I know better. I'd better leave."

She rose from the table.

"Let me know when you're ready to discuss the case," Marc said.

"I'll see you in court," she shot back. "I'll talk about it then."

"But we're not going to court," he said, although he knew what she meant.

"Whatever." The tears began again. "Good-bye!"

Marc watched her walk out of the building, stiffly and not with her usual calculated sway. He sat and looked at his e-mails until he was sure she had left the parking lot. Then he got up and walked to his car.

He had just started the engine when there was a peck on the side window. It was Jenny Jackson. He touched the button to lower the window.

"Well," he said with a rueful smile, "I guess that could have gone better."

"That's what I want you to know," she said. "I think we learned more than you think…And you may have done better with her than you know. We'll see what Kathryn thinks, but I think she'll be glad to read the transcript.

"And one other thing you ought to know. You and Tiff may be fooling Kathryn and Bill. But you are not fooling me. And I don't think you fooled that girl."

Marc opened his mouth to reply, but she interrupted, "Don't worry. I'm not telling on you."

Then she turned to find her car. Marc sat gaping at her, but didn't try to stop her to talk more.

CLAIRE

Claire Daniels, D.Ed. and president of Carolina Highlands Community College, was living through a morning of unscheduled telephone conferences.

The first had been from King Armistead at Southeastern Electronics. King had begun with the usual pleasantries, had continued with how much Southeastern liked to employee CHCC graduates in the trades (she thanked him, of course), moved on to how he hoped that the CHCC Foundation would remain on Southeastern's budget, and finally wound around to what he really wanted to speak with her about. She'd known something was coming.

"I was talking with your Compliance Officer about the hearing you have coming up on terminating that instructor," he drawled.

Claire knew she shouldn't interrupt, but did. "Monica really shouldn't be discussing an internal issue like that with you," she said, not hiding the irritation she felt.

"Oh, please don't blame Monica. She didn't tell me anything confidential. I asked her about it. I saw the news reports a few weeks ago and asked her how it was coming."

"What did she say?" Claire knew she was talking to a contributor, but still couldn't hide the irritation.

"Not to worry, please." His voice was soothing. "She only said there was going to be a hearing, and she couldn't discuss it. This is my fault, but I did ask her if the news stories about the charges got it right. She said she couldn't confirm or deny it, but I got the impression that those really are the charges."

Claire took a deep breath, and forced as friendly a voice as she could manage.

"King, you know I can't discuss it, either," she said.

"Oh, Claire, I do. I do. I just wanted to say," he hesitated, and repeating himself, went on, "I just wanted to say that I know you need to give the man a fair hearing and all; but if there is any chance that you really have someone on the faculty payroll who would do things like that – any chance at all – you know, harass the girls, I should say young women, and have white nationalist ideations, then I don't see how you can keep him.

"I have to push to keep the Foundation in our budget every year, and you can't have your corporate sponsors thinking you even might have racists on the faculty. It would make it harder on me to keep pushing. I'm sure your other corporate partners would feel the same way."

So that was it. The iron fist inside the velvet glove. She was sure Monica had engineered this call and was almost as sure that she and Armistead had rehearsed it. He wasn't her only contact at his company, but he was an important one, because he headed human resources at this plant and she wanted her graduates to continue to get interviews and offers.He knew, and Monica knew, that Claire knew he was.

"King, of course we won't continue to employee anyone like that," she said. "But he is entitled to a hearing."

"I know. I know," Armistead said. "I just wanted you to know how serious we at Southeastern take matters like this. We have to police our own workforce all the time. We give them a hearing, but we do let them go. For something like this, I mean."

"King, I certainly appreciate your concern. And I do thank you for calling," she tried to make herself sound sincere.

"You're more than welcome. And let me tell you, too, that if there is any help I can give you, free consulting or whatever, please call me. Call me anytime."

She thanked him again. What else could she do? But she was seething inside. Monica evidently didn't trust her to do as Monica wanted, and had recruited some outside pressure.

The hell of it was, as she told Peggy a little later, is that it was pressure she felt.

Now she was talking with Larry Kincaid. That was unscheduled, too.

"About your request for a hearing advisor," Larry was saying, "we're going to give you one, but I'm not completely happy about it."

"Oh? Why not?" Claire was genuinely puzzled.

"Ideally, I would do it. Or Megan. But like we told you, neither of us is available. This legislative committee meeting is cast in concrete, and Meg is tied up in a hearing at the college in Wilmington. The only lawyer available is Rachel Jordan."

"Larry, I don't know her. What's wrong with her?"

"As a lawyer, nothing. She knows what she'd doing. My only concern is that she thinks too much like Barry and Monica. The role of the hearing advisor is to make sure the chairperson runs the hearing smoothly and fairly, and if necessary, give objective legal advice in the closed session.

"If Rachel isn't careful, she'll come over more like a member of Barry's and Monica's team than like a fair hearing monitor. If that happens, it'll look horrible on the record if we wind up in court."

"What's the solution, Larry?"

"Well, I'm going to have a talk with her, and read the riot act to her. And frankly, if something happens to free up one of us, I'll come myself or send Meg. But I don't think her case is going to settle, and this legislative hearing is just too important for me to skip. But I'll be fair with you. I don't have a completely good feeling about your hearing."

"Why not?"

"Nothing solid. I told Barry I wanted reports, and he's given me everything I asked for. It all looks okay, but it's almost too good. For example, I don't completely buy this thing about the IT Consultant they brought in finding things on your instructor's computer that the college's IT Department couldn't find.

"Look, Claire, we're under a lot of pressure here. The Community College system depends on the state legislature for money. This is the same legislature that passed the new Campus Free Speech Act. That law is fine with me. It's fine with the system Chairman. I like to think I'm as liberal as anyone, but I believe in free speech.

"I know we have a lot of people on staff here and in our system colleges who are not fine with it. They wanted 'free speech zones'. They wanted strict speech codes. They want to eliminate people who aren't progressive enough. Monica and Barry are two of them. Rachel is another."

He paused. Claire said nothing. But, shifting uncomfortably in her chair she wondered privately how many of her staff and faculty would agree with whether Larry was "as liberal as anyone." She also realized that Monica had been dragging her feet on revising the college speech code to apply with the new law. She doubted Monica's revisions would be approved by Legal Affairs when they finally got them. She hoped he wouldn't bring it up.

"Excuse me," he said. "I needed a gulp of coffee. Anyway, we have enough folks like that around the state that we're getting sued under federal law or under the CFSA, or both. The more we get sued, the more legislature doesn't like it. That's why I have to go to the Committee meeting.

"And that's why Meg has to go to Wilmington. Some over-zealous compliance office expelled a kid for wearing an NRA T-shirt to class. Called it 'hate speech.' Suit got filed before we could handle it. Hell, we didn't even know about it.

"Claire, listen. If your guy up there at Carolina Highlands harassed female students, if he spreads racist propaganda, get him the hell out. I'm really good with that. But we can't have a railroad job. That means we get sued again. That means I have to go back to the legislature, and take the System Chairman with me.

"I'm going to keep up with this the best I can. But you better watch it closely, too, for your own good. Call me if you need me."

"I will," she promised. "But let me tell you something else."

She told him about the call from Armistead.

"Yep," he said when she'd finished. "That's where we are now. Between a rock and a hard place."

She certainly agreed with that.

MARC

On Friday afternoon, Marc found himself in the conference room at the office again. This time, the client would be there. So would Norville, who had agreed to sit in. And there would be an addition to the team, Tammy Cresawn, on loan from Jack Melton, because Jenny and Tiffany were on the witness list.

She was one of their more experienced paralegals, in her fifties, matronly with a round pleasant face and tiny spectacles. But she knew all there was to know about being courtroom paralegal, according to Kathryn. She was seated in front of the laptop with connection with the projector, with the bankers' boxes beside them, where Tiffany usually sat. She and Jenny were seated with their legal pads.

Kathryn brought Mitch into the room, and seated herself in front of the whiteboard. Norville followed a moment after, and took a seat beside Marc.

"All right, people," Kathryn began, "this is a status and planning session. We'll do the witness prep next week."

She outlined the game plan and assignments they had discussed earlier in the week, for Mitch's benefit. He approved everything.

When she reached the expected evidence about what was on Mitch's computer, Marc interrupted with a question.

"Excuse me," he said, diffident in the presence of both Turner and Norville, "but haven't we got that issue pretty much scotched? I mean, we did our own check before Mr. McCaffrey was suspended. Just like the inventory in the office. All this has to be a plant."

Norville answered before Kathryn could speak. "Marc, that would be true in front of a Brainerd County jury. It would be true in front of most judges I know. Most arbitrators, too. But this Hearing Panel will be hard-wired to resolve any doubts in favor of the college. They may not pay much attention to our evidence."

"I know," Marc said, "but it all just looks so fishy."

"We would have a better shot if our guy were able to get access to Mitch's computer. But they won't give it to us. If we go on to court, we can get it then. But who knows what we'll find after the guy they hired finishes with it?

"By the way, Jenny, have you finished checking him out?"

"We have," Jenny said. "Qualifications check out. But if you drill down, he's definitely disposed against us. Positive comments about Antifa on social media. Connected on social media with Bart Stevens and both those guys at the store in Black Mountain."

"Well, we can use that in cross," Kathryn said. "But as Bill says, it won't be perceived as negative by the Hearing Panel. It might make Barry Feldman nervous, though. He's no fool. And Claire Daniels, when this case reaches her."

"Who came up with this consultant?" Norville asked. "Mitch, can you help?"

"My guess is Bart Stevens," Mitch said. "Computer graphics guy at the college. Pretty tight with Monica. There are rumors about them."

"You mean?" Kathryn asked.

Mitch shifted in his chair, looking helplessly at the four women.

"You can spit it out," Kathryn said. "We're big girls here. You mean they're involved sexually."

Mitch's mouth twisted and he spread his hands. "That's what they say."

They moved on to new information. Kathryn told them the latest from Maria Rivera. There wasn't much.

"One of her gripes with Monica is that she eats a lot and doesn't gain weight," Kathryn finished. "Interesting but not helpful."

Marc was surprised to see Mitch's eyebrows lift. "Well, you never know what might be helpful," the client offered.

"What do you mean, Mitch?" Kathryn asked.

"Only what I said. All information is potentially helpful. Isn't that what you told me?"

Kathryn appeared to accept that. Marc wondered. Mitch kept coming up with stuff nobody understood, but Marc always thought he had his reasons. Marc didn't know what they were.

"Now," Kathryn said, making a check on her pad with her pen, "let's talk about YouTube and Twitter."

Someone – they assumed it was the Bean n' Bacon employee Mitch has noticed filming – had put up some of the video from the Thanksgiving party. It began with the guy in the MAGA ballcap shouting out, "Let's make Brainerd County great again!" Someone had edited it to show Mitch and Diana, and also Kathryn and her son. They had carefully omitted the African Americans who were there. The caption was, "White Supremacy lives in Brainerd County!"

The video had been posted on Facebook, and tweeted and re-tweeted. Some of the tweets were pretty vicious. Some were questioning. A few counter-attacked, and a couple of these were over the top. One claimed white Americans were under attack. Mitch said he didn't know whoever had tweeted it.

It had earned a clip run on Channel 13, and a couple of calls to Kathryn and Mitch. They had down-played it. Kathryn had sent word to Margaret and Diana to take no action against the employee who had filmed and posted it. That would make things worse.

"I don't think we're going to hear about this from the college," Kathryn said, "but the Panel will have seen it, especially since it got on television. We just need to realize that. It's part of what we're facing."

"Do we mention it ourselves?" Marc asked.

"No. We don't." Kathryn cocked her head and allowed herself one of the wry smiles for which she was noted. "But I hope they do. That may give us an opportunity to make a point."

She didn't have to explain. They knew.

"Okay," Kathryn said, "let's move on to the latest from Peggy Sturgill."

They discussed what Peggy told them about her boss' contacts with King Armistead. She'd also reported to Mitch that Claire had had a long conference call with Larry Kincaid, but hadn't yet told her what is was about.

"Is there any way to counter this?" Kathryn asked. "Claire Daniels is important. The Hearing Panel's recommendations go to her. She makes the final decision. Bill, any ideas?"

Norville looked around the room, then said, "Well, I know Jim

Douthat, the plant manager. He would be disposed to be friendly to us. But I doubt he'd buck his HR Director. At least, not now."

Norville responded. "If Mitch approves, I can make sure the System Chairman's office is aware that Mitch has contributed to the college. Not as much as Southeastern. But pretty good gifts."

Everyone thought that a good idea. Including, to Marc's mild surprise, the client.

Mitch is evolving, he thought. But he couldn't quite grasp how, or with what effect.

21

HEY, MR. TAMBOURINE MAN

KATHRYN

The following Wednesday afternoon, Kathryn and Marc, with Tammy Cresawn in tow, met Barry Feldman and Monica Gilbert at Carolina Highlands to inspect the hearing room. She had arranged the meeting with Feldman by telephone on Monday while he was still in his office in Raleigh. They had agreed on the room's configuration, and he had promised to pass it on to Monica; but she wanted to actually see the room itself.

The day was cold and blustery, the wind blowing loose some of the leaves that still clung to their branches and sending them skittering across the parking lot. All three wore overcoats. Kathryn carried only her purse. Marc and Tammy both carried legal pads, and the latter also had a tablet computer in a leather case. The campus was busy but the students' mood subdued, thanks to the weather and the exams that would begin the following Monday. The three attracted barely a glance as they walked into the Administration Building.

The hearing would be conducted there, in a large conference room close by the president's office, which was used for staff presentations and large meetings. They met Feldman and Gilbert in the reception area outside the president's office. Bulletin boards featured colorful Holiday decorations, none religious, and announcements of Holiday events.

Feldman was smiling and friendly as they shook hands and exchanged introductions. Gilbert was cool and professional. She considered Kathryn and Marc the enemy, and it showed. Kathryn's history with Gilbert was not good. Years earlier, Kathryn had volunteered — actually had been volunteered by Bill Norville — to advise the college on setting up its paralegal studies department. Monica was relatively new at Carolina Highlands at the time, but had still managed to horn in enough to protest that the curriculum Kathryn recommended didn't have enough "social justice" training in it. She hadn't liked it when Kathryn had observed that she was recommending courses that would turn out qualified legal assistants for North Carolina lawyers, as opposed to working on the staff of the Southern Poverty Law Center, which these days didn't have much to do with law, anyway.

Earlier this fall, Kathryn had introduced Lisa Willingham, who was a conservative television and radio personality, when the latter spoke at the college. Gilbert had sought to limit access to the auditorium, claiming that students wouldn't feel safe around Willingham. Claire Daniels had overruled her, but had asked the Martintown police and the Brainerd County Sheriff's department to supplement campus security. There were a few hecklers, mostly bussed in from Asheville; but the reality was that, in conservative Brainerd County, Willingham had a number of fans among the mostly local student body.

Again, Kathryn's acid remark, made at a meeting with Daniels and Gilbert, that the only persons who wouldn't be safe were the ones who wanted to listen to the speech, hadn't sat well with Gilbert. Too fucking bad, she thought. I don't like her either, and if this were a jury trial, I'd really try to make it about her. Pity that I can't with this Panel.

Monica's assistant unlocked the door to the hearing room, and they entered to find it already set up the way she and Feldman had agreed. The room was already equipped with white boards and screens, and the lawyers had asked for a "courtroom style" configuration, which would enable them to make use of these features, but also facilitate presentation of evidence in a way that a long conference table, or a simple U-shaped configuration, would not.

Kathryn had to give Monica that she'd done pretty much what she and Barry had agreed on. There was a table on the far side of the long rectangular room, behind which were chairs for the Panel. In front of the table for the Panel was a somewhat shorter table that would serve for a computer that could project images on the screens to the Panel's left and right. Forward of the Panel's table, but not so far as the table for the computer, and at right angles to these table, was a small table with a chair for witnesses, situated close to the wall. On the opposite side of the room was a like table for the court reporter.

The rest of the room held tables for counsel and both parties, separated by a podium with shelf beneath it, and behind them a few rows of seats for the small number of spectators that would be permitted. Kathryn looked around, pretty much satisfied, and turned to Marc and Tammy, who merely nodded acquiescence. She was about to voice her agreement, when she noticed something.

"Barry," she said, "there are four chairs at the table for the Panel. Why? It's a three-person Panel."

"That's for the Neutral Panel Advisor provided by the System," Feldman said, his tone matter of fact. "It's in the policy prescribed for faculty hearings."

Kathryn turned to Marc. It was his job to have studied the policy and advise the senior attorney of its contents. Marc stepped close to her and whispered, "It's in there."

Kathryn wheeled on Feldman. "Why weren't we told about this before?" she demanded.

"Kathryn, it's in the policy. I thought you knew," Feldman kept his face neutral, but she caught the shadow of a smug smile twitching Gilbert's lips.

"Okay," Kathryn said, determined not to be thrown. "Just who is this 'neutral advisor'?" This might not be a big deal, depending.

"Rachel Jordan," he told her, "from Legal Affairs."

"I thought Rachel was practicing law in Greensboro." If this was the Rachel Jordan she knew, the news was not good. She had gone to law school with Jordan at Wake Forest, and had found her to be a tireless, and tiresome, advocate of leftist causes.

"She was," Barry said, "but she's been with us about a year. Monica and I agreed this Panel needs someone to help them run the hearing."

"But you didn't tell me," Kathryn accused.

"We didn't need to," Barry said.

"Barry, the problem is that this advisor is not neutral. She's from the prosecutor's office. It's a conflict of interest."

"I don't think so," Barry responded. She's not helping me. We've put up a Chinese Wall. I haven't discussed the case with her, and I won't. She doesn't come in until the day before the hearing."

"She's read the file, hasn't she?"

"Not mine. Now, she has read the report of the investigation, but the whole Panel has done that."

"I take it, then, she's only going to give procedural advice during the hearing?"

"Well, she'll advise the Panel during deliberations. They'll need that."

"Like hell they will!" she didn't try to keep the snarl out of her voice. "I'm going to protest this – on the record. We'll put it in writing."

Barry shrugged. "Go ahead. It won't matter. This is perfectly legal, I assure you. Your research will confirm it."

She stole a glance at Marc, who looked miserable.

"We're still going to do it."

"As I said, go right ahead."

"The room is fine, except for that," Kathryn managed, trying to control her frustration. "You'll get our exhibit notebook this afternoon, as agreed. Thank you and good-bye."

She met Gilbert's eyes before she left, in defiance of the woman's smile of gloating triumph. This wasn't over, and she was damned if it would throw her and her team.

"The hell of it is," she muttered to Marc on their way out, "it probably is legal. But it makes our job harder. And it was hard already. Rachel will coach them on how to screw our client without doing something stupid. That's what she'll be there for."

"I'm sorry," Marc said. "I should have anticipated this. I saw the provision, but nobody said they were going to use it."

Kathryn stopped walking and turned toward him. She willed her tone to be soft and supportive. "No, Marc, we're a team and I am in charge. It's on me." Then she added, "But we're not letting this get the best of us. Let's go get ready to win it."

She just wished she had the confidence she was trying to project.

MONICA

She and Barry had witness preparation scheduled for all of Thursday and Friday. The plan was go over testimony with everyone they were going to call to testify.

The only exception was the former student, the school teacher from Marion, who had begged to come in Saturday, so she wouldn't miss more work. Monica privately thought her a whining little bitch who was already complaining about missing a day on Tuesday for the actual hearing.

But, she conceded, the woman's testimony was promising; so, it was better to placate her, feign sympathy, and thank her sweetly. They would be working some Saturday, anyway.

Today, Thursday, they were doing their hearing prep with Lottie, Corrine, and Darlene. Monica was pleased. It was going well, and as she had predicted.

Corrine had swallowed the theory of the prosecution hook, line, and sinker, and was having fun with it. McCaffrey was an ogler of young women, a sexist who made them feel he was undressing them with his eyes and always uncomfortable in his class. She had never complained about it because she had been afraid to do so, but was speaking out now. She was also sure he was a racist, insensitive to people of color.

She was a little shaky when Barry pressed her to supply details, but gratefully willing when Monica suggested some to her with leading questions, like, "Did you ever notice him looking up a skirt?" Or, "Is it true that he never made any positive references to the literary contributions of African Americans? How did you feel about that?"

When they discussed the incident about May Angelou and Shakespeare, Monica asked if she thought her friend might be offended by the implication that Angelou was worthwhile only as the reflection of a white male, and she immediately agreed that she had. When Corrine left, Barry warned her that they might not be a good idea to lead her that obviously at the hearing.

"We won't have to," Monica said. "Now she'll volunteer it." With my help, she thought. A gentle suggestion spell would be enough.

Darlene was just what they'd feared – a deer in the headlights who really didn't want to testify. But she was so weak-willed that she responded to Monica's compulsion spell immediately, and thereafter was just as susceptible to suggestion as Corrine had been. She thought Darlene would even withstand cross-examination adequately if under compulsion. Still, Monica and Barry agreed that she was not a particularly strong witness, and decided they wouldn't use her unless something went wrong with Corrine's testimony. They'd claim her testimony would be "cumulative", and rely on her prior written statement.

The session with Lottie Watkins came last. Her session was surprising. She arrived in a bulking sweater and loose jeans that did not hide her figure, but did not provide its usual emphasis, her dark hair in its natural waves and not curled or crimped as she so often affected, her make-up minimal. As she took her seat next to Barry, across the desk from where Monica sat in her office, she shifted uncomfortably in her chair, presenting as diffident and a little nervous.

Monica had expected Lottie to be as primed to let McCaffrey have it between the eyes as Corrine had been, but she clearly was not. Her answers were hesitant, and she had to be prompted almost as much as Darlene. Monica struggled to contain her anger. She was considering giving the young princess a big dose of compulsion when Barry saved her the trouble by speaking up.

"Now, Lottie," he said gently, "we understand that testifying is something you're not used to doing. It can be a daunting proposition. But we're here to help you. We can go over everything with you, and prepare you for cross examination. But you have to do your part. We can't testify for you. You have to do it yourself. It's much more persuasive if you tell your story on your own and we don't have to lead you. Do you understand?"

Lottie lowered her head and nodded, saying nothing.

"And something else you need to understand," Feldman went on, an edge creeping into his voice, "is that you started this whole thing.

You made the initial complaint. Look, here's your complaint." He handed it to her. "And here's your detailed statement you gave to the investigating committee." He handed her a more lengthy document, several pages long. "Have you read these?"

"Not in the last few days," Lottie admitted, her voice low.

"Well, we're going to let you read them now. You can keep the copies; we have others. Then we're going to do this again. Okay?"

Lottie nodded again. "Uh-huh."

"And Lottie, you need to understand something else," Feldman continued. "You don't want the hearing panel to think you made this up. That's a major rules violation. You could be suspended, even expelled. You don't want that, do you?"

Her eyes widened. She opened her mouth, closed it, and opened again. "N-no," she whispered. "Of course not."

"Good. Now read these over. We'll wait." Feldman's eyes moved to Monica. He could tell she was seething. "Let me handle this," he mouthed silently. Monica understood, and gave him a jerky nod.

This time Lottie did much better, although Barry had to prompt her to speak up twice. But she told the same story of harassment, sexism and racism that was in her statement without much prompting.

"Good," Barry said when they were done. "But when you get to the hearing, keep eye-contact with the Hearing Panel and speak up. Be confident. I'm told you always are. You can do that, can't you."

Lottie drew herself up and drew a deep breath. "Yes," she said, her voice clear and strong this time. "Yes, I can."

"Good," Feldman said. "Now we're going to tell you what to watch for on cross examination, and we'll have some suggestions on how to handle it."

His eyes flicked to Monica again. Evidently, he wanted her to stay silent. Reluctantly, she did. The preparation for cross-examination took a while. Lottie, she had to admit, did well, and was receptive to Barry's suggestions. She asked a few questions, and they were good questions. The girl clearly was not dumb.

They excused her with a reminder that they would be around the next day if she wanted to meet with them again. Lottie thanked them and left.

"I'm glad you handled that," Monica admitted to Feldman when the door had closed behind Lottie. "I don't know what was wrong with her at first. But you brought her around."

Barry bit his lip before responding.

"Monica," he said at last, "I had to scare her. I shouldn't have had to do that. She still bothers me. In a lot of ways, she is our case. You get that, don't you?"

"She's not all of it," Monica insisted, "we have the other girls, and the computer, and –"

"I know, I know," Feldman said. "But without strong testimony from Lottie, they can shoot holes in everything else."

"Not with this Panel."

"Well, with Claire, then. Or in court. We need this testimony to go in well," he insisted.

"It will," Monica said, her voice firm. "It will."

I'll make sure of it. Even if I have to use the Power.

LOTTIE

Lottie didn't meet Corrine and Darlene that afternoon after class, as she did frequently. She did not take their calls or respond to their texts. She went home, taking her tablet and a few books. Exams were next week, after all. But mostly, she just wanted to be by herself. She wanted to think.

When she arrived at home, she went straight to her room and shut the door. Thankfully, her father was still at work, and for whatever reason, her mother was out, too. There was no one to stop her to engage in conversation. She started streaming music on her tablet, and opened a bound volume to re-read a chapter in her course in Civ. But she couldn't concentrate on the French Enlightenment, and soon closed the book.

Truthfully, she admitted to herself, she had been troubled ever since her meeting at Starbucks with Marc Washington. That hadn't gone the way she expected. She had gone there to flirt with him and tease, and he'd wound up making her feel bad. Marc might think she was good-looking, sexy even; but he didn't want her. He actually thought she was a bad person. Johnny had thought her drop-dead gorgeous, but he had wound up not wanting her, either.

What they had in common, she realized, was that they were serious young men with serious ambitions, and didn't take her seriously. Well, Marc took her seriously, but only because she was going to testify against his client. She didn't think Johnny took her seriously at all.

But why did, all of a sudden, what they thought matter? Lots of guys were interested in her. Black guys, white guys, you name it. She had friends. Corrine and Darlene loved her. There were others, too. But she was kidding herself, and she knew it.

Slowly, stretched out on her bed with her head propped against an over-sized pillow, she faced the fact that Corrine and Darlene loved her because she always had money and a car, so they could run around and have fun. Most of the guys she went with liked her for the same reasons and because she was hot. She wasn't sure anyone was interested in her.

Then came another thought, even more sickening. Was it possible she wasn't interesting at all? As a person, not as a hot chick with a car, whose Dad was a doctor? What had she ever done to make herself interesting to somebody like Marc or Johnny? Not much of anything, she thought miserably. Before she realized she was going to cry, she started crying, sobbing softly so no one would hear.

Damn Marc Washington and Johnny Blake, she thought, crazily linking them even though they didn't even know one another. They were making her cry again.

She decided she wouldn't permit that. She dried her eyes with a tissue and picked up her book. She'd get this hearing over with, say just what Mr. Feldman and Ms. Gilbert wanted her to say, and just move on. Move on!

She opened the book.

But she still couldn't concentrate.

She went down to dinner when her Mom called, first making sure she didn't look like she'd been crying.

At the table, she only picked at her food, although her Mom had made lasagna, which she really liked. When her mother asked what was wrong, she said she was worried about exams, and about the hearing.

"Oh, darling, don't worry about the hearing," her Mom said. "Just do what they tell you, tell the truth about that man. It'll turn out all right. It will."

That really was no help, especially the part about telling the truth; and she almost started to cry again. But she didn't. She just asked if she could be excused. She needed to study, she said.

"Well, that's a nice change," her father, who had said nothing until now, said with a smile. "Go ahead. Study hard."

"Call us if you need us, honey," her mother called after her. She didn't respond.

She returned to her room and shut the door. Flinging herself on the bed, she let the tears come again, but made sure she was quiet. It would be like her mother to come check on her, and she didn't want a conversation right now. At least, not with Mom.

After a bit, she heard the door to the garage close, and looking out the window, saw her mother's car back out. Mom has a Junior League meeting or something, she guessed.

With sudden resolve, she dried her eyes again and went downstairs to find her father.

She found him in the den, sitting in an armchair and reading a medical journal, reading glasses perched on the end of his nose, which was sharp and thin for an African American. A smooth jazz station he liked was playing on Sirius XM.

Seeing her enter, he closed the journal, placed it in his lap, and removed the spectacles.

"Yes, honey," he said. "Do you want to talk about something?"

"Daddy," she said, "do you love me?"

He laughed softly. "What a question! Of course, I love you, Lottie. I love you more than life itself."

"Are you proud of me, Daddy?"

"I am proud of you, sweetheart. I think you're pretty, and stylish, and smart as a whip. But I'd like to be more proud of you, proud of you for more that those things." She noticed he didn't mention the complaint against McCaffrey.

"What would you like me to do?" she asked, just a little above a whisper.

He cocked his head in thought. "Well, I'd like to see you live up to all that potential I know is in that pretty head. I'd like to apply yourself better in school. Truthfully, a lot better. And I'd like to see you interested in something important, not just boys and clothes and having a good time."

"I'm not smart like Becky and Robert," Lottie said, referring to her siblings.

"Don't give me that," he told her. "You're just as smart as either one of them. They just work harder."

She had to change the subject. "You said I ought to get interested in something important. Don't you think fighting harassment and racism is important?"

He looked hard at her before answering. She shuffled her feet nervously.

"Yes, I do," he finally answered. "If someone is doing that, it's important."

"But I'm doing that," she said, defending herself. But she was no longer sure of it.

"Yes, I suppose you are," he said.

"Suppose, Dad? Aren't you sure?" She pitched her voice to sound as hurt as possible.

"Lottie," he answered, "the important question is 'are you sure'. Are you?"

"I am." She answered quickly. But she knew it was a lie.

"Then do just what your Mother said, and good luck with it."

They locked eyes for a moment, then he said, "Anything else you need from your Dad tonight?"

"No, Dad. Not really." Then she added, "Thank you," and surprised herself by meaning it.

"Well, then, I'm going to read just a little more, and then it's bedtime for me." Thursday was a surgery day for Dr. Watkins, and they usually started early. She knew that when he rose early, he went to bed early.

She thanked him again and returned to her room. She changed to her pajamas and set out to cry herself to sleep. She didn't realize her father had tiptoed to the door and heard her muted sobs.

She had a thought that stopped the tears. She sat up and reached for her cell phone. The number she wanted was still in her contacts folder.

There were three rings before he answered.

"Johnny?" It came out somewhere between a whisper and a sob.

"Lottie?" His voice was strong and wide awake. It really wasn't late.

"It's me," she said, her voice under more control.

"Is something wrong?"

"I miss you," she said, even though she hadn't planned to say it.

"Miss you, too," he said after a pause. Then: "But is something wrong?"

"Oh, everything is wrong," she blurted. "Just about everything."

"Can I help?" he asked.

"Johnny, I need advice, and I have no one else to ask."

They talked for a long time. She didn't think anyone in the house heard her talking. She was wrong.

MARC

It was Friday, and Marc Washington was tired and irritable.

The week had been long and busy. There were witnesses to prepare for the McCaffrey Hearing. He'd had meetings with all of the students they'd lined up. These had gone well. The only real problem was that it was not known when their testimony would be reached, Tuesday afternoon or sometime Wednesday; and the Hearing coincided with the first week of final exams. They solved that by getting cell phone numbers, and copies of their witnesses' exam schedules. Fortunately, the college had student witnesses, too; and Kathryn had worked out with opposing counsel obtaining permission slips from the college president for student witnesses to interrupt a test and finish it later, or take it at a later time, alone, if they were called during the time of a scheduled test. Another item punched off the preparation punch list.

Then there was the expert witness to prepare. Marc had offered an expert witness only once, in a case with Bill Norville. Kathryn had sat in on the session with their IT expert. She had offered a few pointers, and would be there with him when they put theirs in the witness chair. So that was good. He had been a little afraid that Kathryn would want him to crossexamine the prosecution expert, but she decided she'd better take him herself. But she'd asked him to review her preparation notes. To his surprise, he'd had a couple of suggestions. To his greater surprise, she'd thanked him and accepted them.

They had saved the client's prep for this afternoon, and the whole team would sit in on that. He really wasn't worried about Mitch. But Norville had told him it was better to worry about every witness until they were off the stand, or in this case, out of the witness chair, there being no witness box in the hearing room.

And, of all things, the asshole lawyer on the other side of the case where the document production ruling had been favorable wouldn't sign the Order Marc had drawn up, insisting on an alternate version that gave him more than the court had ordered. They'd found out about that on Tuesday, in the middle of all this McCaffrey stuff. Fortunately, they had a transcript of the actual hearing, including Judge Sinclair's ruling. But that didn't faze their asshole adversary. He'd insisted on presenting both Orders to the Judge.

Tiffany had had to stop her McCaffrey prep, contact the clerk's office, and arrange to have the matter put on the Friday morning motion docket. And he'd had to work late to prepare for the court appearance. He'd have had to work late anyway, but he didn't need this distraction. Not when the McCaffrey case was front and center.

So here he was, sitting in Judge David Sinclair's court room in Superior Court, waiting for their case to be called, watching a procession of other motions, mostly about child support and threatened domestic violence, getting nothing done on the case for next week, and waiting some more. The only good thing was that Kathryn had let Tiff go with him, so they could go over her testimony in the car going to and from the courthouse, and kill another bird with one stone.

She sat next to him, watching Judge Sinclair at work. At the close of one hearing, she leaned over to Marc and whispered, "He looks like Ichabod Crane. The judge."

Marc suppressed a laugh. David Sinclair did look like Ichabod Crane, at least the Disney cartoon version. He'd never made that connection. He wondered how many women Tiff's age – their mutual age, really – knew who Ichabod Crane was. Not many, he decided. The girl is smart, really smart. A keeper, if he could figure out how.

Then their case was called, and everything was anti-climactic. Marc and his opposing counsel both stood, but before either could say anything, Judge Sinclair beat them to it.

"I've read both Orders, and the hearing transcript," he said. "I'm signing Mr. Washington's Order."

"We wasted a morning for that?" Marc muttered to Tiffany as they left the courtroom.

"It's not a waste," she whispered back. "We needed a break, and we get to spend time together."

"There is that," Marc agreed. "There is that."

He turned to look at her. Strong, regular features, hair tightly curled almost like a helmet, little diamond stud in her right nostril. His eyes wandered briefly over her fine figure as they walked.

Lottie is wrong, he thought. Tiff is just as pretty. No, prettier.

Or maybe he was just in love.

CLAIRE

Shortly after lunch on Friday, Peggy buzzed Claire to inform her that Larry Kincaid was holding for her again. Of course, she took the call. It had to be about the McCaffrey matter.

"News, Claire," Larry said without preamble. "I have news for you."

"I'm all ears," she replied. "Let me guess. You're coming here."

"I wish. But no, I'm going as scheduled. But..." he paused. "But Meg settled her case in Wilmington. There won't be a hearing there, and I'm sending her to Carolina Highlands instead."

Claire was relieved. She had known Megan Stennis for years, and respected her. She didn't know the other woman, Rachel What's-Her-Name. But she trusted Meg, just as she would have trusted Larry. She said so.

"Thank you, Claire. Now, Megan's marching orders are the same as the ones I gave Rachel, mind you. Be sure the hearing is proper. It's got to at least look fair. Don't let the Panel go overboard. We don't care if you get rid of this guy, but we don't want to create any hereafters."

"I understand," she said, "and I certainly agree...Do Barry and Monica know?"

"I'm going to call them on Barry's cell phone right now, and give them the word. They won't like it, but I don't care. They don't run this department. I do.

"Megan will come in Sunday night. She'll meet with the Hearing Panel Monday."

"I'll look forward to seeing her. If she comes in, in time for dinner, I'll take her out."

"I'll tell her that; she'll appreciate it. Oh – Claire?"

"Yes?"

"One more thing. You're not supposed to attend the hearing, but you're entitled to send an observer. If you have someone you trust, I'd do that if I were you. I want this done carefully, including by you."

She thought for a moment. "Well. I suppose I could send Peggy."

"Peggy?"

"My administrative assistant. She'd been with me for years."

"Okay. That's fine, if you trust her."

BART

Bart Stevens caught Monica on her way out of the Administration Building late Friday afternoon. He hadn't been able to catch up with her for the past several days, because she was always with someone. Feldman, with or without witnesses in tow. Claire Daniels, earlier this afternoon. Somebody, all the time. He wanted to know how things were going. He had a stake in this hearing coming up, too, even if he would not be a part of it.

He'd noticed Barry Feldman leave a few minutes earlier, looking as though he'd been eating lemons. They'd nodded to one another, and Bart decided not to ask him anything. He really didn't know Feldman well enough.

He knew that Feldman's hotel room was nominal, that he'd spent most nights with Monica. They hadn't even tried hard to hide it. Bart was envious, but only mildly jealous. He had no claim on Monica. He knew she used him. That was okay, too. He liked the payoffs, when he could get them.

And here she came, banging out the door, her face contorted and thunderclouds over her brow. She was mad about something. But he did know her well enough to ask.

"Hey, Monica," he called.

She turned and stopped when she saw him standing to one side under the overhang of the entrance.

"Yes," she snapped. "What do you want, Bart?"

Well, at least she was speaking.

"I just wanted to know how it's going. With the hearing next week, I mean," he said meekly.

"Right now, lousy. Shitty, really," she said. But she took a deep breath and said more softly, "I'm sorry, Bart. But we got bad news this afternoon."

"What was it?"

She looked around to be sure no one was within hearing. No one was. So she told him about Megan Stennis replacing Rachel Jordan.

"Does that mean you're going to lose?" he asked.

"It does NOT," she almost shouted, and then, catching herself when she saw someone in the gloom across the parking lot turn his head in her direction, continued in a normal tone, "Our evidence is strong. But it does make it harder."

She explained how Rachel would have been their "girl on the in-side" of the Panel, but Stennis wouldn't be. He nodded in understanding.

"What happens if this goes south on you?" he asked, and imme-diately regretted it.

"It won't, Bart. Have a little faith in me and Barry, will you? It won't. It just can't. I won't let it." She sounded confident, but yet – not so much as he would have liked.

But he knew if the hearing went south on them, the college would be stuck with keeping a right-winger on the faculty. And the man Mc-Caffrey was a racist. He knew that. They all were, at heart, even if they tried to hide it.

"Well, good luck with it," he said sincerely. "Keep me posted and let me know if I can help."

Monica smiled at him, fondly he thought with pleasure, and said, "Thank you, Bart. I don't know what else you can do. You've been a tremendous help already. But if I think of anything, I'll let you know. I promise."

Giving him a perfunctory hug, she excused herself and hurried off.

Probably late for another rendezvous with Feldman, he thought.

He stood there for a full minute, lost in concentration. Then he walked slowly towards his car. He had calls to make, but not out in the open.

He couldn't think of any way to help with the hearing, but there were things he could do if it didn't go their way. He knew whom to call. He knew who would come.

22

DON'T GO BREAKING MY HEART

MITCH

After his Friday afternoon meeting with his legal team – he snorted to himself at that thought; he, all by himself, had a legal team – Mitch had dinner that evening with Diana and her family. It was another Bean n' Bacon leftover beef stew evening, with Margaret's cole slaw and corn muffins to go with the stew; and Mitch brought a bottle of Zinfandel for the grown-ups. The boys had iced tea. Margaret's boyfriend Frank joined them, and they sat around the dining room table for a nice meal.

After dinner, when Paul and Steve had gone to watch television, and the dishes were loaded for washing, the adults sat around the dining table with coffee. Everyone wanted to know about the hearing. How was the preparation coming? And was he nervous? He told them it was all going well, he had great lawyers, and yes, he had some butterflies, but was okay, honestly. All true, but incomplete. There were some things he couldn't tell them, and some that he wouldn't.

But he did tell them about the text he'd received from Peggy Sturgill while in the meeting with Kathryn's team, about how pleased Claire

Daniels was about Megan Stennis replacing Rachel Jordan as Hearing Advisor". That meant he had to swear them to secrecy about Peggy, and explain what a "hearing advisor" was, so it took a few minutes.

"Kathryn and Bill seemed to think it was good news," he finished. "Bill Norville especially. He's practiced law pretty much forever, and knows Megan Stennis. He says she's 'liberal as hell, but fair.' They didn't think the other one would be. But Kathryn said they were going to object 'for the record' anyway."

"Why, if this woman is going to be fair?" Frank asked.

"Kathryn said it was to preserve our rights to bring it up later, if we go to court," Mitch explained.

"Are you going to court?" Margaret asked him."

"Only if I lose," he said, then added, "Maybe. Anyway, Kathryn said Peggy understood that Monica Gilbert is pissed off about it."

"Anything that pisses that bitch off is good," Diana muttered, earning a quick smile from Mitch.

Mitch left shortly after that. After she got everything started the next morning, Diana was going to leave the restaurant with Margaret and Becky McCoy, their assistant manager; and she and Mitch were going Christmas shopping in Asheville. It would be another early Saturday morning.

When he arrived at home, he noticed a car parked in the overflow space across from his home. Someone was sitting there in the dark. That raised his internal antenna, but while extending his aura confirmed someone was in the vehicle, which looked to be a late model Mercedes SUV, he detected no hostility. Whoever it was must be waiting on one of his neighbors.

He was surprised when the doorbell rang. He'd barely had time to get his jacket in the closet. When he walked to the door, he extended his aura again. Again, he detected no hostility. He turned on the outside light and opened the door.

He knew his visitor. Knew who he was, anyway.

"Dr. Watkins," Mitch said. "I wasn't expecting you."

Watkins smiled and said, "I'm sure you weren't. But may I come in?"

Mitch stepped aside without a word.

He took Watkins downstairs to the Library (which Diana still called his "home sports bar") turning the lights on with sub-vocalized spells as they went.

"Impressive," Watkins said.

Mitch almost allowed his back to stiffen. Damn, he hadn't meant to use magic; but he was now so used to it, it was second nature. But he had to learn not to be so careless.

"Beg your pardon?" he asked, trying to hide his apprehension.

"Your motion sensors," Watkins said. Mitch's back was to him, so he didn't see the relieved smile. Of course, Dr. Watkins would think this was being done with tech. That was the way the world worked these days.

"Thank you," he said. "It cost enough." And it had, but not in the way that his guest would think.

"Get you a drink, Doctor?" Mitch said at the bottom of the stairs. "I have about whatever you want, including a nice single malt. Laga-vulin."

Watkins hesitated, then said, "Why not? Tomorrow is not a work day. Not this weekend. But just one. I still have to drive home."

Mitch motioned him to the couch while he poured generous snif-ters for both of them. Handing one to his guest, he took a seat in the easy chair to Watkins' right.

"You have a nice home, Professor McCaffrey," Watkins said.

"It's 'mister', not 'professor'." Mitch gently corrected him. "I'm a mere instructor." Then, with a rueful laugh, he added, "And I may not be anything by this time next week."

"That's what I'm here to talk about," Watkins said. "I'm Charlotte's – Lottie's – father."

"I know. How can I help you, Doctor?" He wondered if Kathryn and Marc would approve of this conversation. He doubted it. It could be a set-up. But for some reason, he didn't think it was. Besides, he had always been open to talking with students' parents, and he wasn't going to change now.

Watkins sipped his Scotch, then carefully placed the snifter on a coaster on the coffee table in front of him. "I want to talk with you about Lottie."

"Why now?" Mitch asked.

"Well, Mr. McCaffrey, when your daughter is about to be a star witness in a hearing, and she comes to her Dad and, in a round-about way, asks if she'd doing the right thing, then goes to her room and cries, and then talks on the phone with somebody for an hour, it makes a father wonder."

So that was it.

"Dr. Watkins, what do you want to know?"

"Tell me what you think of Lottie."

Mitch took a moment to collect his thoughts. Then he began, "You start with the obvious. She's a beautiful young woman. She's stylish. She's the leader of her circle of friends. But you know all of that."

"I do. What else?"

Mitch answered without hesitation. "As I feel sure her parents also know, she's quite an intelligent young woman. When she applies herself, when she allows herself to think, she can be as good as any student I've ever had.

"But mostly she doesn't apply herself. It's almost as though she is afraid to." He took a sip from his snifter, and plunged on: "That's what I was trying to do the day this whole thing started. She'd asked a smart-aleck question, and I was trying to turn it into something that would help her understand why we read the classics."

Watkins reached for his snifter. "Mr. McCaffrey, suppose you tell me exactly what happened. Your side of the story."

Mitch did. It didn't take long.

"I believe you," Watkins said when Mitch had finished. "Tell me, are you an Angelou fan?"

"Not particularly," Mitch admitted. "But I've read her. Her essays are better than her poetry, I think. I've always been fascinated by how she found inspiration in Shakespeare. I was hoping your daughter would, too."

Watkins set down his snifter again, and chuckled. "Frankly, Mr. McCaffrey, I've never seen her read anything but a fashion magazine or whatever junk is on her cell phone, unless somebody made her."

"What about you? Are you a Maya Angelou devotee?"

"Never read her. When my nose is not in a medical journal, I read Patterson or Grisham."

Mitch nodded in understanding, and they were silent for a minute.

Then Watkins said, "What about the other stuff they are saying about you? You know, the harassment and the white nationalism?"

"Doctor, you daughter and her buddies traipse around in short shorts and halter tops every time the weather permits. Of course, anyone notices that. But no, I don't mess with my female students. I never have.

"As for the other, that's just bunk. Made up. What some of my faculty peers and the compliance officer have against me is that I don't use my Milton and Shakespeare class, or any of my other classes, to preach about white male oppression, the 'patriarchy' and all that stuff. I don't preach politics at all."

Watkins didn't argue with him. He simply finished his Scotch.

"Damn, that's good," he said. "Thank you. Thank you for talking with me, too."

"Any time, Doctor."

Dr. Watkins rose and extended his hand. Mitch took it.

"Well, I'd better be going," he said. "But I want you to know, I'm not going to try to influence Lottie. She's got to figure things out for herself. A father can hope, but he shouldn't try to force anything."

"Believe me, I know," Mitch said. "I'm a father, too."

"How many?" Watkins asked.

Mitch held up one finger. "Just the one. A son. He's in grad school at Virginia Tech. Just got engaged."

"Like her?"

"I do."

He saw Dr. Watkins to the door, then turned out the lights and prepared for bed. He still wondered what Kathryn would think about this visit.

Or should he even tell her?

DIANA

Diana's Saturday was long, but good. She got the Bean n' Bacon started, knowing that her mother and Becky could have done that without her, but still feeling better for being there. She didn't want to stay in bed while others worked at a business that was half hers.

She went home, changed clothes to something appropriate, which turned out to be slacks and a fluffy holiday sweater, and socks and boots because the weather was chill, applied make up, because she hadn't bothered before, and made sure Paul and Steve had breakfast and were dressed warmly. Mitch arrived shortly thereafter in the Lexus, and they were off.

They were home before dark, and Diana needed to be sure Paul and Steve had dinner before going to Mitch's place. When she arrived, he had grilled chicken and wine waiting, which was nice, but of course he wanted to watch the ACC football championship game on television afterwards. She wanted to know why, because it was Virginia Tech was playing Clemson, and he didn't care about either. He mumbled something about Carson going to grad school at VAT, but she knew he just had a compulsion to watch football. Still, she snuggled up against him with a Campari, and managed to enjoy herself.

But when the third quarter ended with it pretty obvious that Clemson was going to win, he surprised her by snapping off the TV.

"Get your coat, honey," he said quietly. "Let's go for a walk."

"Now?" She was a bit taken aback. Whatever she was expecting — serious conversation, making love, just idle talk — it hadn't been this.

"Yes, now."

Her jacket was only medium heavy. The weather had turned warmer, and something down-filed wasn't necessary. All was quiet when they got outside. The evening was clear and crisp, the stars were out, and she could see the Christmas decorations in the windows of the homes downhill from his place. There was the faint noise of music from one of Mitch's neighbors, where evidently a holiday party was under way.

Mitch had a flashlight for each of them.

"The path isn't lit all the way," he explained, turning uphill and motioning her to join him.

"We're going to the tower? Tonight?" she asked, incredulous.

"Yes, we are. Trust me, it's going to be good."

She was skeptical, but she followed him.

The path was fairly steep. She was glad of her exercise classes, but was acutely aware that they hadn't really prepared her to walk uphill on a gravel path in the dark.

"I'm warning you, buddyrow," she said after a while, "if you think this girl is going to be in the mood for indoor exercise after this, you've got another thing coming."

His only response was a chuckle. After a while, he told her about Dr. Watkins' visit. She listened in rapt attention while picking her way up the path by the flashlight beams.

"Have you told your lawyers?" she asked. "I mean, this could be big."

"Not yet," he said. "I'm a little afraid they'll fuss at me. But I will. They might not even be upset. George -- you know, Kat's husband -- knows Watkins and said he's a good guy."

They walked on in silence and finally reached the tower. Diana was tired and a little out of breath.

"Honey, give me a minute to catch my breath," she pleaded. "I'm not ready to tackle the steps yet."

Mitch reached over and took her hand firmly. He said a word she didn't understand and suddenly they were rising from the ground as though they were in an invisible elevator, and then were deposited at the platform at the summit.

"Is that satisfactory, madam?" he asked.

It was. She didn't even have to say. She just drew close and slipped an arm around his waist. He did likewise.

They snapped off their flashlights to enjoy the view. There was no moon that night, but the sky was crystal and the winter stars were out in all their glory. There were Christmas lights visible in the homes on the opposite ridge. The air was chill, but not too chill.

They stood there for a while, just admiring the view. Diana had a thought, and laughed.

"What?" Mitch asked.

"For some reason, I just thought of that passage in the Bible where Satan takes Christ to a high place and offers him all of the kingdoms of the Earth."

He stepped to one side and looked down at her. "Are you comparing yourself to Christ?"

"No, I'm comparing you to Satan."

"Really?"

"No, sweetheart, not really. Now just hold me."

He stepped behind her and wrapped both arms around her, pulling her close. That brought his groin up against her rump, and after a while, she felt his arousal.

She turned her head to look up at him.

"I told you, buster. You can forget it after I have to walk down this ridge in the dark, this late."

He put gentle pressure on her shoulder and pulled her around. Their kiss was long and satisfying.

"Just close your eyes, sweetheart," he said, "and open them when I tell you."

She did as he asked. She heard another word she didn't understand. It might have been Latin.

"Now you can open your eyes," he said, barely a whisper.

She turned her head to see Mitch's front door before her.

"Did you? Did we?" she asked.

"Yes." The front door opened before them and the lights came on inside.

"Are you that good at this magic stuff now?"

"I guess I am. And I wanted to show you. I want you to understand that, no matter what happens Tuesday, it will all be all right."

Diana walked into Mitch's home, ready to undress and brush her teeth and engage in whatever kind of exercise she had said she didn't want. She was a little scared of her lover and fiancé, she realized. But it was a good scared, kind of the same way you felt around a really tough Marine or Army Ranger. He might be a badass, but he was your badass.

And, she realized as she fell asleep in his arms that night, she really did think it would all be all right. She really did.

And that was good. Really, really good.

23

RED RUBBER BALL

MEGAN

Megan Stennis arrived in Martintown Sunday night too late for dinner with Claire Daniels. She had to content herself with a snack at the hotel coffee shop, which thankfully was still open. She rose early the next morning; and, after a quick breakfast at the same hotel venue, drove to the college and presented herself at Claire's office.

She and Claire spent a few minutes catching up on family and holiday plans. Then Megan got down to business.

"Tell me about the Panel members." She was scheduled to meet with them after her visit with Claire.

The Panel Chair would be Marcia Phillips, the English Department Chair. Monica had wanted Lorna Kaczynski, but Claire had nixed that because Lorna was on the investigation committee. The optics of that choice would not be good; and, besides, Claire thought Lorna too much under Monica's thumb. Megan approved of that choice.

"Marcia is one of those 'go along to get along' types," Claire explained, not bothering to add that Claire herself was somewhat that way herself, Megan thought. "I don't think she privately wants rid of Mitch McCaffrey, but she'll be terrified of doing anything that might open her up to being accused of protecting a racist or a sexual harasser.

"The only thing about Marcia is that she doesn't know anything about chairing a hearing. She's chaired Department meetings, but that's something entirely different."

"Well, that's why she'll have me," Megan said. "What about the others?" "Donna Powell and Teresa Moretz are both committed feminists. They're all in on a woman's 'right to be believed'. They won't want to give McCaffrey the benefit of the doubt."

"Well, as Larry told you, we don't care about that. What we care about is not opening the courthouse door. I don't want this to look like a kangaroo court."

"Even if it is one?" Claire asked, smiling, earning a sharp look from Megan.

"Surely you don't mean that."

"Pardon me. That was a bad attempt at humor."

"Actually, Claire, it really was."

Megan met with the Panel members shortly thereafter in the hearing room. Marcia Phillips she found to be a tall, slender, birdlike woman, fiftyish with graying black hair. She wore a rather severe, dark business pantsuit. Donna Powell was shorter, plumper, and younger, maybe in her forties, with short bobbed blonde hair. She was dressed the way Megan would expect from a music instructor, in a fluffy multi-colored sweater, flowing skirt and clogs. Teresa Moretz, the nursing instructor, was the youngest of the three, likely a thirty-something, her hair flaming red and her spare figure hidden by a white lab coat over a white blouse and black slacks. She wore flats. There was not a set of heels to be found on the Panel.

Megan introduced herself and explained the function she would have the next day.

"I prefer that the hearing advisor do as little talking on the record as possible," she told them. "My primary function is to give the Panel Chair procedural advice so that the record is clean and clear. Marcia, I can confer with you in whispers and by passing notes any time you like, and I can confer with the whole Panel at breaks.

"I want to emphasize that this is your hearing. You will make the ultimate decision on the course of action recommended to the college president. I'm here to help you."

"I haven't done anything like this before," Marcia said, sounding apprehensive.

"I know," Megan replied, "but fortunately the Community College System has a written protocol – call it a script – for the hearing. It's online, but I brought you a copy. I have copies for Donna and Teresa, too."

She handed a slim folder from her briefcase to each.

"So, Marcia," Megan went on, "you can start out by reading this. It simply states the purpose of the hearing, that's designed to give due process to any faculty member who is charged with any policy violation, that the rules of evidence in court do not apply, and that the Chair of the Panel will rule on the admissibility of any evidence. Then it invites opening statements from the lawyers. Then the evidence begins. The college goes first. Then it's the Respondent's turn."

"I've read the summary," said Donna, tapping her copy of the folder. "Like you said, it's available online. It says we can ask questions."

Megan nodded. "You can. But I recommend that you save your questions for when the lawyers have finished, and ask only to clarify. I also recommend that you not interrupt a witness to ask a question."

"Why, if we want to know something?" Teresa demanded.

"If you really need to know something, sure you can ask. But if you wait, chances are the lawyers will bring it out anyway." She looked Teresa to Donna to Marcia, trying to appear as authoritative as possible. "It could be a problem if you appeared to be biased, or have pre-judged the hearing. And one of the worst things we can have is everyone talking at once. There will be a court reporter recording the testimony. We want a clear record that makes us look good, if this hearing is ever be reviewed by a court."

"Why would this ever go to court?" Donna demanded. "It's open and shut."

"Donna, if you say that on the record, it will almost guarantee that it will go to court. So please don't."

She looked from member to member again. Marcia was nodding.

Teresa's body language, with her arms folded, was truculent, but she appeared to be thinking it over. Donna looked downright hostile.

"Look, y'all," Megan said. "I'm not telling you what to decide. I'm here to help you look good. I really am. But Legal Affairs can protect your decision, whatever it is, better, if you save your conclusions until you get into executive session. Trust me. That's true."

"What if we don't like somebody's evidence?" asked Donna. "Can we refuse to hear it?"

"Well, Marcia can rule evidence is not relevant. I suggest she confer with me before she does that. We've found from experience that's better to let each witness say whatever he or she has to say. You don't have to believe any witness, but it's better to let them talk."

There wasn't much to say after that. Megan hoped they would take her advice. That bit about being able to protect the ruling appeared to have got through to all three of them. She hoped.

But one thing she understood. Claire had it right.

They had themselves a kangaroo court. She just needed to try to keep it from looking like one.

MITCH

Mitch woke early on Tuesday morning. He had slept amazingly well. He had used a calming spell on himself at bedtime, and that doubtless had helped.

He had butterflies, but nothing like the ones he remembered from his deployment in Iraq. Whatever happened today, he wasn't going to run over an IED. Of course, if he'd been able sense some things, and do some things, he could do now, he might have had it easier there.

He knew he was going to take some risks today. He felt good about his plans, but he wouldn't know for sure until it all played out. Then there was Monica. He thought he was the stronger magic user. But he didn't know for certain, and he couldn't know what she would do until it happened.

He said his morning prayers and felt better. He made coffee and toasted a bagel for a light breakfast. Diana called with encouragement from everyone at the Bean n' Bacon while he was finishing his coffee.

She had wanted to come to the college in a show of support, but he had persuaded her to go on to work. They wouldn't allow her in the hearing room, and she wasn't going to testify, so all she'd do if she went there would be to sit. She'd do better staying busy.

But the call encouraged him, and her gentle "I love you" made him feel better, too.

He dressed conservatively in a black blazer, gray slacks, white shirt and rep tie under a dark sweater vest. Black shoes, newly shined with spell craft. (A useful spell, that; polishing shoes was not his favorite activity.) A new black leather belt. Diana had insisted he have his hair trimmed last week, and he supposed that had been a good idea. As an afterthought, he threw a raincoat in the Land Rover, to go with the umbrella he always kept there. It wasn't cold, but the forecast said it might rain.

He had arranged to meet his legal team in the parking lot in front of the Administration Building. When he arrived, he found them standing outside their vehicles, waiting on him. There were security guards in the lot, who had placed cones to reserve spaces, and they moved one for him to clear a space next to Mark Washington's Camry.

His was a pretty large group, that included Jenny Jackson and Tiffany DeRatt, who would be witnesses and available for errands, such as going after other witnesses, while waiting, as well as Kathryn, Marc and the hearing paralegal, whose name escaped him at the moment.

After exchanging greetings, they walked to the building together. Mitch carried a banker's box of their evidence to lend Marc a hand.

At the entrance to the building, there was a group of eight or nine students with signs that read, "Good luck, Mr. McCaffrey." That was really nice of them, he thought. And there was another, slightly larger group, maybe a dozen, with signs ranging from "End White Supremacy" to "#MeToo". The security guards eyed both groups suspiciously.

But nothing happened. A few of Mitch's backers called out, "Good luck!" The other group responded with hisses and boos. Neither made a move toward the other, and Mitch's coterie passed by without incident. Other students were coming in to study or take exams, and a few stopped and stared. Most just kept walking. Brainerd County was hardly Berkeley, he thought.

Student and staff traffic in the hallway leading to the suite where the hearing room was located was light. There were a few signs, and some holiday decorations, none saying anything about the hearing. Beside the door to the hearing room was a wall-mounted glass case that announced what was scheduled in the conference room that day. Today, it simply said, "Hearing in Progress. Quiet, please."

Peggy Sturgill was waiting on them, to escort Jenny and Tiffany to a small room reserved for the Respondent's witnesses. The college's witnesses would be kept in a separate room. Because the college would go first, their witnesses were already there.

Kathryn, leading the way, pushed open the door, and they entered to set up shop at the Respondent's table on their left. A court reporter was setting up at a small table directly in front of them. To their right, Barry Feldman, Monica Gilbert, and Monica's assistant Sharon, were positioning their notebooks, pads and devices at their table. Men whom Mitch did not know were hooking up a computer at a table almost directly in front of the "prosecution's" table. He extended his aura and confirmed the computer was his. He sensed his spells were still holding and allowed himself a brief smile.

Mitch had not met Barry Feldman before, and Kathryn introduced the two. Feldman was cordial and polite as they shook hands. Mitch noticed Feldman wore an expensive Navy-blue pin-striped suit and a yellow silk tie with tiny blue dots. He supposed the state paid its staff lawyers well these days. Mitch was expected to shake hands with Monica, too; and did, although he could sense she really would rather not. He let her feel just the barest touch of his aura, and she did the same to him, magical sparring of which no one else was aware, and completely inconclusive, he realized.

Monica was dressed conservatively for her. Her red skirt was tight and short, but not as short as usual, only a hand's width above the knee, and complemented by bright red stiletto heels. Her cream-colored blouse was high-collared and demurely buttoned, although stretched by what he would bet was a push up bra, and her royal blue jacket tasteful. Her only jewelry was hoop ear-rings of sterling silver.

Well, his lawyers were well dressed, too. But Kathryn was not nearly so flamboyant. He thought her conservative pearl-gray suit with flats exactly right. As it occurred to him that Monica's being a show off might come back to haunt her, he stifled what would have been a wicked grin.

They took their seats, Kathryn in the chair closest to the podium, Marc beside her moving from right to left, then Mitch, and finally the paralegal, whose name, Mitch finally remembered, was Tammy some-thing — yes, it was Tammy Cresawn. Mitch noticed that the table for the Hearing Panel, which was directly in front of them, held placards with the names of the Panel Members and hearing advisor.

He heard the door behind them opened, and Peggy entered, fol-lowed by two other college employees whose names he could not re-member. They bore pitchers of water and clear plastic cups, which they deposited at the Panel's table and at each counsel table. The two unknowns left, but he saw Peggy take one of the seats behind Feld-man's and Gilbert's table. He tapped Kathryn on the arm and asked if that was all right. She said it was.

Then there was nothing to do except what the clock on the wall in front of him count up to the top of the hour.

The hearing, at long last, was about to begin.

MARC

If Mitch had a mild case of butterflies, Marc's stomach had lots of flutters. He had only tried a few cases, had a significant role in this one, found the client sympathetic, believed in the justice of his case, and realized the odds were stacked against them. It was a little, he thought, like when he was on the football team at Western Carolina and they were playing Clemson.

Wait a minute, he realized. No, it wasn't. Today, Mitch's team might be the underdogs, but they had a strong defense and would go down swinging. And it was a good, good team. When the Cats had played Clemson, unfortunately, none of that had been true.

That made him feel better, but the butterflies continued. He looked over at the client, and on to Kathryn. They both looked like ice. Man, he wished he felt the way they looked. His phone vibrated. He had already set it not to ring. He had text messages from Tiffany. One said,

"Go get 'em!" The other was just a thumb's up symbol. He texted his thanks, and then the door at the rear of the room opened.

Here came the Hearing Panel. Everyone in the room stood.

A short, plump woman with carefully styled hair and wearing a gray business suit, said, "Pease be seated." She herself sat behind a placard that said "hearing advisor" and he knew that must be Megan Stennis. The others took their seats also. The tall lady whose placard said she was the hearing chair leaned to her left and exchanged whispers with Stennis. Then she opened a notebook, found a page at the beginning, and began reading.

She introduced the Panel and the Hearing Advisor. When she did the latter, Kathryn rose and asked if the Panel could approach the Panel Chair. The Chair, whose placard said she was Marcia Phillips, looked at Stennis, who nodded. Kathryn and Feldman walked up to the Panel's table, and handed a single sheet of paper to Phillips, who took it and passed it over to Stennis, who simply placed it in a folder.

Marc knew what was going on. He was sure the client did, too; but he still leaned over and whispered to him, "This is what we told you about." Mitch nodded his understanding. This was the letter formally protesting a hearing advisor drawn from the prosecution's legal team. Marc and Kathryn had worked it out with Feldman to do it that way, as opposed to making a big deal out of it with oral argument.

Stennis whispered to Phillips again, and the latter spoke into the microphone in front of her, "The record will reflect the Respondent has formally protested the hearing advisor. The protest is respectfully overruled." Stennis must have scripted that for her.

When the lawyers were again seated, Phillips asked everyone present to identify himself or herself, beginning with the prosecution and ending with the court reporter. She also included Peggy Sturgill, who identified herself as the college president's designated observer.

Phillips continued reading, but Marc paid scant attention. It was simply the script for conducting faculty disciplinary hearings prescribed by the State Board. He had read it multiple times over the past couple of weeks. It took a while for her to get through it.

The Chair concluded by saying, or actually reading aloud, "The Panel will now hear opening statements. Mr. Feldman do you wish to make an opening statement on behalf of the college?"

"I do, Madame Chairman," Feldman said, rising and stepping to the podium.

His opening was infuriating, if you were Mitch or on Mitch's side, but completely expected. He said the evidence was going to show and show clearly that Mitchell McCaffrey was a bad actor who harassed his female and minority students, openly consorted with extremists who advocated white supremacy, and conducted his classes accordingly, slighting and demeaning women and minorities. The only possible conclusion was that he was unfit to continue to hold his position as an instructor of young people.

Marc glanced at Mitch. The client was visibly not happy to hear this diatribe. But he was maintaining his self-control and kept a grim half-smile fixed to his face.

Then it was Kathryn's turn. Marc saw her take a deep breath before she began. They had debated long and hard about what approach to take in opening, and had decided to put everything on the table.

Kathryn's voice was clear and strong. She began with Mitch's years of experience in teaching at Carolina Highlands. She rattled off his teaching awards. She promised the Panel copies of letters of support from his former students. She spoke briefly of his military service and his honorable discharge. Marc noticed the frumpy panel member, Powell, frown when Kathryn brought this up.

Kathryn then promised the Panel witnesses who were present and former students, included women and minorities, who would refute the allegations. She promised detailed proof, including expert proof, that Mitch's office was free of anything racist or pornographic when he was escorted out of the college.

Taking another breath, she accused the college of trumping up the charges and playing fast and loose with the evidence. She suggested the college's witnesses would not be credible. They had decided that this approach was not risk-free, but they had to take it. Mark watched the Panel's facial expressions and body language while Kathryn was speaking. At least two of them were frowning.

"Wouldn't it be a shame," Kathryn asked in conclusion, "to dismiss a dedicated and award-winning teacher just because some immature young women decided to act out and make up conduct that didn't happen, and" — she hesitated for only a heartbeat, and plunged ahead

– "because a vindictive and over-jealous compliance officer was willing to manufacture evidence?"

When she said that, Monica jumped to her feet, and practically shouted, "Madame Chair, this is outrageous!" Feldman took her arm, and gently pulled her back into her chair.

Marc was watching the Panel. The Chairperson squirmed in her chair, looking uncomfortable. Megan Stennis' round face was completely impassive. The other two were clearly unhappy. Their faces were contorted, he thought in rage.

That's not good, he thought. But we had to see the lay of the land.

Mitch and Marc

Carolina Highlands' first witness was Gina Tompkins. She was projecting massive hostility that Mitch was able to pick up from her body language and confirmed with only the barest touching of auras. The way he figured it, the truthfulness spell was not likely to do much good with her, because she had convinced herself of the probity of everything she was going to say. It was better, he decided, to just let Kathryn do her thing on cross-examination. If Kathryn cracked her even a little, there might be the opportunity to give her a nudge.

Tompkins was there to summarize the investigation, so her testimony was practically all hearsay anyway. Feldman led her through it, introducing the summaries of witness interviews and the damning neo-Nazi materials supposedly found in Mitch's office. Everything was slanted, even the notes from the interviews of students who were later going to testify for Mitch.

"Upon the conclusion of your investigation, Ms. Tompkins," Feldman concluded, "did the committee reach any determination?"

"Yes. We did reach a determination," Tompkins said, her tone crisp and disdainful.

"Was it unanimous?"

"It was."

"Please summarize it for the Hearing Panel."

"That Mr. McCaffrey had violated the college's harassment policy and its speech code, indulging in hate speech in and out of the classroom, and that, after hearing, disciplinary action, up to and including dismissal from the faculty, be taken." Tompkins was really reading from the committee report, but Kathryn didn't object. Mitch supposed that was because the report was in the hearing record anyway.

"Thank you, Ms. Tompkins," Feldman said. "We pass the witness."

Kathryn began her cross-examination by striking a low key. Tompkins admitted that Mitch had taught at Carolina Highlands for a number of years, that is disciplinary record was clean up to this charge, and that he had won a number of teaching awards, several by student votes. Tompkins answered snappishly, not happy with her answers, but usually not evading them. The only exception was that she pretended unfamiliarity with Mitch's awards. She finally admitted she didn't deny they were genuine.

Kathryn had told Mitch she needed to get that line of questioning out of the way. They needed this information in the record.

Then Kathryn switched gears, and the hearing became more interesting.

"Ms. Tompkins, you interviewed Mr. McCaffrey as part of your investigation, did you not?"

"Yes. We did. I already said that," Tompkins answered, then volunteered, "And contrary to instructions, he recorded it. That alone would be reason to terminate his contract."

Marc willed his face impassive. But he and Kathryn had debated not disclosing the recording for exactly that reason. But they'd decided there was an upside, and went ahead.

Kathryn ignored the comment, and asked, "And during the interview, you asked him whom he had voted for in the last presidential election, did you not?"

Marc was watching the Panel as Kathryn asked. Powell scowled. Moretz sighed with impatience. He couldn't read Phillips, but he saw Megan Stennis bite her lower lip.

"You know we did," Tompkins was answering. "You heard the recording." She smirked, evidently pleased with her answer.

"And you thought that relevant?" Kathryn's brows lifted.

The smirk vanished. "Relevant to what?"

Kathryn opened her hands to each side. "Well, you tell me, Ms. Tompkins. You asked the question."

Feldman rose to object. "Madame chair, the witness is correct. These questions and answers are unfortunate, but not part of the committee findings. We object as irrelevant."

He knew what Kathryn was doing, Marc realized. She was building a record for a coming federal suit, based on free speech violations. He saw Phillips confer with Stennis, and was a bit surprised when the objection was overruled. Stennis must figure the record is worse if the evidence is kept out, he thought.

"I wanted to test his attitude," Tompkins said.

"Attitude about what?" Kathryn's voice was silky calm.

"You know. About women."

"Oh? You can tell that from how someone voted, do you think?"

"Well, he wouldn't answer," Tompkins said.

"What did that tell you?" Kathryn pursued.

Marc saw Feldman begin to rise again, but before he could say anything, the witness responded, "He was trying to hide something."

Kathryn jumped. "So, you did think how he voted was important, didn't you?"

Feldman objected again, and was overruled again.

"Well, not exactly."

Kathryn just looked at her, and she obliged by continuing, "But we know anyway. And we know about you. We've seen that YouTube video from Thanksgiving."

Feldman was on his feet again, but seeing Stennis' stern expression, sat.

"Did that play into your report?" Kathryn asked, adding, "Bluegrass music."

This time Feldman's objection was sustained, and Kathryn moved on to the interviews with former students.

"Isn't it true, Ms. Tompkins," Kathryn asked, "that none of these former students lodged any complaint with the college concerning harassment by Mr. McCaffrey during the times they were enrolled?"

"I don't know that," Tompkins snapped.

Kathryn took a step back from the podium, allowing her jaw to drop.

"You don't know? You don't know?"

"That's what I said."

Kathryn stared at the witness for several heartbeats.

"Are you actually telling this Hearing Panel that you brought these very serious charges against a teacher in excellent standing with this college, and didn't even bother to see if what these witnesses were saying were substantiated by their student files, or by any college records?"

"It wasn't necessary," Tompkins answered.

"Your testimony is that it actually wasn't necessary to test the credibility of these witnesses by testing their stories against their records?"

"That's right. They were probably intimidated into saying nothing at the time."

"Oh? What do you base that little tidbit on?"

"It's common knowledge."

"Commonly held by whom?"

"Everyone knows that white males who harass women intimidate them into silence."

"And therefore you know it must have happened whether there's any evidence of it or not?"

"You could say that."

"Do you say that?"

"Yes."

"And so it's permissible to draw that conclusion without evidence?"

Feldman objected to the question as having been "asked and answered", and Kathryn switched gears.

"But it is true that each of these students did complain about Mr. McCaffrey in one key respect, isn't it?"

"I don't know what you're asking."

"They complained about their grades, didn't they? All of them?"

"I don't know that either."

Kathryn stepped back from the podium again, her hands on her hips.

"So once again, you're telling this Hearing Panel that your oh-so-thorough committee was willing to put forward these serious charges without even bothering to find out if the record contained anything that would cast suspicion on these witnesses' stories. Is that correct?"

"I don't understand your question."

"Oh, I believe you do. Do you deny that each of these witnesses lodged protests about their grades from Mr. McCaffrey?"

"I can neither confirm it or deny it." She must watch television, Mitch supposed. "I can't tell you there is any record of that," the witness added.

"Oh, Ms. Tompkins, there certainly is a record of that, I assure you. In fact, I'll bet the department head, who is our learned Panel Chair, probably remembers most of it."

The room's eyes turned for a moment to Marcia Phillips. Her stricken look said that Kathryn had hit the mark. Mitch had thought it would.

Then Kathryn was on the attack again. "Tell me, Ms. Tompkins, how did you find these former student witnesses?"

"I believe their interviews were arranged by the Compliance and Human Resources Office."

"That's headed by Ms. Gilbert, correct?"

"Yes. That's correct."

Kathryn's hands went to her hips again. "Tell me, Ms. Tompkins. How do you think Ms. Gilbert dug them up?"

Feldman objected, but after a whisper from Stennis, the Chair overruled it.

"I-I don't know."

"Well, there had to be something in the school records that pointed to them, didn't there?"

Tompkins looked lost, and turned toward Monica.

"Oh, you can't ask Ms. Gilbert for help now," Kathryn told her. "You have to answer the question on your own, difficult as it may be."

"Madame Chair!" Feldman protested.

While Phillips hesitated, whispering with Megan Stennis, Kathryn pressed on with a smirk, "I'll help you myself, Ms. Tompkins. If there were no harassment complaints in the records, the only place to look was in the transcripts of their grades, wasn't it?"

"I don't know. I really don't." Tompkins sounded helpless.

Kathryn would up quickly after that.

Feldman whispered to Monica, and decided to forego re-direct questioning.

Tompkins was excused. Mitch was overall pleased. The cross examination had gone well, and he hadn't had to do anything to attract Monica's attention.

But he noticed that Powell and Moretz didn't look happy. That wasn't good.

The next witness was Amanda Atkinson. This was a real, live former student. Mitch had wondered if they'd really call Amanda, in light of the prior cross examination; but he realized Feldman and Gilbert must think they really needed her now.

Amanda Atkinson was a tall young woman, now about thirty, not unattractive but almost painfully thin, with straight dark hair that fell over her shoulders and half-way down her back, bangs down to her thick, dark brows, beneath which were enormous black-rimmed glasses. She wore an outfit that was likely ordered from the "Bohemian" apparel collection on Amazon, consisting of an ankle-length skirt and a fluffy knit top with daggered sleeves.

She was an unlikely candidate to sell a claim of harassment consisting of ogling, or of sexual advances or innuendo; but that wasn't the college's approach with this witness. Atkinson's claim was that Mitch was condescending, abusive and hostile towards women.

As Feldman took her through her testimony, which largely tracked the statement Monica had obtained from her, Mitch's major sin had been in the way he taught Hamlet, portraying Ophelia as a foolish slut, touting the superiority of the male characters, and demeaning and retaliating against anyone he disagreed with.

That was the source of her C in the course, when he'd known she needed a B to get into the "senior" colleges she wanted, she claimed. Mitch was sexist, vindictive, and retaliatory. Mitch could see why she was in the witness chair. She was their antidote to the admissions Kathryn had wormed out of Tompkins. What nobody but Mitch (not even Monica, because he could not feel her extending her aura) could see was that under her calm and confident exterior, Amanda Atkinson was frightened inside. She wasn't telling the whole truth, and was afraid she might be found out. He'd see if there were an opportunity here.

Kathryn's cross-examination began with showing the witness some of her tweets and Facebook posts. Some claimed that accusations of any form of sexual harassment or misconduct ought to be credited and couldn't be questioned. Atkinson acknowledged them and admitted she was proud of them.

Mitch had his eyes on the Panel. The Chair looked nervous, Moretz looked bored, and Powell was frowning with evident hostility. He was glad when Kathryn moved on.

"Ms. Atkinson, tell us who contacted you on behalf of Carolina Highlands Community College in this matter, if you would."

"Umm, I believe it was Ms. Gilbert's assistant."

"And she was contacting you to solicit testimony against Mr. McCaffrey, wasn't she?"

"I think she was contacting Mr. McCaffrey's former students?"

"Oh, surely not all of them, Ms. Atkinson. That would be quite a few. As a matter of fact, you don't know how many, do you?"

"No." The witness said almost inaudibly.

"Please speak up, Ms. Atkinson. Was the answer 'no'?"

"Yes. Yes, it was," Amanda said more loudly.

"Thank you. And Ms. Gilbert's assistant told you that they were calling former students who might be willing to accuse Mr. McCaffrey of harassment, didn't she?"

"Well, she asked me about whether he did."

"Did she tell you that you'd been picked out because you had complained about a bad grade?"

The witness answered, "No." But it wasn't a truthful answer, Mitch knew from the way her aura jumped. He decided to give her a little help. He lowered his head and subvocalized the spell.

"Are you sure about that?" Kathryn pressed.

Amanda looked at the ceiling and swallowed hard. Then she said, "No, I'm not sure. That may have been mentioned."

"May have been, or was?"

Feldman objected, but not before the witness answered, "Yes, it was said."

"Thank you. Let's move on. You testified you are presently a Middle School teacher. What do you teach?"

"Social Studies."

"Not English composition or grammar?"

"No."

"English has never been your strong suit, has it?"

"I'm pretty good at it," Amanda said defensively. She actually believes it, Mitch realized.

"Well, let's talk about what you said Mr. McCaffrey did wrong. You said that when teaching Hamlet, he referred to women as 'nymphos'? Did I write that down right?"

"Yes."

"Ms. Atkinson, did you actually read the play? Or only the Cliff's Notes?"

Feldman objected, and at Stennis prompting, Phillips sustained as to the second part of the question.

"I read most of it."

"Did you read this part? She quoted,

"'Soft you now – the fair Ophelia. Nymph! In thy orisons be all my sins remembered.'"

"I think so."

"The word 'nymph' is in the play, isn't it?"

"I suppose so."

"Do you know what a nymph is?"

"It means Ophelia is a nymphomaniac, doesn't it?"

"It means she is a water spirit." Seeing Feldman begin to rise to object, she quickly added, "You received a 'D' from Mr. McCaffrey on your Hamlet paper, and that brought you to a 'C' in the course, correct?"

"Yes," the witness whimpered. The spell was working nicely.

"And you appealed that to the English Department head, did you not?"

"I did."

"Which was then, and is now, Ms. Phillips, was it not?"

"I believe so. Yes, it was."

"And Mr. McCaffrey was upheld, wasn't he?"

Atkinson nodded glumly. Kathryn was merciless, though. "Speak up, please."

"Y-yes."

Marcia Phillips visibly colored, earning an ugly stare from Donna Powell.

"There was no mention of harassment then, was there?"

The witness gaped like a fish out of water. "I was afraid –" she began, then said, "No, there wasn't."

Kathryn again stood back from the podium. Standing hipshot, she regarded the witness for a few counts.

Then she said, her voice firm but actually soft and understanding, "And what this is all about with you is that you still are upset with the grade you received all those years ago. That's the truth, isn't it?"

Amanda was blinking back tears. "You don't understand," she wailed. "I wanted to get in Furman so bad. This one grade – they wouldn't take me. I had to go to Western Carolina."

Mark leaned over to Mitch and whispered, "The horror."

"Thank you for your candor, Ms. Atkinson," Kathryn concluded. "We pass the witness."

Feldman and Gilbert whispered urgently, but Feldman, despite Monica's glare, said, "No re-direct, Madame Chair."

But Donna Powell didn't want to leave it alone.

"You didn't mention harassment to Ms. Phillips because you were afraid Mr. McCaffrey would retaliate against you. Isn't that true?"

Amanda hung her head, being bound to tell the truth.

"N-no, not really." She blinked back tears again. "I just wanted the grade so bad. I wanted accepted by my first choice."

After the witness was excused, Feldman asked for a recess, so that they could be sure their next witness, an expert, had arrived. The request was granted.

Mitch watched the Hearing Panel file out. Megan Stennis kept her poker face, Marcia Phillips looked thoughtful. But both Moretz and Powell smiled encouragement at Feldman and Gilbert. Moretz wouldn't look at the defense team at all. And Powell turned at the door and looked daggers at Kathryn.

Mitch exchanged a glance with Mark. They both knew. Kathryn had killed it, but it didn't matter. Two members of the Panel were against them, and the Chair wasn't strong enough to buck them.

No matter how well it had gone so far, Team Mitch still needed a knock-out punch.

24

GIMME A TICKET FOR AN AEROPLANE

KATHRYN

The next witness was Ron McKay. He was the college's IT Forensic's expert. McKay was tall, lanky, with angular features and longish lank hair. His blue business suit was rumpled, and he looked unused to wearing it. He wore an iridescent patterned tie that had been loosened at the neck.

He began his testimony seated in the witness chair at the desk directly before the Hearing Panel. Kathryn assumed that Feldman was going to qualify McKay as an expert and have him describe his assignment before moving him over to Mitch's computer, which had already been turned on and hooked to the large plasma screen on the wall to the right of counsel and to the Panel's left. That is exactly what Feldman did, beginning by getting the witness to identify his curriculum vitae and briefly describe his forensic experience. Kathryn noticed that when McKay spoke, he did so with a flat Midwestern accent that confirmed the information on his c.v. that he was from Ohio, and educated at Ohio University, although his business was in Asheville.

After Feldman had offered the witness for acceptance as an expert, Kathryn stood and asked if she might voire dire the witness concerning his qualifications. Stennis whispered to Phillips, who said, "Please go ahead, Ms. Turner."

"Mr. McKay, are you on the approved contractor list for the state community college system?" she asked. He might be, but it wasn't on his c.v.

"No," McKay admitted, adding, "but I'm fully qualified and the college president and the system Office of Legal Affairs, have approved me and my company." Evidently, the question had been anticipated.

"I see. How did you come to be selected for this assignment?" she asked, adding "if you know", although she was damned sure he did.

"I believe I was recommended," McKay answered.

"Do you know by whom?" She was going to have to pull it out of him.

"I believe by Bart Stevens," the witness answered.

"In fact, you know it was Stevens, don't you?"

"Yes," McKay admitted.

"Mr. Stevens is a faculty member here, is that correct?"

"Yes. Yes, he is."

That information set the witness up for later cross examination, based on his and Stevens' Twitter and Facebook histories; but now was not the time."

"Thank you." Looking to the Hearing Panel, Kathryn said, "Madame Chair, we won't object to Mr. McKay's qualifications." This implied that she could, but was being nice.

Stennis whispered to Phillips again. The latter said, "Very well. You may proceed, Mr. Feldman."

Answering Feldman's questions, McKay told the Panel that he had been engaged to conduct a forensic examination of the Respondent McCaffrey's work computer in order to determine whether it revealed any information that McCaffrey had violated college regulations or policies, and described what steps he had taken.

"And did you find anything?" Feldman asked.

"I did."

"Now, Mr. Mckay, before you show us what you found, let me ask you if you had any difficulty in your search."

"A little."

"What?"

"The subject had hidden his activity by saving documents at a location other than his regular documents folder, and hiding the icon, so that an examiner had to go into the whole download record to find them. And he'd bookmarked web pages on a browser he didn't use for anything else and kept the browser icon buried the same way. He also re-named the documents and links so they would look innocuous."

"Does that explain why the college IT Department didn't find these things?"

Kathryn objected to the question assuming facts not in evidence, but was overruled.

"Yes, it does."

According to their own expert, Guy Pollizzotto, the description of what had been done was accurate, because McKay, or Stevens, had done it; but the idea that the IT Department wouldn't have found the hidden stuff with a thorough diagnostic search was bullshit. But that would have to wait for Pollizzoto's testimony.

This whole thing made her seethe. Feldman and Gilbert had denied Pollizzotto access to Mitch's office computer, contending they had satisfied their obligation to give him notice of the evidence against him by providing a timely copy of McKay's expert report. It wouldn't work that way in court – if Mitch let them get to court. And if the computer was still available. She didn't trust Gilbert at all, and didn't trust Feldman much.

But seething didn't help now. She had to focus on the testimony.

Feldman had asked McKay to summarize what he'd found. The witness painted an ugly picture of racist pamphlets, pornography, and links to neo-Nazi and white nationalist web-pages. Kathryn made a best-evidence objection, which Phillips overruled. It didn't matter. They had the computer there anyway.

Then he asked him if the subject computer was available in the hearing room. McKay said it was, and pointed to the computer on the adjacent table. Feldman reminded the Panel that there was a chain of custody affidavit from the college IT director in the College's Exhibit Notebook.

"Now, Mr. McKay," Feldman continued, "can you show the Panel what you've been describing?"

"I can," McKay answered.

"Please go ahead."

McKay moved to the chair in front of the computer, placing his profiles at right angles to both counsel table and the Panel. The desktop of the computer was shown on the plasma screen to the right of the lawyers and the left of the Panel.

When he was seated, McKay asked Feldman, "What do you want me to show first?"

"Please start with a sampling of the documents you found."

McKay used the keyboard's touch pad to locate the hidden document folder. He opened it to show a series of documents titled only with numbers – 1, 2, 3 and so on.

"Please open the first document," Feldman prompted.

"All right," McKay said, clicking, "here we're going to see –" He stopped abruptly, staring slack-jawed at what was on the screen.

It was a sonnet, evidently by Shakespeare. The title was "Sonnet I."

"Excuse me," McKay said. "I may have the wrong folder." He backed out of the file he'd opened. "No this is the correct one. Let me try another document.'

He pointed and clicked again. The screen showed "Sonnet II."

Kathryn looked back across Marc to Mitch. He was watching the screen impassively.

His hands visibly trembling, McKay clicked from document to document so fast the screen became a blur. A blur of Sonnets. One hundred fifty four of them.

"I don't understand," McKay managed, his voice hoarse. "I –"

"Try the web pages," Feldman directed grimly.

Feldman exited the documents folder and found a browser among the menu of programs. He clicked on the drop down menu. It showed a number of bookmarked sites, labeled by letters – A, B, C and continuing.

"Now here is the first one," He said, clicking. "It's –" He stopped abruptly again.

The link had taken him to a YouTube video. The contents were a classic Popeye the Sailor cartoon, "Fright to the Finish."

"I – I – I," McKay babbled. Before Feldman could stop him, he opened site B. It was another Popeye cartoon. He kept going.

On the sixth try, he said, hopefully, "This one will not be a Popeye cartoon."

It wasn't Popeye.

Kathryn stole a glance at Marc, who said, "Betty Boop?" loud enough to be picked up on the hearing record.

The computer's speakers were connected, and Marc's question was followed by "Poop-poop-a-doop."

The court reporter tittered, then stopped herself. Even Teresa Moretz was smiling. Kathryn repressed her own smile, then turned to give Marc a "get-that-grin-off-your face" stare. Beyond Marc, Mitch's face was studiously neutral. Good.

"Please close the program, Mr. McKay," Feldman pleaded. His eyes turned to Marcia Phillips. "I'm sorry, Madame Chairperson. Someone has tampered with this computer."

"Well, I object to that remark," Kathryn said, rising. "Mr. Feldman just introduced the chain of custody. If anyone tampered with it, it's the college, according to this record."

Before anyone else could say anything, Monica's voice came from Kathryn's right, high and shrill, "We did not. It was him. Him!" She rose to her feet, pointing at Mitch. "He's done something to it."

Stennis whispered to Phillips, who reached for her gavel. But before she could use it, Monica, still standing trembling, turned her finger and pointed at the computer on the central table. Her voice was a wordless, "Oooohhh,"

The computer winked out. And then the court reporter's recorder at the table to Kathryn's left snapped as sparks flew from it. It began to smoke, and the reporter had to yank the plug free of the extension court to prevent a fire.

Phillips gavel rapped her table, weakly.

"O-order," she breathed, her voice as weak as her rap. Stennis whispered to her. "Anything else for this witness, Mr. Feldman."

Feldman looked at McKay, who in turn was looking around helplessly.

"No, Madame Chair," He said. "Nothing further. We pass the witness."

Kathryn rose to her feet with a smile. She had cross examination ready, but McKay and Feldman had already made fools of themselves. There was no point, she decided, in over-egging the soufflé.

"No, Madame Chair," she said. "We have no questions of this witness."

"But I do!" The voice was Donna Powell's.

For the first time in the hearing, Megan Stennis spoke.

"Madame Court reporter," she asked, "are you able to transcribe additional questions by hand? And will you be able to replace the recording equipment over the lunch break?"

"Yes, to both questions," said the court reporter.

Stennis nodded to Powell.

"Mr. McKay," Powell began, "do you agree the documents you opened for us contain nothing written by a woman or by a minority?"

"Uhh," McKay said, obviously still shaken. "Yes, that's true."

"And do you agree that the Betty Boop and Popeye films are cis-gendered and sexist?"

Kathryn rose to her feet. "We must object, Madame Chair. These questions are outside the scope of Mr. McKay's report."

Again, Phillips conferred with Stennis, then sustained the objection.

But it wasn't much of a win. Donna Powell had just confirmed what her client faced from the Panel.

Phillips recessed the hearing for lunch. One-half of the first day was behind them.

BARRY AND MONICA

Barry and Monica took lunch with Sharon in Monica's office, lunch consisting of deli sandwiches Sharon had had delivered earlier in the day.

"I don't like the way this is going," Feldman said.

"What's wrong with it?" Monica, now calm, demanded. "You heard what Donna said at the end."

"Yeah, we have Donna Powell," he agreed. "But I'm not sure about

Moretz anymore, not after that fiasco with the computer. What happened to it, Monica?"

His eyes met hers. She knew he was suspicious, but she decided to brazen it out.

"I don't know," she insisted. "That son of a bitch McCaffrey did something, but I don't know what. Or how."

Feldman decided to drop it. "Anyhow," he said, "we can't be sure about Phillips, either; and we damned sure don't have Meg Stennis. I've been watching her. She won't like the record we're making, and I don't either. It will look ugly in court."

"We're not going to court," Monica said, taking a bite of her meatball parmesan.

"Megan will assume we are," he said. He bit into his roast beef, chewed, and after swallowing, said more hopefully, "But we can fix this. We have to get the hearing back on harassment and intimidation. We have to hit them hard with our strongest witness right after lunch.

"We have to call Lottie Watkins."

Monica bit into her sandwich again, saying nothing.

Feldman turned to Sharon. "Can you get her here?"

Sharon nodded. "I'll text her now."

Feldman watched Monica eat. She was going through the sandwich like a construction worker.

"I know Megan Stennis," he said. "I know Larry Kincaid. They don't care what happens to McCaffrey. They just want to avoid a federal lawsuit. If our harassment evidence from current students goes in strong, then the other stuff won't matter. Meg will let the Panel do what it wants."

Monic finished her sandwich and wiped her mouth with a napkin. She reached for her purse to touch up her lipstick.

"Good," was all she said.

MARC

Marc's anxiety level had gone up and down during the morning, but the butterflies began leaping as soon as he saw Lottie Watkins standing in the hallway, when their team returned from lunch. She was his witness for cross examination. The spotlight would be on him.

Lottie was dressed conservatively for her. Her skirt was knee length. Her blue cardigan sweater, quite expensive, was draped over her shoulders and fastened with a silver brooch at her neck. Her white blouse was buttoned to her neck, nothing showing. She wore flats, not heels. She was even, he noticed, wearing panty-hose. Now that was really retro, these days.

But she was stunningly pretty, he admitted. Her dark hair was carefully curled, almost crimped. Her make-up had been applied carefully and conservatively – coral lip gloss, nothing bright red. She had been well coached on how to dress to appear the beautiful and harassed student. Monica's doing, he thought, or Feldman's.

Kathryn grabbed his arm as they took their seats. "Take a deep breath," she whispered, "and settle down. You'll do fine. Take an opening if it's there, but don't argue with her. Stick to the game plan."

When the hearing convened again, Feldman rose and announced the college's next witness was Charlotte Watkins. Monica went to the door and escorted Lottie in and directed her to the witness hair. The court reporter (who had new recording equipment and was a Notary) administered the oath.

As usual, Feldman's first few questions were routine, establishing Lottie's name, including her nickname, address, and age. Then he got down to business.

"You are a current student at Carolina Highlands Community College, are you not?" That was leading, but harmless.

"Yes, sir. I am," Lottie answered.

"In what year?"

"I'm in my second year."

"So, you will finish in the spring?"

"Probably next summer or next fall," Lottie said, squirming in her chair.

"Were you enrolled this fall in Mr. McCaffrey's English Literature class?"

"I was."

"Is that a required course?"

"Well, if you want to transfer to a four-year college." There was polite laughter around the room.

"Is that your plan?"

"Yes, sir."

"Did anything happen in Mr. McCaffrey's class this fall that caused you to make a complaint about him to the Compliance Office?"

"I did make a complaint, yes." More squirming.

"Tell the panel what happened, if anything, that led to your making the complaint." Now he was getting down to brass tacks.

"Well, I asked a question, and Mr. McCaffrey's answer pissed me off."

Mark glanced at Feldman and saw him control a wince. That would not have been Feldman's choice of her words. Not, based on the thundercloud that formed over Monica's features, would it have been hers.

"What did you say, and what did he say?" Feldman kept his voice well-modulated.

"I asked him why we were reading Shakespeare and not something by a black writer like Maya Angelou. We had a writing assignment anyway, and he told me to read a sonnet that Maya Angelou liked and write about that. I thought it was additional work and it pissed me off."

Marc beginning to like her answers.

"I think we can agree that you are African American, can't we, Ms. Watkins?"

"My Dad is. Mom is white. I'm mixed-race."

Feldman kept his cool. "Did you consider the assignment demeaning to you as mixed race, part African American?"

Lottie shrugged. "Not particularly. It just made me mad. I was trying to get his goat, and he got mine, instead. But I understand he was just trying to teach me."

"Do you want me to show you your sworn statement to the committee, Ms. Watkins?"

Marc started to rise, wanting to object to Feldman trying to impeach his own witness. He felt Kathryn's hand on his arm. She was telling him to let it go.

Lottie was answering, "You don't need to. It's wrong. I was mad when I made it, but I'm not mad now."

"Are you saying it's a lie?"

"I'm saying it's true that I was complaining, but I gave the wrong reason."

"Have you been talking to Mr. McCaffrey?"

"No, I haven't spoken to him since that day in class," she said, looking at Mitch.

"What about his lawyers?"

Lottie hesitated just a heartbeat. "I did speak with Mr. Washington, but I wouldn't talk about this hearing. I – I spoke with my Dad. And with Johnny."

Marc thought he might be the only person in the room who understood who Johnny was. Feldman let it go, but was clearly non-plussed. Marc almost felt sorry for him. He had learned already a lawyer's sick feeling when a witness craters on him.

Before Feldman could ask another question, Lottie looked directly at Mitch and said, "I'm sorry, Mr. McCaffrey. You didn't harass me. I'm sorry." Her eyes misted.

Feldman's chin was still on his chest. Next to him, Monica Gilbert got to her feet.

"Ooohhh, you." Her eyes turned toward Mitch and she pointed at him. "It's you! You're doing this. Stop it!. Stop i –"

She stopped in mid-word as something remarkable happened. Her face appeared to get fuller and fuller, rounder. Her body swelled and the buttons on her blouse began to pop off, or loosen. She turned with a moan. There was another snap, and as all eyes turned follow her in her flight out of the room, it was evident that a button on her skirt had given way, and the zipper was, all of its own accord, sliding down with an almost inaudible noise.

Marc's jaw dropped. As Monica waddled from the room, sobbing with mingled humiliation and rage, her now substantial rump was growing, spreading even as she walked. Were his eyes playing tricks on him?

He saw her assistant Sharon hurry after her, and could see, through the door they left open, the lights outside flicker and die as Monica went down the hallway toward her office. Later, Jenny and Tiffany, who had heard the screeching and come to the door of the witness room, would tell him that the spreading and dousing of lights continued as Monica fled, but that as she neared her office suite, the dousing of the lights ended. More, the process of spreading reversed itself, and her retreating silhouette seemed to shrink rapidly, so that she looked herself by the time she entered her office.

But he didn't know that now. He was too busy trying to process what he'd seen.

Feldman abruptly addressed the Panel.

"I have no more questions for this witness," he said quietly.

Marc looked at Kathryn, who nodded.

"We have no cross examination," he said.

Before one of the Panel could jump in, Megan Stennis intervened again.

"On behalf of the State Board for Community Colleges, I am advising the Chair to excuse this witness, and declare an immediate recess. And I strongly suggest counsel meet and confer."

Phillips gently rapped her gavel, and all rose.

Feldman approached Kathryn. "I need to check on Monica, and then we'll talk."

"Sure," she said. "But if I were you, I'd give her a few minutes. Why don't I check with our client right quick, and then I might be able to give you something to take to her."

Feldman considered. "Makes sense," he said. "Let me go release our other witnesses. I don't think we'll need them – today."

Marc looked up at the clock on the wall. It not quite 2:00 p.m. He noticed Peggy Sturgill hurry from the room ahead of Feldman. No doubt, she was going directly to Claire Daniels.

Feldman shut the door behind him. The McCaffrey Team was alone in the hearing room.

"All right," Kathryn said, "let's talk about what we can agree to, to end this."

KATHRYN

Kathryn and Marc left the client with Tammy Cresawn in the hearing room, and went out to find Feldman. When they emerged, Darlene Parker and Corrine Jacobs were walking past them down the hallway, already intent on their cell phones.

Looking back to her left, Kathryn saw the doorway to the Respondent's witness room (really a small conference room) was open. Both Jenny and Tiffany were standing there, wide-eyed and expectant. Beyond them, the doorway to the college's witness room was also open, and Feldman was standing in it. He, also, was looking down at his phone, but looked up as she and Marc approached.

Lottie Watkins had lingered, and was leaning with her back against the opposite wall.

"Let's go in here," Feldman suggested, motioning to the now-empty room behind him. "Lottie, you can go, too," he added. "We won't need you any more today."

"I'll stick around for a few minutes," the girl said.

"Suit yourself," Feldman told her. "But I recommend you not discuss the testimony with anyone. The Hearing is still going on."

Kathryn couldn't blame him for telling his witness that, but doubted it would do any good. Lottie obviously wanted to talk with someone, probably Mitch. But she had Mitch sequestered, for now.

Kathryn and Marc preceded Feldman into the conference room. He followed and shut the door.

No one sat. Feldman began immediately. "Megan Stennis obviously wants this case settled," he said. "Let's see if we can do it."

Kathryn had to admire his professionalism. He'd just been gut-punched when he thought he had a winner. She knew how that felt. It wasn't any fun, for a lawyer.

"All right," was all she said in response.

"Will your client agree to a reprimand for 'exercising poor judgment' or something like that, with mandatory sensitivity training or supervised therapy?" Feldman asked.

Kathryn allowed herself a giggle. "Would you, based on this record?" she challenged. "Would you recommend that to your client?"

"Like I told Lottie," he responded, trying to inject a warning note into his tone, but not really succeeding, "the Hearing isn't over."

"Yes, it is," Kathryn responded immediately. "Come on, Barry. You're not going to put those other two girls in the witness chair now, are you, after what happened with Lottie Watkins?"

Feldman's laugh was more of a bark.

"Well, no," he admitted. "But I'll tell you this: The Panel doesn't think it's over. Donna Powell doesn't think it's over."

Kathryn was shaking her head even before he'd finished. "Maybe not. That's your problem. You know it's over. I know it's over. I'm betting Megan Stennis knows it's over. Even your distraught client" – she was referring to Monica – "knows it's over."

Feldman surrendered. "All right. Tell me what your client will agree to. So far, all I've heard is what he won't."

She told him.

When she'd finished, Feldman made a face, but composed himself and said, "Okay. I'll present this to the college. I think the president will buy into it. Megan Stennis will probably insist on it, I have to admit. But Monica won't like it."

"Oh?" Kathryn said with mock surprise. "Does anyone really care whether Monica Gilbert likes it or not?

Feldman surprised her by saying, "I do."

He excused himself to meet with his client.

Kathryn and Marc left the room behind him. As Feldman walked down the hallway toward the administrative offices, which included the college president's as well as the Compliance Office, they saw Monica's assistant Sharon approach him coming from the opposite direction. The two stopped for a few words Kathryn could not hear, and continued together down the hallway toward the office suites.

Lottie was still standing against the opposite wall.

"Ms. Turner?" she said.

"Yes."

"Is it all right if I talk with Mr. Washington? And I want to talk with the paralegal, too." Kathryn knew she meant Tiffany. She didn't know Jenny Jackson, and evidently hadn't recognized her out of the disguise from the Starbuck's.

Kathryn thought before answering. "Yes. But remember what your attorney, I mean the college attorney, said. I can't advise you not to take his recommendation."

"I don't want to talk about the case. I promise I don't."

Megan

The door to the hearing room through which the Panel had exited led into a kitchen, with a door on the far wall into another corridor with more offices and conference rooms. Megan made sure the Panel had coffee or water, and left them in one of the conference rooms.

"The lawyers are negotiating," she advised the Panel. "You may have to wait a while. I've got to call Raleigh and speak with President Daniels. So please excuse me."

"We have to approve whatever they agree upon, don't we?" Donna Powell demanded.

Megan gave it to her straight. "Frankly, no. President Daniels does, but this Panel is advisory only. But the president I'm sure will insist you are informed, and I know she would prefer you approve. Discuss whatever you want. I'll be back."

"What do you think we should do, Ms. Stennis?" Marcia Phillips wanted to know.

"I'm not allowed to tell you that directly. I am allowed to point out the potential legal ramifications of any decision. But let me talk to President Daniels first."

She heard a buzz of conversation from the Panel as soon as she shut the door behind them. Plainly, Donna Powell wouldn't be happy with anything other than a 'conviction,' and the evidence just didn't support that. She didn't look forward to conveying that message, but she would have to – eventually.

The corridor she was in led down to an L-intersection with another hallway, that in turn led to the administrative office suites from the other side of the building. She used this route to Daniels' office.

When she arrived, she found Peggy Sturgill in the president's office. Peggy was filling Claire in on what had happened that day, and Claire's rather hatchet-faced countenance was clouded in rapt attention. Megan took as seat and listened as Peggy concluded with the Watkins testimony and Monica's meltdown – or whatever it was.

"Do you agree it happened that way, Meg?" Claire asked.

"Pretty much," Megan said. "But damned if I know exactly what happened with Monica. I think my eyes must be playing tricks on me."

"Mine must be playing tricks on me, too, then," said Peggy.

"How is Monica now?" asked Megan.

Claire sat back in her swivel chair with both hands spread to either side.

"I don't know. I think Sharon and Feldman are with her," she said.

"Well, we need to talk with them," Megan said. "I expect Feldman will have a settlement proposal to present to you. But I want us to get Larry Kincaid on the line first, if we can. Will you excuse us, Peggy, while we call him?"

Peggy nodded and rose.

"Ms. Stennis and I aren't seeing anyone right now," Claire called after her. "If Monica and Barry Feldman want to see us, they will have to wait."

They were able to reach Kincaid on his cell phone. He was in his car on the way back from the legislative meeting. He was alone. The system Chairman had driven to the committee hearing separately.

Megan summarized the evidence as quickly as she was able. She decided to skip telling everything about Monica Gilbert, because she didn't believe some of it, even if she'd been there in person. But she did tell him Monica had acted out in a manner embarrassing to the college.

"I take it you asked the lawyers to negotiate?" Larry asked.

"Yes, I did. I hope you don't think I overstepped my bounds."

"Hell, no. I'm glad you did. This was getting out of hand."

"That's what I thought, too."

"And I agree," Claire chimed in.

There was a crackle of static as Kincaid drove through power line interference or something, but they heard, "...have a proposal yet?"

"No," Megan said into the speaker phone. "But I'm sure we'll get one."

"Okay. If you want my input, don't agree to pay McCaffrey anything. Not damages. Not attorneys' fees. And no public apologies or personnel dictates. If anyone gets Monica Gilbert's job, it won't be him.

"Otherwise, it's okay with me to give him whatever he wants. Does that help?"

"It does," Claire spoke up. "But what about Monica Gilbert? I don't see how she can keep her job as Compliance Director."

There was a pause and more static. Megan thought his phone had dropped the call, but then he said, "No, she can't. But I don't want to fire her. She knows the regulations and she knows HR practices. What if we move her down here to the system offices?

"I think I know of a position we can give her. No cut in pay. No confession of wrongdoing implied. And Meg and I can keep an eye on her. I'll speak with the Chairman about it."

"Thank you," said Claire.

"Oh, my," Megan said, not at all sure she wanted Monica Gilbert in Raleigh.

Larry just laughed.

Claire had one more question.

"What about Southeastern Electronics?" she asked. "How do we handle this with them?"

"Leave that to the board Chairman," Larry said. "He can talk to the plant manager."

When the call disconnected, Claire buzzed Peggy.

"Go get Barry Feldman and Monica Gilbert," she directed tersely.

BARRY AND MONICA

When Barry reached the office suite for Compliance, he found the door unlocked, and a stricken looking and white-faced Sharon sitting behind her desk in the outer room. The door to Monica's office was shut.

"Is she able to talk?" he asked in a tone barely above a whisper.

"I'll check," she said in the same tone, picking up the telephone handset. "We fixed her skirt with a safety-pin, and I found her a shirt. She was fixing her make-up a minute ago. I know she'll want to see you." She pushed a button and said into the handset, "Mr. Feldman is here."

She placed the handset in its cradle. "You can go on in."

Barry stepped into Monica's office, and abruptly stopped. Monica stood before him. Her skirt appeared intact, and she still wore the blue jacket. Her make-up had been repaired, after a fashion, but her red eyes said she had been crying. Her hair needed brushing.

The shirt Sharon had found for her — the blouse, with buttons popped off, was hopeless, lying wadded on her desk — was a white tee-shirt with the Carolina Highlands logo across its front in red and blue. It was evidently Sharon's, because it was much too small for Monica's statuesque figure. Her breasts strained at it, and the shirt did not reach her skirt, exposing her belly button. Under other circumstances, it would have been funny. Right now, she looked pathetic.

He had only an instant to take all of this in, because she immediately collapsed into his arms, sobbing against his chest. A wave of pity washed over him. He gently patted her back.

"Now, Monica, honey" — the endearment surprised him when it slipped out — "it's just a hearing. It's not the end of the world."

"Oh, B-Barry," she moaned. "This is s-so humiliating. I'm so embarrassed."

"I know," he said, "but you'll get through it. We'll get through it. We will." He also knew her well enough to know that the tears were largely of frustration. She didn't like to be thwarted. Her normal controlling personality would assert itself soon enough.

She stepped back, already rallying, and not quite successfully tried a smile.

"I had my make-up fixed," she said, "but I guess I'll have to do it all over again." She tapped her lips with a forefinger. "Maybe something can be salvaged. Maybe we can get McCaffrey to accept a warning and mandatory counseling, something like that."

Barry shook his head firmly. "Not a chance."

He told her about his meeting with Kathryn. She looked as though she was going to cry again. But then the door opened and Sharon stepped in.

"Peggy Sturgill just called. President Daniels wants to see both of you now."

CLAIRE AND BARRY

When Barry and Monica arrived at the President's office suite, which was only a few doors down the hallway from the Compliance suite, Peggy ushered them immediately into Claire's office, where Claire waited behind her desk. Megan Stennis sat on a sofa across the room, clutching a pad and pen.

Both did a double take when they saw Monica. Monica's eyes were still red and her mascara smeared. Her hair remained in disarray. And with Sharon's tee-shirt combined with her jacket and skirt, she looked, Claire thought, like a bizarre combination of a Hooters' girl and a middle management executive cultivating a "power" look. But neither she nor Megan commented as Barry and Monica took chairs and angled them so they could look, in turn, from Claire to Megan.

Instead, Meg, as she and Claire had agreed, got straight to the point. "Okay, Barry," she said. "Tell us what Kat Turner says."

Feldman's face twisted in a grimace, but responded immediately.

"It could be worse, I suppose," he began. "She and her client are willing to toss us a bone or two. But they won't accept any compromise findings. They want a finding that the complaints are not supported by credible evidence; they want it on the hearing record; and they want a press release from the college to that effect. They want full reinstatement for the spring semester. That's the bad news.

"The good news is that in return, McCaffrey is willing to sign a release and waiver of all claims against the state, the college, and all of their agents and employees that arise out of the complaint or its prosecution. That includes any claims for damages or for reimbursement of expenses and attorneys' fees."

Monica made a face. Catching it, Megan snapped, "Don't act like that doesn't mean anything, Monica, because it does. For one thing, it means he's willing to release you. Based on the evidence I heard at this pig's dinner of a hearing, it's a really attractive concession. Defending this has cost McCaffrey a bundle.

"What else, Barry?"

"Kathryn says this next part is really important to her client. He wants the college to agree that no action will be taken against any of the students who complained. She said his words were, 'I don't want anything to happen to those three girls. Not a thing.'"

Claire's sigh of relief was audible to the others in the room. She had been afraid that she was going to have to discipline Lottie, Corrine, and Darlene. That would be popular with some students and a few of the faculty, but unpopular with others.

"Oh, he just knows he's guilty and his conscience is bothering him," Monica put in, unable to control herself.

Claire didn't accept that. "No," she said, "he's just being a teacher that cares about his students."

Monica snorted and started to say something, but subsided under Claire's withering stare.

"I don't suppose any of this is negotiable?" Megan was asking.

"No, I'm told it's not," Barry responded. "I've heard that before, and didn't believe it. But I believe it from Kat Turner today. If these terms aren't accepted, then they want to finish the hearing, and will definitely sue if the Panel does anything other than let McCaffrey off the hook."

"So, no confidentiality?" Megan asked.

"He's willing for the formal release he'll sign to be confidential – subject to the Public Records Act, of course. But otherwise, no. Kathryn says he's aware of the libel and slander laws, and that he'll steer clear of those. But he won't agree to a complete gag order. Of course, the hearing transcript is confidential as a matter of state law, as we know."

Megan locked eyes with Claire, and asked, "What do you think? Personally, I like it, based on what I've heard today."

Claire nodded assent. "Let's do it," she said.

"Well, I don't want to be part of it," Monica put in.

Claire was completely exasperated with Monica Gilbert, who she knew to be the architect of this mess, but willed her expression and voice to soften.

"I know, Monica. I understand. Today has been upsetting to you. Why don't you take the rest of the afternoon off, and let Barry handle this? We'll talk in the morning. It'll all turn out all right."

Monica stood, nodding jerkily. But before she left the room, she leaned over and whispered to Barry, "Tonight, Barry? You'll come by tonight? Fill me in?"

Barry felt a flash of heat on his cheeks. He was sure Claire had heard what Monica said. "I really need to –" he began. No, that wouldn't do. He wouldn't return to Raleigh until tomorrow anyway. "Sure. I'll drop by."

Megan rose from the couch as soon as Monica had left.

"All right, Barry. Claire and I are going to tell the Panel what they have to do. You go on and give the good news to Kat Turner and her client."

MONICA AND BART

Monica walked quickly to her office, shoved her wadded blouse into her purse, and donned her raincoat. That would hide the stupid tee-shirt. She told Sharon what had happened, accepted her condolences, and told her to go home for the day. Then she walked to her reserved parking space through the rear entrance to the Administration Building.

Nobody noticed her, except a few students in the parking lot who cast quizzical looks at the raincoat. The rain had subsided and had been replaced by a chilly December breeze. But she didn't care about that.

She was going to go home, have Maria draw a hot bath, prepare a light supper – soup and a salad possibly – and take the evening off. While she waited for Barry, she'd have a drink. Probably two.

Just as she reached her car, her cell phone buzzed. The caller id said it was Bart Stevens. She decided to take the call.

Bart wanted to know what was going on. It seemed that Corrine and Darlene had told other students they had been, for now, released as witnesses; and word had spread rapidly.

Monica was no longer tearful, but her anger had not subsided at all.

"They're going to let the son of bitch off," she said, not trying to conceal the bitterness in her voice. "No fucking consequences at all."

"What happened?" Bart asked.

"I don't want to talk about it now," she said. "I'll tell you later. Not tonight. Later. When I feel like talking."

Bart said he understood, and added, "I'm really sorry, Monica. Maybe I can do something."

"I don't know what," Monica said. "Good-bye." She disconnected the call.

But Bart had another call to make. He knew what he could do.

LOTTIE. MARC. AND TIFFANY

Lottie approached Marc and Tiffany shyly.

"I just wanted to thank you, Mr. Washington," she said, her voice soft. "You started me thinking. Because of you, I spoke with my Dad. I called Johnny, too." She looked down and smiled. "You know, he misses me. He'll be home next week, and we're going to try to make it work this time. I'm going to try, anyhow."

"I'm really glad to hear that, Lottie," Marc said.

Looking up, she said, "I think he and Dad will be proud of me." Laughing nervously, she added, "That will be a nice change."

Then she turned her eyes to Tiffany. "I guess I should thank you, too. I think you must be good for this guy." She motioned at Marc. "You're a lucky girl. And he's lucky, too. You know...you really do look like Condola Rashad. Really."

Tiffany dimpled. "Thank you, Lottie. And good luck to you from me. I mean it."

They shook hands and Lottie walked down the hall away from them, turning once to smile back at them. When she was out of sight, Tiffany pulled Marc into the witness room, which was empty, Jenny having joined Mitch and Tammy in the hearing room.

"I want you to tell me exactly what happened in there," she said.

When Marc reached the part where he said, "and then the bitch's ass EXPLODED," they both collapsed into one another's arms in a paroxysm of laughter, that somehow became hug, and then a kiss.

"Is there anything you two want to report to me?" came a voice from the doorway, which they had left open and forgotten. It was Kathryn Turner, her face suffused by her famous wry smile.

"I guess we're both going to be fired," Marc said.

But Kathryn surprised them.

"No. You're not," she said. "Bill and I have been talking. We've been a little too stringent. You're both going to be reprimanded for not reporting what everybody with three working brain cells knows has been going on to me, as your supervising partner, and you'll both have to sign off on agreements that you'll report anything that might expose the firm to liability. But fired? No."

Someone cleared his throat behind her, and Kathryn turned while

Marc and Tiffany looked past her to see Barry Feldman and Claire Daniels in the hall way.

"We have a deal," Feldman said. "Shall we go in the hearing room and write it up?"

MITCH

It took a little while for the lawyers to jot down the bullet points of the agreement on a legal pad. It only took a moment for Mitch and Claire Daniels to sign off on them. The lawyers explained that there would be a formal document for Mitch to sign tomorrow or the next day, and that took no time at all.

It took a little longer for the Hearing Panel to re-enter the room and listen as Feldman read the settlement terms, and for Mitch and Claire Daniels to affirm them. When the Panel entered, Donna Powell looked as though she had just eaten a bowl of prunes, Teresa Moretz looked composed, and Marcia Phillips looked like a deer in the head-lights, poor woman. Thankfully, Marcia had asked Megan Stennis to chair the rest of the hearing, which evidently was legal, because no one objected. That helped. The Panel all voiced assent to the terms read to them as the findings of the Panel.

Stennis reminded everyone that the hearing was a confidential pro-cess, and that nothing that happened in it could be divulged to third persons. Then she adjourned the Hearing.

It was over. Except that it wasn't, quite.

The Panel members, Feldman, Stennis, and Daniels all exited the building through the back entrance that led to their reserved parking spaces. While Mitch and his team had reserved spots, too, they were all in the main parking lot outside the front entrance to the Administra-tion Building. It took a few minutes for them to pack up their exhibit notebooks, tablets, and legal pads. By the time they finished, the court reporter had departed also.

Kathryn suggested that Mitch hang around, so they could all exit together, in case there were reporters hanging around. That seemed like a good idea to him; and besides, he wanted to help Marc with some of the heavy lifting of what they'd boxed up.

The process of negotiation, agreement, write-up of bullet points, and announcement on the record had consumed most of the afternoon, so that by the time they left the building, sunset was almost upon them. The earlier clouds and drizzle had been replaced by cold, gusty wind. The parking lot was largely empty, but not entirely.

There were people waiting on them, standing in a line in front of their cars, which were only about two hundred feet away from where the McCaffrey team had stopped where the concrete sidewalk met the asphalt of the parking lot. They weren't reporters.

There were twelve of them, all men, Mitch noted, making a quick count. All wore masks. Most were holding bicycle chains that dangled at their sides, but two held metal baseball bats; and one was tapping what appeared to be a blackjack on an open palm. They had attracted a small group of spectators, mostly students, who stood off to the side. Mitch thought he saw Bart Stevens among them, but in the glare of the setting sun, couldn't be sure.

"Tiffany, stand behind me and call E-911," Kathryn said, her voice tense. "Quick!"

Tiffany obeyed, setting the briefcase she was carrying on the sidewalk, and pulling her phone from her purse with shaking hands. Some of the spectators had their phones out, too, Marc noticed; but they appeared to be using them to take photos.

Marc was sure of two things. First, law enforcement would come. Second, while they might arrive in time to make an arrest, they wouldn't get there fast enough to prevent what was about to happen. The line was now moving toward them. They stopped about thirty feet away.

Mitch frowned in concentration. Kathryn noticed and whispered, "What?" He didn't respond.

One of the twelve, evidently the leader, took another step forward, and stopped.

"We only want McCaffrey," he called, his voice slightly muffled by the mask but clear enough. "The rest of you need to quit protecting that racist motherfucker and back away." That he and his companions were all white, and those he addressed included two African Americans, evidently didn't register with him.

"You'd better leave now," Kathryn called, her voice clear and strong. "The police will be here soon. You'll all serve time."

The man took another step, and replied, "Oh, we'll be gone by then. And we'll return him later. Maybe a little worse for wear. Now move aside."

Nobody moved. The masked men, following the lead of the speaker, began to trot forward.

Without warning, the leader turned and, swinging his chain, dealt the man to his left a savage blow across the face. Blood spurted, staining the mask. The injured man staggered and stopped.

Then the man to the leader's right hefted his baseball bat and swung it roundhouse into the leader's side, audibly cracking ribs. The leader sank to his knees, moaning. Another of the attackers, the one with cosh, struck the bat-wielder in the side of the head, causing him to drop to the asphalt, apparently unconscious.

And then they were all into it, twelve masked men beating the hell out of one another, while Mitch stared at them in concentration and everyone else gaped at the spectacle with dropped jaws. The masked men were all kneeling or lying prone, some in the silence of having been knocked out cold, the others gasping and moaning, when the sound of sirens pierced the parking lot, heralding the arrival of three Brainerd County Sheriff's Department squad cars.

Six deputies exited their vehicles. Four began to cuff the masked men who were conscious, and who did not resist; one returned to his vehicle and was heard summoning the Rescue Squad. The sixth, a sergeant, approached Mitch and his entourage.

"What happened?" he asked, looking to Kathryn, and not Mitch.

"These men were waiting on us when we left a meeting here at the college," she said, her voice under cool control. "They threatened my client, Mr. McCaffrey, with kidnapping and bodily harm. Then they started fighting among themselves. Then y'all came."

The sergeant looked around to the others. "Is that what happened? Do you all agree?"

Everyone nodded, and in some way voiced assent, Tiffany and Tammy with shaking voices, Marc hoarsely, and Jenny as calmly as Kathryn. Mitch merely said, "Yes."

The sergeant turned toward his deputies, who were holding the attackers bunched together for transportation, then back to Mitch and the others.

"Well," he said with a sigh, "let me get your names and numbers. We'll likely want statements from you later. Now we need to take this crowd to the ER, and then to the jail. If kidnapping was threatened –"

"It definitely was," Kathryn interrupted.

"—we'll need to report this to the U.S. Attorney's Office. Kidnapping is federal."

There were ambulances at the scene by the time Mitch, Kathryn, and company were able to get to their vehicles and leave. It was now fully dark, and the lights in the parking lot had come on, casting shadows and reflecting off the damp asphalt.

Mitch turned the key in the ignition, and opened his phone while the engine idled.

He was going home. Diana would be waiting. But she would expect a call now.

EPILOGUE

THE CARNIVAL IS OVER

MITCH

On Wednesday, Mitch was called to the Sheriff's Office for a witness interview. It didn't take long. He met with a detective sergeant who took his statement with a recorder, and confirmed his address and telephone number. The detective told him that all of the masked men had, as soon as they were released from medical care, lawyered-up and weren't talking. But a simple internet search of their names had revealed they were mostly from Durham, and belonged to some group that appeared to be an Antifa affiliate.

The detective added that none of the men arrested appeared to have any connection with Carolina Highlands except for Twitter and Facebook connections with an instructor named Bart Stevens. He wanted to know what Mitch could tell him about Stevens.

"Not much," Mitch said. "I've met him, but I don't really know him. He doesn't teach in my department." He decided not to mention Stevens' connections with Monica Gilbert. It was tempting; but if the information came from Mitch, it might be stirring the pot too much, he thought.

On Thursday afternoon, he met with Kathryn in the executive conference room at Melton, Norville. It was pretty posh, with dark-stained walnut furniture and paneling, and a wet bar. He noticed a water pitcher on the sideboard, and took a glass at Kathryn's invitation. He noticed a bottle of the Bowmore Single Malt and several old-fashioned glasses at the wet bar, and raised his brows quizzically as he took a chair across the heavy conference table from his lawyer.

Kathryn eyed the scotch and laughed. "Oh, we use this room to meet with extra important clients, and also for meetings of our management committee. The committee met yesterday after work, and someone must have forgot to put the bottle up. Do you care for a glass?"

"No, ma'am," he said. "It may be five o'clock somewhere, but not here and now. But I need to ask, am I an extra-important client."

"Oh, yes. You are now. Not only do you pay, but also this win for you is a feather in our cap. The details won't be made public, of course. But word will get out. It'll be good for business."

The door opened, and Tiffany entered with the release agreement for Mitch to sign in triplicate. He had already read the copy they'd e-mailed him yesterday, but Kathryn reviewed the terms with him carefully all the same. She took particular pains to explain that while there was no "gag order" in the agreement, he was still subject to the libel and slander laws. Mitch paid close attention, and tapped a few notes into his phone. That seemed to please her.

Mitch signed the agreement, all three copies, and accepted the envelope containing one of them from Tiffany, who left with the other two after accepting Mitch's thanks. She closed the door, leaving him alone with Kathryn.

"Mitch, I wanted just the two of us to talk, because I have some questions that I don't necessarily want Marc or Tiff or anyone to hear, if you will indulge me."

"Sure," Mitch said. "But I can't promise I can answer. Some things, I just don't know."

"Oh, I'm sure you can handle the first question anyway. Its 'what are you going to do, now that this thing is over?'"

Mitch had been thinking about just that, and didn't mind answering.

"Go back to teaching. But first, we're going to have a nice family Christmas. My son and his fiancé are coming. My mother, too. And we will have Diana's family and her mother's boyfriend.

"And we have a wedding to plan. Two weddings, actually; but Carson and Lisa's is a way's off yet. This is the second time around for both Diana and me, so we're not going to be fancy. But we both want a wedding that our friends can share with us. You're invited, by the way. So is everyone else on the hearing team."

Kathryn thanked him and smiled encouragement, sensing that there was more. She was right.

"But there are going to be some changes," Mitch continued. He looked her in the eyes and grinned. "I may write a book."

"About the hearing? About what happened?"

"Why not?"

"No reason, but remember what I said about libel laws," she warned.

"I'll have you review it," he promised.

"Are you going to give television interviews?" she asked.

"Not right away, except for the statement we agree upon," he said. "Maybe later."

"Well, if you want to go on Lisa Willingham's radio or TV show, let me know." Willingham was a commentator that Kathryn knew, not that well, but well enough to speak.

"Maybe. We'll see. I know Diana would freak if I did that now." He leaned back in his chair with hands clasped behind his head. "What else do you want to know?"

Kathryn took a deep breath. "I want to know what happened."

"I beg your pardon." Mitch pretended surprise. He'd been expecting something like this, and had thought through how he would handle it.

"Mitch, I didn't ride in on a tricycle. I saw some things day before yesterday that were awfully, well, odd. And I know Marc and I did well at the hearing. But we didn't do that well. That Panel wasn't going to let you off scot-free. They did, but we had some help. And then that evening, outside. Those men…

"I want to know. Like I asked, what happened?"

Mitch didn't say anything. He closed his for a moment in concentration, opened them.

A coaster summersaulted out of its holder to land next to Kathryn's water glass. An instant later, one of the old-fashioned glasses floated over and settled on the coaster, followed by the Scotch bottle. Kathryn watched goggle-eyed.

"I thought you might want a drink," Mitch offered, grinning.

"As you said, it's not 5:00 o'clock – yet," she said. And then, her voice tinged with amazement said, "So that's it? You're psychic?"

Mitch spread his hands in an exaggerated shrug.

"Maybe. I don't know. I don't call it that. You see, I use spells. It helps if I can say them out loud, but I've got pretty good at sub-vocalizing. Some that I practice a lot, I can make by just concentrating on the words in my head. So, like I was taught, I call it the Talent."

He told her about being trained by Dr. McCormick, and about how being suspended from teaching had actually helped because it gave him time to study and practice. She listened without interruption, sometimes nodding and motioning him to continue.

"You see," he said, "I always thought I would need to use magic in this case. I've been practicing magic for several years now, and I've only found two other people that I was sure had the Talent. One was Dr. McCormick. The other is Monica Gilbert.

"So I knew I had to be ready to counter her somehow."

Kathryn did not look surprised. She told him about what Maria had said at the hospital.

"But I don't know that this makes me feel good as a lawyer," she confessed. "I really think we could have won. Maybe with Claire Daniels. Surely in court later on."

"Kathryn, I needed good lawyers, too. What really broke open the case was what Marc did in turning Lottie Watkins. Without that, we still lose.

"But I had no faith in Claire. Where we were headed was a finding of misconduct based on racial and sexual harassment. Based on weak evidence, I know. But she would have let it stand. At least, I couldn't take that chance. And – I didn't want to drag this out in court.

"Remember, I told you what I was taught about the ethical use of magic. I wasn't going to do anything except defensively, although… although I did finally realize that being defensive doesn't have to be passive. As long as the motive is pure, it's ethical to be aggressive in defense.

"But most of what I did at the hearing was to block Monica's spells trying to compel testimony. That wasn't too hard. I don't think she's a well-trained witch. Well…for one witness, I did use a truthfulness spell."

"Lottie?" Kathryn asked.

"No," Mitch confessed with admiration, "like I said, you guys got that one on your own. I only used the spell on Amanda."

"What about the computer?"

"I took a chance there, and it worked out. Peggy was able to get me access to it at night, so I could work the spell changing what they'd planted. But I told it to delay until after they served their evidence disclosures, figuring they wouldn't pay to have their IT expert come back from Asheville to check it before the hearing. It worked."

"And what about Monica's final meltdown?"

He couldn't hide his smile.

"That was ready to use if the opportunity arose. Everybody kept talking about how much she eats, so I thought she must be using an inhibiting spell to keep the weight off, because she ought to weigh 25 or 30 pounds more than she does; and I found a spell like that in one of McCormick's notebooks, and how to release it.

"She was frantically trying to compel Lottie to go back to her original story, and I was blocking it pretty easily. She was frustrated, and let her guard down. I just released the inhibiting spell, and the weight she'd kept off by magic came on all at once.

"It wasn't permanent. She had her figure back by the time she got to her office. And I really didn't have to do it to keep the benefit of Lottie's testimony. But" – he grinned sheepishly – "I figured she had it coming to her."

"Okay," Kathryn said, "final question. What about the Antifa guys. Was that another spell?"

He nodded. "It was. I suspected something like that might happen, so I had a couple of spells ready. I felt a tingle in my aura as we came out the door; and when they told us what they were going to do, decided to use that one. I could have tried a freezing spell, but I admit they pissed me off. And – well, they had it coming to them, too."

Kathryn was silent for several heartbeats. Finally, she said only, "Thank you."

Mitch leaned forward, deadly serious now. "Kathryn, I've told you this. But you can't tell anybody. Not Marc. Not George. No one. Will you promise me? I know you keep your promises."

"I will."

"You know," he said, "I made that little demo with the Scotch because I planned on telling you the truth, but I didn't think you'd believe me."

To his surprise, she threw back her head and gave vent to a full-throated laugh.

"Mitch, you need to understand this law firm. One of our senior partners, Jack Melton, first connected with his wife when they were possessed by ghosts at a class reunion. Bill Norville is convinced his paralegal – Jenny – is a sort of vampire. And as for me, I saw Bigfoot up in the mountains not two months ago.

"This is not a law firm that's inclined to doubt the paranormal, believe me."

"That's interesting about Jenny," he said. "I sensed something about her, but couldn't identify it. It's not the Talent. And…are you going to tell me about Bigfoot?"

"Some other time," she answered shaking her head, and getting her feet. "For now, I just want to thank you for your confidence in our firm and wish you good luck."

She extended her hand, and he took it.

After asking her to convey his thanks to everyone else, he took his envelope and left. He had a Christmas dinner and a wedding to plan.

MONICA

The day after Christmas, Monica closed the Martintown house. Sheets had been draped over the furniture, and the heat set to keep the pipes from freezing. She had dispatched a small van early that morning that would take the things she was taking with her to the cute apartment she had found in Durham. She had worked harder than she wanted to get everything done, because Maria had given her notice the day after that awful hearing, but the Power had helped, some, when no one was around to see her use it.

Working at the state offices wouldn't be so bad, she reflected. The Triangle offered more social opportunities to offer than Brainerd County. Barry would be amusing. The two were going to Key West for New Year's, and that would be fun.

She frowned as she turned on the ignition in her fully loaded Prius. She hadn't liked the call she'd received from a sheriff's detective about Bart Stevens. He wanted to know if she knew anything about the attempted assault on McCaffrey, and whether Stevens had anything to do with it. Thankfully, the idiot hadn't told her what he was planning, so she could credibly claim ignorance. But the detective had told her the FBI might be contacting her, too. She didn't like that. She might have to do something about Bart...

Forcing her thoughts back to her plans, she reflected that in Durham, she would be around several university libraries. They had to include something about using the Power, even if the librarians didn't know they were "real". Tangling with Mitch McCaffrey had taught her that she needed to refine her skills, and she intended to do so.

Someday, she would have her revenge. Mr. high and mighty wizard and fascist Mitch McCaffrey, and Ms. Smarty-pants Diana Winstead — soon to be, she had heard, Diana McCaffrey, hadn't seen the last of Monica Gilbert.

Not by a long shot. But she could leave them alone for now.

After all, as the saying went, revenge is a dish best served cold.

THE END

AFTERWORD AND ACKNOWLEDGMENTS

In the interest of full disclosure, this novel is, as stated elsewhere, a work of fiction. There is no Carolina Highlands Community College, no Martintown, and no Brainerd County, North Carolina. The North Carolina Community College System has a Department of Legal Affairs, but I do not know how it is run, or what input it gives its constituent colleges on the process of disciplining or dismissing instructors.

Rather the hearing system described herein is an amalgamation of procedures I have drawn from news reports and review of college websites. It is drawn from no Community College with which I am familiar. Likewise, the administrators and instructors in these pages are not based on persons at any college with which I am familiar, but rather drawn from news reports and anecdotes accumulated over time.

The reader should understand that in many cases, students and instructors who become the targets of over-zealous compliance or human resources officers in many cases receive even less fairness and due process than described in this novel. Freedom of expression is very much under assault in American academia, and has been for some time. I put as much due process the novel as I did for the sake of the story.

I would be remiss not to thank all of the friends and readers who have helped me so much in writing and editing this novel. They include Lisa Fuller, Danna Smith (for her word processing and formatting, too!) , Kelly Long, Rod and Mary O'Mara, my loving sister Margaret Studenc, and most of all my friend Sam B. Miller II. I commend Sam's novels to you. They are good reads.

And I always save the most thanks for the support of my loving wife, Deborah. She wouldn't agree with Mitch McCaffrey on much, but she would want to be honest and fair with him.

November, 2020
Robert L. Arrington

ROBERT L. ARRINGTON

practices law with the Kingsport, Tennessee firm of WILSON WORLEY, P.C. He holds A.B. and J.D. Degrees from the University of North Carolina, where he was admitted to Phi Beta Kappa. He is a member of the Tennessee Academy of Arbitrators and Mediators.

But his first love has always been writing.

He and his wife Deborah live with their three cats, Pyewacket, Miss Katie, and BJ. You can find him on Facebook and LinkedIn.

Made in the USA
Columbia, SC
15 January 2021